T0294113

# JAMAICA ON MY MIND

The author and Peepal Tree Books gratefully acknowledge the kind permission granted by FFRR Music Limited to quote the lyric of David Rudder's "Haiti".

HAZEL D. CAMPBELL

JAMAICA ON MY MIND

NEW AND COLLECTED STORIES

PEEPAL TREE

First published in Great Britain in 2019
Peepal Tree Press Ltd
17 King's Avenue
Leeds LS6 1QS
England

*The Rag Doll and Other Stories* and
*Woman's Tongu*e were both first published
in Kingston, Jamaica by
Savacou Publications in 1978 and 1985
respectively. *Singerman* was first published by
Peepal Tree Press in 1991.

© 2019 Hazel D. Campbell

ISBN13: 9781845234405

All rights reserved
No part of this publication may be
reproduced or transmitted in any form
without permission

Supported using public funding by
**ARTS COUNCIL
ENGLAND**

# CONTENTS

## READING HAZEL CAMPBELL

### JACQUELINE BISHOP

Amongst their many virtues, Hazel Campbell's stories chart the vast and rapid changes in Jamaican society, and the different ways individuals have chosen to respond to them. In such uncertain times, whilst it is tempting to cling to the structures that keep one's world safe and ordered, her work insists, time and time again, that no matter how bewildering and dislocating change might be, one needs to confront new realities. I get the sense that she is the all-seeing eye and the all-listening ear, roving over the island, stopping here and there to listen in on conversations. She shows us ourselves: our foibles, when we are at our best, and when we are considerably less so. What stands out is not so much that Hazel Campbell wants to *tell* the story of the Jamaican people, but that she is seeking to *understand* their story. She has been doing this for the best part of fifty years. Her first published story appeared in the *Gleaner* in 1970 and she began winning Festival prizes in 1972. And whilst each story illuminates its specific time, together they show us where we have been and where we are arriving.

★

For example, in the early story, "A District Called Fellowship", people from a rural community are gathering "...because tonight was film show night at the Centre". The Centre and the films shown there loom large in the social life of this community, but what really is this place, the Centre? Such places were part of a programme started by the great statesman Norman Manley in the late 1930s, decades before Jamaica was an independent nation. Manley came up with the idea of the Jamaica Welfare Ltd., a philanthropic organisation which would support development in impoverished rural communities. He struck a deal with the head of the United Fruit Company for a cent for each bunch of bananas exported by the Company to be given over for rural social welfare. The deal was formalised in 1937 and community centres and programmes like the one shown in "Fellowship" were the outcome. So what is being shown in this story is a Jamaica prior to independence and a village still rooted in the past and being forced to confront the challenges of urban criminality. Juxtapose that story with another in this collection, written around fifty years after Jamaican independence, but set in the immediate post-independence period of the 1960s, one marked by the growth of black middle-class housing developments in Kingston. "The Buggu Yaggas" focuses on the confrontation between this new urban respectability and the noisy presence of displaced gay youths. Referencing current news accounts of gay transgender youths living in New Kingston, it is clear that this is still very much an ongoing issue. Hazel Campbell reminds us that what we take to be new often has a much longer history – a reminder even more embedded in the story's title. It is a word of Ewe, West African derivation that takes us back several hundred years into Jamaica's past, and also a word perhaps most commonly found in folktales and proverbial sayings. The new middle class of the housing scheme are both denying and embracing their cultural origins in their use of this word.

It is in this way that you get a sense of the breadth, depth and range of stories covered in this collection. All these decades Hazel has been working, sometimes in near obscurity, writing her stories and looking at a multitude of facets of Jamaican society.

★

If, as a reader, you are looking for easy answers about Jamaican society, this is not the place to stop. Jamaica is not all violence here; it is not all good; it is not all darkness; it is not all light. In fact, the decision as to what Jamaica is, and more so what it is becoming and will become, is left in the readers' hands.

What do I mean by this?

In these stories Hazel Campbell neither gives us answers, nor does she offer solutions. What you get instead is someone who deftly presents issues without passing judgment on her characters, never mind their faults and flaws or how unpleasant they may be. She is the kind of writer who says, *Here are the characters, and here is the situation, and this is what unfolded. Reader, I wash my hands, I have done my job, now it's your turn to do the work*. The book's readers now have to decide what to make of the characters and what to make of how they behave in the situations they find themselves in. If readers are going to take sides, whose side are they going to take? In this way Campbell ensures that the reader becomes implicated in and responsible to the circumstances of the story and, most importantly, is left to wonder what to think, or even to do, at the conclusion of reading.

Take, for example, the story "Jacob Bubbles", a story about two gunrunners, one male, and the other female. We come to know Jacob's story quite intimately, can readily understand how he becomes a gunman, and may well find ourselves in two minds about whether to support him and his Suckdust posse with their M16s used in part to protect the girls and women of the community, or whether we should be rooting for the police to kill him because, after all, he is a notorious gunman. Into this moral morass enters Pantyhose, the leader of the Superduper posse, who fires shots in the air to silence those around her. Should we be rooting for Pantyhose's success over Jacob simply because she is a woman, the only woman who has managed to become the head of a gang because she can handle an M16 better than any of the men, and is beating rival gangs of men at a boys' game? Hazel Campbell does not tell us yea or nay. She instead tells us a story, and we, the readers, are left to grapple with and answer those questions for ourselves.

★

There is also the case of the uptown lady in "See Me In Me Benz and T'ing" who does indeed live on an isle remote and who for a long time, it seems, has lived an unquestioning life, deliberately not seeing what is going on around her. Or, if she is forced to see what is outside her carefully constructed and ordered world, makes one explanation after another that are really no more than justifications for her privileged place in Jamaican society. These are, of course, my ideas about the character, for none of this is explicitly stated in the story. What we see, instead, is a woman inconvenienced by driving through a part of town that she would normally avoid, and coming face to face with the rage of people who are truly "others". But as her cherished status symbol, her Benz, is destroyed, one has to wonder if she ever comes to see the humanity of the poor dark hands that rescue her in her hour of need, or understand the ways in which their unsolicited assistance shows the capriciousness of race, colour and class in Jamaican society, or how seemingly solid class differences are in fact permeated and transgressed on that aggrieved island of ours on a daily (hourly?) basis. My sense of the story is that its protagonist still has so much to learn, and that her sense of class entitlement remains very much intact; indeed may well have been reinforced.

★

But let us not forget that first and foremost Hazel Campbell is a lover of the word, of music and song, of a good calypso, and is a great humourist. In an interview I conducted with her, published in the *Jamaica Observer*'s "Bookends" section, I asked Hazel about her love of music and this is what she had to say:

> I am a seriously thwarted musician/songwriter/singer. I can't sing more than an octave, (lower G to G). I can't remember the words of songs, even those I like. (I often make up my own words.) … I grew up in the Church of God, and for me the music was the best part of the service – always … I love our folk music. … I don't know if I believe in reincarnation, but I have asked the Lord that if I am coming back please, please, please give me the gifts of music and song.[1]

Is it any wonder then that we find calypso lyrics like these at several points in the collection?

> Erma, honey! Is what you do?
> Mek the whole town laughing at you.
> Erma what you doing wrong?
> Calypsonian soon put you in a song.
> Everybody teasing, jeering, sorrying for your man.
> Child, mend your ways
> Crime never pays.

It is instructive how Hazel uses humour. The characters in her stories are rarely trying to be funny. More often than not they aren't even aware of the humour in the situation. It is left up to the reader to find the comedy in sometimes not-so-funny situations. Take for instance the devil's involvement in the Jamaican world – and all the confusion he causes! In "Devil Star" how easy it is for Lucifer to mix in with normal-looking people! If one is not careful, Lucifer is almost sexy, with his bleached-blond hair pulled up in a bun.

But even Lucifer is no match for the Jamaican political landscape, when he shows up in the mismatched political colours of orange and green of the People's National Party and Jamaica Labour Party, respectively. That, in fact, is what singles Lucifer out as not belonging and gets him tossed out of Jamaica – this time around, at least. The moral of the story being: even the devil needs to know his politics before trying to stake a claim in Jamaica!

★

Lucifer, with all his guile and cunning, seems to be busily at work in the fraught relationships between men and women, and particularly so between husbands and wives – who never seem to be on the same page in these stories. Husbands lead lives outside their marriages, cavorting with other women; girls, meantime, are exhorted that "there is so much sinful man waiting to fall a girl", harkening back of course to Eve, the Garden of Eden and the serpent Lucifer. It is no surprise then that the church is an ever-present element in this world, not only doing battle against Lucifer, but being part and parcel of the landscape of women's lives, circumscribing their behaviour, particularly, their sexuality. There are fascinating moments, though, when even the church cannot contain all the repressed sexual and other energies to be found in women. Mother White, wheeling about inside the church in "Easter Sunday Morning", is a wonderful example of repressed energies let loose, and of competing forms of knowledge and belief systems still at work on the island.

★

Something should be said, too, about the code-switching in these stories, not only in language, but also across genres: from gritty realism, to magical realism, to folk tales, to urban legends, to psychologically perceptive explorations of inner lives.

Indeed, outside this collection, Hazel Campbell has lived a whole other life as a beloved author of children's stories. Side by side, the scope of her work is breathtaking and astonishing.

★

What we also see in these collected stories is an author who is always questioning the role of art and the artist in Jamaican society. This is seen most clearly in "Emancipation Park", where the young lovers meet by Laura Facey's contentious nude statues in New Kingston and use the statues to talk through both the meanings of the work and their own lives.

> He paused. "But, as I told you the other day, it's all fiction."
>
> […]
>
> "All art is fiction – painting, music, sculpture, dance…"
>
> […]
>
> "It's all somebody's interpretation of some aspect of life …"

Very true, indeed. All art is fiction, but I would say it is a fiction used to get at a truth, and sometimes is a greater form of truth. One of the ways in which the young man woos the young woman in this story is by showing her the photographs he has been taking. She takes her time to really look at what he has done, shushing him when he breaks her concentrated efforts to understand and validate his vision.

These young lovers are meeting at a place fraught with sexual tension coded in the nudity of the statues. But this time around, the tensions are resolved in a playful manner. The couple, both virgins, head off on a joint adventure full of possibilities, in which art will play a definite role. And it is here, more than anywhere else in the collection, that I believe Hazel Campbell finally lets slip her true feelings about Jamaica: that despite all its challenges, Jamaica is still a place full of new beginnings and infinite possibilities, and that art has a place in the development of the society.

Thank you for your work and your vision, Hazel Campbell.

1.    Bookends Magazine. *The Jamaica Observer*. Kingston: Jamaica. September 8, 2013. Interview: "The Gift of Music and Song: An Interview with Hazel Campbell".

STORIES FROM

THE RAG DOLL

## THE CARRION EATERS

The two old women sat at the table in the middle of the room, working. There were piles of letters to be sorted, entered in a book and filed.

Daphne came from a backroom, walked over to the table and took her seat. She wasn't anxious even to appear to be working. So many stupid letters to be sorted and punched and then placed on the hook in the big book. More letters in the letterbox to be stamped and taken to post office in the hot sun. Such a bother. Not worth the ten dollars a week, she thought.

One of the old women started to speak.

"The young, young bwoy! What a shame! Lawd! An you can bet the parents never even know whey him deh!"

The other old woman sighed and went on punching holes in the letters, importantly.

"The young bwoy that get shot this morning," the first old woman explained, catching Daphne's eye before she looked swiftly away.

"High school bwoy at that. Mam! If the police never reach in time! The poor woman! God only know what dem was gwine do her!"

Stupid woman. Stupid old woman, Daphne thought. Why you don't shut up. Maybe you'd like the young boy to be doing "God only know what" to you… Nobody would…

"Him dead"? the other old woman interrupted her thoughts.

"No. Him in hospital. Have a seat, sir," the first old woman said to a man who had entered the building, asked for Mr. John Ferron and been quietly waiting for an answer.

"A believe somebody in there wid him!"

Can't even take the trouble to find out, Daphne thought. Them suppose to be teaching she an that stupid girl, Lena, all bout the work so them could tek over from them, but all them doing was jealously guarding them job. Won't admit them too old to carry on.

"Hanover Street Baptis have one lovely service last night, you see." The other woman began her story.

Oh, shut up! Oonu can't work widout talk! Thank God the man at the Embassy say that she would hear from them in another month or so… Away from all this… America! Away from these old… A buzzer sounded.

The first old woman had gone to knock at Mr. John Ferron's door to find out if he would see the man who was waiting.

"Him not there. Him soon come back. Wait a little," she said in the direction of the client who had asked for him.

"Coming," she grumbled at the buzzer and looked meaningfully at Daphne as she shuffled to the other door.

Daphne kissed her teeth and walked over to the clerk's desk to pick up a pile of letters which she had to stamp and enter in the mail book.

A man and a woman entered the office. "Is Mr. Ferron in?" the man asked. "Mr. Paul or Mr. John," the old woman at the desk asked.

"Oh! I didn't know there were two!"

"Father and son," the old woman said proudly, as if she was responsible for this fact.

"P. L. Ferron."

"Mr. Paul. That's the father. Tek a seat."

He is handsome, Daphne thought. And such a nice voice. A pity men like him didn't look at her except for one thing. Them look at her and see only a maid who only good to… But she gwine show them. Is only that she didn't get a chance. When her mother died she had to leave school and work, but America next month, maybe. March the latest.

She wasn't no maid neither, not like them old crow. Them two old crow.

Start working wid Ferron and Ferron for two and six a week.

Would believe is them mek the business grow if you hear them talk. Talk, that's all them do. Hanover Street Baptist Church. Wonder what else them know pon Hanover Street.

Sighing wearily, Daphne took up the bundle of letters and prepared to leave the room.

The first old woman rocked her way across the room.

"But Molly, you ever see anything like that Daphne? She hear the buzzer and wouldn't even look up, much less answer it."

"She musbe don't work wid Ferron and Ferron. You no know how dem young people stay dese days? Don't want work. Short frock and money and boy fren. That's all!"

"Who fa pile a things dis?"

"The girl from Casey's. She come in while you was talking to Miss Norma."

"Oh. I was just gwine throw dem off. Come Missis," she called to the girl from Casey's, who had just entered the room. "Move you tings, mek me get on wid the work."

"You can see how old the servants are," the man was saying to the woman.

"Many of these lawyers and solicitors find that it doesn't pay them to move. They're so well established in a particular spot. So they modernise the buildings as much as possible and pass on business from generation to generation. See how modern the facade is, but notice how the old woodwork inside has been preserved. Look at the hand-carving on those stairs. Everywhere cool and dim and musty with age. Look at the panelling in this room. This must have been the hall!"

"Can you imagine them?" his companion murmured dreamily. "The family gathered. Stern papa smoking in the corner. Maybe he wouldn't have been smoking in the presence of the ladies all crinolined and bonnetted. Did they wear bonnets in the house? Maybe Louisa – all the girls were named Louisa, weren't they? – she would be listening eagerly for the clip-clop of the horse on the cobblestones which would mean that her lover, Mr. Bennett, no Mr. Bennett sounds like an old man – Mr. Bogle – no he was a runaway slave, right?"

"You need to go back to school," he told her dryly. "You've got no sense of history."

He looked at her closely and wondered again if he wasn't making a mistake rushing to divorce his wife to marry her.

Who him calling old servant. Why, them wasn't servants at all, not even office maids really. Them didn't scrub floor or anything like that. A little light dusting and carrying water for Mr. John and Mr. Paul and look how much paperwork them had to do. She couldn't even read the name on this envelope M-O-S-E.

"Molly, see if you can mek out dis name."

"Moore. Dat don't belong to Ferron and Ferron. Put it back in the letterbox. That young bwoy won't even read the envelope dem."

"Maybe him can't read."

"Postman can't read? Missis! Tek a seat, mam. All dese people before you."

Daphne came back into the room with a pile of letters. Some were to be delivered by hand. She had to be careful. As she reached for the satchel in which she carried them, her hand bounced over the INFORMATION sign.

Information! Christ! These old crow couldn't tell nobody nothin bout nothin except bout Hanover Street Baptist Church an who dead an bury an in hospital. Look how that Jane face light up when she see the one-arm woman come into the room. She boun to ask her how it happen. She live on dead flesh, on rotten flesh. Old crow, John crow, Jane crow, Molly crow.

"Daphne, why you don't hurry up? You should go to post an come back aready."

"Miss Jones was talking to me," Daphne answered sullenly.

Show off. For the benefit of the clients. Them expect her to call them Miss, too. To show respect. But she wouldn't call them nothin. She wouldn't call them name at all. Miss Jane Crow, Miss Molly Crow. Watch them a look pon the one-arm woman.

See the carrion eaters come.

See them come

Dum, dum.

That was poetry, yes. Like that poetry her Rasta boyfriend tek her to hear the other night at the library. Him like things like that. An sometime him talk like him reading poetry too... Maybe when she went to America she would go to school, night school. Plenty opportunity in America...

Daphne placed her satchel under her arm and walked out through the door.

"I wonder why that young woman looks so angry," the man commented.

"Maybe Mr. Bogle didn't come. There wasn't any clip-clop on cobblestones, nor gently knocking at the door," his companion answered, still dreaming.

## THE RAG DOLL

I

Dessie knelt before the couch in the front room, hands clasped, eyes closed; Dessie, Sister Desdemona, was praying.

Some years before, Johnson, her husband, had deprived her of her weekday prayer meetings, so she now devoted at least half an hour to prayer and meditation in the evenings before he came home from work.

Sister Dessie was a devout churchgoing woman. Johnson was neither devout nor churchgoing – except on the rare occasions when Dessie begged him to attend some special service, and then he would go because he had the idea that what Dessie really wanted was to show him off to her church sisters. But this wasn't entirely true.

True, she liked to show off her husband, but her burning desire was for him to get saved.

For this she prayed night and day.

So Dessie knelt before the big chair in the front room, hands clasped, eyes closed in prayer.

Yes, God had to be praised for the many blessings he had bestowed on her. He had to be thanked for a comfortable home in Independence Park; her own home! Two bedrooms nicely furnished, fenced off from everybody else. He had to be thanked for a steady man who took good care of her. He had to be begged to keep Johnson steady and to make him get saved soon. For if Johnson found another woman! – a woman who would bear him children, he would turn her out and what would she do?

God had also to be begged to help her to say "Thy will be done" with complete acceptance. For when she thought of her childlessness and the cause of it, she sometimes felt stirrings of anger. Didn't God promise to take care of his own?

On her knees Sister Dessie prayed, opening her heart to God. She prayed with concentration, trying to prevent the frightening experience which was occurring with increasing frequency.

Midway through her prayer she seemed to split into two people, one of whom would remain in the attitude of prayer, while the other wandered at will through the years of experiences which made up her life, commenting, sometimes facetiously, sometimes contemptuously, on her thoughts and actions.

When it had first happened she thought she was going mad. She started calling this other voice the Devil, seeing as it tempted her thoughts away from prayer. Gradually she had come to accept it as part of her own self. Dessie talking to Dessie while Sister Dessie prayed.

*You praying fi Johnson get saved. But is pure selfishness you know. That prayer not worth nothing.*

*You not really telling God everything you know. How bout how you mad with fear and jealousy everytime you see Johnson talking to another woman.*

*You can't bear see Miss Nelson with her children and the new baby. Pray bout dat.*

*You malice you neighbour them just sake a dem children. Pray bout dat.*

*Tell him why you run the pickney them from the cherry tree ina the yard.*

*Tell him why you can't suffer the little children to come unto you.*

As it forced her into self-knowledge, Dessie would often find the tears flowing.

*Bawl. A washtub a tears won't wash wey you sins.*

"But a don't do nothing," she would sometimes answer back – aloud.

*The sin in there. Inside you rottening you out,* the voice would reply.

Sometimes there was no voice but she would be aware of its presence watching her. Then suddenly she would find herself completely reliving some important experience in her life and would know that it was this half self forcing her into remembering.

Lately, its favourite subject was the time she had lost the baby she hadn't even known that she was expecting.


II


The neighbours cocked their ears and turned their eyes in the direction of No. 12 as the thin screams rose above the other noises in the lane. The dull thud of blows on human flesh could be heard, as rhythmic and ritualistic as the screams... thump... *whai*... thump... *whai*

Dessie never bawled for "help" and "murder" like a lot of other women. She knew that Johnson had no intention of murdering her, and that the neighbours had no intention of helping her.

As the sounds promised no new excitement, the neighbours returned to their various businesses.

"Cho' why dat fool fool Dessie don't stap har nise!"

"Soun like him beating har little harder dan usual?"

"Him miss las Thursday so him mekking up far it."

"Cho," they said, disappointed.

Somebody turned up a radio. Sparrow was singing a calypso...

*Black up she eye, bruise up she knee*
*Then she will love you eternally*


Soon, Johnson emerged from the side door of the two-room house, jumped on his bicycle, and rode off down the lane, furiously.

Two little boys who were standing by the gate, their bare bottoms showing through their ragged pants, shouted after him, "Black up her yeye, lik out her teet." The few people who were interested enough to listen to them grinned broadly.

"Miss Dessie, you get you regular dose this morning."

"Shut you mout, himpertinent chile. When you get a man tek care a you like Johnson tek care a me… You can talk den."

An impudent laugh was the only reply.

"Dessie, mi dear, a wha you do Johnson dis morning?" another voice asked, falsely sympathetic.

"Ah Rosa, you don't have fi do dat man nothing you hear. De devil in him. Last night, a come from church and…"

Johnson didn't approve of Dessie's churchgoing, especially during the week. While she was at Wednesday night prayer meeting, he ate his cold dinner and fumed.

"Man not suppose to eat no cold dinner," he would tell his friend, Albert, across the road.

"Man work hard all day fi get little food an shelter. Woman mus stay home, look after dem man."

Albert, picking his teeth after his satisfactory meal, would nod in agreement, and from the way he saw Johnson tightening his fist he knew that on Thursday morning Dessie's screams would again be disturbing the lane.

The previous Thursday Dessie had missed her beating because she wasn't feeling well and had stayed home in bed on Wednesday night. Johnson had eaten his cold supper without a word of complaint and had gone to the shop for bay rum to "rub her up". Thursday morning had been quiet in the lane, but the following Thursday things were back to normal.

"Dat woman is getting on me nerves," Johnson told the watchman at the gate as he dismounted and took the clip off his pants.

"She still going to meeting?" the watchman asked. He knew all about the Johnson and Dessie story. All the workers at the tobacco factory knew the story.

"Yes, and leaving cold food fi mi dinner, and when a don't eat it, she warm it up nex morning fi me breakfast. A don't know how a doan dead from bad stomach." He belched acidly to prove its unhealthy state.

"You too sof wid dat woman," the watchman commented.

"What? You shoulda hear her scream when a drop lik ina her skin dis morning."

"Cho dat no serious. She know dat you na hurt har. You have fi do something mek har shame."

"You woulda tink she woulda shame fe de neighbour dem hear har a get lik every Thursday mawning."

"No. Dat is joke now. You have fi do more dan dat fi show har dat you name man."

"What you mean?"

"Which church she go?"

"Is not even church. Is a tent dem pitch pon open land. De parson name Reverend Roy."

"Reverend Roy. Ah oh! Now a understand. A dat samfie man wha have so-so woman ina him church. Listen mek a tell you what we do…"

Next Wednesday evening Dessie locked her door as usual. She was ready to leave for the prayer meeting. As she was about to put the key where Johnson would find it, the impudent girl who lived in the yard called out to her.

"Miss Dessie, why you don't tap go a church an stay home warm up you husband dinner? You like de Thursday mawning lik dem, enh?"

"Shut you mout!" Dessie replied angrily. She didn't want the girl to see where she was putting the key. "It would do you good fi go a church an pray fi you sins before you doom befall you."

"No man not beating me up on Thursday mawning, you hear," the girl laughed.

Because of the girl Dessie forgot that she had the key and walked out of the yard still clutching it in her hand. After a while she absent-mindedly transferred it to her purse and turned her thoughts to the prayer meeting.

The sisters were kneeling on the hard earth, waiting on the Lord.

Many of them had carried pieces of newspaper to protect their long white dresses from getting dirty. Several had already unburdened their hearts. Their whispered prayers filled the tent. An occasional "Praise God" or "Amen" announced the end of another prayer.

Reverend Roy was getting ready to give his sermon.

The sisters settled themselves as comfortably as they could on the hard benches while Reverend Roy opened his Bible for the text. He began calmly enough. Passion had to be built up slowly.

"Brothers and Sisters (there were two brothers – Sister Esmie's two sons aged ten and twelve, who were leaning against each other preparatory to going to sleep), my sermon tonight will be based on the gospel according to…

A hot male voice suddenly came from the rear of the tent. "I have a sermon too, tonight, Reverend…"

Every head turned in the direction of the loud voice, except Sister Dessie's. She had suddenly remembered the key in her purse.

"Our sermon," Reverend Roy repeated, "will be about…"

"You tink it right what you carrying on here?" As yet the speaker could not be identified. Frowning, the sisters tried to concentrate on what Reverend was saying.

"Our sermon," he attempted for the third time.

"My sermon is dat it wrong fi you keep de woman dem ina dis place bout you preaching an praying, an have dem family a yard a starve," the voice bawled. "Can't even get ina dem house."

Someone had started a chorus before the voice had finished.

"*Get thee behind me, Satan,*" they sang lustily, attempting to drown the voice of the unwanted visitor.

Sister Dessie couldn't sing. She sat irresolute, wondering if it wouldn't be better for her to slip out quietly and give Johnson the key so that he would go away. But she was too frightened to move. There was a new sound in his voice which she didn't recognise, so she stayed quiet among the singing sisters and prayed that he would go away

Above the singing his voice could be heard in patches.

"*God is on his throne…*"

"Coulda sing till oona drap…"

"*Get thee behind me Satan…*"

"…want mi woman…"

"*When he calls us home…*"

"Desdemona... outa... outa... here..."

Nobody moved. Only Dessie had heard her name.

"*Get thee...*"

"If you don't come..."

Suddenly six men appeared in the tent. Each carried a stout stick. Nobody saw when Reverend Roy disappeared.

The chorus died on the lips of the screaming sisters. They scattered as Johnson walked up to Dessie, who still hadn't moved, and dragging her by the hand began to use his stick across her back.

This time, as she wasn't sure of his intention, she bawled "Help! Murder!"

When the other sisters realised that it wasn't a general attack, they stopped screaming and calmly watched the beating. For a long time after they would talk about the night Sister Dessie's husband came for her in church.

After that, Sister Dessie stayed at home, on weekdays anyway.

And the watchman at the gate would occasionally wink at Johnson and ask, "How the stomach now?"

Johnson would wink back and say "Fine man, fine. Plenty hot food an ting."

But his laugh would not be genuine. He would never know whether it was a girl or a boy Dessie had been expecting.

### III

Dessie stared through the gates moodily. Everytime she heard the hot belching roar of a motorcycle she hurriedly smoothed her dress and her hair, for Johnson was coming. But when it wasn't him she rested her head on the rails and continued staring out.

"Hi! You! Move from there!" someone shouted. "Get back inside. All a you just waiting fi run wey an gi people more trouble!"

She understood his tone more than his words and backed away from the fence. Because she was walking backwards she fell over a stone. The man at the gate laughed briefly and looked away. Dessie jumped up quickly, brushing off both herself and the baby.

Johnson wasn't coming. Her heart squeezed up in her chest. Was he really going to abandon her in this place? Maybe if she prayed he would come. He would answer her prayer and come… Praying, Dessie looked for the nearest empty bench, knelt down and clasped her hands. She began to pray intensely.

"Baby Jesus in Heaven, I talking to you… You leave dirty water fi me drink an scorpion fi me eat, an you not comin back come see if me dead or alive. Praise God!"

Her voice trailed off and she opened her eyes, got up and sat on the bench, picking burrs off her clothes, thoughtfully rubbing them between her fingers.

There was something else she had to do but she couldn't remember. She frowned in concentration, but the baby started to cry and she couldn't remember. It was time to tidy the baby anyway, so that Johnson would see him looking pretty. She took him out of her pocket and looked at him. He was a fine boy. She thought perhaps Johnson should take him home. This was no place to grow a child. Then she felt very sad. She had done something bad and she couldn't remember. The baby started to cry again. She picked it up to hush it. Then she remembered. She had broken the baby bottle and she had nothing to feed him. In a fit of temper she threw the baby on the ground and began to weep, big waterfall tears splashing sadness on her breast.

"Hello Dessie," Johnson greeted her, trying not to notice the tears. He was late he knew. He wasn't feeling well and had almost not come. But she was a burden he would carry until one of them died. She was a burden he accepted because he blamed himself for her illness.

"The baby ready fi go home," she told him, picking it up and putting it in his hands.

He took the doll from her and sighed. Every week she sewed a rag doll in her therapy class and every Sunday she gave it to him to take home. On his way home over the causeway he would throw it into the sea as he had done the others. Meantime he would pretend with her.

"Tek good care a him, you hear," she said anxiously. Then she smiled. "A can mek good baby, enh? A mek de bes baby ina the class. Everyday a mek, him get prettier an prettier. Don't it is a pretty baby?"

Johnson nodded in agreement. He continued to nod with his sad, patient expression while she babbled on.

## IV

Sometime after Dessie joined the Valley Church of God in Christ, the Sisters began their weekly visits to hospitals. It was Sister Valda, Elder's wife, who had started it. Only seven of the Sisters were housewives and so could find the time to visit during the week. Seven of them, every Thursday afternoon, dressed in white, took their bibles and tracts and went to cheer the sick.

Sister Desdemona never missed a visit. On Thursdays Johnson stayed at work late so she was always back in good time to fix his supper. It was she who suggested that they extend their visits to include the Maternity Hospital.

At first the others were reluctant to do so. After all, few people in a maternity hospital were really sick. It was a place of life, not of death, like the General Hospital. The Bible said take care of the sick and needy. At Jubilee, however, they soon met need of another kind. Many of the mothers, especially the young ones, proud of their procreativity, not yet overburdened by their fertility, were hostile and insolent and would have nothing to do with them. But there were many glad of a sympathetic ear.

"Wha fi do wid de baby? How it gwine get food? Baby-fader disappear when him hear sey me expecting. Never even get clothes fi it. Baby father sey a no fi him. Six more a yard. Ten more. Eight more. Different father. How wi gwine manage? Babyfader no want the family planning."

The Sisters advised where they could and prayed where they couldn't. No mind is as open to conversion as the mind full of problems and fears...

One afternoon, a few months after the Sisters started visiting

Jubilee, Sister Dessie fainted right at the steps of the Hospital. Smelling salts and much excitement were applied and she quickly revived. But she had to take it easy for a few days and missed one or two Thursday visits. When the Sisters discreetly asked what the doctor had said, with much embarrassment Sister Dessie revealed her secret.

The Sisters were a little taken aback. Dessie wasn't so young. In fact, they thought she was past such activity. However they congratulated her.

"The visiting to Jubilee start you in the right direction, Sister Dessie."

"Fancy after all this time," they marvelled. "You husban mus be glad enh! What him sey?"

A slight frown crossed Sister Dessie's face. She wasn't sure about Johnson. She wasn't sure what the doctor had told him all those years ago. She was taking a big chance on that; he had never talked about the miscarriage with her. And she had refused to acknowledge what the doctor had told her.

For several weeks she spat constantly, was sick in her stomach, managed to vomit once or twice and fainted several times. It was Johnson himself who diagnosed her case.

One morning he said, "Dessie, you better go see a doctor. You going on like somebody pregnant."

Dessie smiled with happiness.

"You comfortable? Drink plenty milk and water. Don't harass youself. Get a girl help clean the house. Mi fren them sey you mus get plenty res."

He went out of his way to be nice to her; this was his chance to make up.

When she started to show, he would leave taxi money for her to go to the clinic.

He was a little hurt that she kept him at such a distance. But he understood that she was delicate and he wasn't taking any chances this time. He had always felt guilty since that time she had lost her baby.

So nine months passed.

One Friday morning nobody took particular notice of a pregnant woman entering the hospital. And nobody took special notice of a woman leaving with a baby. That's what the hospital was there for.

Dessie took her baby home.

A boy baby she discovered it to be.

When Johnson reached home that night the house was shut up, tight, and his heart jumped. Dessie gone to hospital? Her time was near.

But when he heard the baby crying he suddenly felt afraid. Something that had been nagging at his mind for several months began to take shape. Dessie opened the door for him and when he saw her, he understood. She had forgotten to take off the pillow stuffing she had been using; she was clutching a baby tightly; and she was mad with joy.

V

Their frenzy rose with the moon. The brighter the sky, the harder they shook the bars and screamed and shouted. It was enough to drive anybody crazy.

Dessie put her hands over her ears to deaden the noise. She was being punished in hell. But she was a saint; how could she be a sinner at the same time?

It was very confusing. Why was she dead? She had done something wrong and now she was being punished in this hell hole.

There was no stink like the stink of hell, no heat like the heat of hell.

She could hear God preaching on the other side and she bawled out, "Parson God, save me!"

Every time she yelled the heat got hotter, until, screaming, she fell to the floor.

Then she remembered. She had broken the babybottle and the baby was crying and there was nothing to feed him. She held the baby close to her and began to sing to it. Eventually it fell asleep. She put it down on the bed and sat on the floor watching it.

She was the angel of God hovering over, guarding the baby. Dessie, the guardian angel of babies. The light in the sky was her halo. Her great fear was that the devil would steal her baby from her. Yesterday a woman had tried to steal her baby.

She had bitten her severely.

## VI

Johnson stood by the taxi waiting for them to call him to come for Dessie.

Dessie was going home. He was very sad. When they told him that the Asylum was changing its policy of treatment and that Dessie, being a mild case, would have to go home and be treated as an outpatient, he nearly died of shock. For the three years he had been visiting her she had shown no sign of improvement. He had buried her in this place. His weekly visits had been like taking flowers to a grave. He hadn't expected her to rise from the tomb. It frightened him.

And the woman he had got to keep house for him had recently delivered his son. He didn't know what he was going to do with Dessie. Nobody wanted a mad woman in their house. Perhaps he would keep her locked in the back bedroom. The woman and the baby would have to move in with him. He couldn't abandon Dessie, neither would he be deprived of his son. It was hard on him.

When he saw her coming towards him he thought that this week he wouldn't be able to throw away the rag doll she was clutching as usual. Then he thought that if she made a doll each week there would soon be no space in his house for people or dolls…

## FIRST LOVE

*FIRST love sweet so till*
*First love! sometimes it mek you bawl*
*First love! sometimes it mek you bawl*
*First love's joy lingers through a lifetime of memories*
*It mek them sey "ole firetick easy fi ketch up"*
*Handle first love with a great deal of care*
*Like a pressed flower even when colour and smell are gone*
*Its brown age keeps the secret that once it bloomed*


– Wha this I hearing bout you an Missa Georgie?
    – Me an Georgie, Mama?
    – Yes, Miss Innocent. You an Georgie!
    – I doan know what you talking bout.
    – You jus mine you step, you hear! That bwoy not fi you. Him come fram mad breed. I doan care what Elder them think bout him. I doan want to ketch you talking to him… An you too young fi man. Plenty time fi man. You mus study you book an pass you exam them. The Lord have great plans fi you. I jus know that –
– Yes, Mama.
She was plaiting her hair and glad that this gave her the opportunity to turn her head away from the scolding voice.
It shocked her that anybody knew. That anybody could have guessed. It must be true then what they said – that the Elders could smell out love even before it started.
She and Georgie. Youth Elder. So different from the other boys. A man among them. She heard that he was talking about setting up his own garage when his apprenticeship finished. She

heard that he already had a lot of tools and she knew that he did odd jobs on people's cars bout the place. He carried around the garage smell on him, even on Sunday. She liked it. It was a man smell.

All the girls in love with him and he not noticing anybody. She too. Funny that morning how she suddenly knew. One minute she was singing peacefully in the choir – the next she was nearly fainting. His face! He had been gazing up at her from his seat in the front bench and his face had seemed to grow larger and larger till it filled the church and nearly suffocated her. Then she knew. As if he had possessed her. And she knew that he knew, though they hadn't said a word to each other. How she loved him! No wonder other people had noticed. Georgie! Youth Elder!

Granny's Sounds across the road started up…

*Eenie, Meenie, Minie mo*
*Reely didn't know that you love I so…*

And her mother in the backyard started to sing almost at the same time in her constant vain attempt to drown out the sounds…

*It's the sweetest name*
*And I love him so*
*Tell it out to all the world…*

Gloria smiled. All the world was thinking about love it seemed. She picked up her books with a sigh. She was going to study at the library. She couldn't study at home because of all the noise rivalry about her, especially on a Saturday.

The Lane people watched her progress down towards the main road.

– Saint Gloria gone study har book.

– Bad mine! A henvy you henvy har.

– Miss Righty a ole her head traight as per usual.

– Think she better than everybody else cause she a go a high school. Cause she pass exam. Cause she tekkin exam.

– Mus a she one bright.

– Mawning mi dear! My! You lookin sweet as usual.

– Lawd, Miss Rosie lucky, sah! The one gal pickney and look how she tun out.

– Get off the street. Go study you book like Miss Rosie daughter.

– A mussy she one bright. Tick out mi tongue after that stuck up gal. She a nuisance. Gloria dis. Gloria dat. Miss Righty. Miss Brighty. Miss Perfect. Yaah!

– Watch you step, daughter! – The woolly tams at the corner shop greeted her.

– Study hard you ear, mi dear. An when you ready fi the other tings member Rudie-I is ere.

Loud laughter. She smiled with them. Most of them she knew. She had gone to school with them. She knew their sisters but there were certain taboos to maintain.

Saints didn't mix too freely with sinners. They could contaminate.

– Bretherin. You ave fi jine church fi ketch dat deh one yeye.

– Gway! Dem ave some daughter ina dat dere church! Whoo-whai-aye! Irie!

– Like-a-who so? Pepsi?

– Sista Pepsi to you, Bigga. Mine a puncture you soul case! A knife flashed out in jest.

She passed beyond range of their clowning. Georgie! Wonder if she would meet him. He never lingered on the streets. Always had a job to do. Only place he was still was in church. Georgie! So intense as if – God-possessed. Georgie! If she didn't stop thinking about him like this she wouldn't pass her exam. The shame of failing now.

— Miss Righty, Miss Brighty, Yaah!

★

The rumours ran up and down the lanes, through the streets, cross the fences, in the backyards. Over in Jones Town rapings and shootings.

Ghost Town shut down. Nobody can't walk pon the street. Las

week it was two streets away. Las night, nex door. Miss Suzie and her daughter. Lawd have mercy!

Multiple rapes. Ten men, six men, eight men – one girl! Oh God! Whispa this one – Louise was in Public. All part of her tear up an jine up ina one! Lawd ave mercy upon us!

Lock up you gal pickney them. Try bolt the flimsy door them. Nobody safe. If a youth ask her an she sey no, him bring him fren them and tek it. Some of de gal them bad. Dem beg fi trouble. All them sinful backless, frontless frock. But some a dem good and innocent – like Gloria.

– What to do to keep her safe? Violence and sin all around. I wish she was a boy pickney.

– Sen her to Green Island Mission House, Sister Rosie. Dem need a mission teacher an she finish her exam them. Is time she went out into the field.

– Suppose she doan pass?

– Nonsense! You ever hear Gloria fail her exam them. She is a good girl.

– An we don't like this thing wid Georgie.

– Yes, Elder.

– She too young, an him doan reach nowhere yet. We don't think the Lord plan this match.

– True. You never even ketch them a talk.

– Is like them talking all the while without words.

– Sen her to Green Island. I will write Elder Mother this very day.

– I doan know what I gwine do without her. But if is the Lord's will. An at least she will be safe from this violence an sin.


– So them sending you wey.

– Yes.

– We doan ave plenty missionary work to do ere?
She didn't answer.

– You want to know why them sending you wey?
No answer. But her eyes dragged the declaration she wanted from him.

– Is cause I love you.

Once again the knowledge of possession tightened her throat so she could hardly breathe. Goose pimples rippled her flesh.

– Them think I not good enough for you. But I will show them. When you reach twenty-one, two years time, I going marry you. I gwine work hard and set up myself and come fi you. You belong to me. An no other man gwine get you.

She stood before him dumb, with the shock waves ripping up her soul and delivering it to him. Dumb before the ecstasy of being claimed, and he didn't even look at her when he said goodbye.

## SEE ME IN ME BENZ AN T'ING;

### LIKE THE LADY WHO LIVED ON THAT ISLE REMOTE

The lady of the house sucked her teeth angrily as she put down the telephone.

"Carl knows I can't stand driving down to his factory," she complained loudly.

"Why doesn't he just send the driver for the car!" she gestured in annoyance. "In a hurry, my foot!"

The maid dusting the furniture nearby didn't comment; she knew her place better than that. In any case she wasn't being directly addressed.

"Don't forget the upstairs sitting room," the lady ordered, suddenly turning her annoyance on the maid. "Yesterday I ran my finger over the TV up there. Absolutely filthy! Don't know why it's so difficult to get you people to do an honest day's work."

Carl had absolutely ruined her day. She would be late for the session with the girls and miss all the nice gossip. Furthermore, Carl knew that she hated driving through the section of the city where he worked. So much violence, and all those people glaring at her in hostility, as if she were personally responsible for the squalor in which they lived. Like wild animals some of them with their uncombed heads and crazy talk. Watching her as if any minute they would attack. No wonder the papers were always full of horrible stories about them. Now she wouldn't even have time to do her nails and she had so wanted to show off the new shade Sylvia had brought back from Miami for her. Damn that Carl!

Quarrelling with the maid, the gardener and the two Alsatians blocking her path to the car, she gathered her purse and her keys and got into the sleek black Benz which had been resting in the double carport.

The 4.5 litre, V8 engine sprang alive and settled into a smooth purr before she eased into reverse, turned it around and put it into drive to make the long trip from home on the hilltop to Carl's workplace by the seashore. It gathered speed as she rolled down the hill, and, as always, she felt a tiny moment of panic at the strength of the horsepower growling softly under the bonnet, controlled only by the swift movement of foot from accelerator to brake as necessary. Carl had promised her this car if ever he was able to buy a newer one, but since 1972, no new models had been allowed into the island, so she had to be content with the Mazda, which didn't satisfy her half as much as the Benz did.

Annoyance returned sharply as she imagined how the girls would have exclaimed when she drove up in the Benz.

"Eh! Eh! How you manage get Carl to part with his car?" they would tease. And she would explain that the Mazda was in the garage so she had to borrow the Benz, pretending with them that it was these great big problems which made life so difficult. Then they would settle down to a nice chat about the Number of Things they were having to do without! And Who had just gone, or Who had decided to! And pass a pleasant hour or so laughing at the kinds of things some people were packing into trailers. And had they heard that Jonesie was working in a shoe store in Miami as a sales clerk! No! God forbid! And *my dearing,* and *oh dearing* each other, they would, with large eyes, contemplate life in the 70s, each realising, but not saying, that they did not know how to come to grips with it.

As she skirted the Sealand trailer parked at the foot of the hill, it reminded her that she must renew her campaign to get Carl to migrate. After all he could even pack the factory machinery in the trailer, and they could relocate in Florida. Lots of other people were doing it. Things were really getting impossible. Imagine, not even tampons in the shops. Good thing she knew many people who were still commuting between America and Jamaica, so she could get a ready supply of the things she absolutely couldn't do without.

As she passed through Half-Way-Tree, she collected her wandering thoughts. She would need all her concentration to get safely through this part of the city. Just last week a friend of theirs had been pulled from his car and savagely beaten because he had scraped somebody's motorcycle with the car.

She made sure all the doors were locked, touched the power button for the windows and turned on the air-conditioning. She was always grateful for the ability to lock-up herself in the car. Lock out the stenches of gutters and overcrowded human flesh. Lock out the sounds of human distress. From the cool, slight dimness of the red interior of the Benz, even the sight of distress took on a sort of unreal appearance, so she could pass through uncontaminated.

A little past Half-Way-Tree, she hesitated a moment before deciding to turn down Maxfield Avenue. She hated cutting across Spanish Town Road, but this way was shorter, and Carl had said to hurry. That was why he hadn't sent somebody for the car. The double journey would take too long. She had wasted enough time already, so she would have to hurry. She was afraid of Carl's bad temper. He would lash out at her even in front of the factory staff if he was sufficiently annoyed. She was sure it wasn't all that important for him to get the car. Probably some luncheon or other for which he needed the Benz to impress somebody. He wouldn't dream of driving one of the small company cars. Not him. No matter how it inconvenienced her.

By the time she reached the first set of lights, the traffic had already begun to crawl. Not much use her ability to move from 0 to 60 miles per hour in ten seconds flat, here. Not much use all that horse power impatiently ticking under her restraining foot. Thank God for the air conditioning.

As she waited for the green light, the billboard on top of the shop at the corner caught her eye. LIFE IS A MUTUAL AFFAIR it read. Somebody ought to tell Carl that. Instead of dragging her through this horrid part of town he should be protecting her. Any moment now a bullet could shatter the glass and kill her.

She spent a moment indulging her overactive imagination, seeing her blood-splattered breast and she leaning back as still as she had seen a body in some film or other. The impatient horn behind her made her suddenly realise that the lights had changed.

She moved off quickly, smiling at her melodramatic thoughts. Actually she wasn't feeling too afraid. After all, didn't Carl do this trip everyday? And if there were problems outside, she couldn't hear.

That group of people milling around outside that shop, for instance, she couldn't see what was creating the excitement and since she couldn't hear either, what did it matter? They were like puppets in a silent movie. In fact she could not decide what they were doing. Was it a dead man they were looking at?

Christ! Her imagination! She really must do something about it. Lots of people getting crazy these days, because of all the stress and strain. They were probably just fassing in somebody's business as usual, idle bitches that they were. Look at those on that other piazza. Wining up themselves and gyrating to some beat loud enough to penetrate her castle of silence. That's all they were good for. And those others milling around the betting shop, race forms in hand. How could the country progress with so many idlers never wanting to do any work? And even those who said they worked couldn't do a thing. She couldn't get Miriam to clean the bathrooms properly. No amount of telling did the trick. No matter how often she told her what to do. No matter what amount of cleaning things she bought.

The traffic began to crawl again as she neared Spanish Town Road. Just at the part she would have liked to pass over quickly. Now she had plenty of time to look out through her smoky glass.

Another billboard. Advertising Panther. Goodlooking youth. Not like the dirty bums cotching up the walls, the streets posts, and any fence strong enough to bear their weight. The Panther boy looked like somebody who would care about life and not spawn too many children. But what did he have to do with these dirty creatures passing as men around the place. Giving all those worthless women thousands of children by the minute. Silly ad. Silly place to put it.

Ah! There was her favourite on the other side. Beautiful clouds and a jet taking off into the sunset – FASTEST WAY TO CANADA – Escape from the closing-in feeling. It was only a matter of time, her friends were saying, before all of Kingston and St. Andrew looked like these dumps around her. Zinc fences hiding poverty and nastiness, hate and crime. Smells she could only imagine. People living, no, not living, existing on top of each other. God forbid that she should ever live like that. That she should even live close to this. Bad enough to have to drive through.

Suddenly she realised that none of the cars were moving, neither up nor down, and that there was an unusual amount of people on the streets, even for this crowded area.

What could be the matter?

Then she noticed the driver in front of her turning up his car windows in haste, seconds before she saw the first part of the crowd running between the cars. Running in her direction.

Oh God! She prayed softly. Had it finally happened? Were they going to get her? Stories she had heard about riots and those who got caught in them raced through her thoughts.

But even in her panic she still felt fairly safe. Wasn't she protected in her air-conditioned car? People were swarming around like the cartoon figures on *Spider Man*, the TV show her children were always watching. And she was looking on at the action, as if she were in a drive-in movie, with a larger-than-life screen surrounding her. But even as she watched, the sounds of their distress began to filter into her castle.

She wondered what was happening, but dared not open her window to find out. Better to stay locked up in the car and hope that whatever it was would allow her to get moving soon.

In the distance she saw something like a wisp of smoke and thought perhaps it might be a fire. But why would the people be running away from it? And why did they look so frightened?

And even as she noticed their fright, it turned to anger right before her eyes. One minute they were running away from something, wave after wave of them. The next, like a freeze in a movie, a pause long enough to allow anger to replace fright.

She could tell by the shape of their mouths that they were angry. By their swoops for weapons that they were angry.

From nowhere, it seemed, sticks, stones and bottles appeared and began to fly around.

The car, she panicked. They would scratch the car, and what would Carl say? That the damn ducoman wouldn't match the shade and he would have to do over the whole car if there was any duco available? Funny how, for a moment, Carl's anger about a scratched car seemed more real than the anger of the mass of people milling around about her.

The traffic going in the opposite direction had somehow managed to move on, and those behind her were frantically trying to turn around to escape the mob.

Tense and nervous, she put the car into reverse and put her finger on the horn hoping that they would clear the way for her to turn around. But all she did was to bring down their wrath on her. The reality of their anger began to reach her when she felt the human earthquake rocking the car. A human earthquake fed by anger. Anger now turned against the Benz, the out-of-place status symbol in their midst.

The driver before her had abandoned his car. The doors were wide open, the people like ants tearing off the wings of an injured beetle. Oh! God! There was one of the mad men trying to open her door to pull her out. To destroy her. She didn't need to hear them yelling, "Mash it up! Mash it up!" She shut her eyes in pain as the shattering sound reached her and the stone which had smashed the windscreen settled on the seat beside her, letting in the reality of angry sounds, angry smells, demented faces and nightmare hands grabbing her.

She didn't hear herself screaming as they dragged her from the car, roughly discarding her to fight as best she could. They weren't interested in her. Only in the Benz. It must be destroyed. The insulting symbol, black as their bodies, inside red as their blood.

Mash it up! Not just a scratch. Damage it beyond repair. Rip out its red heart. Turn it over. And just to make sure, set it on fire. Destroy it forever.

She stood in the crowd and she still didn't feel their reality. She was remembering the day her husband had brought the car home. The first year the factory had made a profit, he had ordered this car to celebrate. *"This is the symbol, baby,"* he'd said. *"The symbol that we've arrived."* That was why, between them, they jokingly referred to it as the Status Symbol.

Her feelings now were tied up with its destruction. Her blood scattered in the streets. Her flesh being seared by the fire. And the sudden roar of the flames as the Benz caught fire, pulled a scream of animal rage from her very bowels.

The roar of the sacrifice quieted the mob's anger. As quickly as they had come they began to melt away.

The lady didn't notice. She didn't hear herself bawling. Neither did she feel the gentle hands of the two old women steering her away from the scene.

"Thank God is only the car!" they whispered, as they hurried her away from the street, down a lane and into a yard. They took her behind one of the zinc fences, into the safety of their humanity. "Sometimes the people them not so fortunate," they murmured as they bathed her cuts and bruises and gave her some sweet sugar and water to drink. "You is lucky is only this happen to you."

They didn't ask her name. It wasn't important who she was. She needed help and they gave what they could without question, fear or favour.

## A DISTRICT CALLED FELLOWSHIP

I

"Quarter pound salt fish, Mass Joe! Look how long me tan up a call quarter pound salt fish! All now the res a food cook, lef the meat kind."

The Saturday evening shop crowd shifted its feet restlessly as the shrill voice made itself heard above the other Saturday evening noises of chatter, domino challenges, and occasional laughter.

This was the signal for all the shoppers to start loudly calling for goods. Calls for kerosene ile, matches, bread, meal, flour, matches, bread, ile, sugar, mackerel – all rolled together to confuse the shopkeeper, Mass Joe and his wife, Miss Neeta.

"Nobody not getting no serve till oonu tap the nise!" Miss Neeta shouted.

Even though they were familiar with it, Miss Neeta's coarse masculine voice always surprised her listeners. There was a momentary hush.

"Now then," she said, taking advantage of the silence, "one bi one. You, Wingy Jerry, what you want?"

The rest of the shoppers grumbled about the service, but more softly now, because Mass Joe's was the only shop in the district and since many of them would be asking for credit, they couldn't afford to vex Miss Neeta.

Mass Joe grinned at the quick restoration of order and picked his teeth with a match stick before helping to serve. He didn't like to sell in the shop and would only serve the already wrapped items like bread and condensed milk, or things from the dry goods section. It was useless asking him for a pound of salt or sugar if it wasn't already wrapped. And as to mackerel! You mus be mad!

Him to push him han into the salt barrel an fish roun fi the fish? No sah! The only thing he was willing to dirty his hand with was the money. So the shoppers ended up waiting on Miss Neeta's pleasure, grumbling to each other, but not daring to be facety to her.

"Whey Rosa?" Mass Joe asked loudly.

"Gone a bush, as per usual." This reply came from one of the men who were standing around outside the shop, idly watching the domino players, waiting on a chance to play.

Mass Joe sucked his teeth. His one girl child, Rosa, was a disgrace to him. Instead of staying in the shop and helping her mother, especially on Saturday when it was busy time, she rarely could be found. The badminded people say it was because she went to bush with the boys in the district. Any of them, or all of them, they said. It was worse since she leave school last year. He would have to find something for her to do soon, since she wasn't interested in the shop. The next thing, she would get pregnant and he would have to start minding some village rascal's bastard. Must be because she was quarter-breed, he thought. His sister did warn him not to get mix up with the half-Chiney woman them call Miss Neeta. But look how the shop prosper since him tek her. And it was she who had suggested that other business, she who had made the connection which was turning out so profitable. Chiney blood know how to run business. If only that pickney Rosa wasn't so wayward.

"That is one dallar and forty-eight cent, an me not writing down nothing more fi you madder. Either you pay me or lef the things!"

Miss Neeta laid a protective hand over the groceries until the girl, who had been trying to trust the things, reluctantly unfolded the two dollar bill tightly squeezed up in her hand. She had been expecting that Miss Neeta would ask for payment, but her mother had told her to try to get more credit if she could.

It was things like this that made Miss Neeta a good business woman. She would give credit, but she could squeeze money out of a green lime when necessary, and always seemed to know when her customer could pay cash. So Mass Joe's shop prospered while the other two shops in the village centre remained closed.

From time to time, some enterprising person, usually a new-comer to the district, would try to set up business, and the closed doors of one or other of the shops in the square would be opened, only to be closed a short time later. Nobody could compete with Miss Neeta and Mass Joe, who sold almost everything the people could want to buy.

A motorcycle which they had heard coming in the distance for some time suddenly came around one of the corners and puttered to a stop in front of the shop.

Silence fell while everybody gazed at the two dreads who alighted and were about to enter the shop. Everybody had heard stories about strangers holding up shops. Over in the next district, it had happened only the other day.

Mass Joe looked anxiously across the street to the two youths who were leaning against the closed shop door there. But their hands remained in their pockets and no sign of life came from behind their dark-glassed faces.

The silent tension in the shop mounted while the two motor-cycle riders entered and casually looked around.

"I, Bredda! A you name Joe Brown?"

Mass Joe nodded, yes.

"You have any beer pan the ice?"

Mass Joe recognised the password and nodded again.

"You have to come roun the back," he said, referring to the little shed he had built at the rear of the shop. It was for drinking people who could afford to buy a couple of rounds, so that not many of the villagers used it. Business could easily be conducted there.

The dreads followed Mass Joe out of the shop.

"What you having?" Mass Joe asked the men as they sat down around one of the shiny-top tables.

"Threeman fi I an de bredda ere," the talkative one answered.

No introductions were made. No names were called at these meetings. Mass Joe didn't really know any of "them". Different people made the arrangements each time.

Mass Joe opened the stouts and a Red Stripe for himself.

The men gulped about half the liquid all at once. Then, wiping his mouth with the back of his hand, the talker started.

"We doan hear nuttin from you this long time!"

Mass Joe didn't answer.

"Is time fi another delivery. We come arrange it."

"Bwoy, things getting tough roun here." Mass Joe scratched his head and talked very slowly.

"What you mean, tough?"

"Well, the owner them a organise fi ketch the goat thief them. An the bwoy them a ask fi more money cause it gettin dangerous."

"Not another cent!" the talker interrupted.

The silent one, who had finished his stout, took out his knife and began to flick it around playfully. It was more of a nervous habit than a threat, but Mass Joe glanced at him and a little sweat suddenly formed on his skin and made him shiver.

He was afraid of any dealings with these people, but urged on by Miss Neeta and tempted by the money, he had committed himself to supplying them and now he had to obey all their orders. Besides, as long as he was involved with them, his shop was fairly safe from raids and organised theft. So he prospered both ways by joining them.

As long as he could supply them, he got good money. On a good night when the boys rustled up to fifteen goats, he sometimes made as much as three hundred dollars after he paid them their meagre share of thirty dollars each. He had been putting this money away in the bank steadily. The last time, the book had shown that he had two thousand three hundred dollars to his credit. He felt very rich. He wasn't sure what he wanted to do with this money. Just to have it was enough.

"We have a passero waiting fi a whole heap a mutton. When you can deliver?" the talker continued.

"About nex week?"

"You a joke! We talking bout tinight. The van wi come to the usual spot at the usual time. See that you ready!"

The two men got up and walked away.

Shortly after, Mass Joe heard the S90 being revved up and he listened with the beer bottle in his hand and a bitter look on his face as the putt-putting of the motor increased sharply and then gradually faded away into the distance.

Mass Joe didn't like being pushed around. He didn't like the short notice they had given him.

He went to the front of the shop and called loudly, "Hi! You two lazy bwoy! Come pack some bottle fi mi."

The two lounging youths across the road very casually walked over and followed him as he returned to the shed at the back of the shop.

Part of their work was to do odd jobs for Mass Joe and run errands as he requested, when they were not actually watching the shop.

The three of them pretended to be packing bottles on a shelf while Mass Joe gave his instructions.

"Whey Randy?" he asked.

"Him gone do some business," one of them answered.

Mass Joe thought about Rosa and sucked his teeth. "Only business him have fi do is help watch the shop. That's what him get pay for. Tonight," he continued, "Miss Cooper, Coolie Man and Missa Warwar. Five each."

"But you did say maybe is nex week."

"Business change. We mus deliver tinight."

"Listen, Bossman. I an I need more bread!"

"What?"

"Money, man. More money."

"You a joke!"

"No! Youthman ere daughter expectin. Have fi buy baby clothes an ting. Responsibility, man. What you a pay a week time cyan do. An dis ya business gettin dangerous. So mek we talk more money, fore we talk more business."

Mass Joe felt cornered. Everybody was bullying him today.

"Not a farthing more. An anytime oonu feel like talkin, member sey a oonu a go a jail. A oonu tief the goat them. Me only sell it. An plenty more youth woulda glad fi get the money."

"But a wha do dis yar man, enh?" one of the youths began.

The other put his hand on his shoulder and said, "Cool it, Iya!"

"Alright, Mass Joe," he continued, "later, as usual? Same place, nuh?"

Mass Joe nodded at them, his vexation showing. He was thinking that maybe it was time he stopped mixing with these thieves. Anytime they started making threats, it was time to stop. Maybe tonight, after they had paid him, he would tell them that he was finished with them. Is that half-Chiney woman get him mix up with these damn criminal.

Angrily, he turned to the shop prepared to use the slightest excuse to vent his annoyance on her.

II

Stella Reid slowly approached the village centre.

She was on her way to Mass Joe to make the usual Saturday purchases for Granny and Aunty Missis.

As she passed the playfield she noticed that some boys were playing cricket. She looked to see if Randy was there, then she remembered that he didn't play cricket and those things anymore. He now went around with Jigger and Rupert, doing what, nobody really knew, except to hang around Mass Joe's shop, hands in pockets, eyes unseen behind the Foster Grant dark dark-glasses they always wore.

When she reached the shop, she looked for him in vain. Only Jigger and Rupert were there, leaning against the wall.

Sensing her unasked question, Jigger, who didn't like her from the day he had tried to touch her breasts and she had boxed him, said, "Looking fi Randy, sister?"

Rupert said, "Him gone tend little business…"

"Yes," Jigger added spitefully, "him gone a bush wid you-know-who," he pointed at the shop while at the same time making suggestive movements with the lower part of his body.

Stella looked away quickly, ashamed that they had so quickly recognised her need for Randy. Since she had left school last year she did nothing but dream of Randy and going to America in that order.

Her mother was getting out papers for her to join her in America, and meantime Granny and Aunty Missis daily warned her about mixing up with any of the village boys; warned her about getting pregnant; and watched her like a hawk. As if they knew she couldn't get Randy out of her thoughts ever since the day, months ago, he had bought her ice cream at the school fair and stayed with her most of the afternoon.

That he had hardly noticed her since didn't really matter.

She had in her daydreams built up a whole myth about him as her boyfriend. The things he would do for her and say to her; and she to him. And she had been satisfied with just the occasional glimpse of him that she got. Only she couldn't help feeling jealous everytime she heard that he was with another girl.

It was very confusing. She didn't know exactly what it was she wanted. She wanted to go to her mother in America. She didn't want to be a bad girl. But there was something she wanted from Randy, too. And now he was with that bad girl, Rosa.

Angrily, she turned into the shop.

Mass Joe watched her enter the shop and wondered with regret why his Rosa couldn't be like Stella Reid. True his Rosa was prettier, and could flash her long black hair about and turn over a man's heart, but that Stella was such a nice girl, a good girl.

Once or twice he had tried to sweet talk her as he had tried to sweet talk most of the growing girls in the village, and he was satisfied that she wouldn't entertain him. She was so quiet, and yet friendly. A girl who obviously had nothing to hide.

He heard she was going to America. That was the best thing. If she stayed in the district too long, the next thing one of the worthless boys would start to breed her and that would be the end of her.

Only a few people were in the shop by this time so Stella got served quickly. Miss Neeta was always quick to serve her because she never asked for credit, unlike so many of the other people. Her grandmother and aunt were no richer than anybody else in the district, but they took pride in not owing any money. As Granny was always saying – only when they reached the stage when they had to box way cow to eat grass would she trust food.

Besides, Stella's mother sent money for them. Every now and then they would bring the American dollars for him to change. Yes, they were good customers.

Stella finished packing the groceries in the big plastic bag she carried and went outside.

Immediately she became aware of the third youth across the street. Randy had returned. She looked in his direction briefly and started to walk up the road to home.

A sudden spell of dizziness attacked her as her blood raced around, acknowledging the fact that he was coming after her.

"Ay! Stella! I hear you lookin fi me!" Randy said catching up with her.

"No!" she answered timidly.

"So them bwoy sey. Mek me carry the bag fi you. It look heavy."

"No," she said. "Granny wi quarrel."

"Cho! Fi you Granny quarrel bout everyting too much. An it mek me no check you, you know. Specially how me no go a church," he laughed. "So what you want?"

"Nothing," she replied. It was nice walking beside him and having him notice her.

"Them bwoy sey you gone a bush wid Rosa!" she said, surprising herself as well as him.

"Cho! No notice them. Them too lie. Me had fi see a man over Islington! Me jus come back."

Suddenly, believing him, she felt happy.

"How I man fi see you if Granny a quarrel and Aunty a watch like a hawk watch chicken. Woulda think you is precious stone the way them gwan."

"Me going to Merica," she said, trying to explain their behaviour.

"Me know. Tell you what. You can tief out tinight?"

"No-o," she said, her eyes round with fright and possibility.

"After them gone a bed, tek time tief out an meet me up a Macca Fat corner. No, not there. That too near to Centre. Up the road at the old post by the guava tree."

"No-o! she said again.

"Yes!" he said, "A waiting fi you. Here, tek you bag fore Granny start quarrel and watch you."

### III

Rosa, crouching in the bushes not far from the road, saw Randy carrying Stella's bag and she knew that he was sweet-talking her. She could tell by the way he held his head, leaning to one side.

He always did that when the sweet talk boiled up in him. It was what he did with her. Jealousy ripped through her belly like a knife and she doubled her fists in anger.

Although she went with any of the boys who caught her fancy, she had singled out Randy as her own. He was so gentle and old-man wise. He never made her feel that he was merely using her body like all the others, but that there was something more, something special about her that he enjoyed everytime.

And that bitch Stella Reid was out to get him. Many other girls wanted him, she knew, but she feared none of them, only that smooth-face Stella, walking like her legs can't part. Sweet smiling like Virgin Mary. Ever since they were in school, she had hated her. She would mark her face for her if she tried to get Randy. Draw a pussy on her face with a knife if she dared to go with Randy.

Fuming, she came out of the bushes and walked toward the shop.

Jigger, the mischief maker, called out to her, "Think fi har ting sweeter than yours?" And he pointed up the road after Randy and Stella.

She spat at them, and they laughed.

"Jigger, mek you never tell Randy bout tonight?" Rupert asked.

"Shh!" Jigger warned, "Me no want him know. Das why me quick tell him sey Stella did want fi see him. Listen! If only the two a we get the goat them, more money ina it fi the two a we, right?"

Rupert nodded slowly, trying to understand what Jigger was telling him.

"But Randy is we partner. Him is we leader!"

"Nobody leadering me, you hear!" Jigger said, vexed. "What Randy have that you an me doan have? You no see't? All we have fi do is pretend to Mass Joe that is the three a we ina it as usual. Him pay we fi three, an the two a we share it. Seen?"

"I doan like it!" Rupert said, "Suppose Randy fine out?"

"Who a go tell him? You? Bet any money him mek date wid the chile deh tonight. While him a pleasure her, we earning the bread. Seen, Iya?"

"Bwoy, me no like it. Randy wicked when him vex."

"Alright, coward chicken. Me one wi go. In any case you know say Randy no really like the business. Him always a say it no worth it."

"Me still no like it," Rupert said, "but me ina it wid you."

"Shh! Him coming back!" Jigger warned.

"I Randy!" Jigger greeted him, "better watch that she-tiger in there. She spitting fire!"

Randy smiled, "Them woman no have nuttin fi bother them, you hear," he said, "except them tail."

All of them laughed at that.

## IV

"Stella, mi dear, you get everything?"

"Yes, Granny B."

"What a wonder. So much shortage these days. You get the saltfish and the mackerel?"

"Yes, Granny, everything," Stella repeated softly. She was still dreaming about Randy.

Excitement at the thought of meeting him later that night

made her almost numb to reality. He would touch her, she knew. Kiss her. She wasn't sure what else. Something sweet, she was sure. Maybe what the girls were always whispering about, that they did in the bush with the boys.

A warning thought crossed her mind. It was what Granny was always warning her about. She had to remember that she was going to America. But she wasn't going to do anything. Perhaps she wouldn't even go to him. It would be extremely difficult to get away from Granny and Aunty. Especially because tonight was film show night at the Centre. She was never to go to such sinful things and they watched her closely to make sure that she did not slip away. She had done this once and they had never forgotten it, or let her forget it.

"Eh, Missis!" Granny's voice brought her back to reality, "mek you look like you see duppy so?"

She would have to be careful not to make them suspicious. Unconsciously, she had already decided to sneak out to Randy.

"Them was mekkin so much nise in the shop, mi head hurting me," she answered.

"Go lie down little, mi dear." Granny was instantly sympathetic. "Mek me rub beer rum pon it and you go tek a little res. Me wi go a tank fe the water."

Stella felt guilty for a moment. Fetching water for the house from the tank was her regular duty and Granny was old, but she didn't know how to stop what she had already started.

Granny B fussed about her only grandchild. She wetted Stella's head with Bay Rum and tied a piece of cloth tightly around it. Then she half-closed the small window in the room to darken it and repeated her advice to Stella to rest.

Stella was glad she had thought of a headache. It meant that she could pretend to be asleep all evening and nobody would notice her or bother her. A cunning she didn't know she possessed began to direct her plans to get away from the house without Granny B and Aunty finding out.

She would say that the headache had got worse and refuse to eat her supper. That would convince them that she really was feeling ill. Never mind that she would be hungry. She didn't feel much like eating anyway. The excitement building up in her had robbed her of her appetite. She was sure that Granny would give her another Bay Rum rub and send her back to bed, full of concern that she mightn't be able to go to church the next day.

It was a good thing, Stella thought, that she slept alone in the tiny room off the hall, while Granny and Aunty slept in the other room in the house. She smiled as she remembered how Granny used to keep the door keys under her pillow until the night she had to go to the toilet in a hurry, and in her haste, Granny had dropped the keys under her bed and they didn't find them in time. They had all been embarrassed by her plight and ever since then the keys were kept on a nail fairly close to the front door. So that was no problem.

Stella lay in the darkening room thinking about Randy, about going to America, and feeling jealous when she remembered Rosa. They had gone through school in the same class, but they had never liked each other. She had always been a little envious over the fuss both teachers and children made of Rosa because she had long hair, was light-skinned and rich. Never mind that she never could do her lessons and was spiteful, cruel and a hypocrite – while she, Stella, was given grudging praise for always coming first in the class. If she hadn't been going to America she would have gone on to high school, perhaps.

She wondered if it was true that Randy had been with Rosa, but he had said no, and she believed him. She was sure that he wouldn't lie to her.

Lord, he was sweet, with his head cocked on one side when he was saying something nice. His lips twitching with the smile that was never far from his face. The newly sprouting beard which he proudly kept stroking. The constant restless movements of his hands, feet and body. Even when he seemed to be still, he wasn't. What would he tell her tonight, she wondered. What would he do?

Stella heard when Aunty came home and she heard Granny telling her about the headache.

"She musbe soon see them things," her Aunty Missis commented. "You know she always sick them time."

"Oh yes!" Granny answered, and Stella could hear the relief in her voice, "True, mus' be that."

They watched her like mongoose watched chicken. Knew more about her body functions than she herself did.

Stella sighed and turned over to continue her thoughts of Randy. Soon she fell asleep.

## V

At six o'clock in September, it was already growing dark in the district of Fellowship. The three youths sitting on the pavement of the closed shop across from Mass Joe's stared into the shadows. Evening seemed darker behind their Foster Grants, and they had been hardly aware when the reality of bush and tree changed to the unreality of shadows.

In a little while, the light in Mass Joe's shop would be put on. He put off turning on the lights for as long as possible to save on the electric bill, he would explain to his customers. Sometimes he would help out the one bulb in the shop by lighting two kerosene lamps and hanging them over each end of the counter.

The three youths shifted restlessly. Two were uneasy and anxious about their plans. The other wondered pleasantly what new delights the night would bring. But there were other thoughts in his mind, too. Lately, the kind of life he was leading had begun to seem increasingly unsatisfactory.

Randy drew some lines in the dirt with a stick. He was trying to draw the large guinep tree behind Mass Joe's shop.

"What unoo doing later?" he asked the other two casually.

He was so busy with his thoughts that he didn't notice their tense reaction to his question.

"Nuttin special," Rupert answered.

"I man gwine sleep early. Tired!" Jigger Toe said, and pretended to yawn.

Randy drew a few more lines. "Film show a Centre later."

"Mm hmm," they murmured.

"Bwoy," Randy continued, beginning to voice what was troubling him, "Iya think say that this life we leading not so good, you know. Something serious wrong with it."

They were accustomed to his philosophising and didn't comment.

"What we doing, really? Since we can't get no job, we sey we offering Mass Joe protection fi a smalls a week time. Protection from what? What we can protect? Ef some real bad man come on ya now, we have fi run faster than everybody else. An what we getting fi it? Couple bottle a beer and enough money fi buy cigarette and dark glasses. Most week we trus out the little money ina fi him same shop fore we get it. My madder still a buy me clothes, an look pan me? Big man, nineteen year old an na work!"

The others shifted uneasily. They were always uneasy when Randy started talking like this. For them it was a nice easy life. The only thing they would wish for was more money.

"Mi shoulda gi *her* money fi buy fi her clothes," Randy went on, his voice growing bitter. "Not a thing fi do roun ya.'

"Hey, Randy," Jigger said, "at leas you get little money when you paint sign fi somebody."

"You call that work?" Randy asked, "One dollar here and there. Whey that can do? Me did wan turn artis, but Teacher Dunn say nothing not into that. And what artis a do a country? You know what me think? Me better go a Kingston see if anything up there fi do. A it mek everybody a go a town. Only fi mi madder so fretty fretty, bwoy, me have fi think bout do something serious. All dis other business we a mix up wid. Me no like it. It not right. An Mass Joe nah gi wi nuttin much. Him one a get rich outa it."

"You can always go help you madder ina her field, plant ground," Jigger said, spitefully.

"Fi what?" Randy asked, "You know how much she get fi the food she plant? Some week she can hardly buy the things she want. No sah, it look like me wi have fi go a Kingston."

Jigger began to fidget. It had got dark enough for him and Rupert to start making plans for the night's activities.

"Mass Joe soon lock up," he said. "Me gone down a road go see if Suzie lef any dinner fi me. A might see unoo later. Film show up a Centre, no?"

Randy still deep in thought, didn't notice his departure. Neither did he notice when Rupert also slipped away a little later, without saying anything.

The sound of the closing door of the shop brought him back to reality.

Mass Joe looked across at him and said, "Alright, later."

"Seen," Randy answered, automatically. For a minute he wondered what Mass Joe meant. Usually he didn't speak to them unless necessary.

As he got up to go, he heard a "psst" calling him. He looked up to see Rosa signalling him from the side of the shop.

He went over to her and she asked with her saucy look, "You a go a film show tonight?"

"But of course, baby," he answered, pinching her arm. "Maybe afterwards?" she asked.

"Maybe," he replied with his ready smile.

Rosa sighed happily. At least that Stella wouldn't be there. Her christiany Granny wouldn't let her go to anything unless it was at them church. Good. She could hardly keep still as she thought about Randy and the things they did together.


## VI


Granny B wakened Stella sometime after six o'clock.

"Come eat something, mi dear," she said; "wi mek you feel better. Is dark aready; me an you Aunty eat long time, but me never want to wake you."

Stella woke up with difficulty. This early evening sleep was like a drug, hard to wake up from. Her eyelids stuck together; she had to make a real effort to open her eyes, and some urgent thought kept teasing her brain, something she had to do. Gradually she came fully awake.

She took her time about getting up and although she was feeling hungry, remembering her plans, she told Granny that she wasn't feeling much better. Her head was still hurting her, she said, and her stomach was upset.

Granny made some mint tea and gave her some crackers. She ate two of the crackers and drank the tea slowly. Her head was confused at the thoughts racing through. She wasn't quite sure now that she would sneak out to meet Randy. It was too risky. And why did she want to go to him?

"Film show up a Centre tonight," Granny interrupted her thoughts. "But is pure Satan business that. Come, Missis," she called her daughter, "mek we say prayers early so Stella can go back a bed. Please God she feeling better a morning fi go a church."

They went through the nightly ritual of prayers.

Because she wasn't feeling well, Aunty read the Bible passage instead of Stella.

They had started reading Corinthians that month and the night's reading was 1 Corinthians, Chapter 10.

*Moreover, brethren, I would not that ye should be ignorant, how that all our fathers were under the cloud, and all passed through the sea.*

Stella hoped that it wasn't a long chapter.

*Neither let us commit fornication, as some of them committed, and fell in one day three and twenty thousand.*

Oh God! Stella felt a shiver of fear. Were they warning her? Did they know what she was thinking of doing?

*There hath no temptation taken you but such as is common to man: but God is faithful, who will not suffer you to be tempted above that ye are able; but will with the temptation also make a way to escape, that ye may be able to bear it.*

And Stella found herself praying in genuine fright – *Lord deliver me from temptation* –

But it was fear of punishment which caused her to pray. Hers was a crisis of being caught between knowledge of punishment and her physical desire for knowledge.

Aunty Missis closed the Bible when she had finished the chapter and prayed a long prayer on the subject of temptation. Granny agreed with several hearty "Amens". Almost as if, Stella thought, they could read her mind and know what she wanted to do.

Afterwards, Stella got ready for bed. She washed her feet at the back door and Granny threw away the water for her. Aunty Missis grumbled a bit about spoiling the child. She always did this when Granny fussed over Stella too much. But if Granny didn't do it, she herself would, so Stella didn't take any notice of her.

Stella took off her day clothes and folded them neatly and put them at the foot of her bed. She would be needing them soon. She wondered if she would actually be able to get out without them knowing.

Granny B and Aunty Missis took a long time to settle down. Longer than usual, Stella thought.

She could hear them talking softly in the next room about the day's events. Then Granny started to sing a hymn. Her favourite, "All The Way, My Saviour Leads Me."

When she was finished, she called softly, "Stella, you all right?"

Stella didn't answer. She heard Granny say, "She musbe sleeping. Bes thing fi her. A hope she feel better a morning."

After a time there were no more sounds except Aunty's heavy breathing and, soon, Granny's snores.

Stella forced herself to wait for what seemed a very long time before she got up and cautiously began to dress herself to go out.

She would have liked to get her sweater because the nights outside were sometimes cool. But it was kept in the trunk in the other room. Instead she put on a T-shirt under her dress and hoped it didn't look too odd. As it was night she was sure Randy wouldn't notice it.

She moved around quietly. If Granny or Aunty woke up and heard her, she would say she was only using the chimmey. If they heard her when she opened the door, she would say that she had to go to the toilet outside.

But her movements did not disturb them, even when her bed creaked as she got up and the door latch made what sounded, to her, like a very loud clack when she pulled it back. She closed the door softly behind her and waited a few minutes to make sure she was safe.

On the road she put on her slippers and set off to meet Randy by the old post, as he had said.

She wasn't too afraid because there was a moon which made the road fairly bright. Her bigger fear was that she would meet somebody who would report to Granny that she had been on the road, or even worse, question her about why she was on the road at this hour. But it seemed that everybody was either at the film show or in bed. She met no one.

Stella walked quickly, hoping that Randy would be there so that she wouldn't have to wait alone. As she neared the old post, she heard a whistling, and her heart jumped for joy and relief.

Randy was waiting for her!

## VII

Randy had made himself comfortable under the guava tree close to the old post. He wasn't afraid of the dark. His many trysts and other night-time activities had made him comfortable with the night. In any case, the moon was out. Under a cloud at the moment, but still bright enough to make him happy with the shadows and the thought of the treat in store for him.

He hoped he wouldn't have to wait too long for Stella. In truth, he couldn't even be sure that she would come. He couldn't be sure that she would be able to get away from her granny and aunty. Not like that bitch, Rosa, who hell itself couldn't stop from getting what she wanted.

He was sure Stella wanted to come. He could always tell when a girl was on heat for him – just begging him almost to do the thing. Even though Stella was so shy and quiet, he could tell. She probably was a virgin too. His body began to stir. Maybe he wouldn't do everything with her. She really was a nice girl and she was going to America and all that. He was full of respect for anybody who was managing to get away from the dreariness of the district. It was what he was hoping to do, too. He felt a little envious as he thought about Stella's coming escape. If it was him getting a chance to get away, especially to America at that, he wouldn't be taking any chances fooling around with anybody. But, he thought with a sigh, is so woman fool fool. Them never seem to know what them really want.

When he heard footsteps coming up the road toward him, he began to whistle softly.

"Randy?" Stella asked, and he could hear how fear made her voice too loud.

"Shh!" he warned. Voices could carry far on a still country night.

"So you get wey?" he asked her softly, holding her hand to reassure her.

She nodded in reply, not yet able to speak. He could feel her trembling slightly and wondered if she was cold or only nervous. For a minute a feeling of panic overwhelmed her and she wanted to pull her hand away from him and run back to the safety of her home; run back to the safety of granny and aunty; back to the safety of being in control of herself; of knowing exactly what to do.

Randy, sensing her need for reassurance, let go her hand and started to talk casually.

"You want to go to film show?" he asked, sure that her answer would be no. But this would give her a feeling that she had some control over whatever or however the night would turn out.

"No," she answered, "mek we walk."

"Okay," he said. "I know a nice place over by Mass Moses pasture. Like how is moonlight it pretty you see. We can walk there and come back."

It sounded so innocent that she relaxed immediately.

They left the road and started on a track through the bushes, and as they walked he put a protecting hand around her and talked of everyday matters, like how he once was afraid of the dark because of all the rolling calf and duppy stories his mother used to tell him. He told her of his ambitions to get away from the district. He told her how he would like to be an artist, learn to draw and paint things really good. He told her how he was sure he could draw her and asked her if she would give him a chance to try. And the magic of his voice, the magic of his words, the magic of the moonlight, the magic of just being with him entered her soul and made her body hunger for the magic of union with him.

## VIII

The film show – a story about some bank robbers – started late, as usual, and the Community Centre was crowded.

Rosa sat in the second to last row of benches as close to the door as she could. She wasn't sitting with the other young people who would be sure to notice any movements she made. Not that she really cared about them, but her plan was to disappear with Randy as soon as he came. Then they would make their own show, she thought with a smile.

But time passed and Randy did not appear. He had said he would be there. What could be keeping him? She thought of how her father had kept on his work clothes instead of getting ready for bed as he usually did quite soon after locking up the shop; and how he had called out to Randy when he was closing the door. She wondered if this had anything to do with Randy's late appearance. She didn't know the details, but she knew that her father and the three boys occasionally had some "business arrangements" which kept them out at night.

Nevertheless, Randy had promised and he didn't usually lie to her.

Outside, a group of men, not interested in the film, were discussing some serious business. Rosa could tell by the sound of their voices the seriousness and tension of their discussion. Then she didn't hear them again. They had either gone away or decided to keep quiet. Rosa wasn't interested. Where was Randy?

She fidgeted so much that the people sitting near her on the bench began to tell her to be quiet. Ignoring them, every five minutes she squirmed around, hoping to see Randy peering in through the door as a lot of other boys were doing. Impatience welled up in her.

She remembered the time they had spent together in Mass Moses shady grove that afternoon. She could almost smell the soft, spicy pimento-like scent of the rosemary bushes they had crushed in play, when she had pretended not to want him for the sheer pleasure of being chased and captured. And afterwards, the fire consuming them which could only be put out by the relief of coming.

Suddenly she could sit still no longer. She would go and look for him.

As she reached the door, she was surprised to see Stella's Granny and Aunt peeping through the door. They were obviously distressed. Granny's hat was back to front over her tie-head and her nightgown was showing under her dress.

"You see Stella in there?" they whispered.

Rosa's eyes narrowed as she had a sudden vision of Randy walking up the road from the shop with Stella that afternoon, his head cocked on one side, sweet talking her.

So that's why he hadn't come. The bitch, she almost exclaimed aloud. Jealousy fragmented her mind for a minute, and she could almost have hit out at the anxious women waiting for her answer. But she quickly gained control of herself.

She would fix that Stella and fix her good. She was sure she knew where they were. They would go to the shady grove; Randy's favourite place. A place she had thought was theirs alone.

"We can't find her," Granny confessed. "We wake up and she not there. So we wondering if she tief out, come a film show."

"She gone a bush wid Randy," Rosa said, with as much spite as her voice would carry.

"What!" Aunty Missis exclaimed.

By this time they were disturbing most of the crowd, some of whom, between shushings and orders to be quiet, were curious to know what was going on.

Stella gone a bush wid Randy, the whisper went around, and some envious people smiled. So Stella was like all the other girls after all.

"What them expect?" a woman sucked her teeth loudly. "Lock up the poor pickney like prisoner. Nature no mus have its way?"

"Come!" Rosa invited them, loudly, "I know where them is." She wanted as many people to follow them as possible. She wanted to catch them doing it, and shame that Virgin Mary, sweet smiling, innocent looking, tight-leg bitch so she could never show her face in the district again.

"I know where them is," she repeated. She beckoned again to Granny and Aunty Missis. They didn't know what to believe. Timidly, they began to follow her, and so did a number of other people who thought that the live drama promised to be more entertaining than the film show.

## IX

Randy had taken Stella to his favourite place. The small bushy valley they called shady grove at the end of Mass Moses pasture. But somehow things were not turning out the way he had planned. Talking to Stella about his dreams and ambitions had set him off in his philosophical vein. He didn't feel much like making love.

Stella, even in her inexperience, could feel that something had gone wrong and wondered if, perhaps, he didn't really like her after all.

Randy thought that perhaps it was a shame to bring her all the way out to his favourite spot and have her risk her guardians' anger and not give her something to remember. But there was an uneasiness in the air, which he couldn't understand. It had nothing to do with Stella or love; it took a little time for him to realise that what was disturbing him was a certain odour in the air – not the John Charles, ceresee bush or rosemary leaves.

It took him another minute to realise that it was the familiar odour of new blood.

Animal blood.

Goat blood perhaps?

Puzzled, he tried to figure it out. As far as he knew, there was only one gang of goat thieves in the area. That meant that somebody outside the area was stealing goats, or perhaps cows. Whatever it was he was curious to find out. Then his mind raced back to the afternoon and evening. He remembered Mass Joe's "alright, later", which he couldn't understand at the time.

He remembered how Jigger and Rupert had been vague when he asked them what they were going to do. Usually they knew each other's whereabouts. Were often together until bedtime, in fact, unless one of them, usually him, had more pressing engagements to attend.

It began to dawn on him that something was seriously wrong. That perhaps somebody had done a doublecross on him. That something was going on that he didn't know about.

"Wait here," he said to Stella abruptly.

"No-o," she said, holding on to him, "A fraid."

"A soon come," he tried to reassure her, "a just gwine check something." From the direction the smell was coming, he knew where they were.

But Stella wouldn't let him go.

"Alright," he said, all thoughts of love gone. "Come, I will walk you back to the road, and you go on home. I have fi go look bout a certain matter. Business."

He held her hand and started to hurry her back through the path they had so recently strolled in pleasure.

They had run only a couple yards when lights appeared at the further side of the field. They stood transfixed with confusion as a lot of noise and shouting broke out.

Before them, ten or so people suddenly appeared, and they heard Rosa's screech, "See them there!" as she threw herself on Stella, transformed to the she-tiger Jigger had called her earlier in the day. They had to pull her off a weeping Stella.

But nobody was interested in Randy and Stella for long. At the other end of the field it sounded as if hell had broken loose.

The villagers huddled together, not sure whether to run away or to move forward to find out what was happening.

## X

Rupert and Jigger dragged the eight goat carcasses over to where Mass Joe was waiting for them.

"Is the las one this," Jigger said.

"What?" Mass Joe asked, "That is only eight. Is fifteen we suppose to deliver. A did tell oonu fi tek five each from Miss Cooper, Coolie Man and Missa Warwar."

Jigger and Rupert knelt down and began to skin the goats with quick expert action.

Mass Joe turned on his flashlight to help them to see better. Speed was essential. Any moment they expected to hear the horn warning them that the van had arrived and, of course, there was always the danger of being found out, although they were reasonably sure that with the film show at the Centre, there would be few people about.

"A tell you," Jigger grumbled, "is like them was expecting we. All the goat them up a Coolie Man was ina the far field and the dog them let go downa Missa Warwar. Is like them was expecting we. These come from Miss Cooper."

Mass Joe didn't like the sound of this. He urged the boys to hurry up.

"An whey Randy? If him was here oonu would a finish aready."

Jigger had his answer ready. "Him stomach was a hurt him. After we catch them, him sey we fi gwan. Him never think him could a go up to the trimming an ting."

"Then him expect fi get pay?" Mass Joe asked.

"No mus!" Jigger answered quickly. "A him catch most a the goat them, and him help wi cut them throat. We did tell him is aright we would a do the res fi him."

Because Mass Joe was so anxious, he didn't stop to think about the limp excuse they had offered him.

"Hurry up !" he urged again.

"Listen, Master," Rupert said, getting angry, "you want come do this a dirty work youself?"

"Jus stop you faciness and hurry up!" Mass Joe repeated. The smell of new blood and the sight of the entrails of the goats always made him feel sick. He hated this part of the operation. The only part he liked was when the money changed hands and he could feel the dollar notes in his hand.

"Hurry up!" he said again. They were on to the fourth goat now and he thought he heard the faint sound of a van far away. They didn't like to wait and they wouldn't pay unless the goats were all skinned and ready for them. The boys would have to carry the carcasses out near the road, where they would be collected, and he be paid.

A light flickered in the distance, and Mass Joe decided that it must be the van approaching. Then he heard the short sharp beep of a horn and against his custom and his stomach, he decided to get down and help the boys.

They were so surprised that for a minute they both stopped what they were doing to look up at him. At that very moment a set of bright lights flooded the field.

Dead goats, rope, long knives, machetes and bloody hands were damning evidence of their crime.

A group of men, all the more menacing because they were faceless behind the bright lanterns they were carrying, advanced on the petrified three.

Fear froze them only for a minute. Then they jumped up and started to run.

"Ketch them!"

"A did tell unno dem bwoy inna it."

"No mek dem get whey!"

"Jesus Chris! Is Mass Joe!"

The lights were springing up all round the field. They were surrounded.

Escape was impossible. "Lik them!"

A stone smashed into the back of Mass Joe's head, and his last conscious thought was, "Is that half-Chiney bitch get me into this!"

## STORIES FROM

## WOMAN'S TONGUE

*Love needs no conju*
*gation*
*really has*
*no gender*
*sex*
*nor person*
*is*
*abstract of*
*you and me*

## THE EBONY DESK

If is one thing I always fraid of is people "dead-lef" things; especially furniture and jewellery. Second-hand things in the pawnshops or the used furniture mart – me? I keep far away from them. For sometimes the people who dead don't really lef them things.

Of course, it sort of different when is somebody close to you, like your mother or an aunt who dead-lef, but even then, I not so sure. Let me tell you bout a thing that happen to me one time. And I have to use me best "pop-style" language to tell you this one.

A little feeling of loss and the salty taste of tears visited me briefly as I watched them unload the desk at my front door. But the trouble we had getting it through the narrow kench of door in these modern town-houses soon made me forget my sorrow.

We had the very dickens forcing it in. Not only was it heavy, we just couldn't find the right angle to get it past the doorway. At one stage it looked like we'd have to cut off the legs, or chop out a piece of the doorway which, since it didn't belong to me, I couldn't even consider.

Eventually, however, with much heaving and pulling and twisting and turning – almost as if the desk didn't want to enter my home – we got it in. I ordered them to place it against the lefthand wall where it seemed to scowl in all its polished black ebony dignity, overpowering the rest of the dainty new wood and plastic town-house furniture with which I had once been so pleased.

I stood as far away as I could and looked at the desk, and not without a feeling of pride. It was, after all, a family heirloom. My mother had inherited it from a great aunt and now that my mother was dead, it had passed to me. My brothers had insisted that I should have it since I was the "writing-one" in the family. It would bring me good luck.

It was quite a large desk. Many inches taller than me and I am five feet nine; about three and a half feet wide and twenty-two inches deep when closed. Its bowlegs were exquisitely carved with the design repeated on the main panels at the back, as well as on the drawers. It had several "leaves", as I think they are called, which you could pull down or pull out to get even more space.

Closed up it looked almost like a small old-time organ with a high back. When you pulled down the front leaf you got lots of writing space. Inside you could store stationery and there was even an inkwell. Yes, an inkwell. When you sat at this desk you felt you should be using a quill and that the letters should come out all beautifully formed, handsomely cursive like the old time people used to write. None of this flat-top, utilitarian kind of modern desk. You wouldn't dream of insulting this desk by putting a typewriter on it. It was a proud desk, made for an age when people took time to make things beautiful, lived in large houses and had time for graciousness, and all those other old time things.

Here, I thought, I would sit and at last turn out the masterpieces which constantly teased my brain, but which I only occasionally managed to put on paper; and then they couldn't actually be called masterpieces, even by me. Perhaps this was the inspiration I needed; the desk to bring genius alive.

My children started complaining about the desk the moment they came in from school.

"It looked better in Grandma's home," they declared.

"Don't you see it's too big for this room?" my daughter asked, with the wide-open, pseudo-sophisticated eyes of the newly arrived teenager.

"But this ya desk too dread, Iya. Is like everywhere I man turn, it eyeing I. You no see't?"

This was my son, another pseudo, a would-be entrant on the

dread scene – in words anyway. I ignored them both. They had no sense of history.

It was true that everywhere you turned downstairs you were constantly aware of its presence. Somehow, even when I was cooking in the kitchen, which was behind the living room, my eye-corner would be aware of the desk.

It had been in the house for about a week, when I began to notice some little changes in our routine. For one thing my son took his "sounds" totally upstairs to his room. He stopped playing his tapes and records in the living room. When I asked him why, he thought for a moment and then said:

"It's like everytime I tune up, that desk start frown-up and scowl-up, like it don't like it."

When I asked him if he was crazy, he laughed and said, DJ style, while doing a little dance:

"*I have a little desk that don't like me*
*Mek I mother say that I craz-ee*
*An I rub an I scrub an I one, two, three!*"

I shooed him away.

Then my daughter stopped entertaining her friends in the room.

"You can't discuss anything," she explained, "without that desk eavesdropping. Even when you whisper it's like it's straining to catch every word."

I started to think that perhaps I had two mad children and dismissed their complaints without another thought.

Everyday I polished my desk, opened up its leaves and sleeves – it had all sorts of drawers and little nooks and beautiful hand-carved decorations. It seemed to glow with satisfaction at the attention I showered on it.

My desk became quite a conversation piece with my friends. Before I knew it I was boring them with tales of how long it had been in the family, and how my mother had taken such care of it. She never allowed us to use it, her "secretary" she called it; and how it was probably worth quite a lot of money, and blah plus blah.

Finally the day came when, on leave from work and armed with many sheets of writing paper, a new fountain pen, which I would fill from the inkwell, bubbling thoughts, my thesaurus and *Concise Oxford*, I sat down, drew down the writing leaf, arranged everything neatly before me and began to write my story.

It was to be about a girl who suffered from the loneliness of being an only child, who never outgrew her intense longing to have a million friends, but who never could overcome her shyness and the habits of her lonely youth and thus could not make friends. The kind of story which could become mawkish, but I was sure I knew how to handle it.

So there I was, everything ready, except that with the first sentence I realised that I had no name for my heroine. The names which came readily to mind sounded too old-fashioned. Annabelle, Glorianna, Miranda; but I wasn't about to name her Kerry-anne or Isher or Mikawa either.

While I sat there thinking, I swear I must have dozed off for I believe I heard a voice saying quite clearly, "Call her Rosebud."

"Rosebud!" Of all the soppy, sentimental names that was the worst.

Rosebud indeed! That name just didn't fit the girl I had in mind. I sat there, pen poised, thinking all sorts of miscellaneous thoughts for about an hour. Then I got up. Leaving everything as it was, I went into the kitchen to fix myself some lemonade, hoping that the break would cause fresh thoughts to flow.

And it did. By the time I had finished sipping my ice-cold lemonade I had decided that the girl's name would be April. Nothing grand or strange or sentimental about that, just the name of a month of the year.

So I went back to my desk to write about April. I got as far as the first few words.

*April was born on a wet rainy morning in...* when my pen ran strangely dry. I unscrewed the cover of the inkwell and I can't tell you how it happened, but that bottle of ink turned over and spilled all its contents over the desk. Ink was everywhere – on my pages, dictionary, thesaurus and worst of all, it began to drip through the crack in the fold and run down the beautiful shiny surface, almost as if it were dripping black blood. As if I had wounded it.

By the time I had finished cleaning up, I was too distressed to continue creating, so I closed up the desk and went about my household chores.

The next day I returned to the desk armed with a new lot of papers and my ink-stained language assistants.

I don't think I realised what was happening until I read the first sentences I'd written.

*Rosebud was born on a wet rainy morning towards the end of April. They named her Rosebud because all the rose plants had sent out such a profusion of buds after the early April showers. Everybody remarked on it.*

I stared at those sentences for a long time. Somewhere in the back of my head the thought began to form that there was something a little strange about this desk. I remembered the comments the children had made and I wondered. Had the desk chosen the name of my heroine?

Everyday I grew a bit more uneasy at the desk. Things I had not meant to write crept unbidden into my story. My hitherto lonely heroine found herself with a brother I'd had no intention of giving her.

I didn't realize how deeply the whole thing was affecting me until I found myself writing about Rosebud's wedding.

The children said afterwards that they had been growing worried about me because I seemed to be constantly muttering while I was at the desk.

The climax came the day they flew downstairs when they heard me shouting, "But I don't want her to get married! She can't get married! That's not what the story is about!"

They found me standing before the desk furiously shaking a finger at the pages and pages of scrawling writing lined out on the lowered leaf of the desk.

I never sat at the ebony desk again. That day I wrote my friend in St. Ann who has a big house and likes antiques, asking her if she would keep the desk for me.

I couldn't yet quite make up my mind to give it away completely, but I certainly couldn't keep it. I told her that the town-house was too small to house it; that it was taking up too much room – which was true.

I don't know if the previous experience made it easier, but this time when the men came to take it away, the desk almost seemed to fly through the door, so easy it was to get it out. No pulling and pushing and twisting and scraping – almost as if it was glad to go.

Come to think of it, you know, my old lady wasn't a very easy person to live with. She was strong-willed and always wanted me to do things the way she liked.

I never knew Grandaunt Jo, but I hear she was quite a woman too.

*"I have a little desk that don't like me*
*Mek I mother say that I craz-ee..."*

My son's nonsense music floated into my mind as I watched them take my desk away. I turned into the house with a sigh, to be greeted by the cheerfulness of my new-wood and plastic modern furniture.

Dead-lef things? Don't offer me any!

## WHY NOT TONIGHT?

Vivette sat beside her mother, longing for the service to come to an end. It seemed to her that the night service had been unusually long and she was feeling sleepy. It must be at least ten o'clock, she thought, and was surprised to see that it was only nine-fifteen when she turned to look at the clock on the wall at the back of the church.

In turning, she got a swift impression of the congregation, still as if mesmerized by the words flowing from the preacher's mouth. She looked at the choir to his left, and they too were sitting glassy-eyed, staring straight ahead. She often wondered what people thought about while they sat through the hourlong sermons. Her own thoughts wandered all over the place, and only occasionally did she pick up a sentence or two, here and there.

However, she was always careful to listen to the text, because her mother would sometimes make comments on the sermon, testing her to see if she had been listening. Vivette had discovered that one sure way to satisfy her was to quote the text.

Her mother's main object in life just now, it seemed, was to see her saved. Vivette smiled slightly as she thought how this desire had probably less to do with a concern for her soul and more for the protection of her virginity. For saved girls did not, were not supposed to get in trouble, and at sixteen she was in the high danger zone.

From her many years experience she heard the preacher's tone change and realized that he was coming to the last part of the service – altar call.

Wiping his perspiring forehead, he began reciting the first verse of a hymn:

*"Where is thy prospect, sinner?*
*What are you going to do?*
*Hope is a blessed soul anchor*
*Offered so freely to you.*
*If it is fixed on the Saviour,*
*On that bright shore you will land,*
*But if in sin you still linger*
*Sad your end.*
*Lost forever! Lost forever!*
*Oh how sad!"*

"Oh how sad!" he repeated, his voice trembling for emphasis. "Oh how sad! Friends, there's no need for that sadness tonight. Jesus has given the invitation. Won't you come to him tonight? Come! Confess your sins. He will forgive you. Why carelessly wait? Why not come to him tonight?"

This was the signal for the choir to begin to sing softly,

*Oh, why not tonight?*
*Oh, why not tonight*
*Wilt thou be saved?*
*Oh, why not tonight?*

The congregation, on cue, rose to join in the hymn as the preacher moved away from the pulpit to rest his voice, hoarse from preaching. He was a visiting preacher and Vivette knew that this part of the service would be drawn out for another half-an-hour at least, as he sought to pull out all sinners to the altar. Sometimes she wondered if the preacher got paid according to the number of souls he saved.

Hymn concluded, the congregation sat down, heads bowed in prayer for the sinners, while the choir softly began another hymn – *"Come home poor sinner."*

The preacher returned to the pulpit and the altar call began in earnest.

"Friends, the altar is here waiting. Jesus is here waiting for you to come to him. Just take that one bold step forward and come to meet him. No matter how black your sins, He will forgive you. Come to him now."

There were always some people who didn't need much urging and three women got up and went to kneel at the altar. The church sisters who were on altar duty left their seats and went up also, because it was their job to pray the repentant sinners through to salvation.

Suddenly, above the preacher's pleading voice and the organ's soft music, there was a voice crying, "Praise the Lord! Thank you Jesus!" Vivette turned her head discreetly and saw that it was Sister Ruby waving her hand in the air and praising God. Vivette wondered why, for Sister Ruby was a longtime Born Again Christian. Then she noticed that one of the women at the altar was Mabel, Sister Ruby's daughter.

For a moment Vivette was shocked. She wondered if Sister Ruby knew what the other young people suspected, that Mabel was pregnant.

She sighed quietly as she felt her mother stiffen beside her and knew she was thinking that she also would like to be praising God because her Viv had got up to meet Him.

It was stupid to have sat beside her. Normally the young people sat together near the back, but they had arrived a little late and the church was almost packed, so she had to follow her mother to a seat nearer the front.

Vivette wondered if she had really got gospel-hardened as the older sisters were always warning the young ones. But the more she thought about the people who said that they were saved, the more she wondered what it meant. Salvation didn't seem to make much difference in their daily lives. They weren't happier or better than many other people she knew.

She had been attending this church for as long as she could remember. From the days when her mother would put a sandwich in her handbag so that she wouldn't get too hungry during the long Sunday morning services. The nights when she would fall asleep and rest her head in her mother's lap – to the days when she was too old to carry sandwiches any longer and would have to wait until they got home to eat; and the nights when she would be pinched awake because she was too old to sleep in church.

Nowadays she was part of the young people's group. Many of them had also grown up in the church, just like her. Some of them had already accepted the Lord and been baptised and were now full members. But something continued to hold Vivette back from this experience. She didn't know what it was.

She was afraid of baptism, she knew. She had watched countless baptismal services in this church where the platform could be raised and the hollow space beneath filled with water to make a pool. Vivette didn't think that she could go through that experience. Sometimes people came up spluttering after the parson had dunked them. And the white dresses the sisters wore had a way of clinging when wet and revealing things one shouldn't see before the raincoat was thrown around them as they climbed out of the pool.

Her mother had assured her that once she accepted the Lord, she would look forward to baptism as the final proof of her new life.

But what, Vivette wondered again, what did it really mean to accept the Lord as your personal Saviour?

It should be an experience similar to Saul's on the Damascus road. An experience so overwhelming it made you temporarily blind. An experience that went through you and made you clean. Made you know that you were immediately, explosively different.

*Now wash me, and I shall be whiter than snow*, the hymn went.

Vivette's thoughts wandered back to the night, a year or so ago, when she had sat in a similar service and had responded to a similar altar call.

It had been a good service. They had started by singing choruses while they waited for the visiting evangelist to come. She liked choruses. They were bright and happy and usually put her in a good mood.

Sometimes the congregation clapped as they sang and the

organist would run a couple of trills up and down the instrument and the church would hum with happiness.

*Make a joyful noise unto the Lord.* She always thought of this line during chorus time.

When they sang songs like We *shall have a grand time, up in Heaven – Hallelujah! We shall have a grand time up in Heaven, have a grand* time, it did indeed feel as if she belonged to something special.

Generally she liked the music better than the preaching and praying. The music was genuine. She would feel more prayerful, closer to God during the singing of a moving hymn than at any other time in church.

So the service had gone on. For some reason, that night she had listened closely to what the evangelist had to say. He had talked about the Judgement Day and the Sorrow of those Unrepentant Sinners who would be banished to Hell. He had warned about Waiting Too Late.

Vivette had heard similar sermons many times before, but that night a feeling of fear of being among those banished to Hell forever had overwhelmed her, and at altar call time, when the choir was singing *Almost persuaded* she had got up and gone to kneel at the altar.

But there her troubles began. Genuinely wanting to give her heart to the Lord, she had waited for guidance from the Duty Sister. Unfortunately, it had been Sister Margaret who had come to her.

That was the first problem.

Sister Margaret began to urge her to reveal her sins to the Lord. She couldn't be saved unless she confessed these sins. But Vivette began to get the feeling that Sister Margaret was more interested in getting some gossip than in helping her to find the Lord. She had been known to divulge secret sins disclosed at the altar.

Next, try as she might, she couldn't think of any sins to confess. For wasn't sin a big thing like fornication and adultery and lust? These were what the parson was always talking about. And murder and malice. She hadn't done any of these things.

As she racked her brains, conscious that Sister Margaret was getting impatient, she remembered that one day during the previous week she had told her mother that she had stayed at school late for netball practice when in truth she had gone to visit one of her school friends. Her mother didn't like her to visit people's homes, so she had told a lie. Was the Lord interested in that?

She had also kept back ten cents from her collection to help pay back some money she had borrowed. That was a sin. Stealing from God. So she had continued searching her soul and had come up with a litany of small crimes that had Sister Margaret sucking her teeth impatiently.

What else did she want, Vivette had wondered, feeling more and more pressured. She hadn't even kissed a boy like some of the other girls. In truth, she didn't find the boys she knew very interesting. But one night she had been woken to realise that her parents in the next room were making love. Through the thin partition she had listened to their whispered words and the creaking of the bed and felt with alarm some unidentifiable stirrings in her own body. Stirrings that made her feel guilty, as if she had done something dirty. Could she confess this to Sister Margaret? No! Never!

So she had knelt at the altar, sweating, for it was a hot night. She had waited for the blinding flash of salvation and none had come. Instead, she had to be content with repeating after Sister Margaret:

"Lord I have sinned. I have been deceitful. I have told lies. I have stolen. I have sinned, Lord. But I am sorry for my sins. Forgive me, Lord. Cleanse me of my sins and teach me how to become a good Christian."

Afterwards Sister Margaret had told her mother that she didn't think that Vivette had "come through" because she hadn't really confessed and therefore could not be forgiven. And Vivette, feeling no different, except perhaps a little embarrassed, had lost some faith in the magic of salvation that the church kept promising.

Besides, she had begun to be critical of the behaviour of those who said they were saved. Sometimes the young people discussed the unchristian behaviour they witnessed and wondered at their elders' capacity for double dealing. That same Sister Margaret, for example, the Most Saved of the Saved. She took great delight in making life as miserable as possible for many people. She delighted in carrying news to the parson so that people could be read out for named sins and suffer the disgrace of having to sit on the sinner bench, until Parson was satisfied that they were truly repentant.

Sometimes, it wasn't even a church member but someone in the family who had publicly sinned; Sister Margaret would still create confusion.

Then there was the time one of the girls had seen Brother Clive coming out of the betting shop with a racing form in his hand and he had threatened to make up a story to tell about her if she ever told anybody what she had seen.

Even her own mother didn't always manage to keep the church rules, usually because of her father who was an unrepentant, rejoicing sinner. Like the very devil, he would tease and taunt them about their Christianity and every now and then would use his authority as head of the house to get them to break the church rules.

Sometimes Vivette wondered if her mother truly obeyed him only "to keep the peace," as she often said – "for the devil himself is in that man" – or if she didn't really enjoy having the excuse to sin.

Like the night, for example, that they had come in from Tuesday evening prayer meeting to find him dressed, waiting for them. He wanted to see the late movie at Palace and expected them to accompany him, no argument. So they had meekly taken off their hats, and changed their white dresses, and gone with him, "to keep the peace".

Vivette had thoroughly enjoyed the show, but afterwards, coming out of the cinema, she wondered if her mother was not afraid that Brother Walker might be waiting outside, leaning on his bicycle, taking note of any church member who was sinning in this way. A couple of people had been read out for this already.

To be born again, it seemed, meant only sadness, long faces, criticism – no joy. Were Christians really not supposed to be happy? Was it only sin which was enjoyable? Did only sinners have fun – like her father?

Even the church socials were no longer pleasant affairs. When they were little, the children had a lot of fun at socials, running about freely and nobody seemed to mind how they enjoyed themselves. Now they were constantly watched. Vivette thought about the social which, against better judgement, the women's group had allowed to be held at a beach. A few brave young souls had donned bathing suits. The sight of so much sinful flesh had nearly given Sister Margaret and others heart attacks as they tried to make sure that the boys stayed far from the girls. The church was obsessed with a fear of sex.

Vivette sighed as the evangelist's voice disturbed her wayward thoughts.

"Sinner, tonight is the night! Suppose you leave this church without cleansing your soul? Suppose this is your last chance? Suppose when you leave this church, tonight is the night He calls you to give an account of your soul. What will you tell Him? What will you tell your Saviour? Why did you put Him off? Why didn't you obey His call? Oh, sinner! Let Him have His way with you tonight."

Vivette shifted her legs, which had started to feel cramped. The altar call was being prolonged, and the choir started a new hymn. Vivette thought how the church people were convinced that some preachers had the gift of knowing when some wavering sinner in the congregation needed more persuasion and would continue his plea until this person came up. Some, it was said, could pick out the exact person who needed to be saved that night.

Vivette shifted again, and her mother, mistaking her discomfort, touched her knee and whispered, "If the Lord is speaking to you, Viv, go up and answer His call."

This was the kind of pressure that of late was causing her to be increasingly rebellious. Always a mild, dutiful, obedient girl, lately she had been surprised at the unruly thoughts which often filled her mind. She was a little afraid for herself at times, because of these thoughts.

Without planning to, she found herself whispering back to her mother, "I dying to wee-wee."

She felt instant pleasure realising that her mother was shocked, but at the same time again felt the little fear. Was the devil taking her over?

But the moments of heart-searching had gone and she listened, very bored, as the evangelist finally brought the service to an end with a long prayer for all sinners everywhere who resisted God's call.

She felt strangely outside of it all. Perhaps it was true what the sisters said. She had heard the gospel too often without responding to it. She was now truly gospel-hardened. Strangely, she didn't really care. Perhaps at next week's service she would start her soul-searching all over again, but tonight, as she walked beside her mother in silence, she found herself wondering what surprise her father had in store for them. She hoped he wasn't sleeping when they reached home. She hoped that Satan had been riding him hard all night and that he had some particularly enjoyable way of testing the faith of his pious wife and daughter as they came home from their church.

## THE THURSDAY WIFE

Shortly after Bertie and Mary got married, things started to get very bad.

Bertie had been a waiter working the hotels in Montego Bay, but he had been laid off soon after the wedding and they decided to move to Kingston.

For a while, they had enough money to pay the first month's rent for their one room and to buy food. But as the days passed and Bertie could get no work, starvation began to stare them in the face.

Still, Bertie insisted that his young wife could not go out to work. She was so pretty with her light-colour skin and brown curly hair, anywhere she went to work the men would want to touch her, and that would cause him to kill. When somebody told her that she could get a job as a store clerk in one of the Syrian stores downtown, he forbade her even to think about it.

Things went from bad to worse. The final blow came when Bertie got food poisoning from the can of sardines they shared over a two-day period. The young wife didn't know that she shouldn't leave the sardines in the can overnight, and on the second day made a sandwich for her husband with it. The leftovers weren't enough to share so she pretended she had already eaten when he came home weary and hungry after another futile day looking for work.

That night, as she held the chamber pot for his vomit and watched him writhing in pain, the thought that he might die and leave her penniless in the big, hostile city, filled her with great fear. So the next day when he was better, but still too weak to contradict her too violently, she suggested that it might be better if she went back to her country village, from which he had taken her a mere six months before. She could stay with her sister. They would give up the room and he could move in with his cousin until he found a job. Then, when things got better, she would come back and they would start again.

They parted reluctantly because they really liked each other and the young love was still burning hotly in their veins, but it couldn't be helped.

For six months Mary fretted in her sister's house. They were all very kind to her and she made herself useful in the house and the shop, but it was not the same. She longed for her husband and her own home once more. And he didn't write. Later she found out that he was barely literate and that it hadn't occurred to him to write her a letter. And although she thought about him constantly, she didn't know his cousin's address to write him.

One Sunday morning as she was washing her hair in the basin under the pear tree in the back yard, her sister came to tell her, mysteriously, that she had a "gentleman visitor". Mary didn't want to see anyone. Of late, some of the country gentlemen, aware of her lonely status, had been trying to "talk her up". She wasn't interested in any of them. So she took her time drying and combing her hair and when she went upstairs she nearly died of shock, because there, sitting on the verandah talking to her sister, was her husband, Bertie.

He had come for her. Things had improved. He had found a job, rented another room and got a few things together. So once again Mary left her country home and went with her husband to start a new life in Kingston.

There was only one thing about the new life that Mary did not like. Bertie had a live-in job. He worked for some white people up on top of a hill and had to stay on the premises for he was chauffeur, baby-sitter, watchman and waiter for their numerous parties – whatever they might ask him to do. He worked hard all week and was only allowed a half day on Thursdays and that was all the time he had to be at home with Mary. For most of the rest of the week, she saw him only in snatches. Whenever he could, he would sneak away while on some errand with the car and drop in for a quick visit.

But on Thursday evenings Bertie came home to spend the night, free until six o'clock the next morning.

And on Thursday evenings Mary bloomed. Early Thursday morning she would wash her hair and plait it, twisting it around her head, the way Bertie liked it. She would thoroughly clean their room and the little verandah which served as kitchen and dining room on occasion. She would make sure that the vase on the bureau was ready, for he always brought her some flowers from the white people's garden. Then she would cook his favourite meal: stewed peas and rice. When everything was ready, she would wash herself carefully and change all her clothes and rest a while, so that by two o'clock when he came she was as fresh as a new bride.

Her heart would lift in anticipation as she heard him whistling as he entered the yard. He would stop and greet anybody who happened to be about, then he would step loudly onto the little verandah, then rap – pam pa pam pam on their door. And, pretending that she didn't know it was he, she would call, "Who's that?" and he would answer, "Who you expecting?" Then she would open the door and he would haul her into his arms and onto their bed and ravish her in the most rewarding ways. Later he would say, as if they were just meeting, "So how you do?" and she would answer shyly, "All right, you know."

Then they would eat and dress and he would take her to a movie or to visit his cousin, or they would go downtown after the shops had closed and walk through the quiet streets and stop for awhile at the seaside at the bottom of King Street, laughing at the antics of the little boys diving in and out of the water as naked as the day they were born.

Afterwards they would stop at a little parlour and buy patties and ice cream and then they would go home for another bout of lovemaking, falling asleep in each other's arms until the clock alarmed at five o'clock next morning and he jumped up to race to catch the first bus so that he wouldn't be late for work – until the next Thursday.

And so it went on month after month. One year passed, two, three, four years. Their love continued bright and shining, fanned into flame on Thursday and smouldering during the rest of the week. No children came to spoil their duet, but Mary was not unhappy.

During this time she learned how to cope with her loneliness. For one thing there was the church, nearly all day Sunday, two nights during the week, with an extra night once a month for the women's meeting. Also, she was a visiting sister, which meant that many mornings she spent the time visiting the sick and the shut-ins, encouraging them spiritually and doing what she could to help their physical needs.

Since all her husband's domestic chores were taken care of at his workplace, she had a lot of time on her hands. She washed and cooked and kept house only for herself, and as Bertie gave her generously from his pay, small though it was, she could always manage to find a little something to take for those poorer than herself and earned a name as an Angel of Mercy. Mary was well satisfied with her life.

The lustfulness of her husband and his liking for the movie house and a drink or two bothered her Christian principles from time to time. But he was so good to her, she felt that she owed it to him to do whatever he wanted on the one day of the week when he could be with her. In fact she took an almost sinful pleasure in breaking the church rules without having a guilty conscience. Wasn't she merely being submissive to her husband as the Bible taught?

Then one Sunday morning, just as she was getting ready for church, without any warning, Bertie descended on her in a taxi, carrying all his clothes and belongings. He had come home. He had left the job in the white people's mansion and had got a better paying one working as a waiter in a restaurant in a hotel uptown. Now he would be with her every day of the week and not just Thursdays anymore.

"Isn't it wonderful?" he asked her, enthusiastically. He had kept it as a surprise for her.

Mary agreed that it was wonderful, but it was with regret that she stopped dressing for church, for they had a visiting evangelist who was hot with the Holy Ghost and made the church walls shake with his message and the strong amens it brought forth.

However, her husband had come home, so she helped him to settle in and set about preparing Sunday dinner, a thing she rarely did, because she had nobody to cook for but herself. And she was happy; for the first time since she was married she would truly have her husband by her side. She might even get him to go to church with her.

A couple of weeks passed before Mary began to feel uneasy. At first she couldn't think why. The first time she thought that it might be because Bertie was around so much, but she pushed that thought aside. How ungrateful to think such a thing!

But her life had been drastically changed by his continuous presence.

First, there was the problem of accommodating him and his possessions. She had to squeeze up her good clothes in the wardrobe and make room for his clothes in one of the bureau drawers. She had to find a place for his shoes and personal things like shaving set and cologne – he was quite a sweet man she thought. The room looked quite crowded now and was more difficult to keep clean and tidy, but he insisted on tidiness at all times, so she was always dusting and straightening or putting things away.

He was miserable about his clothes, she found herself complaining to a church sister. He had even threatened to box her because she hadn't ironed his merinos. They stretched out so easily that she had just folded them neatly and put them in his drawer. But he had taken them out and thrown them about the room, shouting and calling her a lazy woman. She had been so ashamed, for the neighbours could hear every word he said.

He was miserable about his food too, but fortunately he was allowed to eat at the restaurant, so she didn't have to cook for him too often.

She had to curtail many of her activities. The first Tuesday night after he came home, she had dressed herself as usual to go to prayer meeting, but when she was putting on her hat, he came into the room and asked her where she thought she was going. Now that he was home she didn't have to worry with all them church foolishness any more. Mary was so upset she couldn't speak. After that she could only go out on the nights when he was on the late evening shift, because if he came home before her he would always quarrel.

When she tried to explain to the parson why she was no longer as diligent in her church duties, he was very unsympathetic and thundered at her, "Sister Mary, God first! Everything else comes after."

Bertie laughed at her friends. "Where you know all them meek and mild pious woman from?" he would tease her. "Them walk like them can't mash ants, but I bet you everyone of them is as sinful as Satan."

One day he embarrassed her beyond words by ordering her church sisters to be quiet in his house. She hadn't been feeling well and three of them had come to visit her, but when they raised a hymn he had shut them up so violently that they had hastened away without even praying for her.

"Can't stand that dam croaking and wailing," he told Mary when she tried to protest.

Yet he expected her to be nice to his friends. Every now and then some of them would drop by and she would have to fetch ice and fix drinks while they chatted and laughed.

That was the men.

One evening a woman came to see him. A woman whom he hugged affectionately and brought in to sit on the good chair in their room.

Mary was wary of her from the beginning. But he explained the association innocently enough. She was the house-girl where he used to work and she had washed and cooked for him.

Mary and Bertie sat on the bed while Bertie and the woman reminisced and laughed.

"You remember the day when Miss Levy couldn't find her brown wig to go to the party and how we search down the whole place till we finally find it outside and all the dog them playing with it?" the woman said – Corrine was her name.

"And how them used to leave salt fish for we dinner when them wasn't eating in, but we used to tek out steak and cook it," Bertie added his story.

"Remember the day we was going on outing to Ocho Rios and we cook and tek away so much things Miss Levy couldn't help but notice. But we swear it wasn't we but her beg- beg sister who did come up and tek them."

Bertie didn't laugh so heartily at this. In fact he glanced a little nervously at Mary who had started to wonder what else Corrine had done for him besides washing and cooking. The way they laughed and joked together made Mary feel like an outsider, that she didn't know her husband.

Corrine, it seemed, was tired of working for the white people and Bertie had promised to get her a job at the hotel so she had come to find out what was happening.

Mary couldn't help but notice how Corrine's eyes darted around the room, as if she was taking notes about how they lived. Mary decided that she didn't like her.

When she was ready to leave, Bertie offered to walk her to the bus stop and Mary made up her mind to ask him point-blank about her suspicions. But Bertie didn't return and Mary seized the opportunity to sneak away to her church service. When she returned, Bertie was in bed, but strangely he didn't ask her where she had been, nor did he fuss about not finding her at home when he got back.

Shortly after that, Bertie began to stay away from home one night in a week or a fortnight, then one night a week regularly, then two and three nights every week. He told Mary that the hotel restaurant at which he worked had started closing very late, especially on weekends and that they had set aside two rooms for the staff to sleep rather than have them travel home in the wee morning hours.

Mary said nothing. Not even after the night when she suddenly fell ill and on the way to the hospital in a taxi, she begged the neighbour who was accompanying her to stop at the hotel to tell Bertie.

The neighbour was told that Bertie had left for home long ago, as the restaurant closed at ten o'clock.

She never asked him about this.

Gradually Mary found that life had returned to its old pattern of regular churchgoing; Bertie was either not at home or showed no interest in her comings and goings.

Things were like this for some time before it finally dawned on Mary that he was now coming home only once or twice each week. And that since he wasn't wearing the clothes he had there, she had little washing and ironing to do and she didn't have to be constantly cleaning and straightening the house. In fact she was a Thursday wife again – almost.

And still she didn't say anything, for hadn't the parson insisted, "God first and all things after"? If this was God's way of giving her the time to serve Him, then she would accept it without murmur or complaint.

When Bertie began to make excuses for not paying the rent or not giving her any money, she used her savings to buy a sewing machine and went to the Singer classes to refresh her memory of how she used to sew when she was in the country.

She started taking in sewing. She spoiled a few dresses but slowly got the hang of it, and soon enough, between the church sisters and others, she had more work than she could handle. Between serving the Lord and earning a living she had little time to be lonely. She was often surprised when she returned from church to find Bertie in bed on the nights he chose to come to her.

He rarely attempted to make love to her any longer and she was glad, because for both of them it was now a joyless exercise.

This pattern continued. Mary didn't know what he did with his time, and she didn't ask him. But one afternoon, when she returned home after being out most of the day on a mission of mercy, her neighbour told her that a woman with two small children had been looking for her and had waited some hours hoping to see her. When she asked what the woman looked like, she realised it was Corrine, the woman who had visited them some years before. Corrine who used to wash and cook for Bertie. Instinctively she knew that this was the reason why he had all but left her. She wondered what Corrine wanted from her.

Mary brooded on this for some days, and the next time Bertie came to visit her, she broke her vow of silence and told him about the woman's visit. At first he seemed frightened, then angry, then embarrassed, and when Mary asked, "I wonder what she want?" he shrugged his shoulders and said, "I tired. I going to bed."

Mary sat in the best chair, worn now and faded. She sighed. He wasn't even interested enough for them to have a quarrel.

Since he was there she couldn't use the machine, so what could she do to pass the time? It was too early to go to bed. She got up to fetch her sewing. At least she could do some handwork. She sighed another time as she sat down and looked across the room at him lying on the bed in his underwear.

He wasn't handsome any longer. Middle-age was creeping up on him. Then she acknowledged with surprise that she didn't have any feelings for him any longer. She didn't love him. She didn't even like him. It wasn't that he was no longer physically attractive, for she too had put on weight and her stomach had started its middle-age swell, it was more the fact that he was a stranger to her. As if she had never ever been truly married to him. She didn't know him.

She wondered when he would make up his mind to leave her altogether. She didn't know why he bothered to keep up the pretence.

She could not know that Bertie was not asleep. That he lay there wondering how he had got himself into so much confusion. That most of all he was wondering why he had left this good woman to get involved first with Corrine and now with the devil who was out to mash up his life.

He thought of Corrine and her two children, and how lately she had started nagging him, and how the children were getting on his nerves because they always seemed to be crying.

And he thought of Mary, patient Mary, who through all the years had never questioned him when most other women would have made a stink. He thought how she always welcomed him, never turned him away, even though she had more than good reason to do so.

He thought of the other woman who had begun to pursue him. He had met her at the restaurant. She was a customer. She had invited him out after work and he had accepted. At first it was exciting to be with this superior, polished lady, but lately the things she wanted him to do in bed made him feel rebellious.

Corrine, he thought, had come to see Mary because she was wondering why he was staying out so often.

What a mess! The best thing to do, perhaps, was to come back to Mary. He was getting tired of those other demanding women.

"Cho! Mary," he said, turning around suddenly and startling her. "Turn off the light no, and come to bed."

Mary, dutiful as ever, sighed. She hoped he had no amorous thoughts. That night she would not be able to accommodate him.

Perhaps she wouldn't ever be able to accommodate him again.

## MISS GIRLIE

"Wha do you? Me sey wha do you? Wha you a cry fa?"

The sympathetic questions only caused Girlie's tears to flow more freely.

"You musbe have more eyewater than Negril Bay have sea… Stop the noise an tell me what do you!"

"Ivan… Ivan box me up," Girlie sobbed.

"Cho, a dat you a cry so for? Is the first time man box you?"

"An him sen me fi get money an me no know wha fi do," Girlie wailed.

"Which money?"

Glad that somebody was willing to listen to her, Girlie allowed herself to be pulled toward a broken bench at the edge of one of the empty lots facing the beach.

The woman – Miss Winsome – put her fruit basket on a nearby stand, and she and Girlie cautiously sat on the edge of the bench. Knowing that Miss Winsome had a long way to walk along the beach to sell her fruits, Girlie was grateful that she had taken the time to listen to her story.

"Which money Ivan sen you for?" Miss Winsome asked, wrapping her frock between and around her fat legs to keep off the sand flies.

The nine o'clock morning sun was just hitting the expanse of blue sea before them, creating a glare which hurt the eyes if you looked at it too long. The water was so calm that movement was barely visible except when a passing boat disturbed its tranquillity and sent some swells shoreward. The water was so clean, the sand so white, all seven miles of it, that every fish swimming lazily by could be seen from the shore.

Not that Miss Winsome or Girlie noticed the beauty stretched out before them. Born on the beach, they and their friends and acquaintances made their living either from the sea itself or from the many tourists who came to worship sun and sea, or procure sex or drugs. Whatever was the peculiar fetish, it could be found in Negril.

"Is the touris man that writing book," Girlie explained.

"You mean the one that click-clack typewriter, an tear up paper all day down at San San."

"Him," Girlie answered.

Everybody in Negril knew about the Writer. He had been staying at the San San Beach Hotel for two or three months, mystifying them all with his capacity to sit at a typewriter for a whole day, breaking only to drink beer and occasionally to take a swim.

"Him?" Miss Winsome asked. "What him do you?"

"Yesterday evening, when me was a go home, him call me," Girlie said, wiping her eyes with the back of her hands. "You know how them guard man up a San San stay. Them say me couldn't come up with the basket, so him come down pon the beach fi buy a pineapple. But is the las one me did have an it wasn so good. Whole side a it did rotten, so me cut it off an tell him mus tek the good piece an tomorrow, that is today, me would bring him a good one."

"Then is that de money Ivan a fight you for?" Miss Winsome asked. While she talked her eyes remained alert to the movement of people up and down the beach, on the look out for a sale from any passing tourist who might be interested in her fruits and juices.

"No," Girlie answered. "Him say him tired as him was typewriting all day, so him could tek a break an walk down the beach wid me. Me couldn tell him no?" Girlie asked, anxious for approval.

Miss Winsome didn't commit herself. She was waiting for more of the story.

"Well, we walk a little ways, an then him sey is such a nice evening, mek we sit down. So we did sit down and him talk an talk. You know how them white people love talk."

"Hmm," Miss Winsome agreed.

"An then it start to get darkish an me tell him me have fi go home. Everybody did gone off a the beach, and the man them was a get ready fi go out, an me was a think bout Ivan never get him dinner yet. Then him ask me me name and where me live an we jus a talk till, before me know, night reach an me had was to run the whole way home for Ivan was gwine kill me."

"Well, me tell Ivan some foolishness bout say me had was to see a woman bout some flourbag, das why me late, for me never want tell him me was a talk to the white man so long. You know how them man stay."

Miss Winsome nodded.

"Well, it look like eena night somebody tell him say me did deh pon the beach wid the white man, so a morning him vex up an say him want the money me get."

"Den him did pay you?"

"What him fi pay me for? We never did do nothing!"

"You mean you spen the whole night wid the white man, an no get no money?"

"Him never do nothing:' Girlie insisted, the tears starting to flow again. "All we did do was talk!"

"So a wha oonu was a chat bout so?"

"Him was talking bout the sea an its creatures," Girlie said.

"The sea an its creatures?" Miss Winsome threw back her head to let loose a rich belly laugh.

Girlie pouted. For that was how Ivan had behaved, when she had told him the same thing.

"The sea an its creatures!" Ivan had shouted. "What dat ras claat white man know bout the sea an its creatures? What him know bout day an night in a boat what loss the motor. Day an night an you weary an hungry till you can't even talk to the nex man beside you. An fraid ina you skin cause you so far out you no know if them gwine fine you in time, or if you can fine a shore. An the sky jus a swell up with vexation ready fi lash you an the helpless boat an you pray till no prayers no lef. Wha him know bout sea creatures like tingray, an eel, an balloon fish with poison fin, an shark? Shark ever follow him yet like John Crow a wait fi tear dead meat? If you wan know bout the sea an its creatures, ask me."

Girlie would have liked to remind him that the men did not talk to women about such things. That was man talk. Men talked about these things only when they were together. Sometimes when the women were serving them they overheard what they were saying and sensed their fear of this vast watery mass which they fought daily to make their living. But they didn't talk about these things to the women.

The white man had talked for hours, it seemed, not about the dangers of the sea but about its beauty and its usefulness to man. How man could find everything he needed in the sea. He talked of things she could not understand. But she felt pleasure just listening to him as if she was his equal, as if she could understand everything he wanted to talk about. He had talked of loneliness, too, and he had told her about the book he was writing, a very confusing story which she couldn't follow.

"So wha Ivan do?" Miss Winsome recalled Girlie from her thoughts.

"Him vex when me tell him say we never do nothing. An him cuss me an say how me gi it way when everybody else a get money fi do it. An then him say the white man mussi really a battyman fe true, if we never do nothing."

"Is that all the gal them say," Miss Winsome interrupted. "Nuff a them put question to him, but him always say him too busy a write him book. Them say is only man him talk to."

"Den him start box me up," Girlie continued, ignoring the interruption. "An him sen me fi get the money or else…" She was crying again, "An me no know wha fi do. Me never even carry me basket me so confuse."

"Den mek you no go ask the white man fi gi you some money?"

"How me fi do that?" Girlie asked.

"Tell him say you man a threaten fi come beat him up if him no pay fi you time." Miss Winsome got up stiffly and prepared to take up her basket again. "Cho, Missis! You too fenky fenky. Since Ivan want you fi go sell pussy, well, go sell pussy! Plenty hungry touris round the place. An mek me tell you something," the older woman advised in a softer voice. "You don't even have fi gi Ivan all the money wha you mek. After all, is you pussy."

Girlie stayed on the beach after Miss Winsome moved off, drying her tears and wondering what to do. Miss Winsome had said aloud the thing that had been bothering her since morning. She didn't really mind Ivan boxing her. If only he had done it because he was angry that she had gone to a white man. But he didn't seem to mind that; all he could think about was the money.

Ivan wanted her to become a whore! He who was the first and only man she had known in her twenty-four years – childhood sweethearts. Ivan had always treated her as if she was special. I-Queen he called her. And now he was sending her out just like all the other men he used to talk about with scorn; now he was sending her out to sell herself.

Why was money suddenly so important to him? He usually didn't even bother to ask her what she made from her little business. Only borrowing money occasionally if there was some big debt to pay or something big to buy or if he was short of cash. Now money was so important to him it didn't matter how she got it. She knew that many of the women did it for money. Some of them even boasted about the things they did – sodomy and other wickedness. And some of them had brown hair, brown-eye children by the tourist. Fathers who never knew about the existence of these children. But she had never been tempted to do this. She was content to make a little money selling her fruits and the flour-bag clothes she sewed from time to time.

She didn't make plenty money. Sometimes the fruits spoiled and the clothes wouldn't sell. But she got by. And if she got American dollars, Maas Henry would give a good price for them, up to four-fifty if he really wanted them. The thoughts raced through her head. But what to do? She couldn't go home to Ivan without money and she didn't have anything to sell.

Eventually she decided to take Miss Winsome's advice to go see the white man at San San. Perhaps he would lend her the money.

She could hear the clickety-clack of his typewriter even before she saw him working at a table in the outer part of the thatch-roofed bar. He was barefoot and shirtless and seemed not to mind the sandflies, as his fingers rarely stopped to scratch.

Since she didn't have her basket, the guard turned away his head as she approached the bar.

"Hi," the white man said, suddenly realising that she was standing near, waiting to be noticed.

"I don't talk in the mornings," he said, "try me later." And resumed his tapping.

Girlie sat down on the edge of the concrete floor close to his chair and pondered what to do.

An hour or so passed, then he yawned and stretched.

"Since you're still here, go over to the bar and get me a beer, will you. Two, if you want one. Just tell the barman Mr. Tate sent you."

Girlie got up and went for the beers.

"That lady bothering you, sir?" a passing guard asked as he noticed Girlie returning with the beers.

"She's my guest," the white man replied.

Girlie hearing him was pleased and a little proud to be called his guest. His beard, she noticed, was heavily spotted with grey hairs, although there was very little grey on his head. Perhaps that was because his head hair was brown while his beard was much darker, almost black. The white people were so strange with their many different shades of hair colours. For a second she found herself wondering if his hair down there was brown or black, then felt ashamed of the thought.

He drank his beer straight from the bottle, and still didn't talk to her. He was deep in thought somewhere far away.

Noticing that the beer would soon be finished and wishing to delay his return to the typewriter, Girlie hurriedly said, "You can len me a money?"

"Enh?" he said, surprised by the sound of her voice.

"You – you can len me a money?" she repeated timidly. He looked at her for a minute with a strange expression on his face. Then he sighed.

"Must it always be money?" he asked. "Somehow you seemed different from the others yesterday."

Girlie hung her head in shame. Something about her attitude must have convinced him that she needed it.

"How much?"

"Thirty dollars," she said timidly, and when he didn't answer, "Twenty-five, American?" as if she was haggling with him.

"And how will you repay me?" he asked.

She hung her head again, not knowing how to reply.

"Here," he said scratching a note on a discarded piece of paper. "Give this to the barman. He'll give you the money."

"Now go!" he ordered when she tried to thank him. "I have work to do."

Girlie took the note to the barman who laughed when he read it.

"That's all you getting, girl? The really sharp ones get all fifty dollar a time."

Girlie took the money and left quickly, too ashamed to look back at Mr. Tate. When she reached home she thrust the money into Ivan's hands as if it was burning her.

"That's better," Ivan said counting it. "That's for last night. Him never want it this morning?"

"Him was typewriting," she answered, close to tears again, but determined not to let him see how humiliated she was. She wanted to die. Here was her man turning her into dirt. And the other one, the white man she didn't even want, making her feel that she was worth something, that she was a valuable person.

"Member," Ivan shouted after her, as she left the yard with her basket of fruits and her garments, hoping to make a few sales before the day ended. "Thirty Merican is the lowest."

Ivan was feeling good. He could almost feel the putt putt of the outboard motor under his hand. His dream boat becoming a reality. The boat he thought he would never own. Tired of the leaky rowboat and of working for those who owned seagoing boats and could afford to hire men, he had been trying for a long time to save to own a boat for himself. A real boat made of fibreglass, white and glistening, with engine and everything. But always something happened to cause him to spend some of the money he was saving and he never could get the downpayment. And now this gift.

He hadn't thought of it before because he really liked Girlie. From they were small she had been his special girl. He didn't really like the thought of her fucking with the white man. But last night, when they had told him about she and the white man on the beach, teasing him because he had been one of those making noise about the woman them prostituting themselves, he had been surprised. Instead of feeling angry, instead of dashing home to give her the beating of her life, he had found himself wondering instead how much she had got from the man.

He didn't really feel too bad about it. After all it was her choice. She had done it. And if it was just this one white man who seemed to like her, maybe it wouldn't be so bad for her.

He started to calculate. If she went to him every night even at twenty Merican a night, not counting the week when she was unclean – for surely even the white man couldn't be so slack? – he could get three times six nights – eighteen times twenty, that's three-sixty Merican change into Jamaican at four-fifty or five. If the white man stayed for three more months, plus what he had, in three months he could make the downpayment.

Ivan laughed out loud as he took a draw on the spliff he had rolled and it felt sweet all the way down, and up. Then he could get a loan from the fisheries people and catch enough fish, sell at the new depot and look after Girlie in real style, so she could stop fucking the white man and even stop walk and sell. He would set her up in a restaurant, a little cafe where she could sell drinks and things.

Only one thing was wrong. While she was fucking the white man, he couldn't go to her. He wasn't getting into any white man muck. Some of the men didn't mind if their women just came back from fucking the tourist, they would tek them all the same. But not him.

Of course there was always Babs, Girlie's sister. Time she started to pay him back for the many favours he did for her and her mother. He really liked Girlie, but she would have to wait till him get the boat. An when she see what him do with the money, and how the boat pretty, and how him could mek money and set her up, she would proud so till!

Meanwhile, angry, humiliated, goaded by her frustrations into an aggressive selling behaviour, which amazed both herself and the other sellers who knew her as a softie, Girlie had a very good day selling her wares. To appease her anger she had walked farther than usual, even though she had started out later, and it seemed that she found the tourists in a good buying mood that day. In no time at all her fruits were finished and she had sold two of her four flour-bag shirts. She had asked twenty dollars a piece and when one of her buyers thought she meant American and gave her twenty US dollars, she didn't refuse it.

So when she counted her money she found that she had nearly eighty dollars; twenty in US. This was more than she sold for a week sometimes. If she could sell this much everyday, perhaps she could find enough to give Ivan and keep him happy and perhaps pay back Mr. Tate – a little at a time.

Her head ached as she tried to calculate how much she would need. She could add and subtract her financial needs on a daily basis, but the effort to calculate how much she would need to sell to give Ivan some and still keep her business going was just too much for her. All the way home as she walked along the beach, just barely avoiding the evening waves lapping at the shore, she added and subtracted and multiplied until she was thoroughly confused. So engrossed was she in her sums, she didn't notice the white man, sitting on a fallen coconut tree trunk, until he hailed her.

"I was hoping you would pass again, this evening. Where's the good pineapple you promised me?"

Girlie nearly died of embarrassment; her basket was empty and it seemed ungrateful to have forgotten.

"I, me didn't get so much things today," she stammered, "but tomorrow, alright, Boss?" She tried to sound jovial, imitating how some of the other women behaved to the tourists. She even slipped into a pseudo-American accent.

"Come here," he called.

Reluctantly she walked up to him.

"I really meant it when I said that I thought you were different. Don't try that false accent on me. You were the first local person I met who was willing to give me something without a price. Sit down!" he ordered.

Girlie was afraid of his abrupt tone and of what he might want from her. She really didn't want to have anything to do with this man. She had just realised how, with very hard work and a little luck, she might solve her problems. She didn't intend to sell herself.

"It getting late," she said. But since he ignored her statement she reluctantly put down her basket and sat on the tree trunk at least an arm's length away from him.

"I'm not going to bite you, you know. You've been walking far today?" he asked, as she stretched out her legs, suddenly realising how tired she was. The thin dress she wore sucked around her firm thighs, and her full breasts loosely held by her brassiere, jiggled a little as she stretched her hands above her head to take the kinks out of her back.

When she saw him looking at her, she quickly folded herself together, pretending to be writing something in the sand with her fingers.

"You went far today?" he asked again, smiling at her embarrassment.

"Up pass Edenism," she answered.

"Oh? Sales good?"

"Yes," she said. "Better than usual."

"Good! Good! So when are you going to repay me?"

Girlie hung her head.

"I was going to ask you if I could pay it back little, little," she said. "Maybe five dollar a time?"

"Five dollars a week?"

"Maybe not so often."

Suddenly he laughed.

"Sounds as if you expect me to be here for a long time. I knew you were different. Now tell me why you wanted that money so urgently this morning?"

She shook her head.

"Man trouble?"

Girlie opened her eyes in fright. Had Miss Winsome said something to him?

"No…o…o," she said quietly.

"Come on! You can tell me."

She didn't reply.

"Tell you what. I'm a writer. It's my business to listen to gossip and make up stories. Want to hear today's gossip?"

She shook her head expecting something unpleasant.

"Today's gossip headlines… Battyman Tate finally starts talking to a woman. Today's story: Woman goes home late. Her man thinks she was doing it with the tourist with whom she was seen on the beach. So he demands the money – American. Woman doesn't know what to do… How do you like it so far?"

Girlie's eyes filled with tears. He was talking fast and funny, but she understood that he was talking about her and the shame was worse than before.

"Happens all the time," he said, and his voice sounded sad. "So you didn't tell him we didn't do it?"

"Oh! I see. He didn't believe you!" he continued the one-sided conversation.

Girlie hoped he couldn't see her tears in the gathering dusk.

"So what you going to give him this evening?"

"It, it late," she said, not quite able to control her voice and anxious to get away from his probing.

"Oh come on, girl. Don't cry. Here. Here's ten. Will that do? I'm a little short of cash this week, but I should be able to find a ten or twenty now and then just for the pleasure of your company."

"No!" Girlie said, "I can't take any more. Don't shame me."

"You prefer to take the beatings? Look, I like talking to you. You're doing me a favour, an honour, to listen and talk to me. You understand?" Suddenly his voice was angry.

"And I won't ask you to do it. I won't ask you to fuck unless you want to, and I want to; because we are man and woman and not because I'm a rich white tourist with a dirty mind and you are a poor innocent native or you're a whore or anything like that. Understand?"

Girlie didn't really understand everything he said and she was afraid. She understood he was saying that he wouldn't force himself on her and she was grateful for that. But his anger frightened her. She couldn't tell why he was angry. She was more afraid of him than she had been of Ivan when he had beaten her.

"Here," he said, pushing the money at her. "Go on home an cook dinner fi you man." His imitation of the local accent sounded so funny Girlie felt like laughing.

Then he got up and started jogging up the beach in the direction of his hotel away from her.

Girlie walked home, pensive. Suddenly her life was so confusing. So many strange things were happening to her.

She expected that Ivan would be angry with her for staying out late again. He always wanted his meal before he left for the night's fishing. She was surprised, then, when he greeted her pleasantly.

"Don't worry bout dinner," he said, "Babs was here an she cook. Some on the table for you," he said, patting his stomach.

It was then that Girlie understood. Babs had been chosen to take her place at home while she went out and earned money. She didn't ask why he wanted the money so badly but she wished she hadn't been chosen as the sacrifice. She knew that he would put her away as long as he thought she was fucking the white man. The unfairness of everything made her want to cry again. But she wouldn't cry, never again, as easily as she used to.

She would have to be strong. No more weeping. She would do the things her man wanted her to do. Help him to get the things he wanted, even though it meant heartache for her. Girlie didn't actually put these thoughts into words but she felt them, instinctively knowing what her new role was. This was her birthright. Her time had come.

"You bring anything fi me?" he asked anxiously.

Once upon a time, a long time ago it seemed, she would have

asked playfully "Like what?" and they would have romped a little
before settling down to business. That night she gave him the
thirty American dollars wordlessly, ten from Mr. Tate and the
twenty she had made from her sale.

"Him say him will have to give me Jamaican sometimes," she
said.

"It dearer in Jamaican, you know."

"Me know," she answered.

"Bwoy, him must be really like you. Thirty Merican!" he
exclaimed.

"Suppose, suppose him don't pay me everytime, but like pon
a Saturday or so?" she asked accepting the role she must now play.
Scheming to protect him; to protect herself; to protect even the
white man to whom as yet she had no commitment.

"Jus mek sure you get the right amount. Jus don't gi it way," he
threatened her.

"Is all right," she said coaxingly, as if talking to a child.

And he answered, "Yes, is all right, Miss Girlie," as he fingered
his dollars – American dollars.

Then he smiled, and standing tall, patted her head. "Cool,
Miss Girlie. Irie! Cho! Listen, don't worry bout come home early
come cook an so. You know, him might want you stay late an so.
Babs will cook an fix up the place. She no have nothing else fi do.
Is time she tek up some responsibility.

"Yes, is time," Miss Girlie answered, a half smile on her face.
"Yes, is all right," she said again, still smiling and holding back the
tears she would no longer shed.

## SUPERMARKET BLUES

Miss Maud was going to the shop, the Three Tees Super-market. She settled the slightly dirty white hat, which had been down-graded from dress-up church-hat to street-hat, over her thick grey plaits, wiped her face with her hands still greasy from plaiting her hair, and looked around for the plastic bag she always carried with her when shopping.

She lifted her hat to place the change purse under it. She had started doing that since the thinness of her body, coupled with age, caused her to have no more use for a brassiere. Since there was nothing to retain the change purse in her bosom, she now wore it under her hat. In the supermarket she would find a corner, turn her back and, with what she hoped were unnoticeable movements, fish out the purse from under the hat before going to the counter to pay for her goods.

Since she usually didn't take a trolley for the few things she wanted, and walked with the groceries piled in her hands or in a box, getting at the purse was often a complicated exercise. Some-times she forgot to get the purse before checking the goods, and then she had to feel for it right before everybody's eyes. She didn't mind their seeing her; what she was afraid of was that they would follow her and try to steal her money. She wasn't sure who "they" were, but there were so many stories about thieves these days she couldn't help being afraid.

She need not have worried. Her shabby appearance, together with the few groceries she purchased, would never lead anyone to suspect that she had money worth stealing. In fact she didn't.

Her daughter in America owned the house she lived in, along with some eight other tenants. She didn't pay any rent. A regular

$20 a month, an occasional sum from her son in England, occasional gifts of food from her relatives in the country and a Christmas box from the States kept her alive.

She was grateful for this. She was better off than some of the other tenants in the yard, especially the young women with small children. Often it was she to whom the children came for a midday meal of porridge and crackers while their mothers were out "looking work".

Miss Maud shut her door and walked toward the gate. Before she could reach it, two voices called out to her.

"Buy some sugar fe me, no?"

"Wait little, Miss Maud; ef you see any condense milk, buy two tin fe me."

"Ef me see any," she answered, waiting while the two women brought her the money to make their purchases.

"Ef me se any," Miss Maud repeated aloud as she waited to cross the busy main road before the Three Tees Plaza. Of late she talked to herself a lot.

"After them no have nutten inna the shop dem again. Las week me no get no soap powder. Me have fe buy newfangle water soap whey me no like. Me no get no flour neither. Wonder what them no have this week."

Since the shortages started, the rows of empty shelves testified to the absence of many needed items, Miss Maud had fallen into the habit of haunting the two supermarkets near to her every day. Since she didn't have to take a bus, and didn't mind the exercise, every morning at about ten o'clock she visited one or the other, sometimes both, in the hope of finding scarce items.

If she was lucky, she might be on the spot when the two or three cartons of soap powder were opened, and then she would get one. Also, if she waited long enough, and begged hard enough, one of the men who packed goods in the back room might take pity on her and bring out a tin of milk or a pack of chicken necks and backs or a pack of sugar depending on what was short.

Sometimes, too, she had to beg them to package a smaller amount of cornmeal or flour, because the packs on the shelves had more than she could pay for or carry comfortably.

"Life get so hard," Miss Maud continued her soliloquy. "It bad enough that the little money can't stretch, but even when you have it, sometimes you can't get nutten fi buy."

Sixty-six years old, lonely because all her children had gone away, confused by the many rapid changes around her, Miss Maud hurried across the road when the light showed the green "walk" signal.

She arrived on the other side a little breathless, straightened her hat and turned into the Three Tees Plaza.

The supermarket door flew open as she stepped on the mat, making her heart flutter a little. No matter how often she came to here, the magic door which flew open without a touch always surprised her.

She smiled at the young packer who was standing idly by, leaning against one of the take-out trolleys.

"Morning, son," she greeted him. "How tings today, eh?"

"Same as usual, Granny," he replied and turned away. He didn't want to get into conversation with her. The other packers teased him because he was polite to the customers and the older women especially liked to stop and chat with him.

Miss Maud saw that there weren't many people in the store. It was the time when she best liked to shop. When there were too many people in the store, pushing and shoving to get things from the shelves, she got confused and sometimes forgot what she wanted. She never forgot the time, months before, how she was nearly trampled in the rush for rice when a few packs were brought out. They had had to close the supermarket and call the police. Since then she had grown afraid of crowds. When the store was empty she could take her time and if she forgot anything she could look around until she remembered what it was she wanted.

As she hesitated by the turnstile, wondering whether to take a trolley, a handbasket, or simply keep the things in her hands, a woman brushed past her with an impatient "excuse me".

★

Mrs. Telfer was in a bad mood. She was late for work again. Because of the shortages, she too had taken to haunting the supermarkets, three or four of them, three or four times each week, in the hope of filling her grocery needs. What one shop didn't have, she sometimes found in another. And, of course, being on good terms with more than one manager meant that she would get three packs of soap and so on, one from each, depending on which item was short.

But it took up so much time! She was having to sneak out from work at odd times during the day or go in late with some inadequate excuse. Of late, her boss had been staring at her whenever she went in late. He hadn't said anything yet but she was sure that it was just a matter of time.

She wasn't happy about the situation, but what could she do? Personally, she didn't mind the shortages. She could do without many of the things she had to hunt and scrounge for, but her husband and her two sons were forever complaining when she told them that the things they liked just weren't available.

"I don't like this soap. It stinks! Why did you buy it?" her husband would ask.

She would patiently explain that it was the only brand available.

"You just write your sister in Chicago or John and tell them to send you some decent soap," he would command her. "Is better you don't bathe than use this. You smell stinker after you use it," and he would bang the bathroom door to emphasise his annoyance.

"Mummy, you sure them don't have no Kellogs?" her elder son would wail, both elbows on the table, leaning over the porridge he didn't want.

"No, Joseph," she would patiently explain for the millionth time. "There's no Kellogs. Eat your porridge before your father leave you again this morning."

"I don't like this black sugar," the little one would then begin. "It don't taste good."

They nagged her as if all these changes were her fault. As if she could manufacture the things they wanted, the things they had been accustomed to, out of thin air.

If Three Tees manager couldn't find a bottle of coffee for her today, she was sure she would have to move out of the house. She couldn't face that miserable man in the morning and tell him that there was no coffee. She wondered who she could sue for breaking up her marriage.

Not the government. They said it wasn't their fault.

Mrs. Telfer put her handbag in the trolley and pushed it briskly before her.

★

Miss Maud was taking her time over her shopping. She looked at the tightly squeezed-up dollar notes in her hand and tried to remember what her neighbours had asked her to buy. "Tilda want sugar and milk. Valda want soap and milk too," she said aloud, moving around to look for the groceries. A little commotion at the entrance caused her to look back.

A large woman, fat and sweating, had entered with her small child and was teasing the shy packer.

"Morning, George," she greeted him loudly, much to the amusement of the others.

"You leave anything for me today?"

"Wha him have, yu no want it!" one of the grinning youths told her.

"Who sey me no want it?" she laughed. "When you gwine gi me? Enh, Mr. George?" she teased the youth, who was busy trying not to look as uncomfortable as he felt.

"Him ketch fraid. Him can't manage you," another one said.

"Cho! Me fat but me easy fi manage," the woman said, still laughing. Then suddenly she stopped laughing and said in a stern voice, "Me want some chicken back and flour this morning an oonu better no tell me no foolishness say oonu no have none!" she announced loudly to the shop at large. The two cashiers looked at each other and raised their eyebrows.

It didn't take Miss Maud very long to pick up the few things she wanted. She had found milk but looked in vain for onions. The food just didn't taste the same without the onions. And she couldn't afford to pay the price they were asking on the plaza. Furthermore they had married it to yam, or something else.

She had been lucky to catch the eye of one of the store-room packers and had begged him to bring some sugar and a few onions for her. She was willing to pay the 80c or so they would cost and do without something else this week.

She waited almost ten minutes before the packer returned with only one pack of sugar. "But is two me beg you," she protested. "Them gal a yard beg me buy fi them."

"Oonu gwine have fi share that," the man answered rudely. "No more no pack," he said, and shut the door in her face.

"Wha bout onion?" she asked the door.

Sighing wearily Miss Maud walked towards the cashier to pay for the groceries.

★

Mrs. Telfer was looking at her half-full trolley in disgust. Most of the things she had picked up she didn't need – at least not yet, since she had some at home. But it had become a habit with her not to pass up items that might become short in the future. It wasn't that she meant to hoard. But take toilet paper. A month ago that had been reduced to the last roll at home. She'd had to buy box tissues to fill the family's needs, and endure a number of often downright rude remarks from her husband. Now she automatically picked up an extra roll or two everytime she shopped.

This little shopping spree would cause her to overspend her budget again for the week, but she had almost given up the "battle of the balancing budget" as she and her friends called it. It really didn't matter. She would ask Ralph for more money and he would shout at her, yelling that she was asking for more and more money and bringing less and less into the house.

Men never understood. Ralph would talk for hours about the economic situation of the country, balance of payments problems, explain to his bewildered friends that the bad planning in the past had brought the country to its present situation, but ask him to use newspaper instead of toilet paper, as she had once suggested! Mrs. Telfer could smile now as she remembered his comment. And as to his whisky! He still managed to make sure that he had at least one bottle in the house.

Her only consolation this morning was that the manager had given her a bottle of coffee, discreetly wrapped with the price marked on the paper bag so that the cashier could check it without even knowing what was inside. But he had given her no oil.

Somewhere in the supermarket she could hear a woman's voice boisterously abusing somebody for not giving her any oil. The voice was tracing the other person's ancestry back to monkey days in the forest. The people who behaved like that usually got what they wanted, Mrs. Telfer thought. But she would have to starve before anybody got her to behave like that.

A little way from the cashier she paused to check her purse. She always did this since the day she had suffered the embarrassment of not having enough money to pay the cashier after the goods had already been checked.

★

Miss Maud had also stopped to worry about the second pack of sugar which she hadn't got. She was wondering what was the best thing to do. Maybe Little Corner Supermarket would have some. She sorted out the money to pay for the different goods and satisfied that she had it correct, began to move toward the cashier just as Mrs. Telfer started to push her trolley forward. Seeing Mrs. Telfer's half-full trolley, Miss Maud with her few items hastened to get in front of her. In her hurry, she didn't notice the jutting back wheel of the trolley until she tripped over it and, to the horror of onlookers, banged her head on its side as she fell to the floor.

Tins of milk, a box of soap, a pack of sugar flew in all directions. As she struggled to pull herself up on hands and knees, blood began to drip slowly onto the floor.

The supermarket froze. Nobody moved. Not the cashier who had been getting ready to receive the goods; not George the young packer with whom she had smiled when she entered the store; not the manager who had been passing; not the idle packers congregating by the door; and certainly not Mrs. Telfer.

With horror, Mrs. Telfer watched the drops of blood pooling and the old woman kneeling, unable to rise. Somewhere in Mrs. Telfer's head was the thought that she should help the old woman to her feet, find out how badly hurt she was. Something in the way the old woman looked reminded her of her own Aunt Jo, and her heart turned over in sympathy. Yet still she did not move.

She wanted to reach out and hug the bleeding head. She wanted to comfort the old woman who had started to moan, but even later, when she was telling the story, she couldn't explain why she never moved.

Suddenly the fat boisterous woman burst around the corner. Hurrying to Miss Maud, she roughly pushed Mrs. Telfer's trolley out of the way and gently lifted the old woman off the floor. She helped her to stand up and grabbed a pack of toilet paper from Mrs. Telfer's shopping.

Breaking open the pack she took out a roll and tore off a piece which she used to wipe the blood which was trickling down the old woman's face.

"Them can't charge we fi this," she said, tearing off more and more paper. "Come Granny. Look how you mash up you face this big big Tuesday morning. Come we go outside in the fresh air mek me see how it stay."

"Jilly!" she called to one of the small children who had come shopping with her. "Tek up Granny hat and her purse and beg them a bottle, ketch little cold water at the cooler.

"Hurry!" she ordered and kept up a constant chatter, bemoaning the old woman's wound and threatening punishment against the management as she led Miss Maud outside.

With a sigh of relief the supermarket thawed.

"All right," the manager shouted. "One of you idle boys get a mop and clean up this mess. Move it!"

George went to find a container to get the child the water.

The cashier settled herself on her chair and began to punch her machine as Mrs. Telfer unloaded her trolley. Mrs. Telfer's brown face had turned very pale, as if it was she who had lost the blood now drying on the floor.

"I'll pay for the paper," she almost whispered to the cashier, who didn't reply.

## EASTER SUNDAY MORNING

It wasn't me playing the organ that day, you know. It was like those mechanical pianos that play by themselves. My fingers were moving I know, but I wasn't responsible. The organ play louder and louder and keep on playing even when the hymn suppose to stop. I didn't know what was happening down there because my head stiff straight ahead. Lord, it was frightening! And when the notes just start crashing together I was so scared. And then, immediately after that, I found myself playing "Praise God" and the people start singing it same time, as if I had already introduced it.

Not even rector don't talk about it yet. It's like everybody still trying to understand what happen.

Some of us would like to pretend that it didn't happen. You notice how church full up since then.

Yes. It's like it was a sign or something. Like the church renewed. It's real scary.

I never felt so in touch with God since I going to church as on that morning. It was frightening.

I sensed trouble the moment she walked through the door.

I sense trouble through the whole service. We were sitting behind her and she was restless the whole time.

It's when the folk group start singing the Zion songs that she really started getting excited. The moment the drums started she start to twitch.

I don't know. I still think it not quite right to sing them Poco songs and beat drum in church. I don't know. I just not comfortable with it. Mark you, I like accompanying them. You know it's different and I enjoy it. But I not so sure you're supposed to enjoy yourself in church like that. All that clapping and swaying about – almost like dancing in church, and the drums, I don't know.

The scariest part was how Mass Luke find the bunch of burn-up bush right in the middle of the aisle.

You think she came back?

No. They say nobody has seen her since that.

It was the very first time that they were discussing the incident together. Three weeks had passed and the church was still trying to understand what had happened that Easter morning. It was the one time that an incident with so many eyewitnesses didn't have different accounts of what had taken place. Everybody gave almost the same details. There were minor differences only in the estimate of the length of time the incident had taken and the organist had fixed the time almost to a second. It was the length of time it took to play the hymn, "*Oh God unseen yet ever near*", twice.

The universal sentiment was that nobody knew exactly what had happened but that it was very frightening.

The April Easter Sunday morning had dawned as fresh and calm as the dew-covered trees and bushes and meadowgrass in the village of Walkup Hill. Rainfall in March, after a long drought, had brought an outpouring of the signs of spring from a grateful earth. Easter morning praises could be heard and seen everywhere. Birds twittered and chirped and sang whole songs as they darted from tree to tree. Every bush and every weed was painted with vibrant colours testifying to its joy at being alive.

Walkup Hill was peaceful, content and holy as the church bells at St. Peter Anglican church began to peal, summoning the faithful to praise God.

Easter morning service was always special at St. Peter. For some reason, which nobody could remember, the church had combined a kind of Harvest Festival with the Easter service so that in addition to the white lilies and other Easter flowers, the church overflowed with red otaheite apples, bright yellow oranges and grapefruits; sugarcane, yams and sweet potatoes. Green bananas hugged each other in large bunches; voluptuous ripe plantains tempted the touch. The sights and smells injected a special earthy sensuousness into the worship, which no other service had.

When the middle-class people who had moved into the area in and around the village had first attended this service, they had thought "how quaint". But they had liked it, so that the only change now was that the baskets were prettier and more artistically arranged by the Decoration Committee, and everybody was pleased.

It was like this with many things in Walkup Hill these days, a mixture of old customs and new ways as the village changed from a backwoods on the outskirts of the city to a middle-class suburb.

It had started with one man, a lawyer, who had his roots in Walkup Hill and who had built his home right beside one of the many streams which tumbled through the village on their way to the thirsty flatland below. His friends had envied him the peaceful nature of his home, far from the city crowds and noises, and since it didn't take more than three-quarters of an hour to reach the city, the villagers found themselves being besieged by requests for land. One enterprising developer had even turned what appeared to be a rocky hillside into a very charming housing scheme.

Now, in the mornings, the narrow road winding out of the village was busy with fancy motorcars and villagers with their donkeys, often getting in each other's way, as old timers and newcomers learned to tolerate each other. In truth, most of the villagers didn't really mind the change. For one thing, the newcomers didn't plant food, so the tiny market did good business most of the week, and some villagers who used to go to the big market in the nearest town at the foot of the hill now found that they could sell their foodstuff right there in Walkup Hill.

Several village daughters found employment in the new homes. The village shop expanded to take care of the increased demand, and with the cash for the land they had sold, old timers fixed up their houses or bought more animals and tools. Walkup Hill assumed an air of prosperity which other villages further away envied.

The newcomers also took over leadership of community organisations, and since they had money to contribute, or were good at fund-raising, these also prospered – like the new Community Hall and the improved cricket pitch, the toilets in the market, and most of all the churches.

Walkup Hill had two churches. Three really – the Methodist Church, St. Peter – the Anglican Church – and the Church of the Holy Redeemer of the Resurrection. The last named, a revivalist church, usually had the largest weekly attendance, although most of the villagers would tell an outsider that they were either Anglican or Methodist – meaning that they had been christened in one or the other.

Many of the newcomers were Anglican and they quickly took over St. Peter. Attendance used to be small, the church had been looked after mainly by a deacon, a parish rector visiting once a month or less to administer communion and oversee church matters. But in no time at all this changed and soon the congregation was large enough and contributing enough to have its own parson. A rectory was built, facilities at the church upgraded, a few additions made and St. Peter, instead of sitting forlornly on the peak of a hill as it had been wont to do, now stood, its old stone walls softly proud of the new attention, and a sparkling new cross on its roof testified that it was taking over the leadership of the spiritual community in Walkup Hill.

Some of the oldtimers who had kept things together through the years of its backwater existence were a little put out by the new leadership, which tended to ignore them, not out of malice, but simply because they were anxious to get on with their jobs and were impatient with the slower, more cautious manner in which the oldtimers lived their lives.

Anyway, St. Peter became the pride of Walkup Hill and many villagers who had ceased attending, now resumed their membership to the detriment, in particular, of the Church of the Holy Redeemer of the Resurrection.

One such was Mother White. She had come back to St. Peter, she told somebody, because it seemed that the church had got new power, power that she coveted.

Mother White was not an ordinary villager. She could see things and do things – so people said. They didn't actually call her an obeah woman, but it was said that she had powers to cure people of strange illnesses. Illnesses which ordinary doctors could not even diagnose. She could take off evil spirits, and a bush bath by Mother White could cure the most serious disease.

She didn't always practise her calling. Mostly, she was an ordinary citizen like anybody else. But sometimes…

Once there was a girl given up for dead. She came from another village and her people brought her to Mother White as a last resort. Her case was so hard that Mother White had left her lying in the thatch-covered room where she gave baths, and she had disappeared for a whole half day searching for the bushes which she needed.

She returned almost exhausted, with a tale that the spirit riding the girl had followed her and had tried to prevent her getting the right bushes. As she told it:

"Everytime I put out mi han fi pull up the right bush, wha you think come up? Stink weed! A looking Guinea Hen, a find Horse Whip! A looking Rosemary, a find Lovebush! This is a hard case."

She had kept the half-dead girl for two days, giving her baths and potions and the whole thing had ended with a drum ceremony to pin the evil spirit so that it wouldn't follow the girl home.

Since the girl lived far away, the villagers never heard if she had recovered, but nobody doubted Mother White's powers.

Until her own son began to act funny.

It was said that he had given a girl in a nearby village a baby, and had promised to marry her, but during the time that she was sexually unavailable he had taken up with another girl. The baby mother had "put something on him" in revenge.

The villagers looked on curiously to see how quickly Mother White would cure her son. But nothing happened. Ceremony after ceremony was held, but if anything the boy got worse.

One day he ran amok with a machete and was taken away to the asylum in the city.

Had Mother White lost her powers?

It was during this time that she returned to St. Peter, where she had been a confirmed member a long time before.

The first Sunday morning she appeared in church, the new-comers, many of whom had never heard of her, were quite startled.

She was dressed in bleached calico with two or three layers of thickly gathered long skirts. Her head was tied with calico under her hat. When she entered the main doorway she did a kind of curtsy, then walked up the aisle to the altar where she made the sign of the cross and spun around three times, her many skirts billowing around her. Then she walked down the aisle, stopping at the pew which caught her fancy.

She did this every Sunday morning and at communion time she would be among the first at the rail, where after receiving the sacrament, she would walk straight out of the church and go home without talking to anyone.

After many Sundays witnessing this behaviour, the church relaxed since it seemed that she was harmless. Some of the younger members even began to giggle at her performance. Some of the old timers, however, were apprehensive. Later, they would say that they knew something was wrong from the beginning, but since nobody listened to them any longer…

It was a child who first awakened the church to the fact that Mother White was up to no good.

One Sunday morning, on their way home after service, the Wynter family passed Mother White walking her stiff, swift walk through the village centre on her way to her home hidden away in the bushes.

One of the Wynter children suddenly asked, "Why that old lady don't like the communion, Mama?"

"Nonsense. She takes communion, every Sunday," the mother answered.

"But she don't drink it," the child insisted.

"What you mean?"

"Last week I was outside. You member I went to the toilet? And she came out of church and spit out the communion in a bottle that hide in her skirt."

Wynter mother and father looked at each other puzzled, then the mother said quickly, "I'm sure it wasn't that. And, by the way, don't I tell you not to linger when you have to go outside?"

Later, though, she discussed the situation with her husband

who thought that there had to be a simple explanation for what the child had seen.

"Why would anyone want to spit out the communion?" he asked. It didn't make sense.

His wife, however, was sufficiently puzzled to mention it to some other church members the following week, and she asked the same question: "Why would anybody want to keep the wine? It has its place only in church!"

Two oldtimers in the group said nothing, but during the week, they went to the rectory to tell the parson about their suspicion that Mother White was using the church and the communion for evil purposes. That could be the only reason why she was not swallowing the communion wine but saving it.

The parson, brought up in the city, had a modern scientific mind and was inclined to dismiss the story.

"True, the woman is strange, but each of us has our little ways," he told them. "It's just that Mother White is a little more eccentric than most."

Still they insisted that he should at least observe her so that they could be satisfied that everything was all right. Great harm would come to the church, they predicted, if she was really using the communion for devilish purposes. When the parson asked what she could possibly do with the communion wine, they told him in some detail what they knew of her history.

The following Sunday he was away, so communion service was not held. But sure enough, the next communion Sunday, Mother White turned up, went through her usual act and those watching saw how, as she stepped outside the church, she stopped, took a bottle from her pocket and spat out what had to be the communion wine into it. She also wrapped what appeared to be the wafer in a piece of paper, put both in her pocket and walked quickly away.

Parson was surprised and a little worried when he heard this report. He had no choice but to put the matter before the church's advisory committee. He called a special meeting and together with the witnesses they discussed the situation. Nobody had ever heard of such a thing before. They were bewildered and afraid, because the old timers were talking about obeah and devil dealings and they were not quite sure how to handle Mother White.

It was decided that the parson should seek advice from the Bishop, but meanwhile they would withhold the communion from Mother White. As the parson summed it up, "We can't prevent her from coming to church, but we can withhold the communion since we have witnesses that she is not receiving it in the holy tradition of the Church."

"Suppose she makes a fuss?" somebody asked.

"That would only prove that she was up to no good," another replied.

It happened that the next communion service was held on Easter Sunday morning. The church was packed, as usual. Many who hardly attended church during the year made a special effort to be there at Easter and at Christmas. Indeed, one of the parson's favourite jokes was to wish some of his audience Happy Easter at Christmas and Merry Christmas at Easter.

So St. Peter was full. Old timers and newcomers dressed up, feeling peaceful and content with the world as they walked in quietly and took their seats.

Easter lilies filled the brass urns at the altar. Brightly coloured fruits and other offerings wooed the congregation into feelings of worship and praise; the Decoration Committee had spent a busy Saturday and had outdone themselves with the flower and harvest arrangements. They were both celebrating the resurrection of their Lord and reaffirming his goodness in providing mankind with so many gifts from the earth.

The organist entered and began the soft prelude and the congregation sat in expectation of the grand march up the aisle led by the altar boy with the cross, followed by the rector and choir. This was one of the few occasions when St. Peter followed a formal order, for their services tended to be more informal than in many other Anglican churches.

Suddenly there was a rustle at the main door and a harsh voice crying "Holy is God! Holy is the Lord!"

Everybody turned around and there was Mother White. Her
calico skirts looked whiter and stiffer than usual. Beneath tie-
head and hat her wizened features glistened from the oils with
which she had rubbed her face.

In her hands she held a bunch of dried bush, which looked as
if it had been slightly scorched by fire. She also had a single dried
mandora coconut, large, smoothed like a calabash and shining as
if it too had been rubbed with oils. She walked slowly up the aisle
and those sitting near could smell white rum and strange oils as
she passed.

At the altar-rail she plunked her bunch of burnt bush into the
midst of the beautiful white Easter lilies, rested the coconut on
the ground, made the sign of the cross, spun around three times
and then returned down the aisle. At the end of the aisle, near the
doorway, she spun around three times again, then counting off
seven rows from the door, she indicated to those in the crowded
pew on the left side that that was where she intended to sit.

Two people got up and gave her the aisle seat, while others
shifted uncomfortably. Somehow her presence had introduced a
new influence into the church. Many could sense it and it made
them uneasy. The smell of alcohol and strange oils were an
unwelcome addition to the already heady odours in the church.

One woman, outraged at the ugly bush in the midst of the
lilies, plucked it out and went to a side door and threw it angrily
outside. Somebody else spirited away the coconut.

Somehow, after all that, the holy procession up to the altar
seemed something of an anticlimax.

It was already going to be an unusual service that morning, for
the advisory committee had decided to invite a group of folk singers
as part of the entertainment during the service. Many of them felt
that the church could do with a little modernising of the pattern of
its service, a little more recognition of the island's culture. Some
churches, they argued, were even including dance as part of the
worship. The Freedom Singers were seated in the front pews and
the two drummers were already stationed near the organist waiting
to offer their praises in the folk tradition.

Things went calmly enough for the first part of the service. They sang the usual Easter songs of praise and joy for the resurrection of Christ, and the choir did a special number. It was when the drummers for the Freedom Singers struck up that the first signs of trouble began.

The Singers started with, *Me alone, me alone ina de wilderness.*

Those near to Mother White reported that she began to twitch and shake as soon as the drumming started. So much so that two more people left the pew. When they started to sing, *Moses struck the rock,* she got up and began to wheel and turn in the aisle.

A few visitors thought that this was part of the entertainment and were delighted. But the parson, who was a red man, turned redder, and many in the congregation began to frown. Mother White was going too far.

Still nobody made a move to try to quiet her or lead her outside, as had been done on occasion with certain stray persons who had tried to disrupt the service. And after the drumming ceased, she returned to her seat where, after a few more twitches, she kept quiet and the parson with a feeling of great apprehension began his sermon. The main message was that Jesus Christ by his resurrection had enabled Christians everywhere to overcome Evil and the Power of Darkness.

Much later, when they were still trying to analyse it, the congregation agreed that it was from this point that the battle began. Imperceptibly. Nothing spectacular. Just a heightening of tension in the church; a strangely powerful ring in the parson's voice affirming the power of Christ in a way they had never heard him do before; and quite unexpectedly storm clouds shielded the sunlight so that someone got up and turned on all the lights in the church.

Then came the invitation to communion.

"My brothers and sisters in Christ, draw near and receive His Body which He gave for you, and His Blood which He shed for you. Remember that He died for you and feed Him in your hearts by faith with thanksgiving."

Mother White was among the first to move out of the pews to go to the rail to receive the communion.

Organist and congregation prepared to sing *Let us break bread together on our knees,* as usual, but the parson surprised them by giving instructions for the hymn.

"O God, unseen yet ever near, Thy Presence may we feel, And thus inspired by Holy fear before Thy altar kneel."

He recited these words as the faithful took their place waiting to receive the body and blood of Christ.

Mother White was second at the rail and when he came to her, the words *The Body of Christ given for you* just would not come out, so he shook his head and whispered, "Mother White, I cannot in all good conscience offer you this sacrament."

There was a pause as Mother White looked in her upturned hands where there was no expected wafer. She looked up at the parson puzzled, but he was moving on to the person beside her.

The first most of the congregation knew about what was happening was when she sprang up and began to stamp her feet and shout: "I want me communion. I come fi mi communion and I must get it. You have fi gi me."

For a second there was a shocked silence in the church, the singing petered out and the bewildered congregation wondered what was happening.

The parson repeated loudly so that all could hear, "Mother White, I cannot in good conscience offer you this sacrament."

As if on cue, those who had been in the aisle waiting their turn quickly retreated to their seats as if clearing the battleground as Mother White began to shout and stamp in earnest.

As if on cue too, the congregation took up back the hymn and without knowing why, began to sing louder and louder. The louder she screamed and shouted, the louder the organ played and the louder the congregation sang. When they reached the last verse

*Thus may we all thy words obey*
*For we O God are thine*
*And go rejoicing on our way*
*Renewed with strength Divine*

they sang with a fervour and belief that most of them had never before felt in their faith.

Meanwhile the parson stood motionless at the altar, the Host still in his hands, his head bowed in prayer.

But still Mother White shouted and when the hymn ended, the congregation started it all over again, without even a pause. The organ pealed out as it had never done before and the congregation sang as they had never sung before. Small children hugged their parents in fright as Mother White began to foam at the mouth. She spun around not three times but seven times one way and seven times the other. She rolled rapidly on the floor down the aisle and returned as rapidly. She stood up and her body, washed with sweat, shook and trembled. At one point it seemed that her head alone was spinning leaving her body motionless.

And still the congregation sang.

Suddenly, when it seemed that they could get no louder, when it seemed that their very souls were being lifted out of their bodies, the organ made a loud crash of discordant notes frightening everybody, and in the silence which ensued Mother White shook herself violently once more and then, quite calmly and peacefully, took up her hat which had fallen on the floor and walked out of the door.

And without any directive, organ, parson and congregation burst into the hymn:

*Praise God from whom all blessings flow*
*Praise Him all creatures here below*
*Praise Him above ye heavenly host*
*Praise Father, Son and Holy Ghost.*
*Amen.*

At Amen, without another word, as if still on cue, without waiting for the established dismissal, everybody quietly and quickly left the church and went home. No lingering to greet each other and exchange talk and comments on the service as usual, for the emotional experience they had just undergone was too much for discussion yet.

Even the parson, who usually stayed until all had departed, left St. Peter that morning without a word to any of his flock.

As they hurried away the rain clouds dispersed and the bright April morning Easter sun streamed down on them, once more warming them and lighting up the cross on the roof of the church triumphant.

## PRINCESS CARLA
## AND THE SOUTHERN PRINCE
## A C'BBEAN FAIRY TALE

I

*Our Antillean Ark*
*painted Carib blue*
*charts ancient unknown waves*
*even to the centre of the storm*
*The bird of love sent out*
*brings back no branch of peace*
*Our ship sails on*
*forever fixed*
*in storm's eye*
*parking space*
*for desperate souls*

Once upon a time, in the land of Jamrock, a tiny village-kingdom in the C'bbean Sea, there slept a princess named Carla.

There was nothing unusual about the fact that she was a princess, for Jamrock had many princesses, all of them of uncertain royal lineage, and all of them heiresses to no kingdom.

What was unusual about Princess Carla was the fact that she had been asleep for one hundred years.

Princess Carla fell into a trance the day that she was born and nothing her family ever did could awaken her.

She slept through her childhood never knowing the frightening experiences that many other children in the kingdom suffered. Not for her the problems of having no father, no mother, no shelter, no schooling, malnutrition, and other Jamrock ills. In fact, if she were not asleep one could almost say that she was spoilt.

Princess Carla slept her way through adolescence and into womanhood. And during her long sleep she dreamt many dreams.

All her dreams were those her family wished her to dream. The same dreams their parents had had for their daughters and so on for generations back.

In her dreams the princess attended school, learned what they taught her, not brilliantly, but well enough to pass whatever exams she sat. She kept away from trouble and in early adulthood married the first suitable man to stir her interest. She had children, made a home, did nothing unusual, dreamed more dreams for her children and grandchildren and their children, a never ending circle of satisfactory, if unspectacular dreams – for one hundred years.

Members of her family died, were born, left home and returned while Princess Carla slept on, smiling vaguely in the large beautiful white bed they had prepared for her in the middle of the hall in the great house in which they lived.

And while Princess Carla slept, very little changed in the Kingdom of Jamrock. The poor remained poor and the rich remained rich and powerful.

Princess Carla's long sleep was well known throughout the C'bbean. Everybody in Jamrock and the other kingdoms scattered on the sea had heard about her.

They came from far and near and shook or nodded their heads as they gazed in wonder at the smiling princess hibernating in her comfortable bed, dreaming her comfortable dreams.

If the truth were told, Princess Carla was the biggest income source of her kingdom. The visitors needed to be fed, some to be housed, and most were willing to pay for and give a tip for the services of the villagers.

Some of the visitors were envious.

"It's the best thing," they said, "to sleep and dream so comfortably, unaware of the problems of this world."

But others were annoyed.

"What a waste of time," they said. "Surely, something should be done to wake her. She should be up and about making a contribution, helping to improve life around her, teaching others the skills she has learned."

They forgot, of course, that the only thing the princess had learned to do was to dream. But none of their comments bothered the princess. None of them changed her dreams. None of them made her want to awaken from her long sleep and comfortable dreams.

However, towards the end of her one hundred years, the family began to notice a change in the princess.

The obeah priest who had diagnosed her case at birth said that she would live forever, provided she were never awakened from her sleep. The family had thought that this also meant that she would never grow old. That she would continue to make them rich and famous, a continuous attraction for all the tourists and others who liked to gaze at their sleeping princess.

But now there were unmistakable signs that the princess was beginning to age. Her hair started growing grey, then her smooth brown skin began to go blotchy and her body began to lose its youthful, robust look. When wrinkles began to gather on her face and the visitors began to comment on this, the family became uneasy.

Would the tourists continue to come if the princess were only a shrivelled-up old woman? Part of the attraction had been her beauty.

"Let us send for Bongojai," they said.

So they sent for Bongojai, son of the obeah priest who had attended the princess's birth.

But Bongojai, after observing the princess for half a day, could only shake his head and say, "It is as my father prophesied. I do not know what is ailing the princess."

They sent him away and called in Congojai, the rival obeah priest in the village-kingdom.

"It's time for the princess to awaken," Congojai told the family. "She has slept for too long."

"But if she is awakened, she will die!" the family protested. "That is the prophecy."

"Perhaps, perhaps not," Congojai answered. "But if she remains like this, you'll soon have nothing but an old hag on your hands, and who will come to see her then?"

In truth, both obeah priests were worried about this themselves. Many of the tourists who visited the princess also took the opportunity to consult them. The village-kingdom was almost as well known for its obeah priests as for the sleeping princess.

Some of the family were fearful, however. "She must not be woken." But others were willing to listen to Congojai. "How can we awaken her?" they asked. "Nothing disturbs her! Not noise, not heat, not cold, not hunger, nothing!"

"There will come a man," Congojai said, but that was all he was willing to say. Reluctantly he had to admit that this was a hard case. Almost too much for him.

After that the family eagerly looked among the tourists for the man who would awaken the princess. But none seemed to be able to do so.

Somehow the family had got the impression that the man to awaken the princess would be a rich and powerful person who would compensate them for the loss of fame which the sleeping Princess Carla brought them. They sent invitations to many rich and powerful men throughout the world, but those who came turned away when they saw the ageing princess.

"We were told that she was young and beautiful," they complained and quickly packed their bags and left.

Time passed. The village kingdom began to suffer, and the family fretted. Nobody knew what to do.

Then, early one morning, the family awakened to a strange noise in their yard. It was a sound they had never heard before – music, but made by an instrument nobody could recognise.

They crowded the windows and the doors to get a look at the cause of the unusual sounds. In the yard they saw an extraordinary young man. Standing in the first rays of the morning sun, his white T-shirt and short pants seemed to light up and glow.

Goatskin sandals and a floppy white hat completed his costume. Suspended from his neck by a cord was the instrument which was producing the unfamiliar sounds.

The family stared at the instrument which looked like the lid of a large dustbin, from which the visitor coaxed strange metallic ululating notes by beating with two sticks as if he were playing a drum.

"What an odd person," the family exclaimed. "What is he doing here? What does he want? Who is he?"

In answer to their questions the stranger stopped beating his pan, lifted his floppy hat, threw back his head and laughed.

"I come from the Kingdom of Tees, south of you, and I am known as Prince Ralph."

His voice held a kind of magic the family had never heard before, even though they were accustomed to people from many different foreign lands. It held the warmth of the sun and the music of the wind in the trees. It held the song of the waves, the depth of the sea and the freedom of blue skies. It held all the sparkling beauty of a tropic sunrise and it hinted at a kind of happiness none of them had ever dreamed existed. And it made them afraid.

"What do you want?" they asked.

"I've come to see your sleeping princess. Where is she?" he replied.

"Could this be the man of whom Congojai spoke?" they asked each other in whispers. But he was so strange! Surely this could not be the rich, powerful person they were expecting. He looked almost like a vagabond with his strange manner of dress and stranger musical instrument.

"What do you want with the princess?" they asked.

"It's time for her to awaken to make her contribution to the great change which is about to sweep over your land."

"Change?" the family questioned itself. "Had anybody heard anything of any change?" All shook their heads.

But while they stood there hesitating, Prince Ralph began to play another tune on his peculiar instrument.

As he struck the notes on his pan the music he produced was both beautiful and disquieting. It spoke of people dancing with abandon, jumping with joy, and it spoke of sadness. It spoke of hope; and it spoke of despair. But most of all it spoke of the happiness of being alive, of doing things, of creating things, and the family huddled close together in fear. This was not their way.

"Shh!" they chorused without knowing why. "You'll awaken the princess."

And when he heard that, the Prince from the South threw back his head and laughed long and loudly. And the richness of his laughter joined the music of his pan and gave it a new urgency, which despite themselves caused the family to start nodding their heads and tapping their feet.

And the music and the laughter reached the princess in her comfortable bed in the middle of the hall and its urgency penetrated her dreams and for the first in a hundred years her eyes fluttered slightly open.

The family knew at once that something unusual had occurred.

"Princess Carla!" they cried, rushing to her bedside.

And the Prince from the South followed them, beating his pan and laughing in his triumph.

When he reached the bedside, he stopped playing and gazed at her.

"Ah, but she is beautiful!" he exclaimed.

"Not any longer," the family said, sadly.

"Oh yes, she is!" he replied, his eyes creating visions which they could not see.

"Time to get up, Princess Carla," he whispered in her ear. "Time to find out what life is about. Time to face reality instead of dreams."

But the princess had returned to the land of dreams. Only a faint frown showed that she had been disturbed.

"A fraud!" the family chorused in disappointment. "Out before we set the dogs on you!"

The prince left the hall, but he did not go away. He stood in the yard where once again he seemed to attract the now very bright sunlight like a magnet. He seemed to collect the brilliance of the morning and beam it back at all around him – a vagabond turned sungod. His brown eyes glowed, his white teeth gleamed and points of light radiated form the shiny parts of his pan.

Then he raised his sticks and the music poured from him once more. This time, the sweet, high, tenor notes spoke only of the happiness of being alive.

And this time the princess opened her eyes fully. Slowly her dormant muscles were forced into movement. Slowly she arose from her bed. Slowly and shakily she began to walk towards the source of the music.

She reached the doorway and stopped, blinking unaccustomed eyes at the brilliance of the sunlight streaming from the prince.

And when the prince saw her he threw back his head once more and laughed his golden laughter.

"Dance, Princess!" he cried. "You're awake! You're alive"

And the sunlight streaming from him entered her soul and made her warm. His laughter and music kindled her sleepy responses and she wanted to dance. She could feel life and joy flowing through her limbs.

"I don't know how to dance," she said.

"Listen to the music, Carla. The music will teach you how."

So she listened to his music, and she listened to his laughter and didn't even realise when her feet began to move to the rhythms he was producing. She only knew that something strange and wonderful was happening to her. That she was alive for the very first time, and she felt faint with the wonder of it all.

"The light hurts my eyes," she told him. "I can't see you very well. I want to see you."

He stopped playing and gently touched her eyes with his fingers.

Princess Carla blinked twice and looked at the prince. She saw that his eyes were brown and alight with laughter and a promise of kindness. She noticed his long wavy hair and full beard. The prince looked deeply into her eyes and she could feel herself drawing more strength from him. Then he touched her cheek and the contact made her tremble.

"Life is joy and life is sadness, Princess," he told her.

"I'm thirsty," she replied, for she did not understand him.

"Come!" the prince said, striking up his music again. "Not far from here there's a well containing the sweetest water you will ever taste. Follow me," he said, and set off at a fast pace.

"Not so fast!" she pleaded, fearing that she wouldn't be able to keep up with him since her newly-found legs were still weak.

"Follow the music, Princess! Listen to the music and you won't be lost," he cried, as he disappeared along the road before her.

And though she grew afraid when she could no longer see him, his music and laughter continued to guide her and gradually a new confidence came alive in her and made her strong.

Because she was so unused to walking, it seemed to the princess that the journey was very long, but soon the music began to grow louder and louder as if the prince had stopped walking away from her.

Eager to share the joy of which the music spoke, Princess Carla began to run and suddenly around a corner, there he was sitting on a large stone beside a well; brown eyes sparkling.

The princess herself broke into laughter when she saw him. "I was so afraid I'd lose you!"

"Never," he promised, putting aside his pan and taking her hand.

Then for no reason except that they were happy, they both began to laugh so hard that they had to sit on the ground softened by its cover of fallen yellow and pink flowers from the pouis trees which surrounded them. Sometime later, weak with the expression of their happiness they arose from their pink and yellow carpet.

"Are you still thirsty?" the prince asked. She nodded eagerly.

"The lid of this well is heavy," he told her, and she watched his muscles bulging as he slowly but firmly lifted the wooden cover.

"Come," he invited her, "cup your hands and drink. This well is almost full and the water is clean. Nobody else can lift the lid but me."

Princess Carla cupped her hands and drank. As he had promised her, it was the sweetest water she had ever tasted in all her dreams. It went like wine to her head filling her anew with the joy of being alive.

The prince smiled at her obvious pleasure.

"Aren't you thirsty?" she asked.

"It's my well," he answered. But she didn't understand him. "Look into the well," he commanded.

She looked, and then suddenly cried out in delight at her reflection. "Why I'm young!"

"Of course," he smiled.

"But I'm a hundred years old?" She was puzzled.

"What is age?" he replied.

"My wrinkles have gone!" she said in wonder. "My skin is as fresh as a young girl's."

"Age is only in your mind, princess," he told her. "Look at me. How old do you think I am?"

"Twenty?"

He shook his head.

"Twenty-five?"

"No."

"Thirty?"

"No."

"Thirty-five?"

"No."

"Surely you can't be older than that?"

"Perhaps I'm younger than twenty."

"Are you?" she asked.

"What does it matter? I'm none of the ages you guessed, but I could be any of them. It's what you do with yourself that matters, Princess Carla. You were getting old because you were content only to sleep and dream. It was all in your mind."

She looked at him thoughtfully, trying to understand what he was teaching her.

"Look into the well again, Princess Carla," he said.

This time she frowned at the picture she saw in the still water.

There was a group of children, ragged, uncared for, crowding an adult, hands outstretched, begging.

"Who are these children?" she asked bewildered.

"Look again!" he ordered her.

A row of ugly shacks built from a hodgepodge of zinc, cardboard and stones greeted her eyes. As she looked, an old man appeared at the door of one of the shacks, staggered out and sat down slowly and painfully and began to gnaw at a piece of tough-looking bread. Then the group of ragged children she had seen earlier burst on the scene and grabbed the bread from the old man leaving him sobbing in despair.

"Why are you showing me these things?" she asked in fright. "What kind of a well is this?"

"Once more, Princess!" His voice forced her to look again into the well.

More distress greeted her eyes. She saw people living in want, fighting pigs and crows for pickings from the dungle; people sick and dying without care or attention; people fighting; people despairing and she whimpered in pain as the awful scenes unfolded before her.

"Ah Carla," the Southern Prince said, his eyes now filled with a sadness she could not comprehend, "these are things of which you didn't dream. This is reality for more people than you could ever count."

"If this is reality, I prefer my dreams!" she cried.

"No Princess. To hide oneself from truth helps nobody. You will have to face reality and do what you can to help those who need help. That is why you were born and that is why I awakened you."

"Who are you?" she asked for the very first time.

"Does it matter? The time has come for you to live life as it was meant to be."

"No! No! I can do nothing. I know nothing. I can't."

"You'll find out how to do the things you have to, Princess. Don't worry. All it really needs is for you to want to do your part. The rest will fall into place. Look into yourself, Carla. The answers are there, right inside you," he said.

Then he gently closed the lid of the well and took up his pan.
"Don't leave me," she begged him. "Don't go."

"I must go, Princess. But I'll be back whenever you need me.
Whenever you are thirsty, return to the well and you'll find me."

"What is this place?" she asked looking around, anxious to
detain him.

Smiling, he said, "Let's call it Olympus, where the gods live
and are happy."

"How will I find it again?"

"Whenever you need to, you will."

"Suppose I can't find the way. Suppose I get lost!"

"No, you won't," he replied, preparing to go.

"Goodbye for now, Princess. No, not goodbye. I hate that
word. I'll see you again. Remember, whenever you need me I'll
be here. Till then, my Princess."

"When?" she insisted.

"Only you will know that," he answered, and blowing her a
kiss walked rapidly away.

Princess Carla turned to go home. She found herself on a
lonely street, but strangely she didn't feel lonely.

As she walked home the warmth of the sun prince stayed with
her. The memory of his music and laughter flooded her with
happiness and confidence. As she smiled with the people she met
as she neared her home, the light from her eyes touched them and
made them warm. When she spoke to them, music seemed to
flow from her lips and all around her became happy.

II

In time, the family had reason to forget their fear of losing prestige
and fortune if the princess should awaken; for not only was she
as young and beautiful as ever, but she brought new joy, life and
energy not only to the great house, but to the entire village-
kingdom.

During the time that the sleeping princess had been the main tourist attraction, the villagers had grown lazy. It was so much easier to simply gather in the tourist dollars than to tend to their fields and other businesses. Most of the fields had been allowed to fall into ruin and the kingdom had to buy all the supplies, foodstuffs and other things that they and the tourists needed from other kingdoms far and near. As long as there were many tourists bringing in many dollars they had no fear of want, no need to do anything else but scramble for the tourist dollars.

However, when the number of visitors began to fall off, real want began to creep upon them. The long period of indolence had made the people too lazy to revive agriculture or any industry. They began to fight among themselves for the few dollars which came in. Some migrated, and in face of the increasing hardships many began to consult the obeah priests, spending what little money they had in an effort to find some easy solution to their problems.

Congojai and Bongojai prospered.

This was the picture to which Princess Carla awakened. Somehow she felt that she had to do something about the problems in her village-kingdom. She eagerly sought for ways of reawakening the peoples' interest in productive activity. How could she get them to start planting their fields, start making things which they could sell to other kingdoms so that they could buy the things they needed?

So Princess Carla began to talk with the people. She visited them in their homes and encouraged them to work, and such was her charm and her conviction, that slowly they began to respond to her urgings. She sent away for books on agriculture and various homecrafts. She got the women knitting and weaving, preserving fruits and making wines from the fruits they grew.

She sent for various advisers to teach them how to improve their skills. Small factories began to emerge. She organised activities for the children when they were not in school. The strangers who now visited the kingdom came either to help them produce or to buy their goods.

Slowly the kingdom grew prosperous. They sold their surplus food; their craftwork was in great demand; they became in fact a

model kingdom. More visitors now came to admire their industry and to seek advice on how to make their own kingdoms
prosperous.

And flowing over with life and confidence, it seemed as if there
was nothing that the princess could not do. Often she would
remember the picture of the deprived children in the well, and
she would renew her vow that this would never happen to the
children in her kingdom. The great house and the princess once
again became the centre of life from which all good things seemed
to flow. The villagers would point with pride at the great house
and tell the story of the sleeping princess and the good she had
done since she had awakened. Many did not believe until they
visited the great house, spoke with the princess and also fell under
the spell of her charm.

But, there were now two very unhappy people in the kingdom.
As the villagers grew more and more prosperous, they had less
and less need for the services of the obeah priests. And the visitors
were so impressed with the kingdom's prosperity they forgot
about the two old men.

Congojai and Bongojai were so unhappy that they got together
to assess the situation and try to see what they could do about it.

"The princess causing all we troubles," they lamented. "If only
we could mash up her power."

"Send her back to sleep."

"Demolish the sourcement of her wisdom and charm."

"Bring back chaos to the kingdom so that the people will come
to us again."

They racked their brains for an answer.

"What we need to do is to fine out where she get her power,"
Bongojai said.

"Yes," agreed Congojai. "We must set a watch on her. Day an
night."

So they made their plans.

But Princess Carla, happily unaware of their evil plans, continued to do her good work in the kingdom. The people continued
to stream to her for advice and always she seemed to find the right

answers and the right way to help them. Her own family prospered along with the village-kingdom and everybody was happy.

And whenever she felt weak or afraid, tired, or in need of added
strength, she would suddenly remember the way to the well. And
true to his promise the prince was always there when she needed
him.

At a distance she would hear the melody he had chosen to play
that day and she would run the last part of the journey, bursting
into laughter when she saw him, and it would be with them as it
had been on that very first day.

Together they would gaze into the well and he would show
her more visions of life. She would drink from the well and be
revived. Sometimes he played his music and she danced
herself into ecstasy. Sometimes they simply held hands and
talked for hours. He was very wise. He knew all things and all
men, it seemed, and she who had been asleep for a hundred
years listened to his words and drew strength and wisdom
from him.

But unknown to Princess Carla, Congojai and Bongojai had
been spying on her. After a time they met to finalise their plans.

"That Prince Ralph is the cause," they agreed. "Is him mek."

"Wonder is who him? Where him come from? Him magic
powerful!"

"We must fine a way to mash-up the friendship."

"But him too wise. Him will fine us out."

"Mek we work pon the princess," Congojai said. "Get her to
become suspiciousful of him. Get her to bedoubt him."

"How?"

"What every woman want from a man?" Congojai asked.

"What every woman want from a man?" Bongojai puzzled
over this riddle.

Suddenly he snapped his fingers. "Money and love!" he said.
"That's all them ever talk bout."

"Right. But the princess no need no money, and you see how
this Prince Ralph never talk about love. Him never yet tell her that
him love her."

"She think him love her so she don't bother her head."

"Ah! We gwine spoil that."

They whispered together for an hour or so and parted well pleased with the plan they had made.

A few days later, Princess Carla was surprised to see Congojai approaching her in the special room in which she met people.

"What can I do for you, old man?" she asked graciously.

She was not unaware that the obeah priests were unhappy at the present industry in the kingdom. Just the week before, the sun prince had shown her two old men surprisingly like the obeah priests and had warned her to be careful of them. Had warned her to be strong and confident. Deceitful, he had called them.

"Greetings, Princess Carla," Congojai began, wiping the sweat from his brow with his index finger. "The old man jus' a pass this way and stop fi say howdy and congratulation for the miraculous works you working in the kingdom."

"Thank you Congojai," the princess answered, wondering what he wanted.

"But, Princess," he continued, "a beautiful woman like a you shouldn't be alone. You shoulda have a man side a you a help you with all the work." He waved his hand to indicate the whole kingdom.

Princess Carla frowned. Fleetingly she remembered the experience of her dreams, and then she thought of Ralph, her sun prince.

"Yes, princess, a handsome woman like you need a man fi love her up, an warm her up. I bet plenty of them young men a roll them yeye after you," he added slyly.

Princess Carla shook her head and smiled. "But Congojai, I am not thinking about these things. I have too much to do."

"What woman don't want little loving an ting?" he winked at her. "If ah wasn't such an old man, I'd a try mi luck with you meself," he grinned lasciviously. "Woman like a you too juicy fi live alone," he said in parting.

The seed he had sown settled within Princess Carla. She began to think how nice it would be to have a mate beside her. And she

began to think more and more of Ralph. Why not? she mused.
Together they would be able to do even more for the kingdom
than she had been able to do alone. The more she thought about
it, the more attractive the idea became.

And so the next time she went to the well, her mind was
occupied with only one thought.

Resting her head on Prince Ralph's shoulder and gently
stroking his lush beard, she asked about the one subject they had
never discussed.

"What is love?" she asked and didn't understand the sudden
strange stillness of his body. When he spoke it was with a note of
sadness she had never heard before.

"I do not know," he answered.

"Do you love me?" she persisted.

"That's not for you to ask," he said.

"Nor for you to answer?"

It was the very first time that a feeling of disharmony had crept
in between them. He disengaged himself from her and walked a
little distance away. He seemed to be thinking hard. After a while
he returned to stand before her.

"When most people talk about love," he said sadly, "what they
really mean is possession. Too often "I love you' means "I want
to possess you', as if people are things. It also means "I must be
your whole world' and other selfish sentiments like that. You and
I have cared for each other without wanting to possess each other.
Do you want to change that?"

"No! No!" she cried in alarm.

"Oh yes, Princess," he sighed. "You begin to dream of limiting
my freedom; of tying me to your side; of making demands which
no two people should ever make of each other."

"I get lonely, Ralph."

"Loneliness is only a state of mind, Princess. Even though you
cannot see me physically, I'm always with you. You know that.
Have I ever refused to respond to you in times of need. I've always
been here when you needed me. Cannot that be enough?" He was
almost pleading.

"I warned you about the deceitful old men. I can't stop them in their work, but I had hoped that you would be strong enough to resist them. Now... Oh my Princess!" he lifted her and hugged her tightly. "Must you spoil it?" Then very swiftly he walked away and left her.

With a heavy heart Princess Carla returned home. Try as she would she couldn't regain her peace of mind and happiness. The thought kept nagging her – If he loved me he would want to be with me, just as I want to be with him.

Gradually it became an obsession with her. She could think of nothing else. Wild schemes to trap the prince raced through her thoughts and soon enough the consequences of her obsession began to be felt in the village-kingdom.

The princess began to behave strangely. She lost interest in the kingdom. She refused to see those who wanted to see her. She had no advice to offer those who sought her and soon, without her direction and guiding hand, things began to fall apart.

Poor princess! Desire turned obsession, nearly drove her mad. Night and day she tormented her brain. How could she trap her prince into staying with her? She didn't even know where to find him. They met only when he wanted them to meet, because try as she might, she had never been able to remember the way to the well apart from the very special times of need when she suddenly was able to find him as he had promised.

One day the thought occurred to her that if she could find the well, she would find the prince and reason with him. So she called a few of the youths of the kingdom and gave them as accurate a description of the poui forest and the well as she could, and sent them out to find it.

The youths stayed away a long time and while they were gone the princess fretted and further neglected her duties in the kingdom. To make matters worse, a fierce drought began to lay waste the fields, industry suffered, people began to despair, some moved away and those who stayed began to blame the princess for the hardships they were suffering. And as in former rough times, they began to consult the obeah priests once again.

Congojai and Bongojai were happy.

After some time, the youths began to return, one by one, looking very tired and emaciated from their travels. They told stories of the spreading drought and hardships everywhere they went and none of them had found any place even vaguely resembling the description of Olympus which the princess had given them.

When the last youth returned with the same dismal tale as the others, Princess Carla broke down and wept. She wept disconsolately for three days, and at the end of the three days she found herself saying aloud, "Oh my Prince! I need you so!"

And, as if by magic, no sooner than she had said the words than the faint echo of a pan sounded in her ears, the evening seemed to shine more brilliantly, and before she could understand what was happening she found herself running joyously to the well.

But what a strange place it seemed when she found it! The poui trees had lost all their leaves and stood gaunt, stark and dead-looking, twig intertwining with twig. For though the poui like dry spells well enough, they couldn't withstand the fierceness of this drought. The earth was parched brown. The drought had damaged even her lovely forest.

"Ralph! Ralph!" she called, for as yet she had not seen him.

"I'm here, Princess," he answered, slowly raising himself from the ground beside the well where he had been lying.

Eagerly she ran to him, but there was no welcome in his eyes, only a cold hard stare. His brown eyes held none of their usual sparkle. There was no smile on his lips, and it was the first time that they had met without him greeting her with a tune on his pan.

He stood looking at her coldly, ignoring her hands outstretched in greeting.

"I'm thirsty, Ralph," she said, hoping to soften him.

"There's a great drought on the land, Princess Carla," he replied angrily. "What is your thirst beside the thirst of the land? Is that all you can think of? That you are thirsty?"

"Oh, Ralph! Help me! I need you so."

"Your people need you and you have turned your back on

them. You listened to the words of those evil men in spite of all my warnings and look what has happened to your kingdom. I warned you about selfishness…"

"I love you, Ralph."

"Don't talk to me of love," he said bitterly. "There's no need for me to show you pictures in the well any more. You've created them yourself. Look at your land! Look at your people!"

"No! No!" she cried. "Oh give me some water to drink. I'm weak and thirsty."

"Look!" he said as he lifted the lid. "The well itself is dry."

When she looked she could see no water.

"Use the bucket," he ordered, "but be quick. This lid is unusually heavy, and if you're not truly sorry for the havoc you've created, there'll be no water for you."

Eagerly, she lifted the bucket, the first time she had had to use it. She lowered it into the well and felt the rope slipping away into its depth. She heard the bucket clanging against the sides and the sound growing fainter and fainter until there was no more rope to release. She had not found water.

She turned to look at the Prince and met only a hostile gaze and a hollow cruel laugh.

"Goodbye, Princess," he said, and released the lid which smashed onto her fingers.

Screaming with pain and fear she called him to help her. But he had turned his back, taken up his pan and walked away.

"Was it for this you awakened me?" she cried after him. "Taught me how to love? Taught me what ecstasy is? Gave me to drink from the well of knowledge itself?"

Searing pain both of the flesh and the heart gave her the strength to release her hands from the vicelike grip of the cover of the well.

Weeping for her loss, she turned homewards, her fingers dripping blood, leaking the life from her very soul it seemed.

At home, she spoke to no one, but pale-cheeked and almost lifeless she crawled back into her long forsaken bed to sleep once more. But her sleep was fitful.

The family grieved for her as she tossed and moaned, almost delirious with a high fever.

Once she recovered enough to tell them about her prince; to beg them to find him since he was the only one who could cure her pain.

"Tell him I need him," she moaned. "That my mistakes came from loving him too much. Tell him I'll learn whatever it is he wants to teach me. Do anything he wants, if only he'll have compassion on me. I am nothing without him."

So they enquired about all the kingdoms of the South until they found one called the Kingdom of Tees. And they sent many letters seeking to find Prince Ralph. All were returned marked "unknown"!

Then one day a letter by special delivery brought this reply.

> "This Prince of whom you enquire. The name is familiar. There are many Prince Ralphs in our land, but none fitting the description you give.
>
> There's nobody here who laughs in the way that you describe, and although we have the best pan men in the world, nobody here plays the kind of music you describe. Neither do we have anyone who can do the kind of things you say this Prince Ralph can.
>
> If he existed, be assured that we would not allow him to roam, but keep him here for our own benefit.
>
> Perhaps you only imagined him."

They read this letter to the waning princess and when they reached the end, she sighed and closed her eyes, returning to the sleep from which the Prince had awakened her – old and wrinkled once more, and in time forgotten, save for this legend which I have just told you.

STORIES FROM SINGERMAN

## SINGERMAN

"Even as I write I feel us fly outwards, twelve more light years distant from each other, the cultures on each planet-island shrinking, diminishing, almost shrieking out for light, for face, for hand, for help; and that unless we help ourselves confront the contradictions, we lost, we lost, we sibilant and lost."

The shattered language didn't matter anymore… The language of music; both drum and lyric (revealed) the submerged history was similar."

"When the people element is missing, there is no coordination, no sense of continuity, no love…"

Edward Kamau Brathwaite
*CARICOM Perspective* #29, 1985

"West Indians first became aware of themselves as a people in the Haitian Revolution… In a scattered series of disparate islands the process consists of a series of uncoordinated periods of drift, punctuated by spurts, leaps and catastrophes. But the inherent movement is clear and strong."

C.L.R. James *The Black Jacobins* 1963.

## HAITI

Toussaint was a mighty man
And to make matters worse he was black
Black back in the days when black men knew…
Their place was in the back.
But this rebel he walked through Napoleon
Who thought that wasn't very nice
And so today my brothers in Haiti
They still pay the price

CHORUS

Haiti I'm sorry
We've misunderstood you
One day we'll turn our heads
And look inside you
Haiti I'm sorry Haiti I'm sorry
One day we'll turn our heads
Restore your glory

Many hands reached out to St. Georges
And are still reaching out
And to those frightened
Foolish men of Pretoria
We still scream and shout
We came together in song
To steady the horn of Africa
But the papaloa come and the babyloa go
And still we don't seem to care
When there is anguish in Port-au-Prince
Don't you know it's still Africa crying
We are outing fires in far away places
When our neighbours are burning
The middle passage is gone
So how come

Overcrowded boats still haunt our lives
I refuse to believe that we good people
Will forever turn our hearts
And our eyes… away
David Michael Rudder, "Haiti", 1987


I


Once there was a black Starliner, a floating ship in the Caribbean
Sea to which history gave power long before anybody in western
seas would think that power could be black.

The Starliner sailed proudly, flying its black flag. But it had to
make its way in a hostile white-foamed sea. Its course was a lonely
one and its isolated existence helped to breed excesses among
certain of its officers.

Successive captains lost their way in the uncharted waters of
the Caribbean. From time to time the crew mutinied. Once or
twice pirates plundered the Starliner and as the years passed the
ship grew shabbier and the crew got poorer. Nothing, not even
the proud memory of the ancient black moorings from which it
had been so crudely cut off, not even the beauty of the ancestral
art, not even the mixed-up memory worship of the gods of the
forefathers, could save them from the storms which the sea-god
put in their path, year after year after year.

One day, after a long spell of foul weather, the crew mutinied
again, and the baby-faced captain was forced to abandon ship.

As the ship seemed to be floundering, once again on the brink
of total disaster, other nearby ships surrounded it and threw leaky
rafts and bad rations to the crew.

"Steer this way," some of the onlookers shouted.

"No, that way!" others directed.

Some only looked on, because they thought they had no right to
interfere in the ancient Starliner's business. But some modern day
pirates watched in the hope that, although it was only a very poor
ship flying a black flag, perhaps, just perhaps, there might be booty.

II

The Blister crusade created big public bangarang from the minute it was announced.

"*We don't want them samfie evangelist over here. All o them criminal. Look what they doing in they own country. They only coming for the collection, man.*"

"*How you could say that, man? This one different. You watch him on teevee? This one spiritual bad, man.*"

"*Enh, enh?*"

The newspapers pointed out that Mr. Blister already carried on a crusade for one hour every Sunday morning on the local television station as well as on radio. Did he really need to mount a campaign?

"*He racist bad, man. I hear he go preach in South Africa!*"

"*So? Botha and them don't need to hear gospel to change they ways?*"

"*Man, is whiteman mek gospel an he no change. Still hating Blackman all over the world.*"

"*So what we talking now? Politics or religion?*"

"*Is we scarce foreign exchange he go take, you know.*"

Meanwhile, in the evangelical churches which were sponsoring the Blister campaign, the congregations prayed for people to understand. God's word was God's word, no matter who preached it. Colour didn't matter. And some people preached it better than others, like Blister. Blister was a true son of God, the preachers preached.

"Amen!" the congregations agreed and went out to spread the word and gather support.

The local committee suggested that the crusade be held the week following the annual carnival season when the population gave itself up to a bacchanalian orgy of sensuality, let-goism and revelry.

During the weekend and the two days leading up to Ash Wednesday, I-land went mad. By Tuesday, the ground itself took on a life of its own as it pulsated and shook from the accumulated tramping of feet, the heavily amplified beat from the sound systems and the music surging from the steelpans like metallic waterfalls, drowning the inhibitions of doctor, lawyer, Indian chief; policeman, poorman, beggar and thief.

On Ash Wednesday and the days following, piety stepped in to reprove the previous excesses. Those who could, shook off the consequences. Those who couldn't, carried the consequences – for nine months.

The week after carnival the ground was ready for repentance; ready and willing to receive God's seeds.

Since church and state are always uneasy companions, the government was reluctant to be drawn into the controversy, but the Ministry of Labour had to grant work permits. The arguments escalated the matter to cabinet level.

III

But, the Blister Crusade was not the only worry which the government was having. I-land's economy was in poor shape and the people getting sour-faced. Accustomed to near full employment, a fat treasury and porkbarrel handouts, a sudden, swift downturn in fortune was hitting hard. Now, money was a problem; unemployment rising, perks withdrawn and the population getting quarrelsome, unhappy and inclined to start demonstrations before you could say "boo".

Crime, grinning like a mad jumbie, beckoned the youth to join him.

The Blister Crusade could be a Godsend. Blister could be just the thing to keep the people docile. *The Lord's will* and such.

Tempers flared during the meeting which finally gave the go-ahead for the Crusade. There was nearly a cabinet crisis as some objected to the *further exploitation of the people's emotions through the unrestrained religious imperialism of the United States.* Others pointed out that the distraction could buy them a little more political time *to get the house in order.*

A crusade as big as Blister's could divert almost as much energy as carnival – almost.

Somewhere in the planning stage, somebody had the idea that it would be nice if the opening ceremony for the Crusade could become a national event; a nondenominational affair – a kind of healing for all the quarrels which were going on and those waiting to come to the surface.

*"Never mind it have plenty people who doesn't belong to any religion",* a roots newspaper complained. *"Some a we not even Christian!"*

The plans went ahead. All prominent citizens would be invited to the opening service to be held in the national stadium which could hold fifty thousand. In addition, all the radio and television stations would carry the service live and direct so that it could reach every man, woman and child in the country.

#### IV

Eh! Eh! That was scandal and bacchanal in the place for days. Argument hot, HOT! Some pelting blows and cuffing down one another over Blister Crusade. Little most carnival and all get eclipse – little most. Nothing can't out out carnival.

Well, that was the year that Singerman record catch the place afire. When he hit the tent with "Haiti, I'm sorry"; after man blinking they eye like they can't believe what is this they hearing for carnival; after woman waist freeze into one side of a wine for the song not wining; after they listen a little and the mood of the song ketch them; goose pimple running up and down people body and them moving them hand in the air as if Blister Crusade done start already, for "Haiti" soundin so much like hymn people askin, Wait! Singer turn Christian now?"

Singerman have some winey-winey song too, but is "Haiti" popular, man. Everybody singing or humming it.

Even after carnival gone, record shop and sound system still playing "Haiti". In fact, the whole Caribbean start singing it, cause they glad somebody write a song apologise to Haiti for how they can't make up they mind to help or to ignore the brothers and sisters over there. Everybody wringing they hand since Babylon run away, but when some act, some vex. Some saying one thing, some saying a nex. Nobody can't agree what to do, or who to put. Everybody anxious about the anguish of Haiti, but the whole Caribbean fraid revolution. They fraid it bad, like is something you could ketch like yellow fever or AIDS. Anyway, they glad Singerman mek up song saying "I sorry" for them, and Carnival done but everywhere you go you still hearing "Haiti".

V

Opening night for the three day Blister Crusade arrive. You should see the Stadium! It pack! It ram! It jam! You couldn't put one more sardine inside. All Blister man they trying to keep aisle clear. Eh, eh! Try they best. You could feel something go happen.

Prime Minister and Deputy; Oppositions and Side Kicks; men of the cloth; union chief and plenty other kinda chief representing everybody from everywhere in the country. You could just feel something special go happen.

In the congregation all kinda people mix up. It have Indian, it have Creole, it have Blackman, Chinese, Whiteman, Rastaman and everything in between. Everybody jam up gainst everybody. You could tell something go happen. Those who can't get in have they ears jam up gainst a radio or sitting in they parlour watching teevee.

Blister and he man they kinda worried. The crowd big, big and so mix-up that though he like big crowd, he not so sure everything go be all right They usher plan and thing falling down, but the local preachermen saying everything just cool: *Look, the P.M. in the middle of things! What could go happen?*

Well, you remember that plenty people was having controversy and quarrel and thing bout the Crusade, so is how so much people interested?

Is the P.R. people them, man; the Public Relations Arm. You know how they does pretty up everything and give people conscience an such and move them to action an thing? Well, they do a good job advertising this National Healing, so everybody want to see what go happen. But, that don't mean everybody in agreement. What them P.R. persons don't know is that even though you nodding you head, and saying yes, that don't mean you agree or you dipping you finger in the right ink or that you even go dip you finger at all. So, anyway, everybody watching and listening.

Blister start he Crusade. Local preacherman emceeing, introducing the P.M. like everybody don't know he already; identifying all the important people in the congregation. The poor teevee fellows them in pain trying to switch camera and focus and all them other kinda things, but since is plenty of them imported with Blister longside native assistants, everything cool. Let me tell you, is plenty man Blister walk with: teeveeman, usherman, PR man, press agent man, security man, more than when a Head of State visit.

All musician. Blister band bigger than big, big, BIG carnival brass band. Choir four deep. Papa! Must be a whole ship bring them. Blister private jet couldn't hold them and they accoutrements. Impressive, man! Impressive! An Blister – he the chief preacher, press agent, musician, singer and everything wrap up into one. He nearly like God, man.

So Blister Crusade start. He warming up with plenty nice, nice word for we people. How the natives friendly and Christian and he glad all the controversy put aside and people come together in such wonderful numbers to hear God's word. Plenty ole talk and music to soften we up. But of course, you see how he does carry-on on teevee on Sunday mornings so you know how he stay. Oh, they all had two giant teevee screen on two side the Stadium so if you too far back and can't see the real thing, all you have to do is check the screen nearest you, what you can't see with you eye, you watching on teevee.

Blister brass ban hotting up the place with some up-tempo Sankey, so that the young people could enjoy it. But it kinda confusing for the ole time people singing it "ole time style" slowish; while the young people jukkin the tempo, and Blister brass ban somewhere in between, so Stadium soundin like Babel, but it don't really matter. Is the mood, man. Everybody feeling good and the time getting ripe. You could just tell that the Holy Ghost or something was jus waitin to mek something happen.

Well, preachin time reach. And Blister start. You know how he does begin quiet-like, tell couple joke an anecdote. Then he warm up with the open Bible in he hand; and then he start tramping up and down like he playing Tuesday mas in front the judging stand. Then he start crying cause the whole world so sinful. Then when everybody soften up, he pounce and everybody tekkin he advice to come up and get save and solve all they problems; easy so.

## VI

Blister start to preach. Nobody could tell how it start to happen for the Stadium big. Plenty space between building and car park. You would have to have amps big as a house to interfere with that service, but all the same everybody hearing it, clear, clear. Singerman's calypso: "Haiti, I'm sorry!"

Blister frown. He preach little more. "Haiti" still interrupting. Everybody looking round. But is not radio or anything, is real, real sound, beat strong and clear, instrumentals selecting good, good and is now it sounding like hymn.

Blister frowning bad. He preach little more. "Haiti" preaching louder. P.M. whisper to aide who whisper to security who passing on the whisper. Everybody lookin up and down for the source. Blister people anxious. People listenin radio and watchin teevee askin, "What happenin?"

Nobody know. Is not as if is an attack or somethin.

Blister signallin usher to stop the disturbance and tryin to preach same time. He talkin louder, but "Haiti" talkin louder still.

Blister appeal to whoever creating the disturbance to desist. By this time he face red with frustration so he drop on he knees. "Let us pray!" he scream. Heh! Is better he did say *Leh we sing*. Confusion growin cause the place so ram-jam not a soul can tell what going on.

Then those watching the teevee see a man makin he way to the platform. As the lights pick him out, people saying, *But look! Is Singerman, self! What he go do?*

And the voice on the record sweet, sweet, *I'm sorry! I'm sorry!*

Silence from the crowd as Singerman reach the platform. Blister catchin he fraid. "Who this man? What he go do?" Blister gesturin for security who not noticin him. The locals want to hear from Singer. The foreigners fraid the locals. In any case what they could do? Drag Singer off the stage before the whole o his people? Is riot they want to happen or what?

Singer tek the mike and with him pretty smile jus start sing along with the music as if he still in Big Top Tent. And before Blister could close he mouth which did drop open in fright, Singer calmly telling he, "Don't fight it, man, use it. Is we thing this, man."

"All you know the tune?" he shout, and the congregation answerin "Yeeees."

"Well sing it. I will line the words for you."

"All you ketch the music?" He turned to the astonished Blister brass band.

Still nobody don't know where the first music comin from but after a few stumbles, Blister band playin it too.

Then Singerman gesturin to the audience. "Come , brothers," and a line of Rasta with they drums start toward the platform.

Blister like he getting a heart attack on he knees, but not a soul noticing him.

Hear Singer again, "You too, brothers," and a line of Indian with they sitar an they tassa and the other things they does play joining the rest.

Everybody on a track with "Haiti, I'm sorry". Between them it was like Heaven comin down. You know the part where Singer sing *I'm sorry. We misunderstood you,* the goatskin sobbing and the sitar wailing for Haiti and all the oppressed people everywhere.

And Singerman start: "Is revival all you want? Sing!"

"Is renewal all you want? Sing!"

"Is reconstruction all you want? Sing!"

"Sing for peace on earth."

"Sing till the music wash away all the prejudice and evil in the world."

"Sing for Haiti. Sing for South Africa. Sing for all oppressed people everywhere. Sing for we own self. Sing till greed and suffering come to an end. Sing till man stop kill off man and everywhere the children have enough food to eat and can feel like they is people too.

"Sing! Sing!"

Then he start lining the song with some new words.

*"Oh Lord, I'm sorry. Oh Lord, I'm sorry.*
*Fill us with your Glory! Fill us with your Glory!"*

And the people gettin caught up in the thing. Like the whole country stop. Everybody hummin or singin. Brass band improvisin. Rasta and Indian drum makin up message, sitar wailin and the hands in the air wavin in agreement. That was lookin like revival!

Then over the music Singerman preaching.

"Call on your Power whoever or whatever you think It is. It don't matter what you call him, or she or it – God, Buddha, Mohammed, Jah and plenty other one I never hear about. Even if you don't call it anything at all. Call down the Power! Call It down! Call the Power down! Call It down! *"Oh Jah, I'm sorry…"*

"The world need revival. We need unity. We need a healing. Call the Power down before we perish!"

And the hands wavin. All those watchin teevee or listenin, wavin hand too. They feelin the spirit hoverin. You could feel the Power gatherin. You could feel it like lightning plannin to strike, or earthquake plannin to shake down the place or hurricane gatherin to cleanse.

The music callin it down. The singin callin it down. The Power gatherin and the people holding hands and singin "I'm sorry! I'm sorry!"

## VII

But, you know, them people wasn't really ready! Every man, woman an chile have to want the miracle to happen, for the Power only deal with consensus. An though it lookin like everybody agreeing, who could tell who in I-land heart suddenly harden that day? Who could tell who let in Satan with a badminded thought an block the spirit that day? Who on the platform didn't believe that day, or cursing black people that day? Who suck them teeth and think is pure foolishness a happen? Who lookin at Miss I-land's legs and suddenly feelin a different kinda stirring? Who suddenly start thinkin about them pelau waitin in the pot at home?

The Power hear the music and the singin; the Power hoverin an waitin to come down, but the vibes not clear, the vibes not pure. So, is like when you see the first little glimpse of lightning but it don't reach. Is like when you hear the earthquake grumbling but it don't shake. All that happen is a cloud just suddenly cover the Stadium and a piece of rain pelt the place and everybody take up them foot and run for shelter.

It sad. It sad.

## VIII

And so the Black Star Liner continues to wander around the Caribbean waiting, waiting, waiting for something to happen. Not yet Haiti. Not yet Caribbean. Not yet Azania. Not yet world.

## DON'T COLOUR ME

Clifton could barely contain his excitement. At last he was taking Sara home. The kind of home he had always dreamed of owning from way back when he was a boy and his mother used to work for the white people up at the big house.

Not that the house which they had left behind in Hampstead was bad. Far from it. It had been the *talk* of the neighbourhood that a black man, a first generation immigrant at that, could own such a house. But that was by English standards.

This *was* a house! Large! Six bedrooms, four full bathrooms, powder room, entertainment patio, even a small studio for Sara –where she could paint to her heart's content. And ten acres. He could keep a few horses and enough dogs to satisfy his animal-loving sons.

Yes, this was his dream come true. The real estate agent who'd shown him the place hadn't been able to conceal his surprise at the large deposit he had put down and the ease with which he got the mortgage.

He could have bought it outright. English pounds made a lot of dollars in Jamaica, but he didn't want to be too tight for cash until his new business settled down to earn the kind of income he expected.

He hadn't told Sara about the property. They had lived in a rented house in the town while he completed arrangements, had the furniture shipped and the whole house painted, refurbished and decorated to his liking.

Now he could hardly wait to hear what she would say. He was sure it was much more magnificent than anything she had ever dreamed about, and his chest swelled as he reflected how his business sense, his instinct for choosing and selling fine furniture, had brought him out of poverty in England and made him richer than he had ever expected. Now he was able to give her things none of the other men she had known could ever have offered her. He was sure of that.

For a moment he took his eyes off the empty country road and glanced sideways at her face. He never could tell from her expression what she was thinking and this always made him feel a little inferior.

She turned to answer his look with her strange half-smile, combing her fingers through her windblown hair.

Sara was wondering what her husband was up to now. He was like a little boy with a big secret, always a sign that he had some spectacular treat in store for her. Like the time he'd bought her the large diamond and ruby ring for her birthday. Just like Charles might give Diana, he'd said proudly. She wore it only on rare occasions and only to please him. He would beam with pride when people exclaimed at the ring and urge her to show off her finger; she would want to die of embarrassment.

In its box one could admire the deep glow of the ruby and the crisscrossing points of light on the diamonds surrounding it. On her finger it seemed gaudy and overpowering. Too good to be true, like imitation stuff.

She hoped that he wasn't planning anything too permanent. She didn't like Jamaica. It was pretty enough after a fashion, but after nine months she wanted to go home. There was nothing for her to do and she missed England. She missed the change of seasons. Here every day was like the next. Sunshine or rain, that was all, making everything the same boring brilliant green or splashing gaudy colours extravagantly around. Too loud. Just like the people. Sometimes she couldn't tell whether they were quarrelling or being friendly. Everything was so high key and monotonously the same.

People said green was restful for the eyes. The eyes could get too much rest in this place, she thought as she stared at the gently undulating landscape before her.

"Well, here we are," Clifton said loudly, startling her. She realised that they were turning off the main road and approaching large iron gates opening in from two huge concrete columns. When she saw the inscription "Clifton House" her heart sank. It was as she had feared. Clifton had bought a house. No, a whole property, she thought, as she peered shortsightedly into the distance. The house, surrounded by a clump of trees, looked to be at least a mile from the gate. A mansion, she concluded, as they came nearer.

The house was perched on a little hill whose peak appeared to have been shaved off to accommodate it. It had once been a charming house of local stone and wood. Two wings had been added in stark modern style.

Landscaped gardens surrounded the house and gave way to the ubiquitous pastureland of the area.

Clifton parked the car in the circular driveway and running around opened the door for her and majestically waved her out. "Welcome home, Madame!"

Sara supposed that he had seen that in a movie on telly. She smiled, took his hand graciously and stepped out to examine her new home.

A woman dressed in a blue and white uniform and a matching apron and cap had come from a side entrance into the little reception area where the car had stopped.

"Rachel, this is your new mistress, Miss Sara," he announced and watched with pride as the apprehensive look disappeared from Rachel's face, and a look of welcome surprise took its place as she scrutinised Sara. She had expected something different. He knew his people well.

"Welcome, Mistress," she said, smiling and almost doing a curtsey. "Welcome, mam."

"Well," Clifton continued, "hurry up and open the front door, no."

"Yes Missa Cliff," Rachel said, hurrying away.

As the heavy front door was pulled open, Clifton almost dragged Sara inside.

He had brought all their antique pieces from England and these were distributed imposingly throughout the house.

There were his Louis chairs with their ornate carvings and lavish curves – "If Louis didn't sit on it," he used to say with a laugh, I don't want it"; these were just right for the spacious rooms with their high ceilings. He dragged Sara from room to room, immensely pleased with his work.

He had chosen the colours of the walls, the wallpaper for the bedrooms, the drapes, even in the room set aside for her studio. He had spent a great deal of time choosing colours to make sure that it was bright and arty enough to please her.

Sara shuddered when she saw the studio. Red, green and white stripes in sunray bands on the walls; orange carpet... enough to make her feel bilious. She would have to change this she thought desperately.

And the rest of the house? He was beaming with so much pride she couldn't tell him how wrong it all was. The monstrous four-poster bed had followed her to Jamaica. There it sat, bedecked and canopied, dwarfing the master bedroom which was part of the addition and which, with its clean modern lines, called out for sparse modern furniture.

Sara shuddered when she saw the heavy curtains covering the glass windows, shutting out the light; worse, they were paisley patterned. She hated paisley. It was as if he gone out of his way to furnish the house in the styles and colours she liked least. Couldn't he have consulted her?

Looking around the bedroom she wondered how soon she could put a couch in her studio and, under the pretence of work, avoid sleeping in the bedroom as often as possible.

The kitchen was next. Thank God he had left the decorator alone there. Since he couldn't even boil water, as he was fond of saying, he hadn't bothered to give any special instructions. As a result it was the only tolerable place in the house. There was a cheery breakfast corner at one side; she would be using this much more often than the stuffy dining room with its large chandelier and heavy furniture.

"It's so… so large!" she finally managed to murmur. "So overwhelming! How will I keep it clean?"

This comment pleased him. "This is the Jamaican country-side. Plenty of servants around."

"But it's so far from the town," she added. "How will the children get to school?"

He looked at her in exasperation. When would she learn that he had enough money to satisfy all their needs?

Taking her hand he piloted her to the garage, unlocked the double doors and pointed to a shiny new Volvo.

"Your chariot, milady!" And since she didn't like to drive, he added quickly, "The groom will double as chauffeur for you and the boys."

Clifton, knowing that she was bursting with gratitude but shy of expression, wrapped his large arms around her tiny frame and smiled into her feathery mop of hair, his senses responding with delight, as always, to the silky feel of the hair tickling under his chin.

"You really like it, girl? This is the house I always dream about. I nearly call it Clifton Mansion, but that sound too… too… show-off. So I settle for Clifton House. It nice eh?"

He didn't wait for her answer but nattered on about the horses and the dogs which would soon arrive to delight their sons, and the cows which would give them fresh milk and how she would enjoy tramping around and seeing to things. He was sure she wouldn't miss England at all for the cool Manchester air was even better. He had even wondered about a fireplace but decided against it, but if she really wanted one…

II

Sara moved away from her easel, put down her palette and brush and taking off her apron, stretched and yawned lazily.

That would be all for the day. She was too bored even to paint now that there was nothing else to do. The life of Lady of the Manor did not appeal to her. Unlike the *an pair* girl back in

Hampstead, Rachel was a real housekeeper. Then there were the strange girls who moved in and out like ghosts, with disembodied voices as they scrubbed and polished shoes, silver and anything else Rachel gave them to do on the porch behind the house, well out of sight.

When she inquired about anything, Rachel would say the Missis wasn't to worry her pretty little head for Boss had taken care of it already. They always referred to Clifton as Boss or Missa Cliff. She hardly ever saw the boys except at meal times; they were always out riding or running with the dogs. She didn't like the dogs at all because they sometimes barked at her as if she didn't belong.

She looked at the half-finished painting; it was not coming out the way it should. She was trying to paint the view of the field from the back balcony. But she couldn't get it right. She couldn't get the right greens and blues.

The real life colours were so bright they hurt her eyes. Everything in this land was bright. Bright green except where it joined the sky and became bright blue.

On her canvas the colours came out subdued and pale as if she always saw things through the mists which sometimes covered the fields in the early mornings. Looking at the painting more closely she realised that it represented less what was before her than what she had left behind.

She was no better with the people.

One day, after a series of unsatisfactory attempts at putting people in her picture without using a model, she had captured one of the itinerant girls around the house to sit for her.

She had enjoyed painting the girl and chattering with her, and she was quite pleased with the portrait, but when she called Rachel and the girl, her niece, to view it, neither had seemed pleased. When she tried to find out why, Rachel had hurriedly left the room. After some coaxing, the niece, Denzie, told her she didn't like the painting because it was too black. Her colour was definitely not as black as Sara had painted her.

"Look here, Missis," she said, standing beside the portrait on the easel, "that colour look more like Tanya than me. Me lighter than Aunt Rachel and Tanya darker than me and she. All a we is not the same colour," she explained carefully.

Sara had been so confused and embarrassed that it was days before she could return to the studio. When she did it was to compare the canvases which had people in them. She had to admit that she had used much the same shade of black for all of them. It must be something to do with the light. In any case, she couldn't really see why such fine-tuned differences in shade were so important to these people.

No more people, she decided, and went back to landscapes, painting more and more from her memories of England.

Oh, London! She longed to walk the streets, admiring the displays in Harrod's, feeling again the bite of the cold and listening to the eternal drip of rain; she longed to see again the grey-whiteness of snow and a newly clad tree bowing in homage to the rejuvenating rains of Spring; she longed to hear the comforting accents of her people. Even the discomforts now seemed romantic and she felt even more crushed by the alien land she had been forced to adopt.

Once she suggested that she take the boys on holiday back home, but Clifton had looked so crestfallen, "How can we manage without you?" he had asked, and she had smiled, unable to give an answer. She had not mentioned it again.

III

When Sara first suggested that she go to teach at the school for the handicapped in the nearby town, Clifton nearly choked on his spoonful of soup.

His wife work? Why had *he* been working so hard building up the garage and furniture business if not to provide for all her needs? Why did she think he had brought her to Jamaica? What would people say? And just as he was about to become even more successful with the first shipment to London finally ready!

But she had gone out of her way to be nice to him, so that one night, as she stroked his back lightly in the way that he liked after lovemaking when he was on the edge of sleep, she asked again and he said, yes.

Besides it was voluntary work. She wouldn't be paid so it wasn't like real work.

Sara was relieved to have something useful to do. It was a school for deaf children, and she looked forward eagerly to the two days each week when she would go into town and teach them art.

She liked children, and learning to sign was a challenge. An experienced teacher was put in the class to help her to communicate with the children, but since she learned quickly, the teacher was glad to leave her to make her own way.

Without the official teacher, she and the children grew closer. They taught her more signs and responded enthusiastically to the art lessons.

One day she suggested that they draw water; they could draw anything as long as it represented water. She thought that they would draw pictures of the seaside or rain or the river and was pleasantly surprised at the range of ideas they presented.

A dripping pipe, a washpan with clothes, a drinking glass of water, tears even; and the one which turned them all into shrieking maniacs – a boy peeing against a tree. The noise of their howling laughter quickly brought out the principal who restored order and invited Sara to her office.

The headmistress asked her where the assigned teacher was. She was not pleased to hear that the teacher no longer attended the classes.

Sara felt more and more like an errant school girl as she was questioned.

How did she communicate with the children?

Sara explained that she had learned enough signs to communicate and with the older ones she wrote on the blackboard.

How did she tell the class what she wanted them to do?

Sara showed her.

"Do you understand when they ask questions?"

Sara said that she usually did and that the children them selves taught her new signs everyday.

"So how do you tell them to settle down; to be quiet?" Sara showed her, finger to lip and a punctuated half-circular motion; she didn't understand the principal's smile which was quickly controlled.

"I thought so," she said quietly.

"Let me explain, Mrs. Clifton. We're happy for your help. Very happy. I am aware that you've been using your own money to buy materials for the children and believe me we are grateful. With the shortage of funds there's little we can do to provide extras."

"I assigned Miss Willis to your classes to handle communication and discipline. If you don't have training, it can be so difficult. The thing is, you see, the children have developed their own modification of the official sign language, a kind of "patois" sign language you might call it. I am afraid that this is what they have been teaching you." Her mouth twitched slightly. "They can be very naughty children sometimes."

The little wretches, Sara thought, mortified by the principal's tone. But afterwards, thinking about it, she began to laugh. No wonder they were so often amused when she "talked" to them. When she tried to share the joke with Clifton, he got angry. Nobody could treat his wife like that. She should not go back.

Sara ignored him.

In due course she settled in. The assigned teacher returned and with the increased discipline, the children soon got bored with her presence.

There was, though, one little girl to whom she became particularly attached. Eight years old; small for her age, with large, beautiful, sad eyes. Sara noticed her at first because she was so talented.

She lived at the school, one of the many charity cases. At the age of about two she had been found wandering in the compound. Nobody claimed her so the school had taken her in. Two years later a woman turned up claiming to be her mother. She had abandoned the child because she was deaf, but her conscience had always bothered her and finding herself financially better off, she had come for her. She had been able to prove this, so the school had released the child. One year later the child was again found abandoned at the school gate. Once more the school provided a home.

Sara found herself more and more drawn to the child who was as talented as she was withdrawn. She could copy with unbelievable accuracy almost any picture from a book, and her drawing skill and use of colour made Sara determined to help her.

The child was drawn to the teacher too and, gradually overcoming her shyness, she began to seek out Sara to show her new work she had done.

The teachers, glad that the child was at last opening up to someone, encouraged the friendship. But the first time Sara sought permission to take her home for a weekend, the head mistress hesitated.

She explained that she was afraid the child would suffer further damage if she got too close to Sara. She didn't say it but Sara understood that she was hinting that her interest could only be temporary and the child would feel abandoned again. But Sara continued to ask and one long weekend the child, Jacky, was allowed to go home with her.

At first, Clifton was amused and glad that Sara had found a "toy" to occupy herself. He was aware that she was lonely and not fitting in very well, but he could not understand why. He had dreamed of her making friends with the upper-class ladies of the area and giving little tea parties in the fancy living room or on the porch. He had seen himself coming home to the tinkle of china and silverware and soft woman's chatter, and being introduced proudly as Sara's husband. But unless he insisted on organising a dinner or something, the house remained quiet and he was disappointed that so few people came to admire it.

He himself was too busy to cultivate the kind of friends the place needed. That was the woman's business. She was just right for the job, too. What was wrong with her?

One day, after watching her walking around the garden, coated against the chilly morning air, he had wondered if, perhaps, they should have another child, a Jamaican child. Perhaps it would be a girl and cling to the mother and make her happy. He wanted to suggest this to her but somehow the right moment never seemed to come. Watching her with the little deaf girl he was more than ever convinced that that was what she needed to root her; "tie her down" as his people said. For the moment he was content to watch the child clinging to the adult who didn't look much more than a child herself.

But after a time it dawned on him that Jacky always seemed to be around and that Sara was giving him even less attention than before. Then Rachel came to him to complain that she didn't like this addition to her duties and that it didn't look right "for a lady like Miss Sara to have this little deaf pickney traipsing after her".

Clifton decided he would have to speak to Sara but she seemed so happy with the child he didn't have the courage to deny her this pleasure.

Sara was unaware of the displeasure in the household. Even if she had known she would have ignored them; the satisfaction of being needed was too great. They went for long walks stopping to look at things of interest. Sometimes they stopped to sketch them. It was so rewarding to see Jacky, who had once clutched fearfully at her skirts, now roaming on her own, running freely and excitedly sharing her pleasure in a flower, a bird, a bug. Sometimes they took a picnic basket and stayed out the whole day.

Sara began to buy clothes for the child, so that when she came for the weekend Jacky could change out of the drab school uniform. Sara was amused to see how impatient Jacky became to reach Clifton House and change into the pretty clothes waiting for her.

Sara wasn't quite sure when the idea that she should adopt Jacky first came to her; it would be so good to assume full responsibility for her and watch her grow.

IV

Sara and Clifton sat across from each other at their Monday evening dinner table in the breakfast corner where they ate almost all their meals. They were both silent, absorbed by what was foremost on their minds.

Clifton was thinking that it was high time he spoke to Sara about the danger of her becoming too attached to the little deaf girl and the possibility of her having another child as a more welcome alternative.

Sara was wondering how to broach the subject of adopting Jacky. She was aware that Clifton did not particularly like the child, but he was so seldom at home, it couldn't matter very much to him. She wondered if he was in the right mood now.

"I was just thinking…'

"Darling would you mind awfully if…" Both started to speak at the same time.

"You talk first," he smiled at her.

"Would you mind terribly if… if we adopted Jacky, legally?" Trying to ignore the shocked look on his face she went on hurriedly. "She's such a sweet little thing, and I'm really so fond of her company. She's had an awfully rough time. It would be nice for her to have a decent home. A permanent home."

"What!" he exploded. "That little black, ugly, deaf pickney! Never!"

Sara's pale face turned red all the way down to her neck. She couldn't believe that he could have said those words. In her own anger she chose the words that she knew would hurt him most. Words she had never used in the twelve years they had been married.

"She's not more black than you. She's not uglier than you. In fact nobody would have any problem believing she was your child."

She said the words slowly, all her pent-up anger with him spewing out like black bile signalling death. There would be no going back for them after this.

Clifton seemed to shrink as he heard those words. He looked at her, his soul curling up like a snail strewn with salt, trying to protect itself, but only engulfing itself more deeply in its own nasty oozing slime. He, too, knew instinctively that there was no way back.

## VERSION

(In the pop music industry they call it
making a cover version.)
### OR
## THE DEVIL MADE SOME PARTS

Superior Being yawned delicately. In an idle moment he had built a magnificent garden in a section of his huge backyard. It had amused him immensely to create this most beautiful place filled with flowers and fruits the like of which had never been seen in the universe. Apples, avocados, papayas, bananas, sweet-sops, pineapples, plums (red and yellow), mangoes, oranges were only a few of the succulent fruits spread throughout the garden. Flowers so exquisite and exotic, even the angels marvelled at them, added to the riot of colours. Everything in paradise flourished.

But SB, as the angels called him, was bored with his garden. He watched the plants through a season of flowering and fruiting: corrected any little imperfection which he *thought* he saw – really nothing he created was ever imperfect – and then lost interest in it.

One day he was playing with a piece of claydough to pass the time. He kneaded and pummelled it and suddenly realised that he was making it into the shape of an angel. So he concentrated on the design and when he was finished, it looked so realistic he decided to breathe life into it.

Claydough became Plaything.

Plaything could hear and speak and see/but since it didn't eat, it wasn't necessary for it to smell or taste or feel. It was *almost* like an angel.

SB put Plaything in his garden. This was exactly what the garden needed, he thought, a presence to make things happen. He taught Plaything the names of the plants and was delighted by the admiration and praise which Plaything showered on him as its creator. But soon Plaything got sated with the beauty and stopped noticing and praising. It wandered around the garden aimlessly, was docile and obedient to all SB's commands but did nothing exciting. Plaything was a disappointment.

SB got bored again. He called Plaything and asked it why it was so listless. Plaything did not know.

Then SB thought that perhaps if Plaything had a companion, they would talk together, play together and make the garden livelier. Since he was temporarily out of claydough, he put Plaything to sleep (it was a messy job even if Plaything couldn't feel) and broke off a piece of its rib and used it to fashion another Plaything exactly like the first one. SB called them Number One and Number Too.

Number One was glad to see another being exactly like itself when it woke up, and they chatted together and roamed throughout the garden. Number One taught Number Too all that it knew about the garden and life. But soon they became bored with each other and began to go separate ways, much to SB's annoyance.

Number One and Number Too were becoming a bit of a problem. They weren't really angels so he couldn't give them angelic duties, and since they had limited powers they had to be confined to the garden; he couldn't have them wandering throughout the universe.

Perhaps he should put them to sleep permanently; cancel the whole thing, garden and all, and start another project.

SB scratched his head. What to do with these two? Suddenly he thought of Inferior Being. What Number One and Number Too needed was something to make them lively. Something to challenge them. They needed to be exposed to evil. Inferior Being was the perfect one to plan this for them.

"Get IB on the line!" he roared.

The angel who brought the line had to use his powers of levitation; it just couldn't be touched, it was so hot.

"Now IB," SB ordered, "cut that out! Cool off the line immediately, or you'll regret it."

"Just giving you a touch of the temperature down here," IB said roguishly. "You rang?"

"Yes. A bit of a problem. Right up your street."

SB outlined the problem.

"Give me a little time to think about it," IB said, and the line began to glow again so that SB had it put it down quickly.

"That devil!" he murmured.

A little time passed and the red alarm sounded, startling the celestial arena. That line almost never rang.

"That was quick," said SB.

"Yeah," IB agreed. "HOT ON DELIVERY. That's me. Listen SB, I think I can make your two numbers more interesting, but you have to make some concessions.

"Like what?" SB asked suspiciously.

"Well first of all, I think your design needs a certain – shall we say modification."

"Nothing wrong with them," SB said impatiently. "They're perfect. Almost like angels."

"Exactly. Angels have to be the most uninteresting beings in all creation. Unless they're fallen, of course," he added hastily.

"What do you want to do?" SB asked in a frosty voice. "Just give me a free hand. Couple of surprises for you. Will make the whole thing more fun."

"All right," SB agreed, reluctantly. He didn't trust IB at all.

"Another thing. I want you to promise that when you get tired of them, you'll give them to me."

"They couldn't survive a day in your place."

"Don't worry about that. They'll probably love it."

"Can't promise that."

"No deal then."

"Oh all right. Compromise. If they *want* to come to you, I'll let them."

"Fair enough." IB chuckled. "Just turn your back on the garden for a while. I guarantee you won't be bored with what you get. For a time anyway."

"OK. But don't hurt them."

"They don't know what pain is, so how can I hurt them?"

"True," SB agreed. "You always were a smooth talker."

"No compliments please. Give me one of your newly created weeks. And remember, no peeking."

So SB turned away from his beautiful garden to tend his many businesses in the universe.

At the end of the week, he eagerly returned to see what IB had done with his two creatures.

He arrived in the garden just as they were coming awake.

SB rubbed his eyes, he couldn't believe what he was seeing. IB had indeed modified his design. He had made both creatures different so that at the base of its body where the legs met, Number One now sprouted a kind of corrugated baggy three-part protuberance. Number Too had a mound in the same area covered with hair and SB's superior vision told him that the engineering meant that they were designed to fit one into the other, although he couldn't immediately figure out how or why.

Number One's face was hairy where it had been smooth, and Number Too had two swellings in the chest area. SB nodded his head. Reluctantly he admitted that it was certainly a more interesting design.

Then he realised that IB had made them able to smell and taste and feel. Now they could eat; and excrete. SB wrinkled his nose. They definitely were no longer angelic. They were – he searched for a new name – they were… Human Beings.

As he looked on, smiling at IB's ingenuity, the hot line glowed.

"Hi, SB. Like what you see?"

SB scratched his head. "I'm not sure. What's the redesign supposed to do for them?"

"Now, SB, you can have some real fun. They have knowledge of good and evil, but it's not well developed. They don't remember what they were like before. You can put temptation in their way and watch them struggle to obey you. Forbid them to do things, especially those things that their new design makes them naturally want to do. And remember, when you're tired of them, they're all mine." IB rang off with a diabolic laugh.

SB shook his head. That IB, he thought, he'll never change.

SB watched as Number One and Number Too, now sticking closely together, roamed through the garden picking and eating various of the brightly coloured fruits with relish. Number One picked an orchid and put it in Number Too's hair. Number Too was obviously pleased at the gesture. When they were tired they sat under a tree and fell asleep.

When they awoke they looked at each other carefully. First Number One (NO) touched Number Too (NT) and smiled. NT touched NO's hairy face and smiled also. NO touched NT's lips and swollen chest and giggled and jumped away. NT then chased NO and reached out to touch...

"Cut that out!" SB thundered when he realised what was about to happen, right in front of his eyes.

Then he said, "Number One, from now on I'll call you Man. Number Too, from now on you'll be known as Woman. You are free to roam the garden. Anything you want you can have; but man, you may not touch woman, and woman you may not touch man."

The rest of that story you already know. Some parts of the body will always create problems. The devil made them.

## CARNIVAL

When he was a man, he was neat, dapper, beautiful. Not handsome in the way women usually describe men, since none of his
features nor the way they were put together was exceptional.
Nonetheless, he was beautiful. Perhaps it was the intense energy
which flowed from him which made people say, "What a remark-
able man".

When he was a bird, he was large, with a wingspan of eight feet,
or it would have been if one wing was not deformed and unable
to stretch out fully. When he was a bird he was not like any other
bird. He was large but not impressive like the eagle. He was ugly
but not strikingly hideous like the john crow. He was dull grey,
speckled with black, with a long neck and ruffled feathers like a
*senseh* fowl – a very strange unbeautiful creature.

He'd rather have been a man all the time, but that decision was
yet to come.

He was a very bright man; a lovable man. Most men loved him
for the precision of his thinking and his penetrating but rarely
hurtful wit. Most women loved him because he was beautiful,
and, because, early in his life he had mastered the art of making
them feel special.

When he was a man he walked with a spring in his short strides
and a kind word for everybody; a helping hand even before it was
requested. When he was a man he was a very nice man. This was
his mask.

A long time before, when he was a child, small in size, troubled
by bullies, he had honed his mind to a sharp point which made
him the brightest star in school. But even a fine brain such as his
could not teach him how to make a fist big enough to stump a

bully, so he had learned to take his crystalline brain out of a fight to the solitude of the little hill at the back of the school. Sometimes for a full afternoon he would lie under the acacia trees and watch nature's other creatures, himself a giant in Lilliput land. There were the bees and wasps drifting lazily in the warm afternoon air currents whose landing points he liked to guess; there were ants to divert from their food caravans.

Best of all he liked the birds. Their twittering and hopping around soothed him and sometimes lulled him into a sleep from which he would emerge, mind cleansed from its recent bitterness. There was one bird haunting the hillside that he particularly liked. He called it the *woti woti* because of its lamenting song: "Woe to me; woe to me; will I ever be free? Will I ever be free?"

He could never imagine what it was that the bird wanted to escape. Could there be any more freedom than to be able to fly away, far from the things that caused him misery?

Time passed and his limbs grew, although he would always be small for a man. But he found a place for himself in a world where the power of your brain counts for more than the size of your fist; there he flourished, was respected, sought after for advice and quickly rose to the head of any organisation he chose to join.

No-one questioned his authority until a battle-axe of a young woman, anxious to prove her right to a high position in the company, began to buck every decision he made. She went out of her way to try to embarrass him, but, sure of his support elsewhere, he kept cool until one afternoon when, after a particularly stormy meeting where she could not get her own way, she paused before his door to comment loudly, "That short-ass runt think he so smart, but I going to fix he business…"

It was the first time since he was a grown man that anyone had disparaged his size within his hearing, and he was so shocked that he left the building and fled for home, uncontrollably frightened at being so crudely pushed back into childhood.

He was in the schoolyard, the giant bully they called Caesar cornering him, slapping him on the head so hard that his nose started bleeding, blood dripping down his shirt front; the other children running away from him, frightened at the sight of the blood. He, the smallest and youngest, had answered all the questions that Caesar couldn't, and had earned the teacher's praise. He had stood there, knowing it was useless to resist, waiting for the beating to stop.

Wiping his nose with his shirt-tail and fighting back the tears, he had gone up to his favourite place on the hill, and watching the birds which he had disturbed into flight, he wished aloud that he could be one of them flying far away from the misery he was feeling. He had heard them calling him from the school, "Quincey! Quincey!" and he had shut his ears and his eyes and imagined what it would be like to be soaring over their puny heads. Perhaps he would shit on Caesar's head – only they said that brought good luck, unless it was a crow. He didn't want to be a crow. He wanted to be a beautiful, powerful bird.

That night he dreamed; strange because he could never recall dreaming. In the mornings when the other children told their dreams, crossing themselves at the very terrible ones, he would wish that he could join in, but since he didn't really know what a dream was, how could he? But that night he dreamed that he was flying, flying, flying with a strength which his small frame had never before experienced. Even then he couldn't be sure that he was really dreaming, because coming out of the darkness, like his brother's snores, he had heard a voice whispering, "When the acacia blooms for the seventh time, plus three, then will thy wish be granted thee." It was too stupid a dream to tell anyone so he had quickly forgotten it.

The desire for revenge against the battle-axe at the office was still uppermost in his mind when, the next morning, the woman with whom he lived exclaimed, "Eh! But look the acacia. It blooming so quick again!"

"The acacia tree," she repeated, turning to him. "It take so long to bloom but this must be the third time it blooming this year. A sure sign of something. Must be the drought. It pretty though. Eh, but what happen to you?"

He didn't answer because he did not know why goose pimples had suddenly dimpled his skin.

This foreboding stayed with him all day, made worse because he could find no actual source for his fear. He could not concentrate at work and went home by midday. Towards evening he went for a drive, dismissing the woman when she wanted to accompany him. Inevitably he found his way to the beach, lonely at this time of day. It was his favourite adult place to be alone. He got out of his car and began walking. The sense of disaster deepened as the dusk descended; then looking back briefly, he noticed with shock that his footprints had turned to clawprints in the sand. He lifted his arms and felt them stretch into long wings. He tried to flap them and discovered that the right one was flawed; imperfectly joined to the body so that when he tried to fly he could only flap lopsidedly off balance into a semicircle.

He wept bird tears.

Why had this happened to him? Why had he changed from small but perfect man into imperfect bird! His fright deepened. Was it a permanent change? Suppose he was seen? People would stone him. What could he do? In a panic he tried to find shelter, moving instinctively towards some rocks, where, trying to keep his imperfect wing folded, he huddled for the night.

The woman's voice awakened him in the morning just as the first rays of the sun touched him. "Quincey, darling!" she moaned, holding his head where he, in man form, lay stretched out on the sand. "We search all night for you. I think you drown when we find the car but couldn't find you. What happen to you, man?"

Too bewildered to answer, he allowed himself to be taken home.

But, what could he expect? In despair, and wanting to be alone with his terror, he sent the woman away. When she objected, saying that he needed her, he cursed her so sharply that she lapped her tail and walked away like a beaten mongrel. But his own torment was too great to allow him to feel any sympathy for her. Would the transformation happen again? Could he avoid it?

The acacia bloomed for three days; and for three nights, as

soon as dusk fell, he turned into imperfect bird. Alone in his house, looking at parts of himself in the mirrors, he discovered what a monster he was.

The fourth night, nothing happened, so too the fifth. On the sixth night, exulting in his release and his perfect man form, he went for the woman and made his peace with her.

He cut down the acacia in his yard, but could not convince his neighbour to do the same. Time passed and he began to think that it must have been something he had dreamed. It was much too bizarre an occurrence. He could never give the woman an explanation for his cruel and unusual behaviour. Something like that could not have happened.

Two years went by. The obnoxious woman at the office had gone away to be replaced by an equally obnoxious man who made no secret of wanting Quincey's job. The intrigues and the annoyances continued. But this time he was not so accommodating and there were many clashes. So, pushed into a corner one day the rival hit upon the only word which could stop Quincey. "Runt!" he shouted at him in the middle of a meeting.

The next morning the woman had the child in her arms when she looked outside and exclaimed, "So long the acacia don't bloom. But it's pretty, yes!"

Quincey nearly died. He hadn't noticed the tree. But still licking the previous day's wounds he suddenly recognised the pattern. Could it be that wish he had made those many years ago as a child, to become a bird and escape when the hurt got too much?

Full of anxiety he left the house and drove to the far end of the island where a friend had a beach house which he used from time to time. He waited restlessly for nightfall. Would the transformation occur? Would he become a birdman again?

At dusk his question was answered. As the sun went down he turned once more into the misshapen, useless, ugly bird: without even a voice, for when he tried to sing, warble or twitter, he, whose baritone could make a woman forsake the word "no", now could do nothing more than utter a harsh squawk.

It was during the second night of his nightmare in the cottage that the birdman heard the birdwoman singing. He was not surprised. It was as if he had been expecting her; as if he had always known that she existed. Her song was very sweet. Something like the cello pans warming up on a cold foreday jouvert morning, just a little bit sad, but full of promises. Something like the lone tenor playing the road march on the way home from a long tiring Tuesday mas;. playing only the improvisation, because the tune was still beating in everybody's head; sometimes switching to the sad minor key, with a question at the end of each phrase… "Will we meet again next year at carnival?"

In vain he tried to answer her. His squawk sounded harsh and unwelcome to his own ears. He hobbled from one window to the next anxious to see her. But she would not reveal herself and all night long he was haunted by the melody of that questioning song. When morning came the voice was silent and he knew that she too had resumed human shape.

It was midnight on the third night before he heard her again, this time with a very clear beating of the wings. He hobbled to the door, and there in the moonlight on the beach in front of his door was the most magnificent bird he had ever imagined. She was smaller than he was but beautifully shaped; perfect in every limb. She strutted a little, spreading her wings, showing off for him, but when he tried to communicate, his harsh squawk frightened her and she flew away. He was lost in admiration and immediately, irrevocably in love.

At the end of the three days, Quincey returned home. But what a fit of torment now assailed him! He could not forget the birdwoman. Who was she? What did she look like? Was she as beautiful a woman as she was a bird? If he met her in real life would he know her? Would she reveal her identity? Did she know him? He wished the acacia would bloom again.

It did not, of course. Not for a long time.

Eventually, once again, time dimmed the memory of this strange experience, and again he began to think that it was only a dream. There was no one in whom he could confide. Who would believe him? They would think that he was ready for the mad-house.

Life went on. Quincey left his rival at work and started his own business which led him to travel frequently up and down the islands. One night, in a hotel on a tiny out-island, he requested an early morning call in order to catch a flight. Coming out of sleep at the sound of the telephone, he thought he was dreaming when he heard the receptionist's voice. "Good morning, sir. It is five o'clock. You asked to be called."

Immediately his blood turned icy and his breathing nearly stopped. It was the voice of the birdwoman! He would recognise it anywhere. It had the same sweet haunting caress of the birdsong, almost sad with that slight hint of a question at the end of the phrase.

"Are you all right, sir?" the voice questioned his silence.

"The birdwoman," he stammered. "You're the birdwoman. What's your name? Who are you?" he babbled. Only the slight hint of laughter in the voice told him that she was confirming his recognition.

"The taxi will be ready to take you to the airport in half an hour's time, sir. Coffee will be in the lobby."

Quincey got dressed hastily. Only half-an-hour to meet her! He ran down the single flight of steps and rushed into the lobby, eyes searching eagerly for his birdwoman.

The place was empty. He looked around wildly and almost bumped into a bow-legged, dwarfish woman with an incredibly ugly face who was entering the room with a coffee pot and some mugs.

"The receptionist!" He grabbed at her almost causing her to overturn the tray. "Where is she?"

"I am the receptionist, sir," she replied in her beautiful voice, as she turned away to put down the tray.

"The voice! The voice!" he was stammering again. "But... but... It can't be. The beautiful voice! The beautiful bird!"

"Yes?" she said, now looking at him directly so that he could see the pain in her eyes. He could see the disbelief and horror she was reading from his face. He wilted in shame before her gaze.

"I'm sorry... I thought..."

She made a gesture of dismissal. "Do you think any of those travellers really saw any of the sirens?"

She smiled sadly.

"The driver will be with you in a moment. Would you like some coffee?"

He was too bewildered to answer, and watched in disbelief as she waddled out of the room.

A man could go crazy not being able to understand the things that happen to him. If he's trained a certain way he expects things to happen logically. Step by step. Q.E.D. If he does certain things, then certain consequences will follow. A man could go crazy trying to figure out why he is chosen for experiences so unnatural and bizarre he can never be sure that he is not living a dream or that he is not merely a character in somebody's fable.

Quincey hid from himself in hard work. He gave himself no time to think. There was no birdwoman, no acacia to bloom, nothing to feel or think about but work and more work. At night when he fell into bed he was so tired his body went to sleep immediately.

But one evening, Quincey sat in his living room relaxing after a particularly long hard stretch of work. It was just turning dark and the woman was on the telephone.

"Girl, she ugly, you see! I couldn't believe my eyes! And he's a mean-looking, dry-up runt!"

He didn't know who she was talking about, but is that what she would say about him too? Things hadn't been too smooth between them lately. Without warning his thoughts went to the birdwoman, and the sudden return of the pain his mind had been masking caused him to exclaim, so sharp was the blade of its machete.

He didn't want to talk to anyone, so when the woman looked at him curiously he got up to leave the room. He was totally unprepared when their first child started screaming and pointing at him. Then he saw the woman with the new child in her arms gazing at him in horror, and looking down he saw his feet turning to claws.

Terrified he started to hop and flap his way out of the house, not caring where he went, just trying to get away. He crushed the newly fallen carpet of acacia blossoms on the ground in front of his neighbour's yard without even noticing them. He had to escape without being seen.

But his lopsided, fear-driven progress quickly attracted attention. "Look! A mas man. But the costume don't mek good!" People laughed as they pointed at him. "But it too soon for carnival! Where the rest of the band? Where the parade?" Some boys began to follow him.

Suddenly, just as he was sure that they were planning to hurt him, he heard the birdwoman singing. The song was so enchanting that it distracted his tormentors, and knowing that she had come to help him he followed the voice blindly away from the jeering, the scorn and the ridicule. He followed until, exhausted, he collapsed, not knowing or caring where he was.

In the morning he awakened in his friend's beach cottage to the sound of clinking pots and the teasing smell of coffee. He wasn't surprised to see the ugly receptionist waddling into the room carrying two steaming mugs.

"Are you all right?" she asked.

He nodded.

"Why did you wait so long? Didn't you see the acacia blooming?"

He didn't answer. He was trying to get used to the look of her; the dumpy body, the too large lips, protruding teeth, the flat outsize nose. Oh God! She's ugly, he couldn't help the thought.

"Are you the birdwoman?"

"You know I am."

"How did you find out about me?"

"Let's say a little bird told me," she smiled. "The distance between the islands is not great. You can fly from one to the other in less than an hour sometimes. I like to fly. It's like magic soaring above everything. Free from land. Free from people."

"What's your name?"

"If you were asked to give me a name, what would it be? What would you call me?"

He wished she would continue talking. He couldn't hear enough of that lovely voice. To shut his eyes and listen to her was, he imagined, like listening to an angel.

"Angella."

"That's a nice name," she smiled. "It will do… May I stay here, until it's over?"

"Why not?"

"This is the last time, you know."

"What do you mean?" he asked in great alarm. Would he now be bird forever?

"Don't you know?" she asked looking at him in surprise. He shook his head.

"Didn't they tell you when they granted your wish?"

"No!" he said, getting increasingly frightened.

"When the acacia blooms, the seventh time, plus three," she said in a chant. "Trouble is that they never said which tree," she added as if talking to herself. "Anyway, the third time you have to decide whether to stay bird or return to human form forever."

"Human for me!" he cried with relief.

Her face showed great sadness.

"Don't tell me you're thinking of choosing to be a bird?"

"If you were me, what would you choose?"

He hesitated because he wasn't sure what she meant.

"It's okay," she stopped him from answering. "Don't feel badly. I'm a telephone operator and sometimes I fill in at the hotel where you saw me – the deep night shift, where I won't be seen. Too many times I've heard men eager to meet the woman with the heavenly voice. Too many times I've seen the disbelief and disappointment in their eyes when they did meet me. Angels should be pale-skinned, with fine features and have long, flowing hair; not so? I have learned that it is better to stay hidden."

She was trying to hide her bitterness but it showed in her face.

"When I was little, they put me in the church choir because my voice was so beautiful, but they used to hide me behind the taller children. One Sunday I decided that I had had enough of being hidden so when it came to my solo part I stepped out so that everyone could see who was singing. The church was packed. It was a special service. There were many visitors. Lots of children."

She sighed. "I'll never forget that song. The choir sang the chorus "Jesus loves the little children, all the children of the world." You know it?"

She got up and went to the window, and with her back to him, as if she didn't want to be seen, she sang the chorus.

Quincey sat spellbound. Her voice made him think of the smooth sweetness of his favourite ice cream; he thought of banks of fluffy white clouds; of the gentle murmur of a peaceful stream; of the sparkle of a shower of stars; and he thought that if he had ever really imagined an angel singing, that was how it would be.

"I had the first verse about how I was lame and He healed me." She took a sip of coffee and continued as if he was no longer there, just she and the choir and the congregation giggling at the incongruity of such an ugly girl with such a beautiful voice.

"My mother. My own mother was so mortified at the laughter, I believe that if she could have disowned me she would have done so. She actually scolded me for showing myself. That was the first time I realised how unacceptable my ugliness was."

"That was the first time I wished to escape; to become a bird and fly away from the misery I was feeling."

He nodded in sympathy. He was remembering the feelings of inadequacy which had caused him to make a similar wish.

"But, there were worse times ahead. At school they teased me all the time. Nobody wanted to be my friend. They called me "toady". Even the teachers; they would put me to sing offstage, in the wings, while other girls pretended that they were the ones singing the parts of princesses and other wonderful characters. How I longed to play the part of a princess! How I wished to have long hair and light brown skin and be slim and beautiful! I had to be content with seeing my name on the programme as "voice offstage". Sometimes they didn't even bother to put that.

"Once I entered a talent show but I never even reached the stage. I couldn't handle the comments.

"All of my life I've wanted not to be me. When I left school I chose to live on that out-of-the-way island where you met me and to take a job where I didn't have to meet people. I don't want to live with this ugliness which everybody despises. Having a beautiful voice makes it worse. People look at me in disgust, as if they're saying "What a waste of a good thing!" So, if you were me, what would you choose?"

She was quiet for a time, and he didn't know what to say. What could he say in the face of so much unhappiness? How could he comfort her when his reactions had already betrayed his own negative thoughts about her?

"Why did you make the wish?" she asked. "There's nothing wrong with you."

"I was too small."

She laughed, a sound almost as captivating as her singing. "Too small for what?"

He didn't answer. His reason now felt puny when compared to hers.

"Are you hungry?" she asked, a little shyly.

"No."

"Well, what shall we do all day? Two more days to go." He shook his head, because he didn't know what to plan, but she misunderstood.

Suddenly she turned on him, her face twisted with an emotion that made her seem even more repulsive.

"Look! It have a mask I does wear sometimes. You could bear to see me in that?"

She left the room but quickly returned with her face hidden behind a mask painted to represent a "pretty" lady. The lips were precisely outlined, a cherry-red cupid's bow; the Caucasian nose pointedly straight; the eyes still-water blue with long black lashes. A mask given crude two-dimensional depth with rouge, mascara, eye shadow.

"This is your Angella. You like it? You like me now? You could stand to see my face, now?" A harsh shriek, a different voice, came from behind the mask rising higher and higher until it broke with pain.

"You like me face? You like me mask?" she danced before him. "All a we in carnival. Life is one big carnival. One big lie. You like me mask? You like me face, now? You like your Angella, now?"

He put his hands over his ears and hid his face from the agony confronting him.

She took off the mask.

Neither of them said anything for a long time.

"Do you want to talk?" she asked in her normal tones.

He shook his head. He was exhausted from the earlier scene.

"May I... May I kiss you?" she asked with so much humility that he felt touched but he didn't answer quickly enough and so she turned away trying not to let him see the tears.

"It's all right," she said. "Not even God love ugly."

She wouldn't stay in the house so they spent the days apart. He didn't ask her where she went; she didn't ask him what he did all day. Mostly he thought about the things she had told him and wondered again and again what cruel plan caused people to be born and then singled them out for suffering. It was so much worse he thought when the pain came from the heart, because emotional pain was not an easy one to share. People readily sympathised with signs of hunger, or destitution or physical pain, but hardly ever understood how despair can gnaw the human spirit into destruction.

People quickly grow impatient; – "So what if you're ugly; or too small; or too tall; or too fat? So what if you're deformed? So what if somebody broke your heart? So what if nobody loves you? Look how many other people are worse off than you, yet they manage."

It was true, he thought, that some people did find ways of dealing with their deficiencies, but who knows why a particular flaw could become such an obsession that it could hound a person to a premature death? Who but the victim remembers the pain inflicted by deliberate or careless, cruel behaviour? Angella had helped him to understand himself. Now he knew *why* he wanted only to be human, no matter how incomplete he might feel his body to be. He was on the side of life and living it fully. He would not let people's cruelty devastate him any longer. Perhaps they had their problems too. Now he could discard the deformed bird inside him forever. But how to help Angella? Was there any way to help her understand that the physical beauty which she pined for, which was such an obsession, was not important beside the great talent which she had been given, and that only she herself could destroy herself.

Although she shunned him during the days, at nights, when the metamorphosis overtook them, they sought comfort in each other's company. He never tired of admiring the smoothness of her feathers, the delicate pink around her eyes and beak, the queenly tossing of head on her long elegant neck, and most of all her magnificent flying patterns. Because he was earthbound she never went too far away from him. With her flight always came that peculiar haunting sad-sweet song which was both a wonder and delight.

On the third night they did not sleep. He watched her strutting and preening in the moonlight. He listened to her song and he was sad. This was the last time they would share this experience, and he was not sure what she intended to do.

Early in the morning, just before daylight could outshine the moon, as they squatted sleepily side by side on the veranda overlooking the bay, the voice came suddenly on the early morning breeze.

*When the acacia blooms for the seventh time, plus three*
*Then thy wish will be granted thee.*
*Choose now which one will it be?*
*Bird or man? Bird or woman? Forever free!"*

"Man! Man!" he squawked, roused from his dozing.

"Say woman! Say woman!" he urged her.

"May I kiss you?" she asked.

He gaped at her in amazement. What on earth was she thinking of? At such a crucial time!

Once again she misunderstood his look and reason for not answering.

"You were my last hope," she said sadly. "I thought that you would understand. But, like all the others, you lack compassion and courage. I can't go through life with this terrible loneliness; never being close to anyone; never having someone to touch me without scorn or ridicule. Am I always to be only a voice?"

He understood now what she needed from him, but it was too late.

*"Choose now, which one will it be?*
*Bird or woman? Forever free!"*

"Bird! Bird!" she replied. And as she flew into the morning sky his man's voice echoed over the bay, "Angella! Angella!"

## I—CALYPSO

There was a lot of laughter that April Fools' day when the Sunday papers were read. All caused by a three column by two inch advertisement in very bold type.

**PERSONAL
TO ERMA
PLEASE CONFESS
This is to advise Erma to confess her indiscretions to her husband. He will forgive her if she tells all, but he is getting suspicious and if he finds out for himself, trouble!**

The young clerk who took the ad for the paper was new. It didn't even occur to him that there was anything wrong with it. In any case he was alone on the night shift and he didn't want to look foolish by consulting about every little thing. He processed the ad and sent it to the composing room where it relieved the tedium of the night's work by providing a few laughs as to who Erma might be and why somebody had "put her in the paper". Some thought it might be the husband himself, but the clerk reported that it was a woman who brought it in. Perhaps it was Erma's friend? Or her rival? Whoever had done it, it was a good All Fool's Day joke and everybody laughed.

## ERMA ONE

"But Erma! Who could be calling the house so early on a Sunday morning! Answer the phone, no!"

"Hello! 80900. Good morning."

"Erma girl. Is that you! Chile, you read the paper since morning?"

"Eh, eh! Myrtle. You know what time it is? Six o'clock big, big Sunday morning. I just waking up. What happen so?"

"Girl, you name in the paper."

"What you saying."

"Look it here. Big Advertisement. You can't miss it. Erma please confess."

"What you talking bout?"

"Yes, chile. It right here. What you been up to? It also say you gwine get licks if you don't confess to you husband."

"Listen, Myrtle, if you drink mad puss piss, keep it to you-self and don't provoke me peace this Lord's day morning, hear! Why you don't keep you nastiness to youself? Is me one in the world name Erma? If somebody put somebody name Erma in the paper, it have to be me? Well Miss Gossip, I sorry to disappoint you, but is not me, you hear!"

"Girl, I don't know. But you never see smoke without fire and the pig squealing loudest is the one the stone ketch!"

"Myrtle, I warning you. It's a good thing you on the telephone else I'd be tempted to clap you face for you. Leave me alone and go make you husband breakfast. God knows he look like he need looking after."

"Erma, who that calling so early?"

"That Myrtle. She make me so angry. Always putting she nasty mouth on people."

"Who she macoing now?"

"Somebody name Erma."

"You?"

"Not me at all, boy. Not me."

CHORUS
Erma, honey! Is what you do?
Mek the whole town laughing at you.
Erma what you doing wrong?
Calypsonian soon put you in song.
Everybody teasing, jeering, sorrying for your man.
Child, mend you ways
Crime never pays.


## ERMA TWO

"John boy. How you going?"

"Fine, partner. Jus tekkin the morning constitutional, as usual."

"Boy, I admire the way you tek the exercise thing serious."

"Yes, you know. Have to keep the body fit or the women will leave you out."

"How Erma?"

"She okay. Can't get she to join me for the morning walk. She say is only fowl cock must wake up so early."

"You see the Sunday paper yet?"

"No. I usually get it at the corner."

"A big ad in there bout somebody name Erma. I never know you was having trouble with she, boy."

"What you talking bout?"

"See it here. Will Erma confess! Is you put she in?"

"What?"

"But careful, John boy. Mind you get a heart attack this big Lord's day morning."

"I gwine buss she ass, you hear. Give me that."


"Erma! Erma!"

"Hmm? What you makin up so much noise for so early in the morning?"

"Makin up noise? You don't hear noise yet. What this mean?"

"What, John, man?"

"Read this. Is who put you in the paper? What going on behind me back?"

"Pass me glasses. But, John! How you could think this could be me!"

"Me trust no woman, you hear. How much woman you know name Erma? Somebody talk you business. Tell me what going on before I loss me temper."

"But John!"

"Don't, "But John" me. Jesus! Look how scandal ketch me this big Sunday morning. I feel I could buss you ass for true!"

"John! What you doing with that belt? Is who you planning to pelt? You mad? But look trouble this morning! Look me crosses this morning. Look how I lying down peaceful in me bed this Lord's day morning and the man come threatening to sweeten me tea with salt, for no reason at all."

"No reason at all? Erma, you better tell me what going on!"

> CHORUS
> Erma girl! Is it really true
> That you sins at last ketch up with you?
> Erma, how you could carry on so?
> You had the man like sof sof dough.
> Now somebody squeal an you sins reveal.
> Chile, mend you ways
> Crime never pays.

### ERMA THREE

"Hello."

"It's only me, darling. So! Somebody put your wife in the papers!"

"I told you not to call me on a Sunday. What're you talking about?"

"You haven't read the papers yet? There's a big ad. Can't miss it. Erma, please confess. It goes on to say that her husband is getting suspicious and that if she doesn't confess she is going to get her tail cut. Why, Darling! I didn't know you were violent."

"What the hell are you talking about. Is this more of your nastiness?"

"But sweetheart! Why are you abusing me? Why would I want to be nasty. Erma is doing it herself. You think she's so pure and righteous. Not like me, a loose woman, eh? But nobody has my name in the papers."

"Listen, woman! You taking a joke too far. You taking this jealous thing too far. I finish with you if I find out you have anything to do with this. You hear me!"

"Jerry! Oh sorry. I didn't know you were on the phone. Here're the papers. What's the matter, love? You look upset."

"Some people only like to make life miserable for others. Some foolish person phone telling me about some ad in the paper about an Erma. They want to find out if it's you."

"What!"

"Wait. Let me see the papers. Oh yes. Here it is: Erma please confess. But anybody ever see anything like this. Some idle person with money to waste. Imagine anybody thinking it could be you, love."

"Oh, Jerry. How people so wicked. I suppose a whole lot of people will be calling with their bad jokes."

"Hello. Sheila? Erma here… No. I'm all right. I don't want Jerry to hear me. You read the papers yet? … What happen? Girl, I nearly drop dead with fright. Somebody put me in the paper… Yes. An ad saying Erma must confess her indiscretions. Somebody call Jerry first thing this morning and point it out to him. But he so sweet and trusting. He was laughing with me about it."

"Girl! I don't know who could be so wicked to do such a thing, but Sheila, I fraid. Suppose he find out in truth? Suppose he get suspicious?…Yes. I know you was warning me, but you know how it go? I never dream somebody could do such a thing…"

"How you mean stay calm. I biting me nails. You know how them quiet man stay. If he find out, crapaud go smoke me pipe!"

## CHORUS

Erma! Erma! What you going to do?
Jus yesterday I was warning you.
Is play you say you playing
Jus tekkin a lil chance.
Now the whole world know about you and your romance.
Chile, mend you ways
Crime never pays.

## FINALE

So all you Erma that doing wrong
All you who going around fooling with man
You might think you get away
But crime will never pay
Man mek to do what he want to do.
Woman mek to do what man tell she to do.
So woman, mend you ways
And forever win his praise.
And if you think is a lie
Check out me and me sweetie-pie.

## LYING LIPS

"LYING LIPS ARE AN ABOMINATION TO THE LORD."

Joycelyn had to write that line five hundred times when she was ten years old. And, because she misspelt "abomination" after the three hundredth time, she had to write the word five hundred times more in her best handwriting. Nothing else would satisfy her schoolteacher mother.

Joycelyn couldn't remember the falsehood which had earned her such severe punishment, but she never forgot the importance of that maxim, and her lifelong abhorrence of telling lies had its beginning there.

Although she would never admit it, her rigidity about always telling the truth sometimes got her into more trouble than a little lie would have done.

Like the time her new boss, hiding from a creditor and expecting to be protected, had found himself face to face with the creditor because Joycelyn would not say that he was off the premises.

"Who the bloody hell you think you are? George Washington?" he had shouted at her.

She didn't care, even though she got fired shortly after. Her principles had been upheld. As long as she told the truth, she was convinced that things would work out for her.

Besides, there was no such thing as a "little" lie.

She became so notorious that, whenever her name was called, somebody was sure to say: "You mean the woman who always tells the truth?" They called her Miss Truthful behind her back.

Many people were uncomfortable with her constant diet of

raw truth, including Patrick, who, although fond of her, never-theless told her quite frankly that he was afraid of her. She was a woman to get people into trouble, he said. Perhaps that was why the relationship had not gone further than a casual drop-in for a drink or a chat, a meal and sometimes a date.

Tennyson sat at a table for two in the dark corner of the lounge. Normally there would be quite a few people coming over to say hello and offering to buy him a drink because he was an important person and people liked to think he was their friend. But that evening, as he crouched over his drink in the darkened corner, his body clearly said that he didn't want to be disturbed. They thought, of course, that he was waiting for a woman. Actually he was waiting for Patrick, his lifelong friend and the only person he could ask for advice in personal matters.

It never ceased to amuse him that he, who was regarded as a financial wizard, head of an important national institution, could need advice on his personal financial affairs.

People would have a laugh if they knew that his wife, Jean, handled all the financial transactions in the family. He exam-ined books and advised on investments and expenditure, but the only money he actually handled was his monthly spending allowance. Sometimes he wished the national accounts had the same sort of restrictions and accountability that controlled his personal finances. They would be in better shape. Perhaps it was Jean who should be running things, he thought with a tired smile.

Jean was a trojan woman. No wonder they kept getting richer and richer. She didn't spend money carelessly. She bought all his clothes, enough to make him appear well-dressed, but he never had to complain about needing additional cupboard space; nei-ther did she. She paid all the bills; wrote all the cheques.

When they were newly married and she found him indebted to several clothing stores and with a serious overdraft, she quickly set about correcting the problem. She was paranoid about owing money. When she was a teenager, her father had lost almost everything he owned after he had been successfully sued by several creditors. Lawyers and anything to do with the courts frightened her.

It wasn't that he had not been earning enough money, but he was careless about paying bills and somehow the money got spent on other things. Anxious to please his new bride, he had allowed her to consolidate their earnings and take on responsibility for paying bills and saving for their future. There were no children with whom to share, so, as the years passed, their savings amassed, and, wisely invested, had grown into a comfortable income. Her taking charge at home had freed him to concentrate on his career, which had moved so fast that the responsibility he now had sometimes frightened him.

"Hi, Tenn!" Patrick's voice broke his thoughts. "What're you having? The usual?"

"Scotch and soda," he turned to the waiter, "and a refill for Mr. Crawle."

They were both well known. This was their favourite meeting spot for consultation or just the continual bonding that friendship demands.

"You hear the one about the dog that was crossing the train line?" Patrick asked.

"No."

"Well is a stocious dog, see, so him not walking fast although the train coming. Him just a tek him time a cross, so the train wheel catch him an chop off piece of him tail."

Tennyson sighed. He wasn't in the mood for Patrick's jokes, but he knew better than to try to stop him before he had finished telling one.

"Well, Mr. Stocious Dog feel him couldn't do without the tail that chop off, so him turn back an a search and search the train line for the tail and another train no just pass an chop off him head."

"Yeah man!" He started to laugh. "The dog no lose him head over a piece a tail!"

In spite of his mood, Tennyson had to smile.

"So what's up?" Patrick asked after he had taken a sip of his scotch. "I can't stay too long. I promised Joycelyn I'd stop by for dinner and you know how she damn miserable. She don't hesitate to tell you exactly what she thinking. You know what she do me the other day?"

Tennyson tried to hide his impatience to tell his own story.

"We stop by Pegasus to have a drink and buck up on Char-lie B. I made the mistake to tell Joycelyn that he owe me money but kept dodging me. Me dear sar, Charlie B was under two waters and just kept on flashing the concordes right left and centre, buying drinks for everybody, say it was his birthday.

"I should have known what that woman was up to when she started to fidget. Anyway, in a quiet moment when everybody could hear, Charlie B turn to me – you know how he boasty, "So, Patrick. How's business?" Before I could answer, hear Joycelyn: "Bad. He could use that money you owe him.""

Tennyson screwed up his face in sympathy with his friend.

"I nearly dead from shame. And Charlie B not too drunk to be embarrassed. He get very stiff and grand. "How much I owe you, sonny?" I started to mumble that it wasn't important when Miss Joycelyn she pipe up, "Four thousand.""

"God! Talk about wanting the earth to open up and swallow me! All I trying to catch her eye to tell her to shut up. No use."

"So? He paid you?"

"Yes. He just reel off forty of the concordes and pay me, same time. Is not even like it was a lot of money, but he don't talk to me since that, and when you starting up a business you can't afford to antagonise men like Charlie B. He has a lot of influential friends. He can put business my way."

"I cuss Joycelyn hog rotten, but you know she can't understand that is not everything you know you must talk. All she deh pon is – "Hypocrisy doesn't pay. Don't you get your money?" – I mean, everybody know how her mouth stay, but there is a limit, man. I don't know why I bother with her at all. Cho!"

"You might have to disappoint Joycelyn tonight. I am in trouble. Serious trouble."

"Hmh hmh?" Patrick didn't need to say "tell me".

"About ten years ago, there was this girl, named Hortense. I don't know if you remember her?"

"Vaguely. Brown, skinny, long hair, high bottom?"

"Sort of."

"I never forget a bottom." Patrick laughed. "Yeah I remember teasing you about her that night we buck up at Horizons and you protesting, too strongly, that it was business. More like monkey business I thought."

"Well, she was sort of a junior accountant, and… well…" Tennyson was glad for the darkness which hid his embarrassment.

Patrick laughed again.

"Well, to cut a long story, there was a baby, a boy."

"Yours? Jesus Christ! Does Jean know?"

"Of course not. You know Jean. She would kill me. God! The thought of her finding out scares the shit out of me!"

"Well you're doing all right. I didn't even suspect, and I thought I knew most things about you."

"The mother is cooperative and I've been supporting the child. I've managed to do so without Jean suspecting, but now there's a problem. He needs an operation and there's no way I can take out that kind of money all at once without giving Jean a satisfactory reason."

"Why don't you tell her it's a charity case?"

"Five thousand dollars? She wouldn't agree."

"Tell her it's a loan for me."

"She would question you and demand an I.O.U. You know Jean. She's very careful about money."

"What if you had to buy some parts for your car, abroad."

"The car's kept by the Ministry, remember. She drives the other one," Tennyson said, showing his frustration.

"Man you have a problem. Why don't you just tell her. She mightn't take it as badly as you think."

"No, she would throw me out immediately. She's very sensitive about not having had a child. She's often said that she wouldn't take her childlessness as an excuse for any hanky panky;

that any day a woman turned up with a child saying it was mine, she would divorce me instantly."

"Want me to put up the money?"

"No. With your new business you can't afford to. Besides he's my child. I can more than afford it. It's just Jean. I don' want to lose her. The affair wasn't anything serious. You know how it is. You meet somebody and you amuse yourself for a time, but..."

"There must be a way to fix this up. Let me think."


"Patrick, why we have to stop by Tennyson? Every time we're supposed to do something he spoils it. Remember my birthday? All now the dinner don't eat yet."

"Just for a minute, Miss Miserable. I have to collect something from him. He's leaving this afternoon."

"Where's he off to now?"

"Taking Jean on a holiday to Europe."

"You lie? They're so mean I never thought they'd waste money on something like that."

"Stop it. Tenn is my friend."

But you know it's true. They're the meanest rich people I know. Tennyson ever give you a present yet?"

"Behave, no!"

"And look at the big house they live in. Them one. Not a chick nor a child and they wouldn't even adopt one. They're mean in spirit and pocket or they'd take in a child or two."

"Try convincing Jean of that."

"Me! You know I can't stand the woman. She's too self-satisfied and arrogant."

"Cool it no! She's not so bad really. Must you *always* say what you think? I tired to tell you, is not everything eye see, mouth mek fi talk."

"Why're you stopping here?"

"The back entrance. I can't bother drive all the way round the hill. It's a short cut to the house. I won't be long. Coming?"

"No. I'll stay and enjoy the rich people's view. You not afraid of the dogs?"

"No. Tenn knows I'm coming. He'll have them locked up. Besides they got rid of the really bad ones. Jean was terrified the last time one of them bit a man and he took them to court."

"You go on. Never trust a dog. I'm scared of those big brutes."

Joycelyn stayed in the car looking out at the early morning city beneath the hill. A mist, probably smoke, hung over a wide section, dissipating towards the sea. A few people passed her with a "good morning". Helpers, she thought, for the rich who occupied the hill.

A car squeezed past on the narrow road. The occupants looked at her as though she was an intruder.

Soon she got bored and left the car to stretch. She wondered what was keeping Patrick and began to feel annoyed. Once again Tennyson was coming between Patrick and herself although it wasn't really his fault. The problem was Patrick's inability to say "no" to people. She sucked her teeth.

She would tell him a thing or two when he returned. Then she remembered how he was always complaining that she made people uncomfortable with her forthrightness and love of telling the truth.

He had cursed her thoroughly a couple of weeks ago after she had shamed Charlie B into paying him some money which he badly needed. It was so unfair, a man like Charlie B taking advantage of Patrick just because he wouldn't speak up for his rights. Somebody had to stop all this hypocrisy around the place. "Does it have to be you?" Patrick had shouted at her. He had really been angry.

Cho! Joycelyn sucked her teeth again. She couldn't even bother to be vexed about the insulting things he had said. "Keep your mouth shut when I'm around," he had told her, "or I won't be around."

Did people really so hate the truth that it would cause them to shun her? Was that why he would not take their relationship any further? He liked her, she was sure, but he kept holding back from intimacy. But what could she do? That's how she'd lived her life.

At thirty-three it was difficult to change one's way to accommodate someone else.

After the incident with Charlie, his woman had followed her to the washroom and said, "Is long time I hearing about you. I hope to God you never do anything you don't want people to know. One of these days you tongue gwine turn back on you own self."

She had been annoyed at the note of pity in the woman's voice, but still felt that she was right. If she hadn't spoken up Patrick wouldn't have got his money, and he needed it.

The flowers on the hillside leading to the house attracted her attention and, still thinking her baffling thoughts, she went through the little gate which Patrick had left unlatched. The house couldn't be seen from where she was. The hillside was awash with colours from the terraced flower beds covering it. She had heard that Jean Crawle was a gardening nut. No wonder, she thought. She didn't have anything else to do. She wondered if Jean or the gardener would mind if she picked a few buds – just for the pleasure of doing so, because they would be quite faded by the time she got home. Perhaps she would present Patrick with a bud when he returned, turn the tables on him and see how he reacted.

Joycelyn had just bent to pick a tiny salmon-pink rosebud when two things happened simultaneously. A boy about nine years old walked through the open gate and came towards her saying, "Please lady, I begging you a bus fare to go down the hill." At the same time she heard dogs barking, and looking up she saw six or so very large Alsatian dogs descending on her, looking especially ferocious from her foreshortened view of them.

Petrified, she could only scream, "Patrick!" before the dogs were swarming her, smelling, panting, licking, bounding around with the exuberance of animals newly released from confinement. Then they noticed the boy standing near the gate and went after him. She heard him scream and saw him fall and the dogs standing menacingly over him. Their barking drowned out any other sound.

There was so much confusion that Joycelyn lost her balance on the steep hillside. By the time she jumped up, a man and a woman had appeared and they began to scream too. Patrick and Tennyson came rushing down the hillside, and soon after them the gardener. Between them they called off the excited dogs and shooed them back up the hill. Joycelyn heard the gardener grumbling as he passed her about the stupid person who'd left the gate open so that the dogs could mash down his plants.

As she tried to recover from her fright, Joycelyn realised that an argument was going on. The woman was wailing that her son had been bitten by the dogs. The man was shouting that those vicious brutes should be shot and demanding to know what the owners were going to do about the boy.

It was only when Jean appeared, nervously asking what had happened, that Joycelyn went over to the group. They had lifted the boy off the ground. His pants were torn, as was his shirt, and there were scratch marks on his leg with a little trickle of blood already congealed. He tried to walk but had to be supported by the man whose connection with the woman Joycelyn could not determine.

Something about the scene bothered her. She couldn't tell what it was. Was it that the boy did not seem distressed enough? Was it that the adults were protesting too loudly? Was it that she had never seen Jean Crawle so agitated?

They all climbed the hill, the men carrying the boy. When they reached the patio they settled the child on a couch where the man and woman hovered protectively over him, as if he might be mauled again if they did not stay close to him. They were talking animatedly about doctor's bills, and tetanus shots and lawyer's fees.

Poor Jean was in a state! The maid brought out some juice and when Jean tried to pour it her hand shook so much Joycelyn had to take the jug from her. Tennyson tried to protest that he didn't think that the dogs had really mauled the child and turned to Joycelyn for her opinion. She was, after all, the only eye witness.

Joycelyn was about to say that she thought it was all fake, but suddenly she noticed Patrick staring at her in a peculiar way, and although she didn't know what was going on, something was telling her that this time she should keep her truthful opinion to herself. That if she said what she really thought, Patrick would go out of her life for ever.

She hesitated; a lifelong habit struggling with a very human need.

"They did seem to have got to him," she said, her face flushing with the effort.

Was it only her imagination or did *both* Patrick and Tennyson seem to relax? Jean was staring at her with even more frightened eyes.

Patrick pulled Tennyson aside for a consultation.

Jean was talking a little wildly about no problem with the doctor's bills, her husband would pay, and she was sure that there was no need to go to court.

Joycelyn stared at the boy who was quite cheerfully drinking the juice. His face bothered her. Those eyebrows: bushy and shaped a little funny as if he was perpetually puzzled. Why did he remind her of someone?

Patrick and Tennyson returned and Patrick suggested that they settle the matter with a cheque. He reminded Jean that they were due to travel that same day and shouldn't leave with unfinished business on their minds.

The woman wanted ten thousand dollars; this had Jean looking as if she was the one who had been bitten. However, after some argument they settled for five thousand. Patrick had to write the cheque because Jean was still so shaky, but only Joycelyn seemed to notice that he didn't ask for a name when writing. It was when he turned around, cheque in hand, that the slightly puzzled look which his eyebrows gave his face caused Joycelyn to understand at least a small part of the story.

She bit her tongue into silence.

Patrick and Tennyson shook hands heartily. Patrick promised to drop off the boy at the nearest clinic. As he wished Tennyson and the still shaky Jean "bon voyage", he urged them to forget the incident and have a good time. He was sure it was all over.

After they had dropped off their passengers and were finally on their way, Joycelyn spoke. "The dogs didn't really bite that boy, did they? I was there. They never really touched him. It was all a set-up."

"Joycelyn!" Patrick exclaimed. "Why didn't you say so? You could have saved poor Tenn a tidy little sum."

"Come off it!" she smiled.

He placed his hand over hers. "I took a chance on my favourite truth-teller and she came through like a champ."

"What scamps you both are," she said, relishing the promise of his touch.

## MR. FARGO AND MR. LAWSON

Bouncy couldn't any longer bounce. The name came from his younger years when he'd just come to town and was full of energy and seemed always to be on the move.

Nowadays, he walked slowly, with the aid of a cane, but the name stuck. Youngsters called him Mr. Bouncy.

The folks at number forty would always know when he was coming to visit when they heard the tapping of his walking stick on the pavement outside the gate. There would be a pause while he steadied himself and reached up to pull the bolt, then the ringing of the bell at the end of the string tied to the bolt would be the formal announcement of his arrival, every morning, punctually at ten o'clock.

But in spite of his handicap, nobody would go to help him up the six steep concrete steps which joined street pavement to yard. He was extraordinarily proud and would wave away anyone who attempted to help him. Clutching the concrete wall beside the steps and manoeuvring his stick, he would be sweating profusely when he reached the top. There he would pause, take out his handkerchief, wipe his face, and without greeting anybody in the yard, would push straight through the front parlour to the middle room where his bedridden friend eagerly awaited his visit.

"Good morning, Mr. Fargo," Bouncy would say very formally, nodding at the man on the bed.

"Good morning, Mr. Lawson," the man on the bed would reply.

Then they would shake hands and Bouncy would sit in the armchair the women had put beside the bed for him.

Not until this exchange had taken place would Bouncy speak to anyone else in the house.

The two friends usually spent the day discussing the radio news, dozing, occasionally exchanging gossip, eating when the women brought food; but the really important thing was being company for each other.

Nobody could remember exactly when Bouncy and Sojie stopped calling each other by nickname. It was as if the more ageing robbed them of physical dignity, the more they had to compensate by becoming extremely formal with each other.

Bouncy and Sojie had been friends before any of Sojie's children were born and before Bouncy married Miss D and settled down.

They became friends soon after Bouncy, at about age nineteen, came to Kingston to try to earn a living. They met at Molly's bar at the corner of the lane on which they both lived. That first meeting nearly ended in disaster because Sojie, ever pushy, had called Bouncy, a country boy. A fight had been averted only by the quick offer of a round of drinks by one of Sojie's friends. The hostility quietly subsided over the drink and soon they became very good friends.

Most Saturdays and on some week nights too, they had passed the time together at Molly's bar, drinking, philosophising, playing dominoes, and sometimes creating such confusion that Molly was obliged to ask them to leave or be thrown out.

Bouncy was godfather to Sojie's first inside child. Sojie was best man at Bouncy's wedding. In fact it was Sojie who, at Bouncy's request, went around telling all the young ladies who had an interest but had not been chosen that Bouncy would no longer be available. He wore a stone chop on his right ear to the wedding for this effort. When Bouncy was thrown out by his wife, it was at Sojie's house that he stayed until she calmed down enough to take him back.

They were thicker than thieves, people said; closer than if they had been blood brothers.

When Sojie retired from the army, Bouncy left the large dry-cleaning establishment where he worked and together they rented a small shop on the lane where they both still lived and started their own dry-cleaning business.

The day the business was burnt out, they wept on each other's shoulders, got terribly drunk at bars all over the city, and slept side by side in a gutter until Bouncy's wife found them and took them home.

Together they started all over again and eventually succeeded so that they were able to buy houses at either end of the lane and live fairly comfortably with their families.

Generations of floating city tenement people had come and found them living on Golden Lane. Many benefited from their generosity: school fees for a poor but bright child; lunch money for another; doctor and medical bills paid in an emergency; a blind eye for the tenant who couldn't pay the rent for a couple of months. They were such an institution that people called them the guardians of Golden Lane. People said that even when they died their spirits would continue to guard the lane.

Bouncy and Sojie grew old together. When Sojie's son took over the business, they could still be seen every day sitting on stools outside the shop: giving advice, greeting customers, occasionally placating someone irate about a bad job; otherwise they could be found at the Jug Jug (formerly Molly's bar).

It was strange, but as the years passed, Sojie retained his ability to put away several rounds of their favourite "whites" without ill-effect. Bouncy, however, had developed an intolerance and had to switch to what they teasingly called watered-down ladies' drinks, like gin with lots of tonic or an occasional "brown cow". Even then he could manage no more than two or three before becoming quite drunk. During a session, therefore, he would have to nurse one drink for a long time. But somehow the two of them still managed to stay in sync so that, at the end of the evening, one would be as "sweet" as the other.

Then they would walk each other home. Bouncy, who lived nearest the bar, would insist on walking with Sojie all the way to the other end of the lane. Then Sojie would insist on returning the favour and they would turn back towards the Jug Jug. Golden Lane people were used to seeing the two drunk old men at about nine o'clock at night supporting each other, singing and talking loudly, walking back and forth until one or other of the families arrested *their* old man and insisted he go inside, and then escorted the other to his bed.

When Bouncy got a stroke, Sojie spent as much of his time at the hospital as the authorities would allow. In spite of Bouncy's daughter's protests she'd taken care of him after Miss D died – Sojie was Bouncy's nurse during the long period of convalescence. It was he who struggled with Bouncy until he learned to walk again, albeit with a cane. Then Sojie, who had been in good health for most of his life, got sick and although he received the best medical care he became bedridden. He was like this for almost one year. And every day Bouncy tapped his way up the street to be at his friend's bedside.

One night Sojie died. By morning the undertaker had removed the body and the bed lay stripped, and though everybody on the lane knew, no-one was brave enough to tell Bouncy. Not even his daughter.

So it was that at ten o'clock that morning, the mourners in Sojie's yard held their breaths when they heard the tapping of the cane on the pavement. Since the gate was wide open Bouncy didn't have to pause. He struggled to the top of the steps as usual, and if he found it strange that there were so many people in the yard, he did not show surprise.

There was an uneasy silence in the yard and in the front parlour as he approached the room. Suddenly one of Sojie's daughters whispered, "Is a sin. I going stop him." But her sister held her back. They waited, almost fearfully.

They said afterwards that some people at the other end of the lane heard the cry which wrenched Bouncy when he saw the naked bed.

"Mr. Fargo! Mr. Fargo!"

It was such a painful cry; such a lonely cry; such a heartbroken cry that even those who had felt no sadness before found themselves wiping their eyes. One over-bright youth, seeking to hide his own embarrassment, said aloud, "Mr. Far gone!" and was immediately cuffed on the head by two adults.

Bouncy sat in the chair by the empty bed for half a day until his daughter came for him.

The funeral was not held until a week later to allow family overseas to attend and during that week Bouncy did not say one word to anyone. Except for an occasional cup of tea, and water, he refused to take anything. His daughter worried that he too would shortly be in his grave. People told each other that when two people were so close for so long, often one could not live without the other.

On the day of the funeral, Bouncy got up early and bathed and dressed in his best suit. It took him a long time. His daughter was alarmed at how very weak he seemed to be. Nevertheless he would not allow her to help him. By ten o'clock he was dressed and ready, sitting in a chair by the front door as if he expected them to sneak off to the two o'clock funeral without him.

Unfortunately, the car his daughter had hired came late, so that when they arrived at the church, the lid of the coffin was already sealed and the first hymn was being sung.

The singing died momentarily as the tapping of Bouncy's walking stick was heard. People had been wondering why he was not there. He made his painful way up the aisle until he reached the family pew beside the coffin. One of the grandchildren got up and gave him a seat.

The service progressed unemotionally. Sojie had not been a churchgoer, but the minister was making an effort at giving the service some warmth for the benefit of the family who were members of his church. Nevertheless, it was a cold service. Sojie was an old man, eighty-one years of age, and he had been ill for a long time. Grief had petered out. Everybody was now intent only on doing things in the right way.

The minister, as is usual with ministers of this denomination, could not resist mentioning that Sojie had not been a churchgoer. Nonetheless he hoped that during Sojie's long illness he had used the time to reflect and repent and find the Lord so that his soul could go to Heaven. Somehow he managed to make it sound as if he had not.

It was at this point that Bouncy struggled to his feet, turned his back on the minister to face the congregation and with his arms uplifted like Moses delivering the commandments, his walking stick still in one hand, began to shout.

"Mr. Fargo deserve better than this! Mr. Fargo is dead! Nobody can't cry for him? Mr. Fargo gone!" He stretched out the word "gone" into a long wail.

"How many of you he feed and clothes when he was alive? Help you go to school? Pay your rent? Mr. Fargo dead and this is the best you can do for him!"

The minister left the pulpit and tried to lead him away but he resisted and created some confusion until his daughter came and led him to the back of the church where she sat beside him, holding his hand and patting his knee.

They sat until the service was over and the coffin and procession had left the church. Bouncy's daughter wanted to take him home but he became so agitated when she suggested this that she asked the driver to try to catch up with the entourage which had gone far ahead of them.

Easternside cemetery occupied a rocky hillside overlooking the harbour. The graves were dug close together and vaulted in tiers rising toward the sky. No room here for the elaborate marble headstones and miniature houses for the dead as in the old cemetery in the heart of the city. At Easternside, a simple marble slat gave name and dates; that was all.

But, what a magnificent view for those who came to mourn! Below lay the glistening waters of the sea – the exposed side, with its galloping white horses, separated from the calm deep blue of the harbour by the narrow strip of land leading to the airport. Sometimes a passing ship disappearing on the horizon, or an airplane negotiating with the wind as it rose into the clouds, claimed the attention of the mourners and caused them to forget for a moment the permanence of the farewell they had gathered to say.

The new graves were being dug on a particularly steep slope. Sojie's mourners had to pass two which were newly-dug, and mounds of earth spilled onto the narrow path leading to his grave. It was hard on the ladies whose dress-up shoes sank into the soft earth; it was difficult for the weak to negotiate the narrow lane between the graves and impossible for the elderly or anyone who had trouble walking or standing.

Some of the mourners stopped at the largest level path nearest to the grave, where, although they couldn't hear the minister's words, they could at least join in the singing. Those who couldn't risk attempting to get that close stayed in the cars or sat on the ledge at the edge of the driveway and enjoyed the scenery and the late afternoon hill breeze. This was where Bouncy's daughter left him while she went to visit her mother's grave on the other side of the hill. The walking stick did not make a tapping sound in the soft earth; it sank and had to be lifted carefully out of each hole it made. Nobody remembered seeing Bouncy get up off the ledge and nobody could work out how he climbed the steep slope leading to Sojie's grave.

The group of mourners on the level path first became aware of Bouncy when a small slide of earth he had dislodged fell near them. Startled, they looked up to see Bouncy making his way across earth precariously thrown against the hillside above one of the empty graves. They gasped and held their breaths, too surprised even to call out to him, for it seemed that, as with a sleepwalker, any attempt to thwart him might do more harm than good.

The larger group of mourners around the grave had their backs to him and were singing a hymn, unaware of his dangerous progress towards them. But then he reached a point where he could neither get any nearer, because there was a wide gap between the mound of earth and the concreted grave beside it, nor come down safely by descending the mound. The only safe way was to turn back the way he had come.

"Turn back! Turn back!" somebody shouted. Bouncy had no intention of turning back. By this time the mourners at the grave side had become aware of his presence. Singing stopped completely, everybody paralysed, looking up in horror, wondering what else he would try to do, until the minister sternly motioned to his assistant. "Help him to get across."

Two sturdy men climbed the bank and taking Bouncy by his arms carefully helped him to the graveside. Everybody sighed with relief, although some members of Sojie's family were annoyed at the drama he kept introducing into the service. But when the singing resumed, some eyes were wet with sympathy for Bouncy's loyalty and determination and because death is so painful for the living.

But still they did not appreciate the extent of Bouncy's grief. When the service came to the part where they said "ashes to ashes, and dust to dust", Bouncy threw his stick into the grave where it rattled with a strange, uncertain rhythm before settling on the coffin. Then he lifted his hand once more and cried out, "Mr. Fargo! Mr. Fargo!"

The cry rolled around the hillside and returned as an echo, louder than he had said it, as if thousands of the buried had picked it up and repeated it. Chills of fear spread through the mourners, helpless before such naked sorrow.

"Mr. Fargo was a good man!" he shouted again. And again the hillside echoed, "Good man! Good man!"

They finally understood his intention moments before he made the move to follow his walking stick into the grave. Then holding him firmly they escorted him back to the car and his daughter, who quickly took him away.

One week later, many of them returned to the site. Bouncy's daughter had been lucky to secure a grave almost above Sojie's. They felt that the two friends would rest in peace lying in death as they had gone through life, side by side.

## MAMA PALA

Mama Pala heard the noise as she turned the corner and knew that it was coming from her yard. The decibel of the shrieking was so high that she couldn't tell immediately if they were playing or fighting. Most likely they were fighting. No matter how she scolded, threatened or punished, the way they behaved, you would think they were hungry-belly dogs fighting over garbage-can scraps.

Mama Pala stopped to lean against a tree and gather her strength before facing her pack.

It was true, she thought, that they were sometimes hungry, but that wasn't the reason they were so difficult. They were so hot tempered, so bellicocious, that almost anything could excite a quarrel and a fight.

"See my mark dere. Ef you tink you bad, cross it."

Bif-baf – a heavy fist fight would break out as the challenged defiantly stepped across the mark.

"Mama Pala! Jam-jam use-off the water and epec me fi go a stan pipe go catch more. Mi nah go."

"Tek off mi one good pants. Is who tell you you can borrow it. Ole fief."

The quarrels and the fights stretched the yard from corner to corner often threatening to tear it apart.

Sometimes Mama Pala grew so tired of it, she would threaten to leave them if they didn't behave. This kept them quiet, for a while, for they knew that she was the only thing standing between them and destitution, and that though they were poor, she still did her best to provide shelter, food and clothing.

Part of the trouble was that she had too many children.

Fourteen of them.

Family Planning advice – two is better than too many – had come too late for her. Fourteen of them and no father supporting any of them. Some of the children now even had children of their own, crowding the yard which had once seemed so spacious, and all of them either too young, too lazy or unable to find any regular job to be able to help her.

Mama Pala sighed again as a fresh wave of noise from the yard reached her. She put down her basket, packed with food from the market, and went to sit on a large stone nearby. She needed time to think.

She shook her head as she watched Tit running up the road. He was always on the lookout for her and would run to meet her with the latest news from the yard.

His briefs, all that he wore, settled well below his bang-belly, barely covering what they were meant to conceal. "Tell Tale Tit" the others called him, nobody remembering that his real name was Trevor, after her uncle. She could always depend on him to tell her exactly what the others were up to, even though they cuffed him and reminded him what usually happened to "informers".

It was he who had first told her about Melita, the flouncy, long-haired girl, K.G. the big boy was fooling around.

Mama Pala frowned as she thought about Melita. Even before she met her she disliked her. The time she had spent in the yard as K.G.' s woman was the most disruptive Mama Pala could remember. By the time she left, the family was split up into different warring groups, making Mama Pala despair that she would ever be able to manage them again.

Melita constantly criticised everybody and everything the family did. She had lots of book-learning – so she said – and was always showing off with big words and strange ideas. She never got tired of trying to change the family's ways.

She said they were poor because they didn't cooperate with each other and pool their resources. She said Mama Pala should force the able ones to go out and work and force them to give her what they earned. Then she should decide how it should be spent for the good of the whole yard. Nobody was to make any decision or do anything without Mama Pala's consent. And she hinted sneakingly that if Mama Pala was too weak, then K. G. the eldest son should be the one to take charge. That K. G. was obviously too lazy to take on such a responsibility didn't bother her. What she really meant, Mama Pala knew, was that she, Melita, would have the upper hand.

Once Melita criticised Mary because she used her money to buy a pair of mid-calf boots at Ben-down Plaza. The price of the boots, Melita said, could have bought footwear for three of the children. She went further. She said Mary was stupid because she lived in a hot country and didn't need boots which were for people in cold countries to keep their feet warm. The ensuing vicious, high-powered cuss cuss strafed the yard like a M16 shoot out. Mary and Anne, the sister who helped to wear the boots, threatened to cut up Melita's "rassito" if she didn't stop "soaking" around them.

They stopped speaking to K. G..

Finally, Andrew, who had gone visiting in Melita's home parish, returned with a story of how poor Melita's family was, and how they had been glad when she left because she was such a boasty bitch and a troublemaker.

The family mocked Melita so cruelly after that, that she had to leave the yard. K.G. packed to go too, but when he realised that Melita expected him to go out to work to support her, he suddenly discovered that blood was thicker than anything else.

Mama Pala shook her head. In a way she had come to realise that Melita was right. The family needed to improve itself. They had been poor too long. So many things to which they had turned their hands had failed.

Take vegetables. She had given each child a piece of the yard in which to plant callaloo and pak choi and cho-cho, pepper and so on. But goats had eaten off the callaloo; the cho-cho had run away and borne over the neighbour's yard; and the extra water they had to carry was too much for the lazy ones so the rest of the things just dried up.

She had thought long and hard and had many discussions with the children and they had come to the conclusion that it was only people who did business, buying and selling like Miss Miriam, or shopkeeping like Mr. Zacca, or grew things like at Calm Pen, who made money and could live comfortably. They would go into chicken-farming.

But this business needed money to make a start. Even if they followed Melita's advice and "pooled their resources", they couldn't save enough to build the fowl pen, buy chickens, as well as feed for them, *and* the big trough to feed them out of, *and* the big water pan that let out just enough water at a time, like how it was set up at Calm Pen.

They would have to do it up properly, Mama Pala knew. That was the only way to make money. Enough feed and water and medicine and light so that the chickens could eat all night and grow fat quickly and be sold at six to eight weeks.

They needed capital, to use a word Melita had taught them.

The chicken company, which sponsored small growers, laughed at Mama Pala when she visited in the hope of getting them to start her off. They had laughed even harder when she told them where she lived and the size of the yard. They weren't into ghetto backyard business, they told her. Their growers produced by the thousands.

Mama Pala then decided that it was time she asked her relatives for help. She put on her best dress, a bright floral with a pink background, a pretty polyester that Cousin Ena had sent her from Merica. She tied her head with the matching scarf, put on her good shoes that burned her corn toe, and went to see Uncle Willie.

"Howdy, Mama Pala. Which breeze blow you this way? Don't see you for ages."

"Well, you know how it go, sar. Up an down an hard times an all. Still an all, all well. Thank God!"

"Hmm! So how the children? Big man and woman now?"

"In good health. Thank God again."

"You're looking well yourself. I hope them taking care of you. Most of them should be working by this."

"Well you know how it is, sar." Mama Pala hesitated. She didn't like the trend the conversation was taking. "Work is very hard to come by, especial as some of them never tek the learning so good, you know." Her voice was apologetic. "In fact," she continued, "is that I come to see you bout, sar. We get to fine out that we could help weself much better if we get a little start with some chicken. Raise chicken you know, bout six dozen or so to start with. So I come to see if you will len us the money to start up the little business."

"Hmm. How much?"

She told him.

He didn't say anything for a long while, but Mama Pala, accustomed to the slow pace of such negotiations, was patient.

Suddenly he called, "Mirella! Bring some lemonade for Mama Pala here. She walk far. She thirsty."

Mama Pala knit her brow. The lemonade was compensation. She wasn't going to get the money.

Sure enough as they neared the end of the drink, he began to explain that he didn't have any spare money. Some recent expenses, house repairs and so on. But Mama Pala was looking very good. She was so dressed up! In fact she was looking so prosperous he was sure she wouldn't have any trouble getting the loan. Did she have a credit union? Mama Pala shook her head. Well... Perhaps she should try Miss Gloria, their rich cousin in Spanish Town.

For the visit to Cousin Gloria, Mama Pala didn't dress up. She wore a clean, patched yard dress and her ordinary head-tie and sandals. She was ashamed to take the bus all the way to Spanish Town looking like this, but she had learned her lesson. If you went begging you had to look poor.

The housekeeper who answered the door put her in the kitchen to wait.

The visit was one humiliation after another. Cousin Gloria was on her way out and could only spare a few minutes. Cousin Gloria was amazed that Mama Pala had travelled all the way to Spanish Town looking so shabby.

Were things really that bad? Couldn't she find a decent dress to wear? And shoes to put on? That's what happened to people who were careless with themselves and had too many children and too many men. Cousin Gloria had a good time scolding Mama Pala. And what made her think that she was just going to take her good money and throw it away on Mama Pala and her brood?

Finally, when Mama Pala, humiliated beyond caution, was about to cuss-off Cousin Gloria and walk out, Cousin Gloria offered her the money. Half would be a gift. She was sure she wouldn't be repaid anyway, but she supposed she would get her reward in Heaven. The other half would be a loan. They would have to pay interest on this money even if they couldn't repay the principal for a while.

Cousin Gloria was worse than Melita. She twisted and turned Mama Pala upside down with some big words she couldn't understand. She gave instructions which had Mama Pala rubbing the patch in her skirt into a new hole.

Cousin Gloria talked about deposits and interest rates, profit margins and collateral, return on investments, sinking fund, cooperative joint ventures, wholesale purchases and selling price. She demanded that they keep a receipt book and something she called a ledger, which she would inspect quarterly. She would tell them what to do if they showed a deficit instead of a surplus. The only important thing was the bottom line she insisted. They would have to resist the urge to buy clothes and food and spree themselves out of the money until the business began to pay off. They would have to discipline themselves and she would send the accountant regularly to see that they toed the line. She wasn't about to throw away her hard-earned cash.

By the time Cousin Gloria talked herself out, Mama Pala was ready to flee empty-handed. But Cousin Gloria, well pleased with herself, went inside to write out a cheque. She explained that Mama Pala should lodge it in the bank nearest to her, for she would have to open an account so that the business could be run properly.

A weary-headed, confused Mama Pala left Cousin Gloria not feeling as grateful as she should. For one thing she didn't know what to do with the cheque. Should she wrap it up and put it in her bosom as she would do with real money? After all it was only a piece of paper with money words written on it. Would the pickpockets try to steal it? How would the bank know to give her the money?

She was sorry she had started this whole business. She wouldn't know how to do any of the things Cousin Gloria had talked about. The business would fail and Cousin Gloria would come in and start to rule over the family with her iron hand. She would have to ask Andrew, who had reached grade nine, to help her with this keeping of books and thing.

The people she knew did business daily by cash. They didn't write down in any book except for the shopkeeper when he gave goods on trust.

Mama Pala's head hurt as she thought about buying the lumber and nails and zinc and chickenwire and all the things they would need. Then they would buy the chickens and the feed from the Emporium down the road. Then when the chickens were fat probably the Emporium would buy them or they would send them to market on the bus. She wondered if Cousin Gloria would approve this plan.

Meanwhile, when she went to town next day, if the bank gave her the money from the cheque, she would buy some clothes for herself and the children and maybe pay down on the colour TV set they had wanted for so long. That would help to keep the wretches quiet. After all, Cousin Gloria had *given* her a part of the money, so she could do as she liked with that part and maybe the Emporium would trust her some of the things to build the fowl pen.

Mama Pala's racing thoughts slowed to a halt as Tit reached her and started belching out a long story about how badly they had behaved since she left.

Nobody would go for water so the dirty plates and clothes pile up; and nobody never sweep the yard; and there was no floor polish so the floor didn't clean; and they had started to play some games but the others eat-off the food; and they were quarrelling and fighting; Thomas did call Eliza big-batty bitch, an she tell him, him face favour frog; an... an... an...

## JACOB BUBBLES

I

The year that Jacob was born, it rained so generously during January and February that the sugarcane grew fat with water and it took twice as much to produce a hogshead of sugar, so the masters worked the slaves twice as hard and twice as many attempted to escape, only to be recaptured and severely punished as an example to the others.

Later that year the ratoons came out weak, just like the puny babies the slave women bore, and many fields had to be replanted before schedule and the masters, pressured by heavy debts and their colicky dispositions, turned into larger demons, whipping, swearing, maiming, and killing.

The owner backra on Jacob's plantation got sick and returned to England, leaving the slaves to the mercy of the overseer who drove them beyond endurance, for the more sugar they made, the more profits he could skim off into his own pockets.

Many of them died that year, and the backra swore at the miserable rascals for the finality of their escape and the depletion of hands; the slave trade had been abolished, the price of replacement was high, and the birthrate was low.

The year that Bubbles was born, the city fathers decided that they had had enough of Back-o-Wall, the shanty town which too many people thought was the womb of all the criminal activity in the city.

So they served eviction notices on the squatters. Everybody ignored them. Nobody believed the promises of modern, decent shelter to take the place of shanty town at prices that they could afford. And meanwhile? Where would they go? How would they live? When the bulldozers arrived to raze their makeshift shacks, they screamed and threatened and stoned and resisted. Some bullet wounds and one death later, they gave up in despair and left the bulldozers to do their work.

★

In Jacob's birth year, Na Pearl began to dream many strange dreams. On a Sunday evening, when her neighbours from the slave barracks gathered around her doorstep, too tired even to complete domestic chores, she would entertain them with her visionary stories.

"All a we was a live into a village. Not like this ya hell hole barracks we living in now. Everybody have him owna hut, nice nice, an de village surroun wid a fence mek outa de tall bamboo dem. An no backra no de deh; an no canepiece no de deh, an no slave no de deh. All a we plant out one big field wid coco an such de like an we feed we one anoder, nice nice. An in de middle a we village was one great big stool. It tall, it tall, it tall so tell! So das is only a giant coulda siddung pan it. It mek out a guango an carve pretty pretty like how Jabez can mek a tree trunk tell you a story.

"An a big tall king come fi siddung pan de stool. Him dress up! Plenty big gold chain roun him neck. Him have on a long hat mek outa fedda an it follow him like massa dress-up flyway coat tail. An a whole heap a people wid spear an such de like a follow him an all a dem dress up too. An him hol up him head so gran jus like when Benjie cock a crow, an so much man a follow him dat when dem come de groun jus a grumble "blooma bolucha, blooma tiga. Blooma bolucha, blooma tiga". Lord de dream sweet so till!"

"An when him siddung everybady start fi dance. All de young gal dem wid dem bubby outa door, a jump an a prance, an de man dem only have one piece a cloth cover dem private. An den de king get up an start fi dance too, an him mek one almighty leap, an same time de fedder hat drop off, braps, flat a grung. An de whole place get quiet an everybody frighten, for is death fi see de king bald head. An all a we jus a trimble, an me so frighten me jump up out a de sleep."

And the next Sunday:

"Me dream bout one hilltop, high, high up. But is more dan a hilltop. A really plenty little hill pon top a odder hill, till you ketch dis one. De hill top dem look like young gal bubby pinting straight up fore man start fi trouble har an pickney mek dem drop. An pon top a di high, high hilltop is a village same like de village me tell you bout las time. Everyting nice an clean up dere so, an we plant fi weself and everybody belly full an peaceful. An in de middle a de village is a stool fi de ruler fi siddung pan. Him is a very tall, good lookin man, black an shine, an him wear a hat mek outa yellow snake skin wid a tail a swish behin him neck back. An him call we togeder fi mek a proclamation an as him start fi tell we wha fi do, him two front teet drop out, an me so frighten, me wake up same time."

The third Sunday after Na Pearl started her dream telling, even more slaves gathered before her door, for word had spread and many were trying to interpret her dreams. Some thought that they promised better days, while others said they were just an old woman's foolishness. Others just liked to share the thought of the freedom in those dreams.

As they settled on the dirt to hear the current dream, the overseer backra and three drivers appeared. They whipped and scattered the crowd and Na Pearl was dragged off to be tied to the guango tree at the entrance to Hogsfield where everybody would see her in the morning. She contracted a bad cold from the exposure to the night dew and never recovered her strength. She died two months later.

★

In Bubbles' birth year, his father, who disowned him before he was born, and his uncle were both killed in a fight which started in a bar on Lindy Way. Bubbles' father, Papa Tee, and another man had a quarrel and Papa Tee had gone for his friends to help him discipline the man. When he returned the other man was waiting for him with his friends. When it was all over, Papa Tee, his brother Charlie and three from the other side were left face down in the dust. They said that this incident marked the beginning of gang warfare in the city when men and women had to stop walking alone for fear of ambush; when people began to exchange residences according to their loyalties, so that a whole community

would be one in defending itself against the enemy; when crossing
the border into enemy territory could mean one's death. It also
marked the beginning of the time when, if you were a young man
and hoped to survive in the ghetto, you had to get hold of a gun; and
target practice for young boys was more regular than attendance at
school.

In that same year Mother Osbourne got a vision one night and
left home to become a *warner* woman. Dressed up in a long white
robe with a red sash at the waist and a matching turban, she
warned up and down the streets of Kingston. She warned about
drought and she warned about flood. She warned about pesti-
lence and famine. But her favourite topic was the sea of blood
which would wash the streets of the city if the inhabitants did not
repent and turn to God.

They said that she was mad and her children tried to get her put
away, until the night she appeared at her daughter Ida's gate and
warned of the destruction about to visit the yard. The next night
Ida's manfriend came home and found her in the bed of another
man who lived in the yard. Before they could subdue him, he had
chopped up Ida and the man, and three other people. They left
Mother Osbourne alone after that and she continued to walk the
streets and warn the wicked city of hell and damnation and blood
running in the gullies like angry rivers.

★

The night that Jacob was born they say that his mother's screams
kept the slave quarters awake for several hours. They say her
screams could be heard all the way up at the Great House. The
nanas boiled woman piaba and thyme-leaf tea. They gave her
pennyroyal and strong-back to drink, but none of the potions
could ease the pain or hasten the birth. Jacob entered the world
as big as a three month old baby. In a world of puny infants who
often died at birth, the old people regarded his great size and his
lusty crying as an omen.

The backra's comment was: "Good breeding stock. Tell the
mother to give me more like that. Who's the father?"

But even as they approved of his size, they disapproved of his fearlessness. While the slave toddlers learned very early to move out of the way of the horses and mules of the masters as they came trotting by field or quarters, Jacob would stand up, eyes round with wonder, staring as though he were equal. It took several years of flicks from the masters' whips and scoldings by the women to teach him to turn aside or lower his eyes when the backras passed or spoke.

But though he bore the scars of their displeasure, they couldn't quite tame the sureness with which he walked, hotstepping and proud like the fantail peacocks in the backra's garden. Nor could they completely stunt his quick intelligence. The old women fed him with kon-konte, the dried plantain porridge he liked so much, and saved titbits from the pot specially for him, and looked at him and remembered Na Pearl's dreams.

The night Bubbles was born was the same night the bulldozers moved in on Back-o-Wall. His mother felt the first pains as she struggled to save her possessions: a stool and rickety table, a coal stove and a mattress. There was nobody to help her and no money for a taxi fare and by the time she reached the nearest police station to ask for help, it was already too late.

The sergeant on duty helped with the delivery and said with disgust that it was the third one that week. The lady constable who usually dealt with such matters was on leave, but all of them had basic training in midwifery because of the frequency with which the surrounding squatter communities needed this kind of help. So, although he knew what to do, Sergeant Brown was annoyed and the first thing Bubbles heard when he came into the world was the sergeant cursing, "These damn careless people who drop them pickney like cow." His mother named him Brown after the sergeant. Nobody knew Papa Tee's real name anyway.

A number of Back-o-Wall squatters gathered their scattered pieces of board and zinc and hastily put together shelters in the old part of the city cemetery; the living retrieving space from the dead. It was to one of these shacks that Bubbles went home after he was born. A male acquaintance of his mother, Manatee, had offered her a cotch with him. His previous woman had gone back to her country home rather than "tek box from duppy" in the cemetery. By the time his brother was born eleven months later, Bubbles was learning to walk from tombstone to tombstone. He lived off the generosity of neighbours during his mother's brief absence; Manatee would not care for him; he was not his child. They called him Bubbles because he would amuse himself for hours by blowing bubbles with his spittle. Nobody had any dreams for him.

II

Jacob liked the feeling of danger he got from dangling his legs beneath the dray as it dipped and rose and clattered over the rocky surface, flattened grass or lumpy bare earth of the narrow road. It took skill to know when to pull up his legs to prevent his toes from being scraped.

The girl Miriam had gone to sleep. At first she had leaned against him until he shifted her body away and rested her head on one of the sacks. Asleep, she looked even more mawga, almost as bad as the skin and bone puppies he had seen wandering in the streets of Falmouth. She said that she had not had the flux, but even though it had nearly killed him, he was much bigger and stronger. He could not believe that she was eleven years old as the auctioneer had announced.

He had seen her once before on the plantation when her mother had brought her from the great house where they lived to visit with the old nana in the barracks. She had attracted a lot of attention and admiration because of her long wavy hair and smooth brown skin. Jacob had not liked her. She was only a puny girl who worked in Massa's kitchen. The girls who worked in the second gang with him were strong and playful and when the driver wasn't looking it was always possible to play brief games of hide and seek in the tall cane or to feel up their femaleness when they allowed it.

On top of everything she was a cry baby. Ever since the new bacra had bought them and left them in the care of the man driving the cart, she had not stopped crying. When he tried to talk to her, she only shook her head as if she was dumb.

He too was feeling sad at the breakup of their old life; and he too was fearful of the new life waiting for them on the new plantation. Femus, the driver, had told them that it was a coffee plantation called Mount Plenty.

Cross at being saddled with the newcomers as well as his other duties of collecting and loading the dray with tools and barrels and sacks of produce for the plantation, Femus had wondered aloud about what the Massa was going to do with the "lil kench a gal pickney, and the ole fowl", meaning the old woman who had been thrown in to make a bargain sale of eighty pounds for the three.

They had been travelling for a long time. When they left Falmouth, the sun was high in the sky; not long after the noon break, Jacob thought. Now the sun was almost down; about the time when the second gang would have been collecting machetes and hoes to bring back grass to the pens and finishing their daily routine before the land grew black.

Jacob hoped that the new plantation was not far away. He did not like the night, especially in a strange country.

Abruptly, Femus began to shout, "Whoa! Whoa!" and to pull up the mules. The dray came to a halt. He jumped down and steered the mules into a large grassy clearing beside the road. The girl and the woman woke up and they all came off and stretched.

"We a stop little fi res de mule dem and eat sinting," Femus announced.

"Please, sar," Jacob said, minding his manners to his elders as he had been taught. "We is close?"

"Close nuff," was the unaccommodating reply.

"Me wan pee pee," the girl said timidly. The woman took her hand and they went off into the bushes.

Femus went to relieve himself against a tree, and Jacob did the same close by.

"Night gwine ketch we?"

"What a bwoy fi chat! You nyam fowl batty? When we ketch, we ketch."

Femus took a large enamel carrier off the dray. From it he extracted a couple of boiled dumplings and pieces of yam. He shared the food onto the leaves of the nearby trumpet tree and passed it around. The food was not fresh, but Jacob ate greedily. The girl took only a few bites from a dumpling and the old woman nothing at all. She asked for some water and Femus pointed to a covered jar and a tin cup.

"The wuk hard, Mass Femus?" Jacob asked. He was curious about life on a coffee plantation, never having seen anything else but sugarcane.

"No wuk?" Femus answered gruffly. "You ever hear say wuk no hard?"

"Come bwoy," Femus said when he had finished eating. "Help me set up the lantern. Night a come, an me na stop again."

Jacob did as he was instructed. As they were about to move off he shouted, "Wait little, Mass Femus! Mek a pick two guava." He dashed off into the nearby cluster of trees and returned shortly with two green fruit.

"Me couldn't see no more and them pan grung a rotten."

"Lawd bwoy!" the old woman exclaimed, suddenly excited. "You no know say you no fi pick sinthing affa tree a night! Dash it way, less the tree duppy a go follow we!"

"Stupidness!" Femus sucked his teeth.

"Dash it way!" she insisted.

"Oonu hurry up," Femus said impatiently, pulling at the reins. The mules began to move off slowly.

The woman sounded so frightened and was so insistent that Jacob reluctantly threw the fruits back into the bushes.

"You fi spin roun tree time and say, "Ask pardin! Me no wa none!"."

Jacob sucked his teeth and jumped on to the moving dray.

"Tree duppy a go follow you," the old woman warned. "You an all you generation. Bad luck all you days," she ended as if saying a benediction.

They rode on into the darkness, lit only by the lantern swaying at the rear of the cart and the kitchen bitch near the driver. Sometimes they had to dismount to lighten the load for the mules in places where it was particularly steep or the road too difficult. In spite of his bravado, Jacob was glad when Miriam sought his hand to keep company in the darkness as they hustled to keep up with the dray. At such times the old woman clutched an old torn-up blanket over her head and shoulders to keep off the night air and ignored them.

Eventually, far into the night, they made out lights on a hill and knew that they were near the end of the journey.

Femus asked them to dismount again, then he hooted twice, so loudly and unexpectedly that his passengers shivered with fright. Their fright increased as he was answered first by one then another voice, the shouts echoing eerily through the night. Two figures appeared out of the darkness and walked beside the mules as they climbed the steep hill towards the great house. Midway, they stopped beside a building, and by the light of the kitchen bitches, unloaded most of the sacks and barrels.

"Tell Busha me come, an Massa buy tree new one," Femus said and signalled the weary trio to follow him.

Years later, when he remembered that night, Jacob would wonder why he had been so frightened.

The plantation was a new one, just settling into the rhythm of growing coffee. Until their numbers increased, the twenty slaves, including Jacob, cleared the land, planted the fields, tended the nurseries, collected sand and clay for making buildings, made lime kilns, cut wood, tended the animals and worked at all the jobs necessary to establish a plantation.

They were fortunate to have a conscientious and compassionate owner, unusual in those harsh times. There were few whippings on his estate and he kept in check the wanton cruelty which came so easily to the other white men on the estate.

Very early, Jacob showed a liking and aptitude for mason work, so, as the slave population on the estate grew, he was allowed to develop this skill under the tuition of the head mason, himself a slave, an intelligent man, skilled in his craft.

Now, as he moved about the plantation with the freedom granted those with special skills, Jacob felt a sense of pride in the many buildings which he had helped to erect. There was the mill house which had given them so much trouble: the cisterns to catch water, the channels into the mill house; the first drying platform and the barbecue which had crumbled under the first heavy rains. They had discovered then that the gravel stones they had used were too soft and therefore wrong for that kind of structure. So much of their building had been trial and error, a constant struggle of discovery and invention. Jacob had also helped to erect the cut-stone foundation to the great house, only recently completed.

It was while he was working on the great house that he had met Miriam again, grown, but still frail with a perpetually sad face beautifully framed by the long braids twisted around her head.

He had been working on the foundations for a week before he spoke to her. In fact she'd looked so aloof that he might not have had the courage to speak, had she not, one day, in a very impersonal manner, brought him a duckunoo wrapped in its banana leaf, resting in a small packi.

"Mama Leah sey fi gi you dis an she say if you like it she have more."

Like ducknoo! he thought with amusement, and his mouth watered for a bite, but he merely nodded his thanks and told her to put the packi on a pile of nearby stones.

"Hi massa!" the headman teased him. "Smady ready fi start carry straw!"

Miriam rubbed one foot against the other nervously as she delivered her message to the older slave.

"Mama Leah say fi tell you say she leave sinting up a kitchen fi you, sar. She say you fi come fi it."

They all understood. Mama Leah was looking with favour on Jacob for Miriam. She wanted to discuss the matter with the man in charge of him.

Mama Leah had mothered Miriam from the moment she had arrived at the plantation. She had protected the girl from the attentions of both white and black men by keeping her almost hidden in the kitchen and under her eye all the time. The girl's frailty worried her. Since she wasn't sure how much longer she could continue to hide her, she had looked around and chosen a protector in Jacob. The next day Miriam turned up at the mid morning break with a carrier of food.

"Nice!" Jacob said, licking his fingers free of pork fat. She had stood patiently waiting for him to finish so she could retrieve the carrier.

"A you cook?"

Miriam shook her head. "Mama Leah say me fi tell you say a me cook, but me can't cook so good yet."

Jacob nearly laughed out loud at her awkwardness. Her lack of guile was quite unlike the easy flirtatious ways of the other girls on the plantation. To him they appeared saucy, teasing, daring, tempting: easily available. Miriam seemed special.

But in spite of his youth, flesh was not the most important thing to Jacob just then. Like all the other slaves, he hated his bondage even though his skills earned him more leniency than others – he was even sent to work on neighbouring estates. The last time he had done this he had been given two shillings to keep. At the back of his head was the idea of buying himself from his master. The more he thought about freedom the more he liked the idea. As a mason he could earn enough money to live comfortably. So the older ones said. It would take him a very long time to get enough money, but he was determined to do it.

Then there was the satisfaction of building things: watching lime and stone and clay and dirt come together under his hands to form sturdy, useful structures, like the stone wall which he had helped to erect to protect the long steep driveway to the great house.

And he had a dream. He ached to be able to talk to the busha about it, or if he was very, very lucky, to the owner bacra himself. He wanted to plan and build a stone bridge across the river which ran through the main road on the property, and which was often impassable for long stretches during the rainy season. The bridges they had erected out of planks and iron had never lasted more than two seasons. Jacob was convinced that only one of stone and mortar, reinforced with bricks, could be strong enough to withstand the flooded river.

Shortly before his work on the great house ended, Mama Leah summoned him one evening.

"You like the food Miriam give you?"

He nodded.

"She cook good. Nearly good like me," she said with a smile.

He nodded again, not revealing that Miriam had already confessed.

"She a nice gal. Nobody no touch har yet. But that no gwine las. Me anxious fi smady good tek her."

Jacob said nothing.

"Well?"

"Yes mam," he said stupidly.

"Whey you a go do?" Mama Leah asked impatiently. "She good an obedient. You is a strapping, good-looking prosperous young man an you na keep smady. Me talk to Massa aready."

Jacob waited for Miriam until she had finished her kitchen duties.

They walked out for two weeks before he took her to his hut. But the first time, awed by her frail beauty and innocence so different from the women he had known, he could do nothing with her. When the consummation finally occurred, he entered her with the knowledge that she was very special and that he would kill for her if necessary.

One rainy season, the busha, in a rash moment, tried to cross the river when it was in spate and nearly drowned. The owner backra, who was in England, sent out a man who was said to be a great bridge builder. He was very tall, very thin and very pale with hair so blonde he was quickly nicknamed "the duppy backra".

Animosity flared between himself and the mason gang from the beginning. In the absence of the owner he began to introduce punishments hitherto unknown on that plantation. He was especially venomous against Jacob who had unwisely criticised his plan to build yet another wooden bridge. The fact that the bridge did not survive the first rainy season made the bridge-builder's temper even worse. The owner backra sent instructions for a stone and mortar bridge and, knowing little about local materials, the duppy backra had to rely on the local gang's experience. Jacob saw a few of his ideas put to use.

One day Jacob was scouting the property for stones of the particular kind they needed. He was almost at the edge of the property where it joined the hilly forest land when he heard "pst! pst!" He peered into the bushes but saw no one. He dismounted and stood beside the mule, puzzled.

Suddenly two men appeared beside him. He hadn't heard them approaching. Two short, black men. Maroons, he thought immediately. He was a little afraid of them. They got money for capturing and returning runaway slaves according to their treaty with the white men. Not that he was a runaway, but he had heard many bad things about them.

"You a run way?"

Jacob was annoyed. "How me fi a run way wid de Backra mule? Me is a mason. Me a look fi stone."

To his surprise they were able to tell him that he would find the kinds of stones he described in an old river bed "We coulda use a mason up so," one of them said.

"But onoo suppose fi ketch runway," Jacob answered in surprise.

"That a fi we business. Tink bout it. Up so you free!"

From that day Jacob's life became a torment between the urge for freedom, the desire to see the bridge finished, and caring about Miriam, for the maroons had made it clear that he could not bring his woman. He tried not to think what would happen to her if he ran away. She would be punished for his escape, he knew. What form that punishment would now take, made him break out into cold sweat.

On the other hand, if he were free, perhaps he could convince the maroons to allow him to rescue her, especially if they liked his work.

Many times he met the two maroons at the foot of the hill. They became his friends, sharing their jerk pork, spicier and sweeter than anything Jacob had ever tasted, and the coffee which he had started to steal for them. They talked so much about freedom and the deeds of the maroons and how a man could be a man up in the mountains that sometimes Jacob could hardly swallow, but still he could not make up his mind.

Eventually the decision was made for him. One day he met his friends at the edge of the forest, as usual. They were talking when suddenly the two men vanished. One moment he was talking to them, the next they weren't there. Jacob looked about him in bewilderment. It was a few minutes before the approach of the duppy backra on horseback made him realise why they had disappeared. Jacob was accused of plotting to run away and whipped all the way back to the busha's house. He was flogged till there was no more skin on his back, and in an almost unconscious state tied to a tree for all to see his disgrace. But that night, even as Miriam shivered and wept for him in their hut, his maroon friends came for him.

### III

Bubbles was a puny child; undernourished, bang-bellied, nose running from a constant cold; miserable in the early years before he learned to fend for himself. At ten, he could barely pass for seven or eight.

He had smooth mid-brown skin and Papa Tee's naturally jherri-curled, really black hair; the kind of person they call "coolie royal"; and though his mother and the women in the graveyard loved him for his pretty looks and his air of helplessness, their struggles to keep life going for themselves and other numerous offspring meant that there was little that they could do for him.

His pretty face helped when he went begging downtown, mostly outside restaurants. Which woman leaving the dining room satiated with a company or man-paid-for meal could resist the appeal in those large eyes?

Every year he was enrolled in the primary school, but he rarely attended for more than six weeks in a year. He had no shoes, no clothes, no money to buy lunch. In any case, he hated school. Nobody insisted that he attend.

Instead of school he spent his time swimming with other unclaimed urchins in the warm currents released into the harbour from the power station. One summer, when he was twelve years old, he attended a special camp for underprivileged boys like himself where he learned the rudiments of reading and writing and the beginnings of an exciting theory which taught him that all men were brothers, equal under the law and entitled to a fair share of all the world's wealth; that he was a unit of labour and therefore of immense value to the state. He was given a whole set of rights which he had never thought about. It was intriguing but it didn't change anything for him, and when the boys were invited to enrol for evening classes, he lost interest.

Besides, ·it was time for him to join his community gang. Feared throughout the city, the gang known as Suckdust made sure that all males, twelve and over, living in the Coalyard area were fully committed and knew how to protect themselves and the community. It was the only way to survive. The more enterprising youths were chosen as official members of the gang.

At fourteen, after months of clandestine practice, Bubbles could handle a "dog" or a beretta or any of the small weapons which fell into his hands better than the police with their formal training. He had two ambitions: to own a gun, and to get his hands on an M16, the king of the underground weapons, but his gang had only two of these and only the top ranking could touch them.

At fourteen he left his graveyard home for good after a fight one night with his stepfather, Manatee, who had just given his mother another beating. Bubbles hated this man who kept everyone around him in constant fear of his temper, threats and assaults.

One night, while carrying ganja to a ship outside the harbour, some members of the gang came across an abandoned canoe. When they examined it they found that it was half full of a variety of hand guns and paint cans full of bullets. Somebody had either missed or was late for a rendezvous. The windfall was later distributed to everyone's satisfaction. The event sparked a whole week of celebration.

It was during this week that Bubbles, armed with his new strength, went to visit his mother. She was sitting on a tree stump in the yard and tried to hide her face when she saw him coming.

"A the dutty man do you so?" he asked angrily, when he saw the bruises on her arms and her swollen face.

"Is all right," she said. "No bother."

"Whey him de?"

She didn't answer. Her eyes showed her fright. "You ongle gwine mek it worse," she pleaded with him.

"Dutty man!" he shouted. "Whey you is! Come out an face real man if you bad! Is the las time you beat har up."

"Lawd Jesus!" his mother exclaimed when she saw the gun in his hand. "No, Bubbles. No!" she begged. "Bubbles! Bubbles!"

"Dutty man!" he shouted again, ignoring her. He fired a shot into the flimsy wood of the door.

The noise attracted several people, so there were many who saw Manatee emerge from his doorway, a sharp machete in his hand.

"Because you get gun you tink say me fraid a you? You stinking little pissin tail bwoy! You a go dead bad, jus like you puppa. A who you a call dutty man?"

He rushed towards Bubbles, machete raised to chop, but never had time even to feel the three bullets which ended his life.

The police arrested Bubbles. No witness came forward so there was no real case against him. If you wanted to continue living in Coalyard, if you wanted to continue living, you didn't see most of the things that happened. However, the judge sent him to reform school. He was still under legal age, and there was widespread alarm in the country at the growing violence and the involvement of young boys in criminal activity. Bubbles stayed at the school for two days, mostly out of curiosity.

Coalyard covered several acres in the northern section of the city. As well as the coalyard from which the area got its name, it included the city's main burial ground, which gave its protectors the alternate name of "Duppy Gang".

People said that the coal yard had been selling wood and coal, produce and small stock since the days of slavery. But, with the increasing popularity of kerosene stoves, and the emergence of other more comfortable markets, the actual area used for these purposes had shrunken. The drays and donkey carts laden with crocus bags of coal no longer came in from the country parts; people no longer came with their paper bags to buy a chamber pot of coal; the trucks of goats and pigs appeared only at Christmas time now. Only the sooty residue of coal now reminded of its former use.

On the side furthest away from the cemetery, Coalyard shared a road boundary with another ghetto community known as Slow Town. Nobody knew why it had this name. In an area of extremely scarce resources but numerous people, a natural rivalry had sprung up between the two communities. Perhaps it had started when they both shared the single standpipe which had been situated on the boundary line before the authorities put in a network of standpipes to serve the fast-growing communities. Perhaps it had started when people from Slow Town got more of the jobs when the slum upgrading and road-building projects began. Slow Town had supported the party which was then in power. Slow Town's gang was known as Superduper Posse.

By the time Bubbles was nineteen, he was deputy leader of the Suckdust gang. Police bullets and ambushes by other gangs reduced leaders rapidly. If one was competent and ambitious, one could quickly achieve authority.

That was the year when a police bullet ripped through his groin while he was on a mission one night. The doctors patched him up so that he was able to pass water, but Bubbles had lost his balls.

For technical reasons, the court dismissed all the charges brought against him. Bubbles went a little crazy after he was freed. If you wanted a quick death, all you had to do was to hint that he had been emasculated. Two policemen paid for his loss with their lives. A few people who uttered the word eunuch in his presence disappeared. A dance in another community was shot up because Bubbles heard that people there were calling Suckdust the "ballsless posse". Everybody walked in fear of Bubbles. He was angry, fast and never missed.

Finally, the leader of Suckdust ordered him eliminated. He was too crazy. He was drawing too much official attention to the area. Bubbles heard about the order and went straight to the leader's yard, called him out and beat him to the draw. Nobody disputed his right to succeed. You had to respect a man so fearless.

After that he calmed down a little. The claims of leadership were too demanding for craziness if he was to survive. A little of the desire for revenge had been satisfied, but the bitterness never left him.

As time passed, Bubbles created a small court around himself. For his personal protection he had with him only one man, a friend from childhood whom he trusted. No other adult male lived in his compound. Five women and their dependents lived in various units in the yard. They cooked and washed and carried out other domestic chores for him. It was whispered, very softly, that he had paid two of them to name him as their "baby father". They were also his watchmen and his spies, keepers of bullets and concealers of ganja, guns and stolen goods when the police chose to raid the area. They were well taken care of.

The rest of the community protected him too, for he came to be regarded as a fair leader provided you didn't cross him. He was generous with money, particularly to women in need. They said he had a soft spot for women and would be very hard on any of his men who abused women in Coalyard. Growing in wisdom as a leader, he did not, however, chastise them for abuses outside the community, but it was known that he disapproved of wanton cruelty to women and legend had it that if Bubbles was present on a mission, women would not be molested.

He was also a good negotiator with the community's political bosses, and since the party which Suckdust supported was now in power, he was able to get improvements like a community centre for the youths, equipment for sports and additional standpipes. His growing notoriety in the city as a marksman, feared alike by enemy and authority, also gave the community reason to be proud. No other gang dared touch anyone from Coalyard without expecting quick reprisal. Coalyard respected him as much as it feared him. It was proud of him inasmuch as it wished for peace.

One morning, getting up late as was his custom, Bubbles was greeted by the news that one of his informants wanted to see him.

"What!" he exclaimed when he heard the news. "Man if a joke you a joke, you know say me no like them kinda joke!"

"But is true, Bubbles," the informant protested, and hastened to fill in the details.

"Superduper go pan a mission las night cross the waters. But them run ina one patrol, two jeep; an the police an soldier bwoy dem clap dem. Hotfoot dead. You know him sista, the one dem call Pantyhose, whey always a falla dem bout the place? Well, a she lead dem outa the trap for she know de place good. Dem say a she tun back an lif the M16 affa Hotfoot body. Dis morning dem have a meeting an she still a hol on pon the sixteen an fore dem know what a' clock a strike, Pantyhose a de leader!"

"Rahtid!" Bubbles exploded. "Then we no gwine have fi change them name to Panty Posse!"

He was amused but also insulted. The ghetto gangs were tough. Many people had been outraged that Hotfoot had allowed Pantyhose to run with the gang so freely. She was said to be tough too but she was still a woman. She was Hotfoot's half-sister and they said that he had been sweet on her from they were small, but to allow her such liberties! She had sometimes been used as a decoy and distraction for the posse's activities, but to be gang leader! Impossible! That wouldn't last long, Bubbles thought.

Bubbles sat over his late morning breakfast of fried dumplings and callaloo washed down with beer and thought about this twist.

"Hold a Stripe, no," he invited the bearer of the news. "So, how them man tek it?"

"Some a dem a screw, but a she hol de sixteen an dem say she know how fi use it. Hotfoot did teach her every ting."

"So whey Quicksilver? Me woulda think a him woulda turn chief."

"The police bwoy dem hol him. Him in a KPH. Dem say him well bad. Dem shoot him an Tie-tongue and Lesley."

"Rahtid! Is a big haul that! Rahtid!" he said again. "The police bwoy them must be feel good enh!"

He thought for a while. "So, Slow Town man them unda panty rule. Raas!" He stretched out the exclamation into a laugh.

He leaned over his now empty plate stroking his chin and thinking hard. His face would not grow a beard, only a few strands of hair which he kept shaved. The clean face had served him well on occasion. Who would suspect a nice, clean-faced, coolie-royal man in a crisp three-piece suit of intention to rob a bank?

He was picking his teeth with a matchstick when he heard a slight commotion at his gate. He was curious but knew that the women would deal with the situation and tell him what he needed to know.

Soon one of them approached with the news that Panty hose had sent a message.

"She wan talk to you," a slightly out-of-breath youth who was with the woman explained.

"Say what?"

"She de pan fi dem side a No Man's Lan, say she want a meeting."

"Who wid her?"

"Bout four man. Police lash dem las night."

"Raas! Tell her me soon come."

For some time an uneasy truce had existed between Suckdust and Superduper for the practical reason that both Coalyard and Slow Town shared the same entrance from the main road into their communities – the road and the roundabout now called No Man's Land. During previous war times between them barricades had been erected blocking the roads which gave direct access to the communities and a line of shacks burnt out so that the boundary was very clear. Either side caught lingering in this area was regarded as the legitimate target of a mugging, rape or shooting.

Gradually, however, they came to realise that the hostilities not only cut them off from each other, but from services which they needed. A broken main needed to be fixed, the fire brigade needed access, food needed to be delivered, midwives needed to deliver babies, but nobody of sound mind, no taxi, no bus, not even a handcart man would voluntarily enter the area, so they had had a formal meeting and called a truce. Violence in the immediate communities got less; the barricades were removed, and they turned their destructive energies against other enemies. People from either side were still cautious when using No Man's Land, but at least they could do so without being used for instant target practice.

Bubbles took his time about putting on his shirt and his Clarke's booty. He was not about to allow a woman to take the lead in any negotiations, so he deliberately dawdled for nearly an hour. When he thought that enough time had passed for Pantyhose to get the message, he chose five of his men to accompany him. They checked their guns before leaving, uneasy diplomats going to a hostile conference. Not that they expected any direct hostility, but they had heard that Pantyhose was still wearing the M16.

Protocol demanded that Bubbles wear his too. He also gave his bodyguard one of the other M16s that his gang possessed. It helped to show the superior strength of his armoury. The Superduper Posse was known to have only one. Perhaps that was why Pantyhose had risked her life to rescue it from the police. Bubbles knew that Superduper's arsenal consisted only of 45s and some 22s and some homemade items from bicycle parts. He had mainly handguns too, but he had six more M16s broken down in a trunk hidden in an old latrine in his yard. This was not the time for them to be used. To bring them out would attract too much attention. The security patrols would step up their harassment.

Bubbles walked down his street toward the meeting ground.

Behind him were his deputies and a crowd of the curious who knew that they had to keep a respectful distance.

The gangs would meet in the dusty roundabout which separated the road into their two communities. They didn't need to fear the patrols for the various itinerant sellers of food, cigarettes and other commodities on the sidewalks for a mile in either direction would pass on the word of any approaching problem in time for them to cover themselves.

"You call me?" Bubbles shouted to Pantyhose who was waiting in the shade of a duppy cherry tree on Slow Town's side of the road.

"We can talk?" she replied using the rifle to point to the island in the roundabout.

Bubbles noted that Pantyhose carried the rifle with the ease of familiarity and immediately felt a grudging respect for her. She was dressed in the dark green fatigues which was standard night mission costume for the gangs. It confused people. Made them think that they were soldiers.

She was sweating freely in the hot midday sun. Her shirt was torn at the tail and Bubbles saw blood stains on her right shoulder. He realised that she had not changed since the gang's disaster the previous night; that in true leadership fashion she was organising her posse, putting them back together on some path before allowing herself any rest, and his respect grew. Her eyes were red. He wondered if she had been crying for Hotfoot. His death must be hard for her, Bubbles thought.

"So what happen?" he said when they faced each other. He was deliberately, insultingly casual, his curiosity concealed behind his dark sunshades.

"Me know say you hear already say that the raas claat police and soldier bwoy them kill Hotfoot last night."

She was a strapping woman in her early twenties, not fat, but big-boned and at least three inches taller than Bubbles.

"So?"

"Three man ina KPH, an three missing."

"So?" he asked again.

"Me jus wan tell unoo, official like, say that we have a meeting this morning an from now on a me a rule."

"You a mek joke!" Bubbles said with a laugh.

"No. Me well serious. An don't think say that because me is a woman the posse get sof. We badder than ever." She adjusted the shoulder strap of the M16 as if to prove her point. "Me did jus wan fi tell oonu meself, so every body know what's what."

She moved away as if to depart, then turned back swiftly to face Bubbles again.

"An a nex thing. Me know say oonu gwine want fi call we Panty Posse, Pussy Posse and all them kind a name deh. Me know how oonu man think, but no bother with that. Seen? The man them na go like it. Me name is Inez. Memba that. Figet bout the Pantyhose business. The posse still name Superduper. Me na call oonu Duppy Gang."

Bubbles stared at her, one hand casually on his rifle, the other stroking his chin.

"That's all?" he asked as if surprised. He was in fact a little puzzled. He had thought that she might have summoned him to ask for help. Instead, here she was issuing a challenge.

"Enh, enh! Jus memba say me can shoot better than all a oonu put together. A Hotfoot teach me an him was the bes."

Again Bubbles felt growing respect for her. There was no hint of sadness in her voice when she mentioned Hotfoot.

She pulled herself up appearing even taller than she really was and turned away to be followed by her scowling lieutenants.

Bubbles also turned around. Scratching his head he said to his men, "Oonu hear the lady!"

They all laughed loudly and started walking towards home. But before Pantyhose was fully out of hearing, someone in Bubbles' crowd shouted, "Go way! Panty Posse!"

There was an instant reply of four shots. Suckdust's followers scattered, hugging zinc fences or lying on the ground. All except Bubbles and his immediate party. They knew that there was no real danger; that the Panty Posse had fired in the air; a warning only.

"Cease! No bother!" Bubbles restrained his followers. It was a minor incident, not worth a waste of bullets.

The uneasy truce might have held while people waited to see how the Panty Posse developed – in spite of her warning, that was the name that stuck – but suddenly the party in power announced elections and the political bosses called for serious action from both gangs. Coalyard and Slow Town were one voting district and heavily populated. Both parties wanted all the votes possible, but the area was unpredictable. The side which could intimidate most usually decided victory.

"Mek sure the votes swing my way," both gangs were told by their faceless bosses. "Anybody not fi we, can't stay."

Pantyhose laid the first ambush. Some Coalyard youths returning from a dance hall session and moving carelessly through No Man's Land were shot at. The only casualty was a finger on the right hand of one of the youths. It was an announcement rather than a killing spree.

The barricades at the entrances to both communities went up immediately: old tyres; a twisted rusted bus chassis; tree stumps; the only way to enter was by a slow climb if not given passage by the watchmen. Footpaths at scattered points of the areas were the only other entrances. The audacity of the ambush shook Bubbles. The following night two shops in Slow Town were the target of gasoline bombs thrown by a daredevil rider on a Honda 750 who couldn't be stopped. The fire brigade turned back when it met the barricade.

Next two girls from Coalyard were raped by ten men.

All of Suckdust's M16s were brought out for that reply. A dance was raided: two dead, several wounded.

People began to move out in fear of their lives, but now the order came "Nobody is to move". Too many moves meant lost votes. The gangs began to threaten those who wanted to move. The really timid and desperate left everything behind and ran away. The bosses were not happy. The gun population increased. Fear spread beyond Coalyard and Slow Town as the increased supply of guns began to be used all over the country for purposes other than political intimidation.

The really big explosion came on the night that some Slow Town men and women were at the cinema which served both communities. They had taken to going to the cinema on alternate nights.

The show was a horror movie about monsters from space eating up earth people. Three youths hoping for a free show climbed the wall at the back of the premises and followed a well-worn path across the ceiling where a large hole allowed easy viewing. The ceiling tiles, weakened by many such excursions, chose that night to give way, depositing the three on the heads of the frightened patrons. Their descent showed up grotesquely as large shadows on the screen as they passed through the projector's beam, adding to the audience's terror.

In a minute the Slow Town inhabitants were breaking down the exits and running for their lives. Instinctively they ran towards the nearest entrance to home and safety – No Man's Land. Sanity, however, returned when they remembered the danger of using that road, especially at night.

It was while they were milling around, some fifty-odd of them, embarrassed but trying to discover what had happened in the cinema, that the only plausible explanation began to take shape. There was instant anger when they confirmed for each other that the incident in the cinema was really an attack by Suckdust.

Anger grew as they discussed the matter. A quick decision was reached; several figures melted into the darkness. The rest turned away to take the longer route through the footpaths which led home.

Suddenly the darkness was lit by several burning shacks and cries of alarm spread through Coalyard. Then the guns started playing question and answer games; sweeping for targets, dollying in crazy bursts of excitement.

Flames shot up in Slow Town. The combustion was so great that many people outside the area feared that the whole city was on fire. The police and the army were brought in to try to get the fire engines through the constant sniper activity which kept them out.

They could not pass the barricades. Even the security helicopter, with its bright searchlight hovering to help the ground troops, was ineffective; whenever it came too close, the M16s were turned against it. It was a warning to the authorities. This was their fight. They wanted no interference.

Nobody ever knew the full count of those killed that night. Next day the combined police and military patrols removed five bodies off the streets and out of the burnt-out buildings. There was speculation that some were given secret burials. The police carried out a thorough search of the unburnt buildings, took some people off to jail, beat up others, discovered small amounts of ammunition, but were unable to pacify the area.

As news of the war spread throughout the city, as the strength of the gun power became known, as the impotence of the authorities to contain the battle and its companion criminal activity was discussed, public opinion became so strident that even the faceless bosses became afraid. The monsters they had created had emancipated themselves. Orders were given to contain the gangs. They had outlived their usefulness once they could not be controlled.

While Coalyard mourned and Slow Town wept over their dead, a permanent patrol of soldiers and police was installed in a tent on the roundabout's island.

Bubbles was humiliated. He had led his gang through a previous election and there had been nothing as vicious as this. Superduper had not had such firing power and Suckdust had been largely unchallenged.

But this Pantyhose woman was deadly. She was determined to prove herself better than any man. That his gang should be held in check by one led by a woman! It was unthinkable. The hitherto cringing men of the Pantyhose Gang were now holding up their heads and boasting. Now it was Suckdust who walked around on the defensive.

Bubbles thought hard. Too much loss of face would cause his gang to want a change in leadership. This could mean his life. He began to plan a major manoeuvre to boost morale. The target would be the patrol post at the roundabout. He chose three experienced men for the diversion; Cubal, Bolo and Shanty. Himself and Sharpus, the only one he really trusted, would carry out the main action backed by Pablo and Redwood.

Like most overt military operations, the post's routine had quickly become well known. If there was no trouble they drove through the streets of Slow Town and Coalyard at three hourly intervals. At nights they used the tank backed by the helicopter, or travelled in three jeeps, well-armed and shooting at the slightest suspicious movement. Both communities were under curfew from seven in the evening to six in the morning. If there was trouble, all the vehicles converged on the spot and at such times only two men were left to guard the camp.

It was a simple matter for Cubal, Bolo and Shanty to start a shooting spree about two miles from the camp. While the jeeps were rushing to the spot, Bubbles and Sharpus would divert the attention of the guards by throwing a gasoline bomb which would set fire to the shed they used as a latrine. While the men were busy with this they would enter the tent and pass out the boxes of tear gas grenades and ammunition to Pablo and Redwood who would be waiting to transport the booty to a safe place.

It was a quick, smooth operation. Bubbles was proud of his men. They gathered at the agreed hiding place, an old hut far from the scene of the diversion, to count their gains and gloat over the ease of the operation.

Bubbles and Sharpus showed off the magazines for the automatic rifles that they had captured. They couldn't use them but it would be a severe embarrassment to the authorities. They waited for Pablo and Redwood to appear with the boxes. One hour later they were still waiting. Bubbles began to worry. The patrols would have started their search. The helicopter had arrived and had already made one pass over the hut. It was time for them to move out of the area. More worrying minutes passed. Bubbles began to suspect that something had gone wrong. He gave orders and they melted into the darkness to search for Pablo and Redwood; in spite of the curfew experienced fighters had no difficulty moving around.

Sometime later some Suckdust searchers came across Pablo and Redwood tied up in the shell of one of the burnt-out buildings. They had started moving towards the meeting place as agreed but had been jumped on by Pantyhose herself and a couple of her men. They had been tied up and the boxes taken away. It had been a quiet, efficient, totally unexpected operation by the Panty Posse.

None of Bubbles' men had ever seen him so angry. His spittle frothed as he cursed some of the vilest badwords even the most seasoned among them had heard. He was so angry that the caution essential to good leadership deserted him. He wanted immediate and total confrontation. All his firing power against hers, but Sharpus begged him to be sensible. Not only would Pantyhose be prepared for an attack, but the police and military would soon be swarming all over the place and would be only too happy to wipe them all out. In fact they would have to go into hiding immediately.

It was during the hiding period that another plan was made. If Pantyhose had not humiliated him, Bubbles would not have agreed, but she had proven herself to be more man than woman. No punishment was too harsh for her. No abuse too great.

One week later Pantyhose and three of her men: Bedward, Teddy and Three-finger Jack, who had lost two fingers when a homemade gun exploded in his hand, were returning from a small uptown mission. They were pleased at their take, thirty thousand Jamaican dollars and six thousand US without even a shot fired. The donors had been very co-operative. It had been a very good tip-off from their contact. Drunk with their success they stopped to celebrate at a friendly bar a little outside their neighbourhood. While the men were drinking stout and sharing a spliff, Pantyhose excused herself to use the toilet at the back of the premises. She was always meticulous about her privacy, never flaunting her sexuality before her men, a little prudish even.

Five minutes later the men heard her calling out to them to go on without her. She had some business, she said. They were surprised but she insisted that she was all right and would make her own way home. Since they had learned not to question her decisions, they finished their drinks and left.

What they couldn't see was that she was being held by two Suckdust men, a gun at her head and one in her back.

She didn't go with them willingly. They had to push and drag her through the yard behind the bar, into the gully and up the other side to a waiting car which sped away to the rendezvous.

There was no furniture in the hut except for a small stool on which Bubbles sat waiting, gun in hand, both judge and executioner. He would be the guard while his men took multiple revenge and disciplined Pantyhose with the ultimate insult a man could offer a woman.

They pushed Pantyhose onto the floor, Bolo ripping off her shirt in the process. She fell without resistance, sizing up the situation. Instinctively she knew that they were not planning to kill her; would not kill her unless they became frightened; that the plan was humiliation and that the best way to survive was to take the punishment as best she could.

Indeed she was not even really afraid of them. Her feelings were more of anger and contempt. She had beaten them and this was the only way they could handle it.

"Stay cool! Stay cool!" she kept telling herself, but as she watched them fumbling with zippers and underwear, awkward in their anxiety, each wanting to be first, anger exploded.

"So, the woman them a Coalyard dry-up, mek oonu have fi a tek it by force outside now?"

"Shut up!" Pablo warned as he tore at her pants. Cubal and Sharpus were still pointing their guns at her. She drew up her knees and kicked Pablo across the room. He came back, knife in hand, slashing at her pants and tearing it off.

"Bitch!" he screamed. "Try that again and you dead."

She realised that resistance was only making them hotter so she changed her tactics. As he forced her legs apart, she said in as threatening as voice as she could manage, "The man them have them orders you know. When them ketch oonu, them gwine chop off oonu buddy, piece by piece. The woman them a go do it."

The hot organ which had been forcing entry into her suddenly began to lose its power.

"Bitch! Bitch! Fuckin bitch!" Pablo screamed, grabbing the knife which he had abandoned, but Sharpus held his hand, and the cold, deadly voice of Bubbles stopped him.

"Mek a nex man go on. An oonu hurry up."

"Gag her!" Pablo said, his voice was hysterical as he stuffed his shame into his trousers. Sharpus took up her torn shirt to carry out the order but she bit him and cried out, "None a oonu no ha no mother? Oonu no ha no sister?"

It was then that Bubbles, the point of his gun shifting around his men, suddenly got up and said: "Enough! Cease! Oonu can't manage her. Me wi fix her business."

They looked at him in surprise. They couldn't imagine what he was planning to do.

"Me say fi stop!" he raised his voice at Cubal who had taken Pablo's place and was preparing to thrust. He pulled Cubal by the neck of his shirt and pointed the gun at him.

"Me will handle this," he repeated. They said that Bubbles' angry voice could put a chill in hell. His men recognised that voice. When he spoke like that you obeyed or you died.

They looked at each other in bewilderment.

"Get up!" he ordered Pantyhose.

She scrambled to her feet, trying in vain to pull up the shreds of her pants. Her breasts were bruised and there was blood on her belly where the knife had cut her.

"Wait!" he ordered his crestfallen men, and pointing the gun at Pantyhose he said, "Outside."

Now she was truly frightened because she didn't know what he had in mind. Perhaps, after all, he would be foolish enough to kill her. Neither side would survive the bloodletting that would follow. They both knew this.

But when they were outside, he took off his shirt and gave it to her. She put it on, wordless now. It fitted closely and was barely long enough to cover her naked bottom.

"Me woulda len you me pants but you too big, it not gwine fit you," he said. "Here." He gave her the gun in his hand. "You mighta need this fi reach home. But no bodder use it less you mus."

"You mad!" she exclaimed as she fitted the gun into her expert hand. "Mek you think say me won't use it pon you?"

He shrugged. His life was no longer safe. There were four disappointed and shamed men waiting for answers that would make sense of his actions. He had no sensible answers for them. He had forfeited their trust. Now he could only rule by added force and terror and he knew that could last only for a time.

"Get out!" he said, showing her another gun in his left hand. She hadn't seen the movement which had brought out the second gun. "You never hear say that me lef han badder than me right?" he asked. "Me a go bus two shot, but no notice it. Gwan."

Creature of the criminal night she melted into the darkness, and he heard her voice saying, "Me gwine member this." But he couldn't tell whether she meant the abduction or his attempts to help her.

After that night, Bubbles lived as if he was a marked man. He expected treachery from any source. The women guardians were told to be even more careful. Nobody could enter the compound without first surrendering their weapons. Among his men he was always tense and, even as they whispered rebellion among themselves, they knew that he wouldn't hesitate to shoot the minute he suspected any of plotting against him.

The urgent need to abandon the hut that night had prevented any discussion. His men were not fooled by his brief explanation that he had shot at Pantyhose but missed. Bubbles never missed. He was right in supposing that his days of leadership were numbered. The threat would come from Pablo who since that shameful night had assumed an especially boastful attitude.

Bubbles rarely went on missions with them any longer. A man could easily get shot in the back or be set up for capture by the law. They began to make mistakes. One night, they were caught breaking into a supermarket and Pablo was shot dead. The rebellion, temporarily leaderless, lost its momentum.

Although he had suspected Pablo's intention, and would not have hesitated to shoot him, Bubbles was sad when he heard of his death. He sat for a long time contemplating the futility of the game they were playing; directed and controlled by the big bosses, who were faceless like ghosts, who risked nothing at all. Not even their names could be called, for who would believe or give evidence?

Nomination day came and both communities were heavily involved in a show of strength: intimidating, threatening, booing, and promising the better life that their particular bossman had sold them.

But it wasn't only Bubbles who kept out of direct action.

Pantyhose too, who, before the rape attempt had never sent her men on a mission unaccompanied, was now scarcely seen on the streets.

A kind of wait-and-see attitude set in among the gangs, so that the area that was expected to go up in flames showed only a few smoke signals. Nobody could understand what had happened, though the security officials praised themselves for having at last brought the gangs under control. There were still some minor skirmishes and some missions, for people had to eat, but the scale of violence was so reduced that the bossmen became alarmed. How could their side ensure victory if the gangs had stopped doing their work?

Election day came and though there were threats from diehard party followers and several ballot boxes were stolen and electoral officers intimidated, the only shots fired in Coalyard or Slow Town were by a policeman alarmed at the size of the crowd which had descended on the polling station he was guarding.

When the results for the island were known, Slow Town's party had won.

Bubbles sat in the front room of his house listening to the sounds of celebration coming from Slow Town that night. Two of the women and his mother were with him. The room had no light, reflecting their gloom. It wasn't just that their side had lost, but that he had a sense of the futility of all their efforts. He was twenty-four and he had a strong feeling that he wouldn't live to see twenty-five.

His mother, mistaking the cause of his sadness, said:

"Them can gwan mek noise. Tidday fi you, tomorrow fi me. By a morning the bossman them figet say them help them get in. Wait and see."

Bubbles nodded. It was true. Life would not improve for the majority of the ghetto people, no matter which side won. A little more talk; a little more work for some, perhaps; but never enough to make a real difference. The only way was for the ghetto people to help themselves. He recalled the lessons when he was twelve. But how could they help themselves when they spent all their time fighting one another? The recent campaign had created so much bitterness; there had been so much loss of life; could they ever forget? And if the gangs gave up their guns and the war and lost the support of the bosses, how would the communities survive? This kind of thinking confused him.

The very next day, the new power ordered peace in the ghettos and declared amnesty for all gunmen provided they turned in their guns. The word went out that if they didn't obey, the full wrath of the security forces would be turned against them.

Tired from the battle and lacking the forceful leadership they had once enjoyed, a fair number of gunholders did turn in their guns and when the new boss declared that he wanted a peace ceremony, the communities agreed without protest.

Immediately the organisers went to work. It would be a spectacular event to show the world that what had been almost a civil war had truly come to an end. The acknowledged gang leaders would be there; the clergy would be there; reggae stars would be there; and since Slow Town and Coalyard had been among the worst offenders, the party would be held on the roundabout and roads in that area.

There were some in the gangs who wanted to maintain the badman image; who wanted the war to continue, but they reluctantly had to agree that the time was no longer right and that it would be better for them to keep a low profile, for the time being, anyway.

Celebration day arrived. The women from both sides cooked kerosene tins of mannish water, curried goat, boiled bananas, rice and peas and chicken. Donations for the feast poured in from the business places, glad that the gangs had decided on peace. One firm donated a truckful of drinks; and the boxes housing the amplifiers were so big it seemed as if all of Kingston would be sharing the musical part of the celebration.

The next day's papers would show the climactic moment when four of the leaders of the ghetto gangs held hands on the stage while the crowd cheered. There was another picture of Bubbles and Pantyhose in a symbolic embrace of peace.

The next day's papers would carry another story also.

As Bubbles and Pantyhose embraced and their followers cheered, she said to him, "Me have something me want show you up a yard."

"What?" he asked suspiciously, from habit. He had not seen her since the night they had tried to discipline her.

"Jus something," she replied.

In the spirit of the new peace he agreed to accompany her, so they left the celebrations in full swing and walked up the street which led to her home. Only the henchmen noted this.

"You know," Bubbles said as he looked around, "Is the first time me come over Slow Town bout five year now."

"Me know," she replied. "Is really time we stop the foolishness. Is only the big man a profit anyway. Is like duppy a follow the res a we."

"Me did want fi wear a dress," she said, irrelevantly, "but me did think say nobody never see me in a dress so long, them wouldn't know me."

He smiled politely.

"So me put on this outfit instead. You like it?"

He looked at her white shirt and pants stuffed into blue boots and wondered why it was important whether he liked it or not.

"Me wear white fi show the peace. Battle time done."

Bubbles looked around him curiously as he walked with Pantyhose. Slow Town had suffered the same scarring and destruction as Coalyard. They were both war-torn and desolate with burnt-out shells of houses, abandoned huts, junk and debris everywhere. Some sections looked like the ghost towns of a western movie.

He wondered again how they could be so foolish as to destroy each other solely for somebody else's benefit. People who didn't care about them. When war suited them they declared it. When peace suited them they demanded it.

"Puppets on a string": a phrase from a popular song jumped into his head.

"Puppets!" he said aloud. "That's all."

"Come in no," Pantyhose invited him. They had stopped before a neat concrete nog house with a short walkway, red and shining from a recent polish.

"You house nice," he said, as she opened the door with her key.

"Everybody out a street," she said unnecessarily.

He wondered what it was she wanted to show him so urgently, and why she was behaving so strangely.

"Me a give up the posse," she said. "Me a go settle down. Open a shop at the corner and turn respectable." She laughed loudly. "Me might even start go a church. New Converts a open back them church since the violence stop."

He smiled. He wasn't very interested in her plans. He didn't know what plans to make.

"What bout you?"

"Me don't think bout it yet," he lied.

"Come in here," she said, leading him into a small bedroom. There was a dresser with bottles neatly arranged and a vase with gerberas in the centre. The bed had on a heavy pink chenille spread. It didn't look like the headquarters of a tough gang leader, he thought.

"Me have drinks, if you want some."

He noticed that she seemed to be getting more and more nervous.

"You did want to show me something?"

She laughed.

"Me kinda nervous, you know. Is long time me no have no man. Not since Hotfoot dead. Him wasn't me real brother, you know. We did only grow in the same yard."

"Anyway me never did get fi say thanks that night when you stop the man them from rape me. Me no know what woulda happen if them did get them way. All now we wouldn't de ya. Me never tell nobody you know. You was a real gentleman. Me did think say that maybe we coulda jus figet everything."

Bubbles backed away from the outstretched hand in amazement. He knew that woman's look. The look which said that she was ready to offer herself, the most precious gift she owned. It was so unexpected that he nearly laughed out loud.

She got up from the bed, pulled back the spread, settled the pillows and started to take off her clothes.

"Jus as cheap we tek the little privacy while them all outa street." She was sure of a positive response.

Bubbles collected himself He wasn't sure why, but in his new mood of uncertainty he felt he might as well play the game with her. He had no interest but perhaps she could be of use to him in the future. Long ago he had learned how to cope with similar situations: with women who felt that they had to have intimate contact with him and who for one reason or the other it suited him to accommodate.

He went over to the bed and sat on the edge. Pantyhose pulled him down. Suddenly transformed into a trembling animal, she unbuttoned his shirt and forced him to take it off. In order to prevent her taking off anything else he went to work on her immediately, kneading her breasts, touching all the right places expertly.

It was funny, he thought, almost with contempt, how all women were reduced to animals at times like this. He could never have imagined that this was the powerful woman who had so frustrated him; mocked him. He could hardly believe that this was the same woman now wetting his fingers and writhing and moaning at his touch. Assaulted, yes; forced, yes; but never this giving, this yielding, this complete abandonment of self to another.

"Me no do this so long, me hungry," she panted, pulling his head down and kissing him wildly.

After a while she whispered. "Come we do it now, no." He didn't respond except to increase the pressure of hand and the rhythm of his fingers.

"Me can't discharge like this," she moaned, so he moved his head downward.

"No! Do it now!" she exclaimed and grabbed at his trousers. There was nothing to feel. He shifted away and continued stroking her but she had stopped responding and when he looked at her she was staring at him.

"Jesus Christ! Me never did believe them. Is true what them say. Them eunuchize you! Me never wan believe them." Her eyes were a little wet; there were tears close by, but he didn't see them.

What he thought he heard was contempt and suddenly his old mad reaction surfaced. He got up abruptly and went to stare through the small window, his back to her. She wanted to hold him close like a mother, to comfort him, to tell him that it was all right, but she read his reaction as rejection and her mood suddenly changed to anger.

"Cho! you shoulda tell me say you couldn't do it, and me wouldn't bother waste me time!"

The tensing of his shoulder muscles warned her a second before he turned around, animal rage on his face, gun in hand.

"Stop it!" he shouted and fired hitting her in the belly.

She was almost as quick. There was a gun under her pillow. Her first shot went through his right arm and the gun fell but in one motion he retrieved it with his left. He fired again and the bullet, jerking her body as it entered, caused her return shot to lodge in his heart. He cracked his head against the bedpost as he fell.

"Hell!" he thought. That he had survived so many battles only to be killed by a woman!

In his waning consciousness he thought he heard her calling him, weakly, "Bubbles! Bubbles!" But then it could have been his mother. It sounded like his mother's voice calling him that day he had shot Manatee.

The crack on his head opened a memory path leading back through his life and the lives of all the ancestors: to Papa Tee, a regular bullbucker and duppy conqueror chopping at human flesh; swearing at mothers with babies he had no intention of supporting; swearing in frustration in the line at the docks – no work this week, again! The blood leaking from him belonged to all of them – to Johnson, Papa Tee's father working the piece of land on the hillside which barely gave him enough to eat; to Cris-Cris, digging earth and coughing blood in a strange Spanish-speaking country; to Maas Sam, the obeah man at whom ghosts laughed; to William, chased off the estate because he asked for more wages; to all of them passing swiftly back into time; back to Jacob, the runaway slave pausing under a tree to rearrange his human burdens so that he could make a faster escape into the forest, up into the mountains to freedom.

Jacob realised that Miriam would not be able to walk any further. In fact she seemed to have fainted away. Her eyes were closed and she was barely holding the infant. Any moment it would roll out of her hands. He would have to carry her. They could not stay there. It was too close to the plantation. He did not doubt his strength but what would he do with the infant? He was still too far away from the first lookout to expect to run into a patrol which would help him carry them up to the town. He cursed his stupidity for not bringing a companion, but he didn't want them to know lest they objected and he hadn't expected to find Miriam with a baby and so weak. What could he do?

The faint moonlight and his nose led him to a guava tree close by. As he reached up to pick the fruit, a distant memory flared for a moment. "You fi spin roun tree time." He shrugged it away, picked a fruit and rubbed it with his fingers as he thought about his problem.

Suddenly the image of women working in the field floated into his head. They had babies safely tied in slings on their backs.

That is what he would do. Make a sling for the pickney, put it on his back and carry the mother in his arms.

He looked around. What could he use for a sling? It had to be cloth. His shirt was too short. He couldn't use the blanket as he needed to keep Miriam sheltered from the cold mountain night air. He looked at her clothing. He would have to use her under-skirt. Lucky that she still dressed as if she was a privileged kitchen slave.

He lifted her frock and fumbled for the string which he knew tied the petticoat at the waist. How many times had he done this under different circumstances. He half-expected her to slap away his hand in mock dismissal, as she used to do, but she remained in her faint. He would have to go fast. She needed help; woman help.

His nose wrinkled in disgust as he pulled off the petticoat and smelled the unpleasantness of a bleeding woman, but he couldn't afford to be finicky now.

He tied the petticoat this way and that over his shoulder, trying to get it right before putting the baby in. Eventually he felt that he had a satisfactory hammock and, putting the still sleeping infant in it, he carefully put his arms through, trying to remember that it wasn't ground provisions that he was carrying. He hoped the child would not suffocate. Then he bent down, lifted Miriam and started his arduous climb.

NEW STORIES

## DEVIL STAR

It was the first of times. It was the last of times. It was even the first time at last; and some were saying, "Cho! Jamaica nuh sweet again". There was looting and there was shooting. There was pillaging and there was rummaging. There was ravishing and despoiling. Some wined and dined; some could only lick their lips and pine. Some dipped their fingers in voting ink; blood-red, not blue. Some dipped themselves in healing streams which had no power to "put it back". It was deejay time. It was Dance Hall time. It was slack lyrics time. It was mayhem, noise and corruption time, for it seemed that Satan himself (herself?) had taken up permanent residence in shack, shanty, concrete nog and high rise.

In hard times, the Church prospers more than Satan, for the sinful can easily be convinced that they're being punished for sins of commission and omission; so the church benches full-up on Sundays and the balm yards pack-up on Tuesday nights, for some think that if they pray loud enough or shout loud enough or trump hard enough or get the right set of tongues to communicate to the unknown, something bound to break the drought, the famine, the badluck, hard times and the waywardness – all of which, as we know, worse than any obeah.

★

Devil Star had received Devil of the Month award, again – eleven times in a row. Now, all he needed was to bring home to hell another ninety and nine souls to win the coveted Devil of the Year award. He scanned the globe and shook his head. There were so many places ripe for picking; so many places in which he could find the required ninety-nine that he yawned in boredom. Eventually, he spun the globe having decided that wherever his finger pointed when "eeny, meeny, miney mo" ran out would be the chosen spot. The last 'mo' found his finger pointing at Jamaica.

"AAhh!" he exclaimed. "Wicked! Wicked! Nice, warm place with a lot of sinners."

Then, getting into character, he started to deejay:
*Cheap will be the reaping*
*Why? It's almost like cheating*
*I'll hardly have to work*
*I won't even need my fork!*
*So bretheren and sisteren,*
*Expect the I*
*Dancehall and reggae*
*Plenty sun and fun*

He wiggled his hips and grinned. "Piece a cake!"

He practised a few steps of the old Bogle and the newer Gully Creeper popular dances, and made Usain Bolt's "To the World" gesture before his full-length mirror. "Unoo see me, though? Cho!" He laughed uproariously.

"Let me see," he said aloud, as he examined his reflection. "I don't want to be conspicuous, so…" He snapped his fingers once and looked at his mirror image dressed as a devil.

"Naw," he said, "them don't have halloween, and is not Jonkunnu time yet. And this little too realistic, even for Jonkunnu."

He snapped his fingers twice and looked at himself dressed in a business suit. "Eenh-no! Them wi run me. Too much chickeeny business going on up there."

He snapped his fingers three times. "Ahhh!" he said with great satisfaction. "Ah bad! Ah bad. Ah reely reely ba-a-ad!"

He turned and twisted, admiring himself more with each move. The hem of his baggy jeans rested on the top of his five thousand dollar (plus GCT) sneakers. The waist rested comfortably on his hips exposing the top of his multicoloured boxer shorts. He was wearing a short, bright-green merino under a long orange fishnet vest. A gold chain of the cargo variety hung from his neck.

He patted his head, very pleased with the haircut, a fringe of a blonde topknot with the very closely shaved sides etched with the inscription "devil star".

"Whee whoo!" he whistled himself. "Mi own modder would'n know me. See how me trash an' irie. Me is the Don of dons. Me a tek life, mon!"

★

A streak of lightning hit earth and the thunderclap awakened those still asleep in their foreday morning beds.

"Lord! Please don't let it rain," Mother Cassie prayed. She was in charge of food and drinks for the group gathered in the square waiting for the bus which would transport them to a Portland beach for the day's outing.

Elder had decided to top off a very successful week's membership recruiting campaign with an outing which would provide both worship and relaxation for his fledgling flock.

Elder believed that the best way to worship was to be out of doors. He was already regretting the time when the church would be able to put up a building and stop meeting under the tent. He liked the exposure to the stark reminders of God's power, like the clap of thunder which had just caused people to huddle together in fear and exclaim, "Lord! Have mercy!"

The outing was also a fund-raising event. At one thousand dollars a head, food and drink provided, it wasn't a bad deal for the city dwellers starved of healthy entertainment. So good a deal that many who had no intention of joining Elder's church had paid their money and were anxious to be off.

Mother Cassie was a bit worried. She had provided food and drink, with a little to spare, for seventy people, the number the bus could comfortably hold. However, motherly soul that she was, she wondered if there would be enough food for everyone. "Sea breeze have a way to mek people really hungry," she fretted.

Shortly after the thunderclap, a group of some twenty or more people suddenly turned up in the square. They were coming directly from their Friday night session gloriously bedecked in all their dancehall finery – underwear turned outerwear, indeed almost "no-wear" for some. They glittered and shone in cloth and jewellery. Colourful costumes matched even more colourful hair, curled and crimped and gnarled with unbelievable artistry.

"Hail, Sista! Dis a de tent church outing?"

"Yes?" Elder replied, before the sister addressed could answer. He suddenly sensed trouble.

"We a come wid you. Whey de @%#★★ (expletive deleted) bus? We tiad. Up all night a dance. We ave fi ketch a shut eye pan de way."

"I don't understand," Elder said sternly. "This is a church outing."

"Hmn…hmn. Me know. We pay we money. See de ticket dem ya. Sista Webb sell we."

Sister Webb, who was in charge of ticket sales, came forward reluctantly.

"Eld… Elder, the bus did have more space, an we did need more money fi make a profit, an some a the people say since we a PNP them not coming and mi brother say him an him fren them did in… interested, an dem pay dem money an…"

"Sister Webb!" Elder raised his voice, astounded. "We? PNP? What kind a nonsense is that.? We don't belong to any political party! We are God's people! That's the only party we know!"

Sister Webb looked duly chastened. "Me know, Elder, but…"

"You sold tickets to these people?" He made it sound as if she had invited doo-du to his outing.

But before he could say anything more the bus arrived with grinding gears and air-assisted braking.

"Raaay!" The dancehall group shouted as they noisily and gleefully boarded the bus ahead of the church people. Elder turned his head away from the sight of the women' posteriors, skimpily encased in batty riders, mocking him as their owners boarded the bus. There was nothing he could do now. Sister Cassie was in a state of great confusion. As well as the driver, she would now have to feed – she counted quickly – more than ninety people. She didn't have that much food.

The last dancehaller to board the bus grinned broadly at her. She glared back at him and frowned at his back. His head had something written on it, but in the light of the early dawn she couldn't read what it said.

★

Elder prayed silently that the day would soon end. What a day it had been! He had hoped that once they reached their destination the dancehall group would have gone their way and left him in peace, until it was time to go home. Or (and this was a very private prayer for he didn't want to look foolish if the prayer wasn't answered), that somehow he and his group would be able to win a few of them to salvation.

Not so. First, it was a secluded beach with no nearby entertainment. The dancehallers therefore proceeded to provide their own entertainment with loud music from their many boom boxes.

Sister Webb also had a boom box. She tried to outplay them with some gospel cassettes, but, lively as they were, they could not compete with the dance hall volume and slackness.

In an effort to protect his flock from temptation, Elder led them away from the sinners onto a little hillock overlooking the beach. There they tried to spend time in meditation and prayer. In the midst of Brother Max's very loud prayer, however, some young people began to giggle. The giggling soon developed into the kind of laughter that gets more uncontrollable in the face of disapproval. In vain did the sisters screw up their faces trying to silence the young ones. Indeed, when they themselves identified the source of the laughter, they had to press their mouths shut to prevent any sign of mirth from showing.

Elder stopped the prayer and gave the youngsters a severe lecture, but the more he talked, the more they laughed, and when he discovered the source of their mirth he was momentarily at a loss for words.

On the beach below them, the dancehallers had decided to go for a swim. The cause of the laughter was a gloriously fat mama rolling slowly towards the water. Layers of fatty folds rolled around what seemed to be a naked body.

Elder was outraged. He rushed down the hillside and accosted the woman.

"Lady," he began, "this is a church outing. We are decent, God-fearing people. We cannot have this kind of wanton behaviour in our midst. What will people think! I rebuke you! You'll have to go elsewhere with your indecent exposure."

Fatty stared at him in amazement.

"Ah who you a chat to? Me?" she asked. "H-indestant exposure! You no see me well cover up inna me bikini? She lifted a fold of flesh to reveal a bikini bottom stretched so tight it provided little covering for the main point of interest. When she released the fold you couldn't see anything but flesh. Likewise, the bra was a string enclosed by fat with two petals barely covering her nipples.

"But anybody ever see my dying trial?" Fatty continued, arms akimbo . "A mussi wife you a look!" She was now fully incensed. Her voice grew louder with each phrase and the folds rolled with indignation. "No bodder wid me. Me like me man dem look like man! Me nuh romp wid mirasme baby!"

Laughter washed the beach. Elder's face burned. Fortunately, his flock could not hear the exchange. He ground his teeth in frustration. This was enough provocation to make a saint start swearing.

"You coming for a swim, Parson? Tek off you clothes, nuh. Fatty want fi see what you have underneath it."

"Yeah, Preach. Show we you stuff."

Elder fled.

The outrageous behaviour continued all day. Although the church members tried their best to keep the groups apart, by late afternoon, some of the younger flock had drawn closer and closer to the dancehallers. A few had even entered a very wild impromptu dance contest. When Elder saw the wining of the almost bare bottoms and the suggestive dance moves, he turned aside to pray even harder.

There were other problems too. Having paid their money, the

dancehallers felt it was their right to eat as much as they wanted. They ate off most of the food and the church group had to be satisfied with very small portions. Tempers simmered. All manner of sinful things continued to happen. Smoke from cigarettes and weed floated in the air, already sweetened with the smell of rum. And it wasn't only the fried chicken and rice and peas which made Brother Joe smack his lips from time to time. Quarrels erupted and there was one fight which nearly ended in disaster.

Finally, at five o'clock when Elder declared that it was time to leave for home, the bus wouldn't start and they had to wait for hours while the driver and two dancehallers, who were mechanics, tried to fix the fault. Sister Cassie had to dip into the profits and send to a nearby district to buy bread and tins of bully beef to feed her charges.

"It's like Satan himself in our midst today," Elder told his people as they waited. "Pray that nothing worse happens!"

And strolling casually past him with a wide grin was a man he hadn't noticed before. He winked at Elder who shuddered without knowing why. "Pray!" he repeated softly. "Pray hard!"

★

It was past eleven o'clock before they could leave. The mechanics could find no reason why the bus wouldn't start, and just as they were about to give up, the engine miraculously sprang to life. When they boarded the bus, Elder breathed a sigh of relief; the nightmarish day would soon end.

Two miles into the return journey, people had settled into the repose they expected to keep until they reached Kingston. Apart from their manner of dress, it was now difficult to tell the groups apart. Elder's followers were intimately mixed with dancehallers as everyone tried to find a comfortable place. They were sitting three in a seat meant for two; they squatted in the aisle and even sat in each other's laps, making the kind of flesh contact that Elder deplored. He knew too well where this could lead. In truth surreptitious petting had already started.

Elder closed his eyes to say yet another prayer. He prayed that the bus would safely navigate the many steep winding places on the road and that they would reach home without any incidents. When he opened his eyes, he noticed the strange man with the big grin staring at him. The hair on Elder's neck rose. Something was very wrong but he could not tell what it was. He looked away quickly.

Devil Star's grin grew wider and wider. It had all been so easy that he had decided to give himself an extra handicap – leading Elder's flock astray. He had until a minute before midnight to lead them to hell, thirty-five more minutes and five more souls to add to the lot on the bus. Excluding Elder – who might not succumb – that would give him his ninety-nine souls.

"Hmm-hmm," he shook his head, rejecting the immediate idea which came to him. "Too easy. I can get more fun out of this."

Just then, the bus swerved dangerously and there was an enormous screeching of brakes. The sudden stop woke everybody up and there was immediate consternation. Voices were raised in alarm wanting to know what had happened.

"What the *&+%$# (more deleted expletives) the idiot tink him a do!" the bus driver exclaimed as he dashed down from the coach to see a car dangerously perched on the edge of the precipice.

"Help! Help!" Voices were screaming.

The bus quickly emptied and willing hands pulled five people from the car, which, as soon as the last person was out, rocked gently and then eased itself over the edge of the precipice – almost as if someone had pushed it. There was silence among the people as they listened in awe to the crunching sound of the vehicle crashing from one rocky ledge to another on its way to the beach many metres below the road.

"Unoo fi say, tenk God!" a voice came out of the darkness.

It seemed to unleash the fury of the driver of the car. "Tenk God, mi headside!" He was almost weeping. "Mi jus buy de car an get dis job fi carry dese people go a airport. It don't even insure yet!"

"All we grip dem gone!" another voice wailed. "All the nice, nice roast breadfruit we was tekkin back!"

"But how you so fool-fool fi a try pass me pan dis lil kench a road. Me neva see unoo till de las minute. Good ting me brakes soun or else de whole a unoo would gone over."

Another little silence as they contemplated this near miss. Just the week before thirteen people had been killed in a road accident not too far away from this very spot.

"Ah mi unoo want tun into accident statistics," a voice said humorously. A few people laughed, but there was a general mood of thoughtful sobriety as they returned to the bus. The driver had agreed to take the stranded travellers to the next town. There was no point in them standing by the roadside at that hour of the night, and there was nothing they could do about the car and luggage until morning.

Elder seized his opportunity. As they tried to settle down, he began to preach.

"We have just been delivered from a very close shave with the grim reaper," he began. "Many of us spent the day in riotous behaviour forgetting to praise the Almighty who gives us life and health. Sometimes the Lord uses incidents like these to bring us back to the paths of righteousness." Elder felt himself growing warm as the words welled up in his mouth.

"True word! True word!" someone agreed, while others added loud amens

"Preach it!" a screechy voice urged.

Elder was happy. Perhaps more good would come out of this than he had thought. All was not lost. Maybe he would return with more converts than he had left with in the morning. How many were on the bus? He did a quick check. With the additional five it must be about a hundred, he thought.

Suddenly his eye caught the grin that seemed designed to torment him. It made Elder's blood boil. He felt as if the man was challenging him. Devil Star looked down at his watch and nodded at Elder. Elder also glanced at his watch and saw that it was seven minutes to twelve. Time was running out, he thought, although he had no idea what this meant. Feeling cornered he raised a hymn he thought suitable for the situation.

*There were ninety and nine that safely lay*
*In the shelter of the fold*
*But one was lost on the hills away*
*Far off from the gates of gold*

His followers who had been duly chastened by the near accident quickly took up the hymn, improvising different drawn-out harmonies around the tune.

*Away on the mountain wild and bare*
*Away from the tender shepherd's care*

Elder, with his hands clasped, did a slow rock to the rhythm, very pleased with the response.

Devil Star bent over with laughter. Suddenly Fatty's voice broke into the song.

"Is a PNP song that. We nuh want no PNP song in 'ere. Unoo hear me! Me tell unoo them was PNP."

"My dear lady," Elder began, but Fatty was on her feet shaking off those closely packed around her. Perhaps she was still smarting from her earlier encounter with Elder and glad of another opportunity to embarrass him. She had a bottle raised menacingly in her hand. "Sing dat song an a better de whole bus did go over the cliff."

"Go way!" a voice challenged her. "What wrong wid a little Christian song?"

"Me is JLP an me no want fi hear no PNP song."

"You an who else?"

"Nuff a we a JLP. No PNP song nah sing in here tinight!"

Someone with a sense of humour raised a new song:

*Don't board de wrang train*
*Don't board de wrang train*
*De devil is the driver*
*Will take you down to hell.*

"Unoo stap de nize!" the bus driver shouted. "Unoo mek me so confuse me cyan even see where the bus a go!"

They ignored him. In no time at all it seemed the bus had divided into two factions. Quarrels were breaking out all over. Even Elder, beginning to lose his temper, pushed aside a drunk man who kept leaning against him. The devil had indeed taken over.

"Mek we see who is who," Fatty continued her tirade. "Stand up fi you position. Who is not fi me an the JLP is against me." The bottle was still menacingly raised.

"Fight! Fight!" People began screaming as fists began to fly. "Stop de bus! Stop de bus!"

The driver braked and wearily placed his hands on his head as he bent over the steering wheel. He opened the bus doors, expecting the worst.

Devil Star suddenly jumped to his feet. "Drive! Drive!" he ordered in a thunderous voice. Round the next corner was the spot he had chosen for the bus to go over the precipice, thus giving him all ninety and nine cantankerous souls to take home to hell and win his prize. The driver had to keep going. It was almost midnight.

The bus grew silent for a moment as all eyes turned on him.

"Who you?" some of the passengers demanded as if they were seeing him for the first time, and, in the nature of crowds, glad to find a common enemy. Devil Star found himself isolated between both factions.

"Declare you han!" Fatty stood ready to pounce on him. "You a wear de two party colour, green fi JLP, orange fi PNP. State who you for, for you cyan be fi de two."

Devil Star looked around, bewildered. The grin had disappeared. He glanced at his watch, one second to midnight. They were going to spoil his plan. It had been such an easy, entertaining, perfect plan.

"State you position!" Both sides were now accosting him. "Head or bell, one or the other. Cyan be the two."

As they reached to grab him, ready to tear him apart, he

disappeared in a puff of smoke. Intense heat and sulphuric vapours enveloped the bus. Surprised and panicking, the passengers tumbled out of the bus. As they stood outside coughing and trying to understand what had happened, something bright like a star seemed to streak out of nowhere and crash into the earth with a very loud thunderclap. Frightened beyond telling, many fell on their knees and began to pray.

## I CAN MANAGE

I live by myself in a gated apartment complex. There is a security guard and friendly tenants. I can manage, but my children do not approve. "You are too old to live alone," they say. But I will not allow them to dictate to me. How old is "too old" anyway.

At night, I usually watch television until it starts watching me. Eventually, I will go to bed. Some nights I sleep on the couch. Why should that bother anybody?

My favourite shows are the ones that make me laugh. Like one called *Fraidy Thief*. Even the idea of a thief being afraid is amusing and his adventures on the show are even more so. He never successfully completes a burglary. Everything scares him – a shadow, a sound. Even his intended victim fearfully whispering, "Who's' there?" causes Fraidy Thief to scamper away. He is a very unsuccessful criminal.

One night, while laughing at the antics of this inept Fraidy Thief, I suddenly realise I am not alone. Standing inside my door is a young man who looks a little like the Fraidy Thief in the show I am watching. His cap is turned backwards, revealing a slightly bulging forehead. His face is clean, only a few scraggly hairs promise the beard to come. He is a good-looking robber-man. Or, rather, robber-boy. He is wearing a black tee shirt with the legend "Toy Boy". There is a gun in his hand.

"What do you want?" I ask. He waves the gun around. Strangely, I am not afraid.

"Are you Fraidy Thief?" I ask.

He looks confused.

"Am I on TV?"

I look to see if there is a camera behind him. I think maybe I am on reality TV. It could happen!

"Turn it off," he orders. I feel for the remote and turn off the set. He looks at me with disdain, as if thinking that I am old and foolish and probably a waste of his time.

"Where's the money?" he asks.

I start to get up, but he points the gun at me. I tell him it's in a book on the dresser.

"In a book?" he asks. He gives me another condescending look.

He goes over to the dresser, yanks the book and a few notes float to the ground. There's only J$5000 to pay the day's worker, the woman who cleans house for me once a week. He quickly counts it.

"That's all?" he asks, pushing the money into his pocket.

"I don't have any more."

"Where's your purse?" he demands. He is trying to sound menacing, but his voice is basically pleasant. I can't place his accent.

"In the top drawer."

He finds the purse, turns out the contents and snorts at the few coins which he quickly discards.

"Where's the bank book," he asks, as if we have mutual funds. I stare at him.

"How much in it?"

"I don't know," I say. "Not much. I have to go online to check it."

"Online?" he asks.

"The computer." I say.

He hesitates and I wonder about his education.

"Over the Internet," I add.

"Oh, yes," he says.

He doesn't look any older than my eighteen-year-old grand-son who is my tutor for the computer and the cell phone which is smarter than me. I have a feeling robber-boy is new at this. He is nervous. He is sweating. And he doesn't seem very bright.

"Which bank you use?"

I tell him.

"Find out how much you have."

I turn on the computer, which is right beside me, while he looks around the room.

"How did you get in?" I ask. I have three locks on each door.

"The door wasn't locked."

I'm getting careless, I think. Senility setting in. I hate that word and what it implies.

I wonder if I could email somebody for help. Despite my grandson's coaching, I don't use IM so I wouldn't even be able to find somebody online, and, many people don't read their emails right away. I know that much. I don't know that many people either.

He stands behind me. The computer groans and beeps and flickers.

"Why's it taking so long?' he asks.

"So it stay, sometimes," I tell him. "It's old, like me. I could be your grandmother." I am still not really afraid of him, even though he waves the gun around a lot. I am stalling for time to think. I would like to help him get out of this with a clean slate. I don't think he means to hurt me, and I don't want him to go to jail. He is somebody's grandson.

"Why're you doing this?" I ask. "You don't look like a thief."

"No questions. Hurry up!"

I am tempted, but I don't lecture him. I was a teacher before I retired. I know youngsters hate lectures. I am hoping that the computer will say, as it sometimes does. *Error. Unable to connect.* But, of course, it doesn't. The balance is J$63,005. My children have deposited my monthly allowance.

"So, how you get the money?" he asks.

"I go to the ATM."

He squints at me like he is thinking hard. "You still drive? You have a car?"

I hesitate, then I nod. I now know how to get us out of this situation. I don't want him to be caught. And I don't want him to panic and set off the gun.

"Get your car key. We're going for the money."

"Now?" I ask. "It's after eleven o'clock."

"So? Don't they always open?"

He's not really dumb, I think.

I have trouble standing – severe arthritic knees. He sees me struggling to get up and comes to help me with his free hand. This confuses me. What's his story? I wonder. He lacks the roughness and evil demeanour I associate with robbers.

I waddle to the chest of drawers and fish out a set of old keys. I make sure he doesn't see them. My plan is taking shape. Despite the security guard, a few cars have been stolen from the compound recently. Everybody is puzzled and nervous, and on the lookout for the car thieves. My neighbour's car alarm starts squawking at the lightest touch. If I try to put a key in his lock, the alarm will alert the guard, my neighbour and others. They will all come running, and my would-be thief will have to disappear. I am counting on him to escape in time.

As for me, they won't have any trouble believing that a scatterbrained old woman forgot that she no longer owns a car. The rusty keys will be proof enough.

I pick up my handbag and walk out unsteadily. My apartment is on the ground floor. He walks behind me as I slowly shuffle out to where the cars are parked. I really need to use my cane to help me walk, but I have been resisting this. I am grateful he doesn't poke the gun in my back as I see robbers do on television. I imagine he has hidden it in case anyone sees us. That's what I would do.

"Hurry up!" he says in a whisper as I fumble with the keys. In the semidarkness he can't see how rusty they are.

I select one and lean against the car as I try to insert the key in the lock. There is an instant loud shrieking which frightens me. I lose my balance and fall.

"Shit!" he exclaims. He hesitates and I can tell that he is inclined to help me up. What kind of idiot is this?

"Go!" I command as I wave him away. "Run!"

He is at least smart enough to obey. He disappears before the security guard and tenants come barrelling towards the car.

There is a babble of excited and concerned voices and questions. The car's alarm is turned off. From the ground, I tell them in a frail voice, "I was just going to drive to the store to fetch some milk."

They help me up. "But, Granny," the security guard says. "You can't drive. You don't have a car."

"This is my car," I reply defiantly. "See, here are my keys."

The area is now brightly lit. They look at the rusty keys and shake their heads.

They lead me back to my apartment where the door is still ajar. "I'll call her daughter," says the neighbour who keeps an eye on me. "She can't live alone any longer. She can't manage."

I can manage. I dealt with that young burglar, didn't I? Better than any of them would have been able to. He got away. No shots were fired. I hope he mends his ways. I don't want to see my grandson in prison.

## IT'S TIME

"Wake up, dear. It's too hot. Time we went in." Rachel poked her husband who was dozing in his wheelchair.

"Call Fairy," he mumbled.

She shook the bell they used to summon the caretaker, vigorously. Fairy would say she didn't hear the bell if it only tinkled.

In the kitchen, Fairy grumbled, "A person can't get two minutes to themself. All day long they ringing that damn bell. Never mind," she consoled herself. "The house soon finish, then…"

She went to the couple who were taking their morning sunbathe on the porch and pushed Neville in the wheelchair, while helping his wife who walked with a stick to their bedroom. "Anything else?" she asked.

"Some lemonade would be nice," Rachel said. "All that sun has made us thirsty."

Fairy grunted and left the room.

"She has got quite surly of late. Have you noticed, Neville?"

"Maybe, she's tired of looking after us," he replied.

"She's well paid for her services."

There was silence for a while.

"Neville, we need to talk some more about that thing we were discussing last night."

"What thing is that?"

Rachel sighed. She wished he wasn't so forgetful. Last night they had discussed her fear of either one of them dying before the other. She couldn't bear the thought of him leaving her, nor the thought of leaving him all alone.

"This year," she rehashed the conversation he didn't remember, "we will both be 98. Most of our friends are gone. It's been a good life, but maybe it's time for us to go. I don't want to continue until we can't move or help ourselves or each other."

"Hmn," he said, and she didn't know if he was following her.

"I don't know how long our money will last."

"It should last a long time," he said, suddenly perking up at the mention of money. "We made some good investments."

Another round of silence.

"I haven't checked our bank book for some time."

"Fairy granddaughter has it."

He chuckled when he used the name they had given the caretaker shortly after she had come to work with them some years before. Her name was actually Fairy and Rachel had said, "We are too old to have a fairy godmother, so you'll be our fairy granddaughter."

And so she had turned out to be: looking after them and developing their trust to the point where she was solely in charge of withdrawals from their account to pay bills, keep the house, buy what they needed and pay herself.

When Fairy returned with their lemonade, Rachel said, "Fairy granddaughter, please bring the bank book. We have to start planning our expenditure more carefully."

The tray with the glasses suddenly tilted and Fairy had to steady it to prevent the juice from spilling.

"It's… it's in my other bag. I… I left it at home this morning," Fairy stammered.

"No problem. Please go home and fetch it. We'll be all right until you get back."

Fairy seemed to hesitate, so Rachel said, "Just lock the door when you leave. We're going to take a nap now."

A few minutes later, Rachel whispered to Neville, "Did you see how she got flustered when I asked her about the bank book? I have a feeling something is wrong. Why would she have it in her bag at her house? I am going to call Cecille at the bank and ask her to check the balance. We have been careless about it."

"You said we could trust her," Neville replied.

"People change."

By the time Rachel finished a very disturbing conversation with her contact at the bank, Neville was asleep.

"Neville! Neville! Wake up." She shook him. "It's bad. Really bad."

"What's bad?" he asked, sleepily.

"Oh, Neville, pay attention. The girl has stolen most of our money!"

"Who has stolen our money?"

"Fairy. She has taken out a million dollars over the last six months. There's very little left."

"Call the police! Call the police!" he kept repeating.

"Calm yourself, Neville. Let me think."

After a while, she said, "Perhaps it's time to put my plan in action."

"What plan?"

"Last night when we were talking about it, you agreed it was the best plan."

"What plan?"

Rachel went to sit on the bed beside him. She held his hand as she talked.

"We're 98 years old this year. We have had a good life. We can't expect to live much longer, and neither of wants to die and leave the other."

"What are you saying?" he asked. He looked at her through cloudy, watery eyes. He could hardly see now, but he smiled and said. "You are a beautiful woman. I'm glad I married you."

"Yes, dear," she said. "I'm glad I married you, too."

She got up and wobbled with her walking stick to the desk in the room, took up a pen and wrote on a pad. "I've written a note for the police," she said. "Listen –

"*This morning we discovered that our caretaker, Fairy Gentles, has stolen most of our money from the bank. When we accosted her, she threatened to kill us. If anything happens to us, you know where to look for the culprit.*"

"Very good, mi love," Neville said. "Who is the culprit?"

Rachel shook her head, but she smiled as she folded the note and put it in an envelope.

"It's perfect. Just like that movie we watched. She won't get away with it."

The two glasses of lemonade Fairy had brought for them were still on the table, untouched. Rachel opened a drawer, took out a small packet and emptied the contents into the glasses. Then she took two capsules from a vial. Her hands shook as she pulled them apart and emptied the contents in the lemonades. She walked unsteadily to the bathroom and flushed the empty packet and capsules.

She returned to the bedroom and used the straws in the glasses to stir the contents until she felt certain that her additions were absorbed, then she took one and brought it to the bed.

"It's time, Neville."

"What time is it?" he asked.

"Here's your lemonade, dear."

He took the glass and slowly sipped through the straw. "Bitter," he said, making an ugly face. "It's warm."

"Never mind, dear. Just drink it."

She waited until he finished, put his empty glass on the table, then stirred and drank from hers quickly, making sure there was some left for testing.

When she returned to the bed, Neville was lying on his back with his eyes closed. She was glad she had thought of adding the sedative; he wouldn't feel anything.

She checked that the note to the police was hidden under her pillow then lay down beside him. She snuggled up and rested her head on his shoulder, too bony now to be comfortable, but this had always been her safe place.

He mumbled softly and she answered, her voice fading at the end, "It's okay, dear. We're going home, together."

★

Fairy had found her husband. "They asking for the bank book. They're going to find out we thief the money! What we going to do?" she wailed.

"Calm down," he said. "Stick to the plan. We were going to do it, anyway. We just kill them now instead of later."

## HAUNTED BY LISTS

As far back as I can remember somebody was always telling me: "Make a list of the things you have to do; of what you need to buy; where you have to go," et cetera, et cetera.

You see, I am extremely disorganised, although I like to think that there is organisation in my apparent disorganisation; my own unique style of getting through each day.

I hate making lists. I am a scribbler by nature, so I do make jottings on various pieces of paper but I would probably have to make a list of where I put these jottings in order to find them again.

My first job was as a temporary clerk in a sales department. Inventory! I hated it. No surprise that my first evaluation included "not well organised". When I told my boyfriend, he tried to help me by insisting on calling each morning for me to read him my "to do" list, accounting for each hour of my day from the time I woke up until I went to bed. It even included finishing lunch ten minutes to the hour to take care of bathroom business. I don't know the name of the phobia for fear of lists, but by Thursday, that week, I was stressed out from making lists, by Friday almost screaming. On Friday night I had a nightmare. A bunch of lists with stick arms and feet chased me into a backyard pool where I woke up just before I drowned. That same weekend I dumped said boyfriend.

Then I went to college and bumbled through until the second year when I joined a study group led by this fellow who would win any championship on list-making and organising time. Adrian was his name. A nerdy fellow. I can see him now, racing across the campus, the wind lifting his hair. He was always in a hurry to get to the next place on his list.

There were five of us in this group – four girls and him. He was the automatic leader, not because he was male but because he was so organised. We never wasted time just chatting in our group. When others complained that group work was a waste of time, we boasted how productive ours was.

We met four afternoons weekly, and Adrian planned each of our four-hour sessions down to the minutes we would spend on each topic. When we complained of feeling stressed by the intensity of our sessions, he added breaks, strictly ten minutes only. Gossip, bathroom, snacks, anything besides what was planned for the session had to be crammed into those ten minutes.

We teased him about his list-making, but we got in so much work we were the top group in that year. These were pre-electronic gadget days. He always had a yellow legal pad for his lists. We would watch in amusement as he ticked off each item as it was completed.

One afternoon he had to leave us for a few minutes – some emergency – and we took the opportunity to examine his yellow pad. His whole day was planned in detail, hour by hour. There was a tick beside completed tasks and here and there a comment, like – good, needs attention, waste of time, and so on.

When he returned, we looked at him in awe. Sharlene, ever bold, said, "Tell me something, Adrian, when you're dating a girl, do you write down when you're going to have sex, and for how long, and when you finish d'you tick it off on the pad beside the bed?"

He grinned at her. "What you think?" He never got mad at our teasing. I guess that was not on the list.

But he was brilliant, and the next year it was our great loss when he took up a scholarship in another country.

After college, I joined the civil service, and though I did my work well, always the negative comment: "needs to be more organized". I ignored it. If the work was somehow getting done, I told myself, perhaps they should just leave me alone.

I lost touch with my friends from college, but I continued to hear about Adrian. He had become Dr. Adrian and was rising fast in politics in his island.

Time passed and I was assigned to be part of a mission to a four-day conference on climate change in Adrian's island. I was delighted when I recognised him at the head table at the opening session. He looked very respectable in his jacket and tie – hair now cut close, neat beard and his smile just as big as I remembered it – but still nerdy. I watched him, curious about this different persona. He no longer had a yellow pad, but I guessed that his smartphone was now bearing that burden.

At the first break in proceedings, I approached his chair where he was busily tapping on his phone, and said quietly, "I see you're still making lists."

He looked up, startled at first, then, when recognition came, he jumped up and hugged me. "Pansy!" he exclaimed. "Long time! Just look at you. All grown up and beautiful as ever."

He held me at arm's length and I could tell that he was liking what he saw. I was surprised. I would never have thought that he would notice me in that way.

The rest of that conference remains a blur. There wasn't much for me to do except take notes; our mission leader was very competent and liked to do things herself. But other experiences are still very clear. At nine o'clock that first night, my phone rang. It was Adrian. We chatted for a while, catching up on each other's lives. He was divorced and he seemed interested to hear that I was not married. He ended by inviting me to have breakfast with him in the hotel dining room next morning.

I found myself dressing with great care that morning and bemoaning the fact that I had left my favourite perfume. I should have made a list, I thought, and smiled.

We had breakfast together – and lunch, and dinner. Somewhere along the day, I realised that when people stopped by our table to talk to him, and he seemed to be very popular, they all had a sort of smirk as if they thought he was on a date with me.

When he made his presentation on climate change, I realised, again, how competent and knowledgeable he was. I overheard a conversation implying that his party was grooming him to be their next prime minister, but when I asked him about this, he shook his head. He was not interested in serving like that, he said. He had been offered a university post which he was thinking of accepting. He would make himself available to his government as a consultant.

For three days I sat in that conference trying to concentrate on the proceedings. Whenever I looked up, it seemed our eyes would meet. Somehow, during the social events, like the concert and film sessions, we always seemed to be sitting next to each other. It felt like there was a powerful magnet pulling me to him. It confused me.

On the free afternoon of the final day of the conference, he invited me to go to the beach with him. I had brought my swimsuit hoping for just such an opportunity. The beaches there were famous. I don't remember much of that swim except the anticipation of what had to follow. Seems neither of us could deny the attraction.

Our lovemaking in his room that afternoon was perfect. Afterwards, when he was still holding me like something precious, a memory suddenly bubbled up and I burst into laughter. I could see bewilderment on his face rapidly turning to alarm, so I said: "Do you remember when Sharlene asked you if you made a list of when to have sex, and if you ticked it off afterwards? I was waiting to see if you were going to reach for your phone to make a tick."

He started laughing, too. "She asked me about having sex, not making love to a beautiful woman."

Our laughter rekindled passion and we started all over again. I had a feeling it would be some time before that day's list got any attention.

Two months later we got married. The only lists I ever enjoyed making were those leading up to our wedding. I still have trouble making lists, and he still divides his life into daily lists, but somehow we manage.

## EMANCIPATION PARK

"So now they putting the slackness on the front page!"

"What slackness, Mama?" Melissa asked as she came into the room. She was about to leave for work. Just one week into the new job, she didn't want to be late.

"I hope you not walking past those disgusting statues when you go to work."

Melissa had already heard her mother's opinion of the two naked figures in the monument recently erected in Emancipation Park. She had read the outraged letters to the editor; the principal concern being that the man and woman, who were much larger than life, were explicitly naked. She had not seen them, since her route to and from work took her in the opposite direction. She would take a look, but she couldn't tell Mama that. Apparently, groups of people gathered around the statue daily to gawk at the figures. That made it seem even worse to Mama.

"Look at them! Them don't have nothing better to do than stare at nekkidness!" She pronounced the word with a hiss.

"I leaving now, Mama."

Mama looked her over keenly. Apparently, she passed inspection as she didn't comment.

"What time you coming home this evening?"

"It's school tonight, Mama. Not before nine o'clock, maybe."

"You want me to come and meet you at the bus stop?"

"No, Mama. Suppose the bus late? You would have to be standing there waiting. Plenty people around at that time. I will be safe."

Mama screwed up her face. No young girl should be walking alone on the streets at that hour of the night. Even though Melissa was twenty-one years old, she still thought of her as a young girl. She didn't approve of these night classes, but it was a way for Melissa to get higher education. Since they couldn't afford the university fees, she couldn't very well object, but she worried about her. "So much sinful man waiting to fall a girl." She hoped and prayed that Melissa kept her head focused and didn't meet any of these wayward, out-of-order men. Hopefully, one of the promising young men in the church would become seriously interested in her soon. That was her daily prayer.

But Mama need not have worried. Melissa had learned all the lessons she taught and kept them constantly in her thoughts. Men were evil. They only wanted one thing from a woman and when they got it, they would disappear. Any girl who opened her legs to a man before she was married was a slut – on and on. Melissa knew that Mama's obsession stemmed from her own mistake and betrayal; the mistake and betrayal which had produced her; the mistake and betrayal which had made her family kick her out when she got pregnant when she was eighteen.

Melissa didn't know who her father was, and when she asked, Mama behaved as if she was committing treason. She had even given Melissa her own surname, so there was no easy way to trace him. Only her light-brown skin colour with a slight yellowish tinge; thick, almost straight hair and the telltale slant of her eyes betrayed the fact that her father had to be Chinese. She sometimes wondered who he was, how he and Mama had got together, and if he would ever know of her existence.

Later, at work, Melissa examined the picture in the newspaper her mother had been reading. The bronze male and female figures were huge – more than three metres tall – standing in a pool of cascading water and proudly showing off all their private parts.

The photographer had cleverly taken the picture at an angle which partly hid the man's genitals. The woman's breasts, however, were very prominently displayed – large with very erect nipples. They were both gazing up at the sky, "their nakedness symbolic of a rebirth, freedom from slavery, and their faces expressing the expectation of a new dawn". The statement had obviously been written in defence of the commissioning committee's choice of this design.

Melissa quickly turned the page lest any of her co-workers saw her staring at the picture, nor did she join the conversations about the sculpture. But her curiosity intensified; she would change her route that evening and walk past the park. She wouldn't even have to go into the park as the monument had been placed in an alcove at the entrance and could easily be seen from the sidewalk.

At five o'clock, Melissa hastened out of her office. She had an hour before her class started, enough time to pass by the park and catch a bus to the Evening Institute.

She didn't need to ask the location of the statues. There was already a small knot of people gazing up at it. Some were munching on snacks as if at a picnic and making jokes, but some stood looking up at the huge figures as if they held some vital secret for mankind.

Melissa stood at the edge of the small crowd. The sight of the man's very prominent genitals made her uncomfortable. She felt her face growing hot. She turned away and bumped into a photographer, camera pointed in her direction. She immediately panicked, blush disappearing and her face turning very pale. What would Mama say if they published a picture of her looking at the statue?

He seemed to understand her problem. "Don't worry," he said. "I didn't take a picture of you."

She nodded at him, not sure if she should thank him, and started to walk away.

"It's all fiction, you know," he said.

She paused to stare at him, not understanding what he was talking about.

"The man. Nobody is that big. I mean, I know he is larger than life, but those genitals! Somebody's wish list, perhaps."

He laughed out loudly and some people turned to stare at him. It was not a sound she was accustomed to. In her house, loud laughter meant an invitation to DISASTER. "Chicken merry, hawk deh near!" was one of Mama's favourite sayings. There was always a hawk in Mama's version of life, hovering, waiting to destroy happiness. Like a lot of other things, Melissa had learned to repress laughter.

She fled before the photographer could see how embarrassed she was. She had never talked about anything sexual with a man. Indeed, she had never talked about sex with anybody. She could only listen to her mother's frequent harangues which didn't give her any information anyway. At one point, when she was younger, she had believed that even thinking about a boy could make a girl pregnant. What she knew had been picked up here and there from books, surreptitiously read, and listening to other girls talk. She thought about sex as an ominous force in a lurking future when she would be properly married to a man acceptable to Mama.

Sex was something bad; something that made the parson's voice crescendo to great heights of condemnation as he regularly threatened to place any of his congregation found in fornication or adultery on the sinner bench at the back of the church – a spectacle for all to see.

Melissa didn't learn much from that evening's class on Caribbean cultures. Confused thoughts swirled around in her head, and when she reached home, she was glad that Mama, who was waiting up for her, could not read minds.

At five o'clock the next afternoon, she lingered at her desk, not sure what she wanted to do. She had no classes that evening and her bus stop was in the opposite direction, but her thoughts continued to linger on the statues and the photographer. What did he mean by saying that they were fiction? She wondered if he would still be there.

And he was. Her heart did a little skip and jump when she saw him, and she walked a little faster, pretending that this was her regular route and she was just casually passing by.

"Hey!" he called out when he saw her, and when she didn't stop, he hurried to join her.

"You're not stopping today?"

She looked at him and tried to control the blood rushing to her face. He was quite good looking, she thought, as her eyes explored his face and body. Early twenties, she guessed; unusual brown eyes, lighter than his skin colour; puss eyes literally twinkling with whatever was amusing him. He was comfortably dressed in khaki pants and a blue polo shirt with his newspaper logo prominently displayed.

"Are you always here?" she asked boldly.

He grinned at her. "Assignment," he said. "Human interest. Did you see the picture on yesterday's front page? I took it," he said proudly. "I'm here between three and six o'clock. You'd be surprised at the range of expressions on people's faces and the things they say. It's like a shrine, or something."

She didn't comment.

"One day, a mad man stripped naked, jumped into the pool and posed like the statue." He laughed his happy laugh. "His penis was very big, too. Maybe he was not so mad."

There was no controlling the blush now.

"You're a virgin, aren't you?"

Her face turned even redder.

"You don't need to be embarrassed. That's a good thing."

"What makes you think so?" she asked, suddenly once more bold.

"The way you were looking at the statue, and your blushing. I've seen it all – the blushing, the giggling, the finger pointing, the mouths open in wonder. You would think this represents an alien species and nobody has ever seen naked people."

She could think of nothing to say.

"I'm a virgin, too," he said, as if making a confession. His eyebrows were raised in expectation of a reply. She said the first thing that came to mind.

"What's wrong with you?"

He laughed. She couldn't restrain a tiny smile, his laughter was so infectious.

"Not a thing. Despite popular opinion, like everything else, that too can be controlled."

She continued to stare at him.

"Many priests are truly celibate."

She didn't say anything.

"So," he said chummily, "We are two of a kind – strange creatures in a wanton land. Maybe, we are the aliens."

More silence from her.

"Aren't you going to say something?" he asked. "Something witty, perhaps."

They were now at the corner of the park; she would have to cross the road to continue her journey. They paused.

"Why?" she asked.

"Why what?"

"Why… you know. Why you never…"

He put his hand under his chin, one finger resting on his cheek and leaned his head. Then he smiled.

"It's something I've had to think about. When I reached high school, in grade seven, they gave us boys sex education lessons – obviously designed to scare the wits out of us. The pictures of diseases and what they could do to the body and the discussion of health problems related to sex did scare us off – me, for good, it seems. I'm a very disciplined person. Or, maybe it's just that I never met a girl I wanted to take the risk with." He looked at her keenly.

The blush started again, up from her neck, rushing to her face. "And before you ask anything more, Palmella is good company, when needed."

"Who is Pamella?" she asked.

"Oh come on," he said. "You can't be that naive. Palm-ella," he gestured with his hand and laughed really loudly as she hurriedly dashed across the road despite the oncoming traffic and the honking car horns.

More confusion in her thoughts; she couldn't get him out of her mind.

In the way of mothers who live vicariously through their children, Mama quickly picked up that something was changing for her Melissa.

"How you so quiet?" she asked when they were eating dinner that night.

"Mama! I'm always quiet."

"Enh enh? I talking and you not hearing a word I'm saying."

"Of course I'm hearing, I just don't have anything to say."

"So, what I was talking about?"

Melissa had vaguely heard the name Irene, so she made a quick guess. "Sister Irene and the church supper next month."

"Ha! I knew you weren't listening. I was telling you that Sister Irene son, Desmond, get scholarship to go to university."

"That's good," Melissa replied – too late.

"So, what him name?"

"Excuse me?"

"The problem with you young people is that you think we older one born yesterday. I know that look of distraction. Who is he?" This time the question sounded more like a criminal interrogation.

"I don't know what you're talking about," Melissa lied. "I have a test coming up and I'm trying to concentrate on that."

"Oh!" Mama replied, slightly placated. Despite her misgivings, she couldn't argue with education.

Melissa went to bed and dreamed she was a model posing for a flashing camera. The photographer wore a blue polo shirt and kept laughing and spoiling the pictures.

For the next two days, she fought the urge to see him again and went back to her regular route from work so she wouldn't have to pass the park.

On the third afternoon when she came downstairs from her office on the third floor, already late for class. She was in such a hurry that she missed the figure sitting on the couch in the reception area until he called out, "Hey!" and got up.

She stopped so suddenly that she nearly fell over. Her bag and notebook fell to the floor.

"How you just passing me, so?" he began in his cheerful way, as he bent down to help her retrieve her things.

"Hi…" she managed to stammer when they were both standing. "H… How… How are you?"

"I am very fine. Thank you for asking," he replied, with a little bow, and in such a formal tone that she realised he was teasing her and gave him a nervous smile.

"I'm going your way, so I thought we could walk together."

Oh, gosh! she thought; he couldn't know that that was not her normal route.

"How did you know where…?"

"I'm a journalist. I investigate. You didn't come yesterday, nor the day before."

"Do you know my name, too," she asked.

"Yes, Miss Melissa Ferron. You just joined Pinkham's Services as a trainee. You are twenty-one years old, and I am hoping you will tell me the rest…"

She raised her eyebrows and he said, "…like where you live and so on."

The thought of home and introducing him to Mama made her shudder. She just knew he was not a churchgoer, and that was the first question Mama would ask.

The security guard standing in front of the building looked at them curiously, then winked at Melissa as they passed her.

"And what is your name?"

"Whew! I thought you were never going to ask. Did I scare you?"

When she didn't answer, he said, "It's Hydrew, spelled with a 'y'. Please don't laugh and always remember to pronounce the 'h'. Some people just call me Hy. Which is as anonymous as you can get. 'Hey, Hy! What's up, man?'" He laughed, softly this time, more like a chuckle.

"Ironically, my parents imagined I would be somebody great – like an athlete or a Prime Minister, so they thought I needed to have an unusual name – so they combined theirs – Hyacinth and Andrew."

She couldn't decide if he was joking.

"It could be worse," he added. "My father could have been named Mendel or something such."

She decided to be honest with him. "You know, I can't tell if you are serious or not."

"Oh, I am serious. Look at my face." She looked at the face he was making and had to smile. "Just call me 'Hy'. 'Hey' would do too, although I prefer 'Drew'."

They had reached the point at which she had to turn north to catch her bus. She was going to be really late for her class.

"I have to turn here. I go to the Evening Institute. I am late."

"Can't you skip class this evening? I have some pictures I want to show you."

"If it's more naked people, I don't want to…"

"Of course not!" He sounded indignant. "That's work. Some other things you might like."

It was surprisingly easy to talk with him. Without making a conscious decision, she turned in the direction of the park.

There weren't many persons looking up at the statues that evening.

"Ah," he said. "They're beginning to lose interest. Thought it would happen. My assignment will soon end."

He pointed to a ledge a little away from the monument. "Come, sit here with me. Look out for bird doo-doo, they're always around looking for the crumbs people leave behind."

She noticed that a few tame-looking black birds were sitting on the fence behind the ledge, their eyes darting about, but the area was clean, so they sat a little distance away from each other as he placed a large envelope between them.

"I have dreams of becoming a great photographer. Some day, everybody will know my name. I won't even need another name. Just Hydrew. My parents were right."

Suddenly he was shy. "You can tell me if you don't like them," he said, as he opened the envelope and placed it in her hands.

"I don't know much about photography."

"You don't have to know about the technical details. Respond with your soul, with your feelings."

For a few minutes, they were silent as she pulled out the stack of photographs and began looking at them. He started humming a tune she recognized as Bob Marley's "Redemption Song".

"You know, people can't decide whether the statue should be singular or plural."

She paused to look at him.

"Is it one piece of art and therefore singular, or should it be plural since it's two people?"

"I can't look at the pictures and talk," she said.

"Sorry." He grinned at her sheepishly, like a little boy.

The pictures covered a range of topics – landscapes, seascapes, animals, sunsets and sunrises – both in colour and black and white. They were all quite good, she thought.

"I don't like the name *Redemption Song*," he said.

"What?" she asked, slightly annoyed at the distraction.

"The monument – its title is *Redemption Song*, but maybe *Free at Last* might have…"

He stopped talking when he saw her expression. She was making a face inherited from Mama – eyes and mouth narrowed, nostrils flaring – a stern look designed to stop any malefactor in his tracks.

He put up his hands, ran a pretend zipper across his mouth and started tapping a foot on the pavement. She realised that he was actually nervous about her reaction to his pictures, and wondered why it was important to him.

She returned to looking at the photographs and quickly saw how he excelled at taking pictures of people. Some of them looked almost like paintings, as if he had used the camera to see into their souls and capture what they were thinking at a particular moment.

After a while, she looked up at him. "These are pretty good."

"You think so?"

"What are you going to do with them?"

"Not sure, yet. Maybe a book, or an exhibition, or both."

"They are very creative. The people are almost like paintings rather than photographs."

"There is an art to taking people. Either you take a candid shot before they realize what you are doing and get a chance to mask their thoughts or actions, or you take a portrait after you have talked them into relaxing and revealing something of themselves. Otherwise you're only taking a false pose – you know, 'say cheese'." He paused. "But, as I told you the other day, it's all fiction."

"What?"

"All art is fiction – painting, music, sculpture, dance…"

"I don't understand…"

"It's all somebody's interpretation of some aspect of life – not real life itself. So your statues can only represent something – not reality, but an appeal to feelings – anger, reverence, hope, lust – all of those emotional kinds of things."

"My statues?"

"Yes." He grinned. "I've started thinking of them as your statues. The man and woman are giants – in more ways than one. Maybe what we would all like to be, but cannot be."

"And your photographs? Don't they capture reality?"

"A fleeting moment in time, frozen as if it can forever be real. The real thing is never exactly the same all the time, you know. Even the same landscape – different every shot, even a short time later. A breeze will have changed the contours of the leaves. A bird will have flown in or out of the picture and so on."

He was quiet for a few minutes. She wished she could think of something profound to say to prolong the discussion, but she wasn't even sure that she completely understood him.

"You think they will allow us to take our wedding picture in the pool before your statues?"

"What!" she exclaimed.

"Oh, I intend to woo you, and go down on one knee, ring box in hand, and ask you properly when the right time comes. But, for now, just imagine it. You, looking extra beautiful in your wedding dress. Me, handsome in my tux – I'm warning you from now that I'm getting married in a tux – We're both wet, sitting at the edge of the pool kissing, right under those outsize genitals."

Several kinds of feelings nearly overwhelmed her – outrage at his brashness, confusion because he could so easily mess with her head and make her heartbeats speed up, then finally amusement at the picture he had just painted. The more she thought about it, the funnier it seemed.

HAZEL D. CAMPBELL. NEW AND COLLECTED STORIES

"The newspaper will carry it on the wedding page. Headline – Emancipation Park Statues Breed Love. Caption – Popular photographer, Hydrew, and his bride share a kiss under *Redemption Song* where they met."

He started laughing and a picture of Mama's face looking on at the scene he had just described flashed into her mind, and, for the first time that she could remember, laughter, starting deep inside, welled up and burst from her – strong and free.

The birds sitting on the fence behind them suddenly flew away, startled by their laughter – and she didn't even remember to look up to see if there were any hawks circling the sky.

## THE BUGGU YAGGAS

Before she died, my grandmother used to tell us stories about the "black heart" man. He lurked in dark, lonely places to catch young children with the object of cutting out their hearts to use in his "black arts". Maybe something bad once happened and much later it morphed into a scary story, a folktale told to young children to prevent them wandering in places where harm might befall them.

I wonder if, in future years, children will be told about the Buggu Yaggas of my youth, as if they are only folk tales too. But the Buggu Yaggas were real. Very real. As to whether they were all bad? I couldn't say.

I don't know who gave them that name which quickly caught on. I was about eleven years old when the Buggu Yaggas came into our lives. I was living with my family in a middle-class housing scheme where the houses were built close together with hand-kerchief sized lawns and minimum space for a home garden. But, there was a large park at one end of the scheme where we children played with our neighbours, and where the community held parties and communal activities. This was before the Internet and iPads, cell phones and video games began to keep most of the children indoors. We loved the park with its shady flowering trees, pretty flowers, green grass for picnics and benches to hang out with our friends. It was a pleasant neighbourhood. A good place to grow a child, the adults often said.

Our father died when I was eight years old, soon after Dolly was born. He left our mother, Clara, my older brother, Richard, and the baby who we called Dolly – when she was born she did indeed look like a doll – and me. I have suppressed most of the memories of that time. I remember our mother always crying; having to help mind the baby; and Aunt Hopie, my mother's sister, visiting and staying with us very often. Then one day our mother started smiling again; that was when Uncle Freddie came into our lives. Our new father, she said. He moved into our home just about the same time that the Buggu Yaggas moved into our park.

The park was protected from the gully which bordered it by a chain link fence, and neighbours looked out for one another and the children, so it was deemed safe for us to play or hang out there when we got tired of home.

After the Buggu Yaggas captured the park, everything changed. We could not go to the park. We could not walk on the streets in the scheme alone, and if we did, we were cautioned to get home as fast as possible. Most of all, we were cautioned not to speak to any of the Buggu Yaggas.

When I first heard that name, I thought it was very funny. I did not know what it meant, but I learned that Buggu Yagga was an old-time name for disorderly persons. But these Buggu Yaggas were more than that. They were despicable persons: homosexuals, transvestites, drug addicts cast out by their families. I learned these words by eavesdropping on adult conversations. There were other words used to describe the Buggu Yaggas too, but I knew that even to hear them, much less to repeat them, would send me straight to hell.

The Buggu Yaggas, at first a small group and a new phenomenon, wandered about capturing unused spaces in the city which could accommodate them and their activities, and they liked our park.

Our neighbourhood was not accommodating. The police were often called to get rid of them, but the gully behind the park was their safe place. Whenever there was a raid, they would simply disappear into the gully and reappear after the police left. When some of the men from the community tried to reason with them and get them to move away, they were met with hostility, they were jeered and stoned and the whole thing soon escalated into a mini war.

We children were fascinated by these Buggu Yagga men, and all the talk about them. We were afraid yes, but fascinated. Many of us young girls got our first glimpse of an adult male's body by peeping through our curtains, for when the sprinklers came on they would strip and bathe right there in the open park. I think the attraction for us was that it was all so forbidden.

The community tried everything they could to get rid of them. They turned off the sprinklers. They repaired the fence by the gully, which was quickly torn down again. Nothing could stop these Buggu Yaggas. The more they were rejected, the bolder they got and their numbers seemed to be growing. They stole from our homes, especially women's clothing drying in our backyards. It was entertaining to some and disgusting to others to watch groups of four or five of these mostly young men walking through the scheme dressed as women in wigs, tight dresses, midriff blouses and short shorts showing off their hairy legs wearing high heels which made them walk like clowns. The children laughed quietly while the adults fumed. In a way, they were faceless. I don't know if anybody saw them as anything more than a nuisance.

Soon the park began to look very shabby as food cartons and bottles and other debris littered the space, and some of the plants grew brown or dried up. Sometimes the Buggu Yaggas romped. They played football and cricket and other games, loudly. Sometimes they fought one another, loudly. Whatever they did was loud. As their numbers grew, they were like an invading army and all we could do was to try to protect ourselves from them.

About the time the Buggu Yaggas came into the scheme, life became increasingly chaotic for my family and it was only when I was much older that I was able to put the details of events into some kind of order.

Our father's death affected all of us, but moreso my brother Richard, who was eleven years old. For more than three years, he tried to fill this gap as best he could. He would try to fix things around the house. He would cook when our mother couldn't. He would check my schoolwork, very annoying at times, but he kept us going when all our mother did was cry. We had a day-worker who came in to clean the house once each week, but it was Richard who took care of us. One day, when he was about fourteen years old, I watched him clearing a drain in the yard and I thought he was nearly looking like a man.

Then Uncle Freddie arrived – and stayed. At first, things were great. He was tall, good looking and charming. He took care of us. He never came home without a treat for us children. He always said how pretty Dolly and I were. He would lift up Dolly, hug her and play games with us. He took us to the movies and the beach and concerts. When his friends visited, he showed us off, like a real father. He fitted in with the community and joined the campaign to get rid of the Buggu Yaggas. Our mother was happy and so were we.

Except for Richard. I guess it would have been normal to expect that Richard would resent this new male, usurping both his father's and his own authority in the family. He began to withdraw and sulk. As time went on, Richard barely spoke to anybody at home and stayed out as late as possible. There were many quarrels between himself and our mother and eventually Uncle Freddie too when he began to nag Richard about staying out late and almost everything he did or didn't do.

But there was something else going on that we could not have known. All we felt was Richard's bitter hatred of Uncle Freddie. Sometimes I would see his eyes red as if he was crying, but he would not answer me when I tried to find out what was troubling him. Our mother seemed to be constantly scolding him about his poor grades and attitude towards Uncle Freddie, and sometimes she mentioned drugs. Then she began to blame Richard for Uncle Freddie's changed behaviour. They had started quarrelling a lot and she was no longer smiling and happy. It was very unpleasant. I tried to shield Dolly from it all as best I could. When they were at home, we mostly stayed in our room, me reading and she playing with her toys.

One evening, Richard came home very late from school. He came into the kitchen where my mother was making a snack for

Dolly and me. He picked up one of the sandwiches and our mother started her usual scolding. Richard lost his temper. "Leave me alone!" he shouted at her.

Uncle Freddie stormed into the room. "Enough of this. I won't allow you to be so rude to your mother. You need some licks to settle you," he threatened Richard. He started to take off his belt and Richard spat at him. As the spit rolled down Uncle Freddie's cheek, I froze. So did our mother and Uncle Freddie, for a moment, at this barefaced insult. Uncle Freddie tried to grab Richard who dodged him and ran out of the house. Uncle Freddie ran after him but couldn't catch him. When he came back into the house, Uncle Freddie was cursing and shouting what he would do to Richard when he caught him. He was waving the belt around like a mad man. I grabbed Dolly and hurried to our room.

Richard didn't come home.

They searched for him for a few days. Eventually, after my mother confessed that he was unhappy at home, the police told her he had just run away and would come back when he was ready, so they stopped searching.

After this, things got even more unpleasant. Neither our mother nor Uncle Freddie noticed us much. They seemed to be either quarrelling or not speaking to each other. When nobody remembered to bring food or cook for us, I started preparing simple meals for myself and Dolly from whatever was available when my mother remembered to go shopping. Things like fried eggs and sausages. We ate a lot of cheese sandwiches. I was very proud when my first attempt at cooking minced meat could actually be eaten. I even learned to cook rice without turning it into soup. Weekends, when Aunt Hopie took us to her home, were the only happy times we now had.

All this was happening at the same time the Buggu Yaggas were still living in the park. Uncle Freddie was very vocal about this disease in our community. He had joined the Neighbourhood Watch of men who patrolled the scheme for protection against the Buggu Yaggas, who were getting even bolder. They now stole anything not fastened down. They broke into cars and kept us hostage, locked in our homes. Every house in the scheme was now securely grilled – windows, doors, verandas.

But, one night the police raid was successful. They attacked the Buggu Yaggas in the park and in the gully at the same time and arrested some of them.

Two days later, our mother was in the living-room watching the evening news. When we heard her screaming, Uncle Freddie, Dolly and I rushed to her. We found her pointing at the television and making a funny noise, like she was choking. When she could talk she kept repeating, "Richard! Richard!"

Eventually, Uncle Freddie calmed her enough to understand that there was a news item about the police raid on the Buggu Yaggas and that she had recognized Richard among those arrested.

Uncle Freddie made some calls and left the house. We stayed with our mother, who sat not moving or talking. We watched whatever came on the television for a while. When Dolly got sleepy, I took her to bed. I didn't hear when Uncle Freddie returned. Next morning the house was very quiet. Nobody spoke, neither in the car nor when we got out at school. Later that day, it was Aunt Hopie who came for us at school and took us to her home.

She wouldn't tell us what was happening at our house. But by this time I had become expert at eavesdropping to find out what the adults were up to. Each time the phone rang, I listened to find out if it was my mother. I told Dolly to keep quiet when I heard Aunt Hopie saying, "Clara, you have to stop crying and talk to me."

She listened for a while, then I heard her ask, "But how could he have been with them, so near and you never knew?"

I don't know what my mother answered, but after listening some more, Aunt Hopie said, "Okay", hung up, and told us to get dressed. Richard had come home and our mother wanted us there.

I was happy to hear that he had come home, but shocked when I saw him. His clothes were dirty. His white merino had turned brownish and his pants were torn. His hair was uncombed as if he was growing locks. He looked wild, just like one of the Buggu Yaggas. I could hardly recognise him.

Dolly and I only stared at him. He nodded at us, said "Hi" and went back to looking through the window. Our mother had been crying, I could tell.

"He won't go to his room and clean up himself," she wailed. Aunt Hopie tried to talk to him, but he ignored her. After a while, looking upset, she left us. Dolly and I went to our room and the house became very quiet. I didn't hear any movement or talking between Richard and our mother. It was getting dark when Uncle Freddie came home. As soon as I heard his car door slam, I knew there was going to be trouble.

I heard him shout, "Boy, why you still have on those dirty clothes? Go and clean up yourself."

"What for?" Richard asked. His voice was loud and challenging. "So you can do what you want with me?"

There was silence for a short while, then our mother asked, "What does that mean, Richard?"

I didn't hear his answer but soon they were screaming at one another. I heard words like "molesting", "my room", "liar", "abuse", and some others I knew were so bad that I shouldn't be listening. Neither should Dolly. I shut the door of our room and tried to distract her by reading to her. The loud voices continued and then all was quiet for a while. Just as I began to relax, shrieking and shouting and banging with the sounds of shattering glass started. It was awful. I knew something very bad was happening. I was so scared, I wanted to vomit, but I had to take care of Dolly.

We crawled into the closet in our room to hide. Even then, we could hear the commotion. We covered our ears for a long time. I don't know when Dolly fell asleep, her head in my lap. I don't know if I slept. My eyes were open when Aunt Hopie found us in the closet. She burst out crying, and couldn't stop saying, "Thank, God! Thank, God!" Seemed she had been searching for us but never thought to look in the closet. It was morning and I didn't know what had happened during the night.

Aunt Hopie packed some of our things and led us carefully

through the house to her car. She sort of shielded us as if she didn't want us looking around. She took us to her home, helped us to get clean, fed us and put us to bed. I was afraid to ask her what had happened and she didn't give us any explanation. I think we slept for a long time. When we woke up, Charlene, one of her neighbours, was in the house babysitting us, I suppose. Late in the evening, Aunt Hopie returned. She looked very tired and sad. She told us that our mother was in the hospital, but would soon get better, and that we would be staying with her for a while.

We didn't go back to school for the rest of that term. It was near summer holidays anyway. I passed the time by reading and rereading every book I could find. Dolly mostly stayed beside me quietly hugging her teddy bear; sometimes she just slept. About three weeks later, we went home. Dolly, who had hardly spoken since that awful night, asked, "Is Uncle Freddie at home?" Aunt Hopie said "No." And Dolly started crying, "I hate him! I hate him!"

"He's not coming back," Aunt Hopie reassured her. I was happy to hear that. I was very afraid of him.

When we got home, our mother was sitting on the couch in the livingroom. Her eyes were open but it didn't look as if she was seeing anything. We ran and hugged her, but I immediately knew something was wrong. She didn't respond. It was as if we were hugging a warm statue.

Nobody ever directly told me the details of what had happened that night of fear. Gradually, from bits and pieces of information from different sources, I gathered that after Richard left the house again, there had been a big fight between our mother and Uncle Freddie. The neighbours had called the police who found her lying on the kitchen floor bleeding from stab wounds. She had fought back because he, too, was wounded. She was admitted to the hospital and he treated and taken to the police station but they had not arrested him, only taken a statement. Neighbours said they heard when his car drove up to our house. They saw him go in, then he came out a little later and drove away. Nobody ever saw Uncle Freddie after that. Days later, the police found his car in bushes along the lonely Port Royal Road. There was blood in the car but they never found his body.

That same night, the Buggu Yaggas totally deserted our park. All they left behind was their usual rubbish heaps. People wondered if they had anything to do with Uncle Freddie's disappearance. The police searched for them, but it seemed they had just vanished. Uncle Freddie was presumed dead, and Richard became "a person of interest" for the police. They told us that if we saw him we should contact them immediately.

Our mother didn't recover. Aunt Hopie came to live with us and we got a full-time household helper because our mother needed attention when we were out, and gradually things returned to some kind of order in our lives. I missed Richard and was very sad about our mother, and Dolly, who had to be sent for counselling. She was so young I never knew that she was absorbing so much of what had been going on. She had frequent nightmares and it was more than a year before she started to talk and interact with us like a normal child.

Our mother lived her catatonic existence for another two years. We tended her as best we could. Sometimes I would read to her from one of my story books while Dolly listened. I think that's when Dolly too began to love books. But our mother never showed any sign that she heard, as she never responded in any way. The doctor said that she had retreated from life. Aunt Hopie suggested that I read from the Bible for her. I usually read from the Psalms because I loved the way they sound like music. She didn't respond to them either, except once, when I had finished reading Psalm 23, she whispered, "I didn't know," and started crying like a kitten in pain. It was horrible to watch her. Dolly and I ended up crying too.

As time passed, we put the tragedies behind us as best we could. I often thought about Richard and hoped he was okay, but we didn't make any attempt to find him, lest the police were still interested. After a while, the Buggu Yaggas resurfaced, but not in our neighbourhood. I don't know if they were the same ones, but they were annoying people the same way in different parts of the city. They would take over empty houses until the police evicted them. Sometimes they lived in the gully areas. They became quite a nuisance in the city, accosting people, demanding food and money, getting bolder and bolder as their numbers grew. They even split into different groups. Every time there was a news item, I read it carefully and searched the pictures, but nothing ever suggested that Richard was still with them.

Eventually, some charity organisations managed to reach them, and those who wanted it were given housing and counselling and opportunities to become "regular" citizens. Many of them were quite young; teens and early twenties. Many had run away from home, some because of abuse or because they were ostracised for being homosexual or drug addicts. The Buggu Yaggas were, in fact, a sort of refuge for abused boys like Richard.

One day when I was in lower sixth form, just past my eighteenth birthday, a car stopped at our gate. I didn't recognise the young man who came into the yard and knocked on the grill. Aunt Hopie went to answer the knock. When I heard her exclaim, I rushed to her side. It took me a few moments to realise that this was our brother, Richard. He was taller, well dressed, hair cut, a young moustache and beard on his face. He resembled our father.

He greeted us by name and came onto the verandah when Aunt Hopie unlocked the grill. We all stood looking at one another awkwardly.

"I've come to tell you that I am leaving the island today," he said. "I am actually on my way to the airport. As you can see, I am doing all right now. Somebody is sponsoring me."

We stared at him, not knowing what to say.

"Where's Dolly?" he asked.

"Dolly!" Aunt Hopie called. "Come here a minute."

When she realised who he was, Dolly threw herself on him and hugged him so tight I could see it was uncomfortable for him. But he hugged her back.

When she released him, he said, "Well, goodbye, I don't want to be late. You'll hear only good things about me from now on." He quickly kissed Aunt Hopie and me, both of us still too surprised to respond. When he reached the car at our gate, he turned and waved before he got in. If he was still "a person of interest" for the police, nobody would recognise him now and I presumed he had changed his name.

That's the last time I saw Richard. For some years before we sold that house and moved away, we would get a card at Christmas, always addressed to me. But the only thing he ever wrote was "Love, Richard". There was never a return address. The last one had a picture captioned "My Family". There were two adult males, one barely recognisable as Richard, looking prosperous, and two boys about nine or ten years old who looked like twins. I was happy for him.

As I write this, many years later, I am still vexed, hurt and perplexed by some of these memories. Richard was about fourteen years old when Uncle Freddie came into our lives. Why had he put up with the abuse? Why didn't he say anything? What dire consequences had Uncle Freddie threatened him with, if he talked?

I wondered how Richard had managed to stay hidden with the Buggu Yaggas, living so close to us. Why had our mother not realised that something more than just resentment was seriously wrong between Uncle Freddie and Richard? This had haunted her to her deathbed. Her last words had been, "Tell Richard, I didn't know."

Eventually Aunt Hopie cleared up some of the other things that puzzled me. When I asked her how it was that we had never seemed to be short of money, she said that my father's insurance policies and investments had provided enough for us to be comfortable for some time. In fact, she thought it was the money that had attracted Uncle Freddie, and that had been the reason for some of the quarrels with my mother, who had not married him, and wouldn't allow him to get his hands on it. That was the only sensible thing she had done, according to Aunt Hopie.

These many years later, my sister, Dolly, seems to have fully recovered. She is now married with two children. Aunt Hopie is spending her declining years with her and her family.

As for me, this question haunts me. How can one know, before one is in too deep, that Prince Charming is really an ogre? I console myself by living in the worlds I create in my books. This will have to do.

## MISSIONARY WEEK

It was the first time that I was visiting my mother's home in a deep rural part of Jamaica. It was the first time she was returning home since she had left as a young girl, and she was received with much excitement.

"Miss Maudie granddaughter come home!"

"What a way she favour Aunt Rob and Kytie!"

"Her daughter cute enh!"

She took some time to show me around the sights of her childhood village, exclaiming at the changes; some good, some not so good.

Along the way, I became curious about a small, derelict building in a little valley, which looked like it had once been a church. It had obviously been out of use for a very long time. The roof had caved in; there were bushy shrubs all around the collapsed walls, and tall trees crested where perhaps a steeple once stood. The tips of some lopsided weather-beaten boards at the back showed the remains of what perhaps had been the pit latrine. There was a crude, nearly illegible board sign fastened to a tree near the road with these strange words:

L CIF R CH R H

O NO  NTER

My mother promised to tell me the story of this abandoned building – later. So, as dusk descended, while we were roasting corn set on wire above coals enclosed by some big stones, she – helped by a few of her cousins, an aunt and an uncle – told me the story. There was a very old man sitting with us, somebody's great grandfather, and he introduced a measure of drama by squeaking "Lies! Lies!" whenever a new person took up the story. They would shut him up by giving him another corn. I wondered how he ate the corn for there were only a few teeth scattered throughout his mouth.

I am giving you my embellished version of the story because there had to be much more to it than the barebones they gave me. Quite in order, since I am telling you a story that somebody heard from somebody who heard it from somebody…

★

Missionaries from the USA – all white, well-meaning people who had answered the call to go out into the field and save the heathens – had introduced this denomination to Jamaica. The Caribbean headquarters of the church was in Kingston, but several small churches had been started by lay persons, deacons and such, usually small farmers in different villages throughout the country. These were very passionate men, who, not being theologically trained, preached their own interpretation of the bible. Mostly they preached about sin, and the wages of sin – "all who died in sin were destined to roast in hell, forever".

Mostly they preached against sex, in all its forms. I grew up in this denomination, so I know. Before I knew the meaning of, or the difference between fornication and adultery, I knew that they were terrible adult sins, perhaps worse even than murder. I remember one sermon that pointed out that it was the fornication (or maybe it was adultery) with Bathsheba that led David, a man after God's own heart, to murder her husband, Uriah. The flesh was Satan himself at work. The snake tempting Eve to discover her apple and then tempt Adam into sin and damnation.

The deacon who started this church in my mother's village was a very zealous man. His sermons about hellfire were very convincing, and in no time at all, he had got enough followers to build this church on land owned by his family. Of course, he got financial help from the approving principals in the USA. Some villagers were not very happy with this project, as not everyone had building skills and could get work building the church – and deacon was getting American dollars, which he wasn't sharing equitably. Malice against deacon, and therefore the church, was a strong undercurrent for some time.

However, despite this, the church prospered, and, as attendance grew, missionaries from overseas would visit the village from time to time to deliver the true sermons, which didn't differ much from the hellfire messages of the deacon, but were much more impressive. These missionaries were committed to pouring salvation down the throats of all, like medicine if necessary, but they understood how to sweeten it with entertainment – music and singing. These were pre-keyboard/electronic equipment days, but they brought banjos and harmonicas and at least one full-voiced singer. So, with their banjo playing, soul-searching music the church rocked for the week of their visits, and many more souls were saved and the church grew.

As I said, these were well-meaning, very religious people; usually a pastor and his wife with an entourage of two or three backup persons who played the thrilling music and sang awesome songs. The whole village would turn out to hear them, even the dissenters. People came from other villages, too. There wasn't much else by way of entertainment in those days.

The missionaries also came with prejudices they themselves seemed unaware of, but if the Lord had called them to minister to these heathen, black people, who were they to resist His call?

Life in the village was very simple – no electricity or running water. Everybody had to use the outhouse. But they were prepared to put up with the backwardness, the physical inconveniences, the mosquitoes and other nuisances in the name of the Lord's work.

Their visits always caused a stressful but pleasant flurry of activities for the church members. There were no nearby hotels or guest houses so the villagers had to accommodate them for Missionary Week. The main speaker and his wife stayed in the deacon's house. Deacon and his wife gave up their bedroom and bunked with the children. Others in the visiting party stayed in homes, which, though poor, could provide fairly decent accommodation.

The week before they arrived there would be meetings and

much cleaning of premises and inspections, for it would be a disgrace not to make the visitors as comfortable as possible. Church members made it their duty to spoil these messengers of God to the best of their ability. There were always willing cooks, and laundry women and shoe polishers and errand runners – even some to empty the chamber pots as the visitors could not be allowed to use the lowly pit latrines at the backs of the houses. Commodes were borrowed, their wooden frames polished, the inner chamber-pot scrubbed to perfection, then discreetly placed in a dark corner of the rooms the visitors would occupy, beside a table with a decorated basin and ewer and a small towel hanging on the arm.

On this particular missionary visit, a single lady, a very tall, imposing sister, accompanied the crew. She was the main singer that year, and when she sang at night service the church rang, like an angel was singing. As news of her lovely voice spread, more people came every night just to hear her, and went away feeling blessed.

This was Sister Pam's first missionary visit and she had not anticipated some of the inconveniences. She started keeping a journal, thinking it would both amuse as well as prepare others for these kinds of circumstances. These she left behind, and touted as a great reader, they were shown to me.

On Monday night she wrote:

> I am writing by lamplight. The service tonight was intense. The congregation shouted a lot of amens and a few persons came up at altar call. I hope there is better attendance tomorrow night. I expected that it would have been packed like a tent meeting, but Pastor Henry says it will pick up as word gets out to the surrounding villages.
>
> Tomorrow we will meet with the women for counselling. Honestly, their way of life seems so different I don't know what we will be counselling about.
>
> The place is quite pretty. Most of the houses are built on a hill overlooking the farms set out in a haphazard way with plants I don't recognise. Everything is extremely green and the sunlight piercing.

*I am not happy with the food. Lots of starch – they call yams, sweet potatoes here and yams are a different kind of starch. Also they cooked the chicken with a lot of oil and heavy spices. I had to ask them to hold back on the pepper in the future. May the Lord give me the strength and patience to last the week. I never was a country gal.*

On Tuesday night, she wrote:

*My skin is on fire with mosquito bites. Good thing I brought only long skirts, it was all I could do to not scratch during the service. More people came out tonight. They seem to appreciate my singing, but then they seem to appreciate everything we do and say. Forgive me Lord, but it is almost a kind of hero worship I am sensing. Pastor Henry likes to give jokes and they laugh themselves silly at everything he says. I am not even sure they understand him. I am having trouble understanding some of their speech. Very embarrassing. I find myself having to ask persons to repeat, slowly. The meals continue to be bountiful but not very palatable. I did not know that bananas could be eaten green! They boil them.*

Wednesday night:

*More and more people are attending the service. Lots of Praise the Lords and amens and clapping when we sing. They join in the familiar hymns and quite spoil it sometimes, but it's all to the glory of God, so be it. Several persons came to the altar tonight. Pastor is pleased with the way things are going. I long for a good bath. I can't even describe bathtime, too embarrassing. Modesty is apparently not a consideration here. The deacon's wife accompanies me to an enclosed zinc area at the back and waits to pour water over me when I am ready to wash off. She means well and won't take no for an answer. I am feeling very puffy. Sat on the commode for a long time tonight, but nothing happened. It's not very comfortable.*

Thursday night:

*This is getting serious I haven't had a bowel movement since I came here. I am afraid I might get sick and there are no doctors or hospitals nearby. I wonder what I should do?*

*I tried eating more veggies, but didn't like the greens that look like spinach that they call callaloo or something like that. Otherwise they put the veggies in with the meat, or boil them tasteless. Everything is too oily.*

*Last night there were one or two squawking critters on the walls in my room. I learned that they are croaking lizards. They're supposed to herald rain. Some fell before morning so perhaps the lore is true. At first, I wasn't sure if I should be frightened, but I surely wasn't fixin to do battle with them, and since I sleep under a mosquito net, I figured they couldn't reach me so I said my prayers and went to sleep.*

Friday night:

*The children here are very strange. They either stare at us as if we are aliens or they do weird antics to attract our attention. One actually put her hand in my hair. I can't imagine why. At the youth service tonight, they hardly responded and when you talk to them they won't look at you. Jake tuned up his banjo fingers and tried to get them singing some lively choruses, but their voices are not sweet.*

*Pastor's wife asked me today if all is well, she said I looked peaky. I confessed my problem and she said I should have spoken sooner. Pastor, being experienced in the possibilities of discomfort in these backward places, travels with several bottles of relief for various ailments. If nothing happens tonight, please Lord I need the relief, she'll give me something that will work quickly.*

★

On Saturday night Sister Pam was so uncomfortable she could barely reach the high notes which so thrilled the congregation. At bedtime, despite a warning that one spoonful would be enough, she eagerly swallowed two big spoons of a red medicine from Pastor Henry's stock and was abundantly relieved early on Sunday morning in the chamber pot in the commode in her room.

Later on, feeling fit and chirpy, she happily accompanied the group to the final Sunday morning service. She was dressed from neck to toe in white, and with her blonde hair, if she'd been just a little smaller in size, she could have passed for an angel – so the congregation whispered.

Everybody was in high spirits. The week had gone very well.

The collection was never great, so there was no disappointment at the minuscule amount. Most importantly, many new souls had been added to the Kingdom. Pastor Henry kept everybody laughing – even if they didn't quite understand his jokes. When he preached, his words were very clear, but when he was giving jokes, in his fast talking American accent, few could follow the story. But as soon as he began his joke: "There was a man (it sounded like 'meen') who wanted to be a preacher..." all the villagers started snickering. By the time he was finished with the joke, everybody, who was not actually laughing, had silly smiles on their faces. So, breakfast, which they all had together in the little hall at the back of the church, was a pleasant meal. In truth, the missionaries appreciated the villagers' attempts to make them comfortable, even though they were mostly all glad the visit was coming to an end.

The morning service started. The small church was packed with people dressed in their best clothes to hear this last message. So many people were in attendance that they had to borrow benches from the nearby school for seats on the outside. Inside, those who had anticipated the heat had brought their fans, others fanned with their hands or any makeshift item they could find. Sweat poured, but they didn't mind, for the music was sweet and they could feel God's presence.

Before the sermon, Sister Pam thrilled them with a soul wrenching rendition of "I Surrender All". Amens, Hallelujahs and Praise the Lords echoed off the hillside and spread through the little valley. It was after this impressive solo that disaster struck. The second spoonful of laxative suddenly demanded Sister Pam's attention. There was nothing to do but quickly repair to the outhouse at the back of the church. She beckoned to the deacon's wife, who became quite flustered by the whispered request. But, sensing the urgency, she escorted Sister Pam, as discreetly as possible, to this somewhat shaky-looking haven. Sister Pam shuddered as she looked at the small, lopsided outhouse and tried not to think of lizards, spiders and rats, as well as roaches and other insects which would, no doubt, have made this their home. But there was no alternative – an accident was near. She had to be quick.

Deacon's wife summoned another church sister and the two stood guard outside so no one would disturb her. A quick look around showed that the inside was clean enough; the wooden seat seemed to have been scrubbed and polished, the wooden floor swept, but there was no time for further inspection. Sister Pam hastily prepared herself and plopped down on the seat which immediately began to creak. Before she could think what this meant, the whole inside of the ramshackle structure collapsed.

The cracking, splintering sound of the collapsing boards of the latrine shrieked above the hallelujahs and amens in the church. The congregation poured out to witness the most horrific scene ever beheld in that village.

With the deacon's wife shrieking and holding her head in her hands, the men, as soon as they understood what had happened, tore down one of the still standing sides of the latrine and ropes were speedily fetched. They hurriedly lowered the ropes several feet down to poor Sister Pam who, after her first loud screech, was quietly whimpering in disbelief. Modesty forgotten, Sister Pamela managed to tie the rope around her waist and hold on as she was slowly pulled to safety. The line of men had to pull hard, for she was a strapping woman.

The congregation gasped as she emerged. Plastered in filth from head to toe, she looked like the devil himself rising from the pit of hell. There was much screaming and cries of "Lord, Have mercy!" The deacon's wife and some other women fainted.

The water tank was almost empty by the time the women got her clean enough to dry her off and put on new, hastily fetched clothing.

That was the end of Missionary Week – and the church. The story spread over the whole countryside, and in the manner of such tales got inflated and enriched. Those who still held malice against the deacon for excluding them from the building of the church were gleeful. Sister Pam morphed into Lucifer himself rising from hell to warn the people that this church was a false prophet. No wonder Sister Pam had such a compelling voice, they said, for Satan was a good singer (wasn't he a fallen angel?) and could take any form he wished.

Thereafter, people shunned the church. The deacon moved away and the premises fell into disrepair. You couldn't convince the villagers that it wasn't the hand of Lucifer shutting down the church, for Maas Nathan was a good builder. None of the other latrines he had built had ever just collapsed like that.

Then I could translate the weather-beaten sign
LUCIFER CHURCH
DO NOT ENTER

## LUCKY DREAMS

When Morgan was in upper sixth-form, an expatriate teacher from Britain said something that would stay with him the rest of his life. The teacher pointed to the members of his class and said: "You are all philosophers here."

Morgan thought that philosophy always referred to high academic theory. Didn't university scholars do doctorates in philosophy covering a wide variety of subject areas? It wasn't something for the ordinary man, let alone students in secondary school.

As the years passed, Morgan began to understand what the teacher meant, especially as he grew prone to deep thought about the many puzzling things in life – his and others. He thought about the lives of the people he knew; people who tried hard but were poor; people whom Fate seemed to punish whether they were good or bad.

Morgan had a beef with Fate: capricious, mean, traitorous, yet at the same time seemingly impartial and foreordained. It made no sense. Often he wavered between his Christian teachings and the idea of life which nobody could predict, or change.

Could one make choices that would defeat the machinations of Fate? Would his wife have left him if he had moved to the affluent area of the city as she wanted? Had Fate placed him in this neighbourhood to help students finish school and get some out of ghetto poverty?

Morgan had come down in life. His *The Corner Shop* had served the community well for many years. But, as times got harder, people were finding it difficult to buy, or pay for the items he would "trust" them. Goods were increasingly expensive, so finally he closed the shop, rented part of it to a drinks outlet, kept the smaller part and applied to sell lottery.

Things were quiet for a while in Morgan's little lottery shop, until one week it was announced that the winning ticket had come from his shop. People in the area rejoiced. It gave them hope. One of them could win millions of dollars, even though the winner was not identified as coming from their community. Winners were no longer advertised in order to protect them from criminal activity.

Morgan's shop got a banner which said, in large letters: LUCKY LOTTERY TICKET SOLD HERE, and underneath, in smaller type, Week 12, 2015, and underneath that in larger type – $128,000,000.

It was an impressive amount, and for a few weeks after that, sales increased. People like being associated with success, even if many warned that lightning would not strike twice – not so quickly, anyway.

The lottery business was profitable. People had to pay cash for their bets, and somehow they found the money, every day, sometimes four times each day. Sometimes the amount of cash passing through the shop frightened Morgan, and he was glad when the armoured car came to collect before he closed shop. But despite his increased commissions, he preferred how things had been before, and was happy when the sudden interest tapered off.

Although some of the other games were popular, it was the *Lucky Yabba* which drew the biggest following. The company's advisors had chosen this name, predicting that it would become popular because it would subconsciously remind Jamaicans of the Anansi story about the lucky pot which would spit out an endless supply of food provided it was never washed. *Lucky Yabba* was low cost, but rewarding in its own way.

People had their own routine for choosing their winning numbers; a significant event like an accident, which they called a "rake" or, more popular, a lucky dream, could feed a family for a week. *Lucky Yabba* was like a precarious salary. If you didn't work, you didn't earn and if you didn't place your bet, you couldn't win.

When Morgan's church said he had to give up selling lottery tickets because it was gambling, he stopped going to church. Weren't they the ones preaching about the transfer of riches from the wicked to the deserving? His head got confused when he tried to justify his decision using this premise, for the people betting in his shop could be both wicked and deserving.

People came three or four times a day for their *Lucky Yabba* ticket – one ticket was only $10, which couldn't buy much of anything else, anyway. Four times a day, people had hopes of winning enough to satisfy their needs for another few days. They stayed to see the draw and the winners left with broad smiles on their faces.

Morgan knew most of them and their stories – like Letitia who insisted that she be called by her full name and not Letty. It was a more dignified name and she was a dignified lady. But the men in the shop were always teasing her. She would cross the street in her loose-fitting short shorts and skimpy blouse and grin when the men noticed her. "Letty, where you drawers? Only cheeks mi a see."

She would lift up the sides of the shorts to reveal more of her bare skin and the string around her hips which suggested that she was wearing underwear. "Mi have on mi baggy!" she would retort.

"That a nuh baggy! ...That a stringy! ... Or a thongy! ... Or a *bare* essentials." The men would high-five each other for their clever replies.

Morgan, seated behind the counter, appreciated the men's company. It kept him feeling as if he was part of the community and mitigated the loneliness of the house behind the shop when he locked up and went home, empty now that his son had left for college.

When he opened the shop doors at 7:00 a.m. – though Jolene, the girl he employed, didn't come to work until 8, he felt gratified that he was opening the doors to another day of opportunity and survival. Watsup, trundling his handcart to the market, would wave as he passed the shop and shout: 'Morning, Mass Morgan', and Morgan would nod his balding head like a benign patriarch.

He was known and loved by the community for his generous help to anyone who needed it. All he demanded was proof of real need – doctor's bill, lab-test invoices, school fees and needs, exam fees etc. It was the people he loved. They were like family. He had watched many of them grow from childhood to maturity. There were now too many bad eggs forming gangs and giving the community a bad name for criminality, but most of the people were decent citizens just trying to make a life for themselves. He liked the fact that they were so tough, rising above the complexities of their daily lives, frequently with irrepressible laughter. Their humorous interpretation of life was, many times, the only thing that kept the tears at bay.

Most weeks, women like Letty won something, even two draws which kept food on the table for their children. When Letty's rent was due, she came every day and seemed, mysteriously, to know when her number would play twice in one day. She would bet all her earnings from the first draw and scoop up a decent sum from the second or third or fourth draw. When she didn't win, she shrugged her shoulders and promised herself that "Tomorrow is a next day". When she won a satisfactory sum, she would "let off a money" on the men whose teasing she liked, telling them things like: "Here, go buy a baggy fi you old woman." Or: "Unoo look thirsty. Go buy a drinks."

Between draws, the shop always had at least three or four men just hanging around. Morgan had put a long bench against one of the walls and they sat there, mostly older men, glad of a place to sit and watch people's familiar routines, even as they discussed the mysteries of the wider world. In a way, they kept the shop safe. Morgan paid for protection from the area enforcers, but every now and then an unconnected young fool, tempted by the flow of cash, would take it on himself to try a lone robbery of one of the businesses in the area, but not in Morgan's shop – there were too many permanent witnesses.

They served another purpose too. *Lucky Yabba* numbers were mostly chosen according to the patron's dreams. The shop had a chart listing the numbers linked to the subject of dreams.

1. *Ghost, milk, clothes, rice, anything white*
2. *Anus, sitting, bed, crab*
3. *Dead, duck, tongue, bride*
4. *Egg, blood, wine, breast, sexual intercourse*
5. *Thief, dirt, spider*
6. *Strong man, iron, running*
7. *Married woman, hog, heaven, and so on to number 39.*

Your dream was the ticket to your winnings.

People had their favourite numbers which seemed to play regularly for them. Others, uncertain which number to buy, would discuss their dreams with the men on the bench and they would collectively agree which number the patron should buy. Sometimes it worked, sometimes it didn't. But a good part of the thrill of all of this was the entertainment, like a Reality Show.

Patron (*entering shop*): Ah don't know which number fi buy.
Old man 1: What you dream last night?
Patron: Mi dream mi was a young girl in school an we was playing
      a ring game an mi fall down an bruise mi knee.
Old man 2: Young gal is number 16.
Old man 3: Buy 27 fi accident.
Patron: Them don't have nothing fi pickney a play?
Old man 1: Enh enh. What else was in the dream?
Patron: Mi nuh memba.
Old man 3: Ef is nuff a you was a play, you could buy 25 fi crowd.
      (a school dreamed played number 20.)
Old man 2: She shoulda buy that, too.

One day a woman came in with a strange request for help. "What number fi buy when you dream you dreaming, but you don't know what you dreaming?"

Nobody could decipher that puzzle so they advised her to play eenie, meenie, minie mo on the chart, or just let the machine choose by buying a quick pick.

Yardie was another regular on the premises. His real name was

Peter, but when he started sweeping the yard, he quickly became known as Yardie. Nobody quite remembered when he came to be the sweeper of the area in front of the shop. There were always crumpled tickets littering the ground. People threw away their losing tickets, ignoring the bin at the side. The discarded dreams would make the place look even shabbier until it was time to close the shop, and Jolene, who sold the tickets, reluctantly did the sweeping.

One day, without invitation, Yardie, armed with a coconut frond broom, swept away the tickets from the morning traffic. Morgan was surprised that he didn't ask for payment. The third day of his self-appointed task, Morgan called him into the shop and told him that he would give him a small amount to continue sweeping. Truth was that Yardie had discovered that when people won, they were invariably in a generous mood, and when they saw him lingering in the yard they would give him money. He never begged. After all, he used to be the handyman when *The Corner Shop* was a real shop. He had not worked since it closed. Sweeping gave him a legitimate reason to be there now; nobody could call him a beggar, even though he might look like one dressed, as he always was, in an old T-shirt, shabby, patched pants and scruffy half shoes.

From time to time, when Yardie found himself with enough to make a small $10 bet on the *Lucky Yabba* game, he would purchase a ticket. But, he claimed, he had never had a dream in his whole life – NEVER!

Old man 3: How you mean you don't dream?
Old Man 1: Everybody must dream
Yardie: Not me.
Old Man 2: You sleep?
Old Man 1: If you sleep you dream. Simple.
Yardie: Me don't dream, mi tell you.
Old Man 4: So which ticket you a go buy?
Yardie: Mi just gwine close mi eye an point mi finga pon the paper
    an any number it point pon, mi buy it.

Yardie's system never worked. He never won a game, and after a time it became a joke to tell patrons, "Yardie buy that number, it not gwine play." The regulars took this advice seriously.

Then one morning, Yardie hurried into the shop, his half shoes threatening to capsize him. He was later than usual and his face glowed with excitement. "Ah dream! Ah dream! Mi get a dream last night!" he announced.

The shop was immediately interested.

"How?" Everybody was curious.

"Me nuh know. Pure gunshot last night, gang warfare, so mi couldn't sleep til morning and mi sleep late, so must be in the morning when sun come up mi dream."

"So what you dream?"

"Mus be the gunshot-dem. Me dream say me see a coffin an a dead man in it. An a lady dress up in white, like a bride was bawling an kissing the dead man."

"You know the man?" somebody asked.

"Me noh know a who. Was jus a man," Yardie replied.

"Number three," the advisors chorused. "Dead and bride is number three. Bet all you have pon number three."

Yardie bet $200 on number three with money he had borrowed from his daughter, without telling her why he needed it. He could hardly wait for the midday draw. The machine closed off five minutes before the draw was broadcast on television. Many came in to buy their tickets at the last minute and waited to see what number played, so there were usually quite a few people anxiously watching the TV above the counter. Word of Yardie's dream was passed around like a curiosity, but nobody was tempted to bet on number three. Yardie's bad luck was well known.

So, when the number three ball dropped into the winning slot for the *Lucky Yabba* game, a big shout went up in the shop. Yardie had won $5,200. He collected his winnings with a shaking hand. The four old men on the bench each got a beer. Morgan declined. He told Yardie to save his winnings. But, against everybody's advice, Yardie put the maximum single bet, $500, again on number three in the next draw at 4:30. He collected $13,000 and new respect from the old men. While he was staring in confusion at the cash in his hand, as if he didn't know what to do with it, Jolene gave him a paper bag from the stock Morgan kept for just such occasions. He grinned at her, stuffed the money in the bag and hurried away.

The yard was not swept that day, but the next morning, Yardie showed up, as usual, and started sweeping. They could hardly recognise him. He was wearing a new T-shirt, new trousers and new sneakers. And he'd got a haircut and shave. His daughter had insisted, he told them. His ladyfriend had trimmed and shaved him. A man with money could afford to look decent, his woman said.

There are no secrets in a small community, and since many knew the legend that Yardie's number never won, when news of the change in his fortune spread, people began to call out as they passed him. "What you dream, last night, Yardie?"

He merely smiled, because no more dreams came to him. He tried number three a few more times, but didn't win. Sometimes number three played, but never when Yardie bought it. People quickly forgot his good fortune, and things went back to normal.

Morgan's shop had other successes in some of the other games. Somebody won second prize in the big Lottery game and there were impressive wins here and there, but *Lucky Yabba* continued to be the favourite of the community. One day Morgan read a newspaper feature which complained that poor people were treating *Lucky Yabba* like subsistence wages, placing small bets which could yield just enough to satisfy their immediate needs. The article gave examples of people who depended on a win to feed their children or send them to school. What kind of life was this? the writer asked. It led to more idling among the so-called deprived, the feature concluded, and was counterproductive to the economy.

The next day a comment on this feature argued that the country should be thankful for *Lucky Yabba*, for it was only the widespread belief among the dispossessed that one could win "a money" to get by that was preventing riots and anarchy in these

342     HAZEL D. CAMPBELL. NEW AND COLLECTED STORIES

hard times. Morgan thought that both conclusions were correct, but he didn't think things would change for the many unemployed people in his area. Many had given up, but some who wanted work could find none.

The churches in poor communities continued to preach against gambling, and the reliance on *Lucky Yabba*, not realising (perhaps) that this was sometimes the source of their offerings, as people gave thanks for their wins.

One morning, some months later, Morgan was surprised to see Yardie hurrying in before the 8:30 draw. "Ah get the dream again," he squealed.

"The same dream?" Only one old man was there so early.

"Yes! Yes! A coffin with a dead man an a woman in white clothes like a bride kissing him."

"Number three," the old man reminded him.

"Mi daughter give me $500 fi buy the ticket."

With a thoughtful look on his face, the old man also bet $10 on number three.

Number three played, and they both collected their winnings. It played again at 12.30 for both of them. Yardie, who had recklessly used $10,000 from his first win to buy tickets for this second draw, couldn't count his cash. He stuffed the money, $260,000 into the paper bags Morgan gave him – he needed three.

"You nearly clean out all the cash," Morgan said with a chuckle.

By this time all the other old men had come in. News spread fast and more people came to hear about Yardie's good luck. Although they understood the principle of gambling and that a game of chance was unpredictable, many believed that, somehow, the results could, and sometimes were rigged by an entity they referred to as *The Man*. Just who he was nobody knew or cared. He could be the owner of the lottery company or his agent, luck, God, or some capricious imp amusing himself by manipulating their lives. Was *The Man* again showing special favour to Yardie?

When Yardie announced that he would bet on number three

one more time, there was a noisy debate as to whether number three would play three times in a row. Many advised him to take his winnings and go home. The common wisdom was that lightning might strike the same place twice, but three times was unheard of. When Yardie's daughter heard the news, she hurried to the shop and, after a loud quarrel, she collected his earlier winnings but left him $1,000. Eyes wild, like a man possessed, he bought two $500 tickets.

As the 4:30 drawing drew near, there were many more people than usual in the shop. They wanted to see, first-hand, if Yardie's winning streak would continue. Some placed cautionary $10 bets on number three. A few bet larger sums.

The old men shook their heads. It had never happened and would never happen that a number played three times in a row. Morgan was nervous. There were just too many people in his little shop. Even with the overhead fan it was hot, and the noisy chattering upset him. The noise hushed when the Lottery company's introductory music heralded the third drawing for the day. *Lucky Yabba*, because of its popularity, was the last game drawn each time. People fidgeted. There was a low murmur when persons who had tickets for other games didn't win and sucked their teeth and threw the ticket on the floor.

Then, the bright voice of the attractive woman who conducted the draw, announced:

"And now, it's time for your all-time favourite game: *Lucky Yabba!* Hold on to your dream tickets folks!"

People literally held their breaths as the numbered balls spun in the machine, and when the winning ball dropped, it was number three. The shop erupted into celebration for Yardie and the adventurous who had also chosen that number. There was much laughter and backslapping, as well as envious grumblings from the doubters who had not placed a bet.

In a daze, Yardie collected his $26,000. Together with his earlier wins, he now had what was a fortune. Some people, hoping for a handout, stayed until Morgan gave him the money. They were all so engrossed in discussing the history of *Lucky*

344     HAZEL D. CAMPBELL. NEW AND COLLECTED STORIES

*Yabba* and the phenomenon of three draws in a row of the same number, that nobody noticed the nervous, sweating youth under the hoodie until he waved the gun in Yardie's face and demanded the money. Yardie clutched his paper bag of money to his chest. He had no intention of giving it up. So the youth shot him and fled, too inexperienced to realise that with a gun in his hand, nobody in the shocked, frightened crowd would have prevented him from wrenching the money from Yardie's dying hands.

In the moments of freezing silence that followed, one of the old men spoke in the hushed, awed voice that the situation seemed to demand. "Is him owna death him was dreaming bout. Him say him was thinking bout getting married if him win plenty money."

## ABOUT THE AUTHOR

Hazel Campbell was born in Jamaica in 1940. She attended Merl
Grove High School and obtained a BA in English & Spanish at
UWI, Mona, followed by Diplomas in Mass Communications
and Management Studies. She died in December 2018 as this
book was going to press.

Before her retirement she worked as a teacher, as a public
relations worker, editor, features writer and video producer for
the Jamaican Information Service, the Ministry of Foreign Affairs
and the Creative Production and Training Centre; later she
worked as a freelance Communications Consultant.

Her first publication was *The Rag Doll & Other Stories* (Savacou,
1978), followed by *Women's Tongue* (Savacou, 1985) and then
*Singerman* (Peepal Tree, 1991). Her stories have also been pub-
lished in *West Indian Stories*, ed. John Wickham, 1981; *Caribanthology
I*, ed. Bruce St. John, 1981; *Focus 1983*; and *Facing the Sea*, ed. Anne
Walmesley, 1986.

After *Singerman* she concentrated on writing for children. Her
publications include *Tilly Bummie, Ramgoat Dashalong, Juice Box
and Scandal, Follow the Peacock* and others.

Hazel Campbell wrote of herself in 1990: "Child of the 1940s
when nationalism was raising its head in Jamaica, I attended
schools where patriotism and budding political movements were
regarded as extremely important. In spite of the pervasive use of
foreign texts, we were encouraged to think Jamaican. This consciousness has remained with me to the extent that I get physically
uncomfortable if I am away from Jamaica for too long a time.
Perhaps that's why I never migrated and why my work reflects
almost a 'romantic' view of Jamaica – its people, landscape and the
very peculiar aura which makes it difficult to understand; difficult
to live in; but nevertheless such an enchanting country."

She lived for much of her life in Constance Spring.